J.McCOY
DOUBLE-BLIND

BOOK THREE: NYCHTA'S FAVOR

aethonbooks.com

NYCHTA'S FAVOR
©2024 J McCoy (AKA Eligos)

Aethon Books
www.aethonbooks.com

Print and eBook formatting by Josh Hayes. Artwork provided by Francell Garrote.

Published by Aethon Books LLC.

Aethon Books is not responsible for websites (or their content) that are not owned by the publisher.

ALSO IN SERIES

———

Want to discuss our books with other readers and even the authors?

JOIN THE AETHON DISCORD!

CHAPTER ONE

They called it the Summit.

Despite being lofty, the name fit. A meeting of the minds of opposing factions that Nick and I had been working toward uniting for nearly a month. Spreading rumors of the Court, utilizing Nick's charisma by having him go out of his way to aid the Adventurers' Guild in their newly established interest in climbing the Gilded Tower for resources while I vouched and fought alongside him as Matt, all the while whittling away at Sunny's loyalists as Myrddin, poaching or otherwise eroding his confidants and trusted underlings until the power he held in the Order of Parcae was a shadow of its former self, all bark and little bite.

He still had holdouts, of course. Enough that we needed to take the threat he posed seriously. With his native gravitas and willingness to commit to decisive action, Sunny was a captivating leader, the sort people naturally flocked to. But he was too volatile, and as such made more enemies than he could realistically track.

I'd effectively negotiated myself out of the room. Serving as a heel to Aaron, harassing, undercutting, and otherwise toxically edging him out until Tyler—who, according to **<Cruel Lens>**, wasn't planning on giving the other guild leader much of a chance to begin with—apologetically told me to take a walk.

As the kind of empathetic person who gave more of an ear to someone who was being shouted down, Tyler would be more open-minded toward whatever Aaron had to say now, while Aaron trumpeted the Order's prime objective of instating the Court and stopping the Transposition while subtly pinning every underhanded action the Order had ever taken on Sunny.

We'd played our cards perfectly, and an alliance was almost guaranteed.

It would be temporary and likely to fall out—the Order and the Adventurers' Guild were simply too different because of the caution of the latter and the dubious morality of the former—but with me and Nick smoothing the edges on either side, we had a real shot at making progress now.

The month had flown by, every day a gaussian blur of negotiations, combat in the tower, and extracurriculars with my newly formed strike team. It was both more and less work than before. I was doing less of the nitty-gritty myself, taking a back seat and letting Nick take the spotlight. As he should. According to a recently uncovered prophecy, Nick, my oldest friend, was the avatar of legend after all—strongly implied if not directly stated to be a manifestation of Arthur. *The* Arthur, namesake of Arthurian legend and lore.

If you're rolling your eyes at the word prophecy, congratulations, you're adequate on the uptake. This was all a sham, of course. With this system, nothing was free, nothing was accidental, and the only handouts given were bestowed with the expectation that something equal or greater in value would eventually be returned.

The interest always came due, eventually.

In our case, the primary cost of Nick's sudden uptick in status was a simple one. With the so-called prophecy centering on the classic setup of retrieving a powerful sword from its upper reaches, the tower wanted to be climbed. There was undoubtedly something sinister or questionable driving that desire. But, at least in the short term, it gave us a greater goal that served as an excuse to shore up our forces and get organized.

Nick and I had pushed into the mid-thirties of the tower on our own at first, intending to limit the complexity of adding outside players before we realized the unfortunate reality. The Gilded Tower simply wasn't the adaptive dungeon. And while its early floors had been almost trivially easy, the population of Users plummeted past the twenties, while the number of monsters, hazards, and traps only grew.

The increasingly dangerous ventures culminated with the two of us walking out of the absolute death trap that was floor thirty-four, covered in the blood and viscera of countless monsters, nursing multiple wounds and nearly overdosed on health potions before we'd accepted the grim reality of the situation. If the dungeon kept up this exponential ramp, it simply wasn't something we could feasibly handle on our own. Even a large-scale organization like the Adventurers' Guild or the Order would likely struggle, eventually.

Realistically, we needed two of them. Two competent, well-organized groups of Users capable of pushing through some of the most difficult scenarios and encounters the system had on offer outside of the Transposition itself.

Which brought us here.

What's taking them so long?

As I stared up at the distant building where the Summit was still taking place on one of the upper floors, I could feel my confidence fraying at the edges. I'd coached both Aaron and

Nick to the best of my ability on Tyler's inconsistent truth-sight. But it was still possible he'd caught them out and things were getting heated. I'd left Azure in the room, and he'd alert me if things went terribly wrong.

But the time they were taking made me nervous, regardless.

"Maaaaaaatt." Iris droned out from behind me. She'd put her hands on her hips and was glaring in my direction.

"Yeeeeees," I drew out, mocking her.

Her knitted-together brows grew tighter. "I thought you wanted to spend time with me."

"I do."

"And that there was nothing more you could do about the meeting."

"There's not."

"Then stop dragging your feet and come on."

My sister took my hand and led me through the orchard of gray-blue trees with golden blossoms sprouting up from the asphalt. Ever since Iris had awakened to her system abilities, she'd been more assertive. In my opinion, it was a well-earned improvement. She was a support role with a strong architectural focus, and she'd put her abilities to use almost without rest around the region, building everything from barricades to repairing buildings.

We passed through the section of my region where the trees that came with our bonus were heaviest, giving way to more mundane urbanity beyond.

Only there was a recent addition, recognizable not only from its sprawling shape and scale but the simple blue cross that crowned it beside oversized letters in a clear font.

Region 14 Hospital.

"That... wasn't there before." I said slowly.

Iris shifted uncomfortably, a lock of curly hair falling in front of her face. "People are always getting hurt around here.

And I know, the Adventurers' Guild has their own infirmary, but we have more than a few doctors in the region with nowhere to work after the big one in thirteen went dark with the rest of the region... and I thought... it was a good idea."

"Is it just the bones?" I asked, still staring at the building. I had spent little time in my own region lately, but it felt like Iris's latest creation had gone up almost overnight.

"There's some guts. Not completely filled out, but there's a lot. It's converted from some abandoned flats, so it's still wired to the same endless source of electricity powering the rest of the dome with backup solar-powered generators, and there's a bunch of medical equipment. We even have a top-of-the-line MRI machine."

I glanced at her and she flushed and looked away.

"No, I didn't make it. Even if I had the materials, anything that complex is still a little too difficult for me. It was donated," Iris said.

"Kinsley?" I asked.

Iris nodded. "She's been very supportive of this venture. Other than reserving a basement addition for her people's research and lab work. Probably because of... you know."

I didn't. But I could guess. I'd been gravely wounded on the tail of the first Transposition event, and while both old and new allies had interceded and taken care of me, their intervention didn't change the fact that they'd had nowhere to put me. The nearest hospital was in Region 13, a region that was now completely off the map and covered in dark clouds, which no one had wanted to venture into for obvious reasons. With her considerable resources, Kinsley had managed to throw together a last-minute home care set up in a mostly sterile environment. From the accounts I'd heard, given the severity of my condition, it was still a close thing.

It was obvious what happened here. Not only had Iris seen

and considered that problem, she'd come up with a solution that solved it for everyone in our region, and potentially neighboring regions beyond.

That was just the sort of person she was.

Iris shifted uncomfortably from how long I'd been silent. "Sorry. I know you don't like hospitals."

"No. Just wrapping my mind around the fact that this was all you." I smiled and mussed her hair. "From the looks of it, you did exceptionally well."

She perked up at that. "Oh. Really?"

"Really."

"Do you want a tour?"

To the far right of the more pedestrian grays and whites of the hospital, there was a splash of color outside what I guessed was the pediatrics wing, a sprawling mecca of wood and multicolored plastics. I pointed to it and Iris flushed. "Let's start there."

After a short walk, we arrived. Fresh peat shifted under my shoes as I stepped within the wooden beams that encased it. One of the tall, considerable trees that were native to our region had been planted in the center, providing shade. The carefully crafted area was complete with climbing ropes, a tall swing set, and railed wooden fort-like structures. The sprawling, maze-like fort led out to a mix of spiraling and straight tubes. It felt like the sort of playground that didn't really exist anymore, blown up to a grand scale by the mind of a child.

Which was likely exactly what it was.

"Sensing the architect put a little extra attention here," I signed, taking it all in.

"Started as a way of giving kids cooped up in hospital rooms with nothing communicable something to do." Iris shifted from side to side, looking down shyly. "But it got away from me a little. Is it too wasteful?"

There was a pang of guilt when I realized her accomplishment *embarrassed* her. I could relate, slightly. I felt similarly every time I spent a large amount of Selve on an expensive item at a crafter or the store. We'd come up with nothing, and though our prospects and resources had risen astronomically, the trauma of scraping by with almost nothing for over a decade had left its mark.

"Dunno," I said blandly, walking to the base of one of the taller structures and grabbing a handful of rope before I looked back at her. "Gotta stress test it to be sure."

Iris's face brightened and she chased after me, grabbing onto the rope net and taking the lead as we climbed to the summit. She took me through the wooden palisades not with the enthusiasm of a child but the eye of a designer, pointing out how even though it looked like a winding maze, everything flowed easily to one outlet or another, demonstrating the stability of a rope bridge as we passed over it.

I finally lost patience when she sat on the base of a slide and began regaling the temperature resistance of this particular blend of plastic composite. While she talked, I reached down, grabbed her shoulders, and shoved her down it.

An affronted cry turned to muffled giggles echoing up through the plastic as my sister slid down her creation.

I waited long enough for her to clear it, then followed suit. Despite being a little too tall, I slid down easily, the plunge smooth and frictionless.

She was waiting for me at the base, trying to look stern.

"That was rude," Iris signed.

I smirked. "Considering all the thought you put into it, I just figured you should experience it for yourself."

"It's not for me. It's for kids in the hospital and the region," Iris insisted, staring at her knees.

"Why can't it be both?"

I lounged on the base of the slide, reclining somewhat as I considered what could be happening in my sister's head. With the Ordinator clusterfuck, infiltrations, and the long string of disasters that followed the system's appearance and subsequent dome that locked us all in, I hadn't been able to spend much time with her. But this change in her—a sort of knee-jerk refusal to partake in leisure activities—had started before the dome itself.

At least part of that was my fault. After a breaking point, I'd been honest with both of my siblings about our previous financial situation, purely because I couldn't handle it all myself. They'd both risen to the challenge in their own way, and as a result, our family had survived.

But the abridged childhood that resulted had taken a toll on both of them in different ways.

I spoke slowly, signing the words to ensure she caught them. "You know, even though it might not seem like it, our situation is far better than it used to be."

"How can you say that when there are monsters now?"

"There were always monsters. They looked and acted like humans, but they were there, lurking beneath the surface, sowing chaos."

"And events where a bunch of people die."

"Before there were hurricanes, earthquakes, and natural disasters. Was it really that different?"

Iris squinted at me irritably. "Yes."

I ran a hand through my hair. "Okay. Fine. I'm being a little reductive—" I ignored Iris as she signed "A little?","—but just take a second and look at the good. We're not an eviction notice away from disaster. Mom hasn't had a drink in months. And for the first time we have real allies, people willing to go to bat for us. And sure, maybe the world we live in has changed, and there's a lot that's scary and new. But it's not all on me, you, and Ellison anymore."

"Even if that's true, I have responsibilities now," Iris signed, visibly grappling with what I was saying.

"Of course you do. And I'm not trying to diminish your accomplishments, or take those responsibilities away. Given what you've already managed, that would be both short-sighted and cruel." I thought about everything she'd been through, the bullying, the close calls, and I pulled her to me, hugging her gently. When we parted, I annunciated carefully, making sure she could read the words. "What I'm saying is after a job well done, like this," I pointed to the playground and the hospital beyond, "it's okay to let yourself be a kid again. Even if it's just for a moment. It's okay to want things for yourself and enjoy life. You're a selfless person, and I think at some point you connected that selflessness to depriving yourself of simple joys. You never ask for things, or do anything that might inconvenience others."

"I don't want to be a burden," Iris whispered.

"There's a difference between being a burden and taking time to let yourself be happy." I jerked a thumb toward the playground. "Now get back up there. You gotta make sure it's safe, right?"

Iris opened her mouth, undoubtedly about to insist that her creation was in fact, safe, when she seemed to connect my advice with the suggestion. She smiled and scampered off. Not long after, I heard her laughter ring out again and again.

The relief it gave me was a fading balm. According to my brother, one of the few Users inside the dome with future knowledge, Iris was important. He'd been cagey on the details. Ellison generally was, even before he'd lived multiple iterations of the same timeline.

And in my experience, "important" was a double-edged sword.

If she was as important as he thought, I wanted Iris to have as many carefree days as she could before her life took a more difficult turn. Maybe my fears were in vain and Hastur's intended outcome of stopping the Transposition altogether would succeed swimmingly.

But I had to do what I always did.

Prepare for the worst.

A violet notification light appeared in the corner of my vision. I focused in on it, expanding the semi-transparent messaging user interface.

<Ellison: FBR.>

It was a text code we used in the old days. The closest analogue our family had to a "Code Red."

Fucked beyond reason.

My pulse, relatively calm moments before, picked up speed. I started to type out a longer message, asking him what was happening. Then I realized the significance of the acronym. Ellison had used code in a direct system message. Which meant one of two things. Either our communications were compromised, or he was in a situation where he needed to be as brief as possible.

I matched his brevity, starting with the most pressing question first.

<Matt: Are you hurt?>
<Ellison: No. Not really. Something didn't go my way, but I'll be fine. We have a bigger problem.>

The next message came in before I could respond, chilling me to the bone.

<Ellison: Was supposed to meet a particular person at a specific time, but they weren't here. Knew I was coming. Left something nasty for me. Something changed in a big way.**>**

I didn't even want to know what my brother considered nasty. It was also like him to understate his injuries. Ellison had lived through this timeline more than once, the loop starting from a few days before the dome came down, and as a byproduct he'd seen the worst the system had to offer. He wasn't able to share much without risking the butterfly effect, but what he had shared had been chilling.

<Matt: Drop a pin.**>**
<Ellison: No. Forget about me and LISTEN. Something happened that wasn't supposed to happen. Which means we're off-route.**>**

The chill slowly manifested into fear. Ellison had been waging a mostly solitary war, using his knowledge from prior loops to protect us from the larger threats and putting a stop to catastrophes before they came to bear. If this version of the present had somehow diverted from his prior experiences, he'd be hamstrung in his ability to act in that capacity.

<Matt: Retreat and fortify?**>**
<Ellison: Wellness check. Lipreader first, then everyone else who matters.**>**
<Matt: On it.**>**

One final message came in, distracting me. I'd been scanning the playground, trying to find Iris. She was still giggling and happy.

> <**Ellison:** Could be a false alarm. Just... the last time this happened? It turned out to be really, really bad.>

The feeling of impending peril grew stronger.

I banged on the side of the wood paneling lining the playground hard enough that Iris would feel the vibration and come down. The tube slides were slightly transparent in the direct sunlight, and I watched a dark shape slide down the spiraling tube until Iris popped out head first, a half-smile on her face.

"What?" she said, hesitating when she saw my expression.

There was a creaking noise above her. It seemed to come from the playground itself, toward the top of the slide. A loud thud followed as another dark shape leapt into the tube Iris was still supine at the base of and descended directly toward her.

I ran.

CHAPTER TWO

Time stretched thin.

There was a blur of darkness behind her, something almost imperceptible to the eye. The sound of a low moaning growl combined with the smooth swish echoing down the plastic slide was profoundly unsettling. If my sister had all her senses, she would have heard it too. But while she was astoundingly perceptive in countless other ways, no amount of wishful thinking could change the fact that my sister was deaf.

The button at my pocket popped open with the flick of a thumb and I drew **<Broken Legacy>**, flipping the tip of the blade between my fingers and preparing to throw it. The weapon housed one of my summons, and if I could thread the needle between my sister's upper torso and the exterior wall of the slide behind her, it would place a giant pissed-off wolf between her and whatever the hell it was hurtling down the slide.

What if you miss?

An intrusive voice whispered, forcing me to hesitate for a fraction of a second. Iris had no context for what was happening. From her perspective, I'd gone from lounging to running straight for her. We had a lot of trust, but she was still a kid. I was experienced enough to know I could hit my mark—I'd spent plenty of time with the blade and made more difficult throws in the past from greater ranges—but that wasn't accounting for human error.

If she flinched? It was over.

I wouldn't make it in time. Whatever it was had reached the bottom, and I could see nothing more than a maw filled with countless teeth homing in on her, glistening with saliva.

There were options. Not many, but a few. All of them involved breaking my own rules.

I did it without hesitation.

<Command>, a new Ordinator ability, extended from my fingertips in a nearly imperceptible spear of blue light. It met temporary resistance from Iris's mind, like she was poking at it, unsure of what it was but accepting just the same.

Roll over the right side NOW.

My sister responded immediately, awkwardly scrambling off the side just as a twisted, nightmarish amalgam of teeth and flesh snapped viciously at the bottom of the slide. It was an asymmetrical abomination, and what little I could see of it was impossible to make sense of. Devoid of an obvious target, I plunged **<Broken Legacy>** in the sickly yellow flesh above its mouth.

It squealed, shrieking as Talia took form and ripped into it in a mess of growls and guttural tearing. A yelp followed.

"It's strong," my summon warned, pained voice speaking directly into my mind.

"How strong?"

"I may only buy you a small window. Run!"

I was already scooping up Iris, leaving a small, child-sized imprint in the peat as I held her to my chest and ran.

There was more movement at the corner of my vision, monstrous and hulking.

Whatever they were, there were more of them. I reached in my inventory and grasped the flight charm, intending to fly directly back to the Adventurers' Guild meeting hall.

A shadow loomed overhead, shattering my focus. A macabre raven with five eyes stared down at me, pumping its wings above. Several others circled at a higher altitude.

Shit. They look agile, and the charm takes a while to wear off. Can't risk flight.

Iris said something, but I couldn't hear her, my mind too full, trying to simultaneously send out an emergency message to everyone I knew and get a grip on what was happening and why.

Outside of dungeons or other realms of Flauros, native monster attacks were rare. Which implied that this thing was either someone's creation or under their direct influence. They were targeting either Iris or me. I had a hard time believing the former—Iris was too valuable of an asset to kill, at most an antagonistic third party would want to kidnap or take her hostage. But the latter made little sense either. If I was out and about as Myrddin, there was no shortage of people who'd want to swing at me given the price on my head. But here in my home region, I was acting as Matt.

Matt, who held the status of leader of a region that traded mostly on the value of its enchantable lumber and was heavily connected with both the Merchants' and Adventurers' Guild? He was supposed to be almost untouchable.

Apparently not.

I finished the emergency message and fired it off slipshod to every friend or acquaintance who owed me a favor in my contact list, embedding a location pin, praying that we'd have backup before it was too late. A landslide of messages returned, all of which I ignored as I ran, pressing into the more heavily wooded area for cover and making as much ground as I could.

In my arms, Iris squirmed, face contorted in panic as she whisper-cried and began to hyperventilate. I swore internally and swerved, ducking beneath a branch and planting my back to a large tree. I looked down at her and mouthed, "Deep breaths, kiddo," demonstrating by taking a few exaggerated inhales and exhales myself.

She was still ghostly pale, and scared, but she caught on quickly, breaths spreading out and normalizing. "Head hurts. What's happening?" she whispered.

The headache was an unfortunate side effect of **<Command>**. Unlike most of my abilities, it wasn't subtle. The target would feel the influence as coercion, and a successful cast meant they were forced to carry out what I commanded in a painfully short-term window. And if the actions went against character, they'd come back to themselves, clearly understanding what had transpired.

"Figuring that out. Watch my back?"

Truth be told, I wasn't really expecting her to. Iris had been shielded from most of this since the beginning, outside of some of the early event and riot, and as an unfortunate byproduct this was her first real brush with mortal danger. She'd be doing well if she didn't freeze up completely.

It was more about giving her something to do, blunting the trauma of helplessness.

Still, Iris nodded, her lips tight and quivering.

I took a half second to scroll through my messages until I spotted Grit and Ire, the hired mercenaries who escorted me whenever I left the region as Matt.

Grit's messages were mostly expletives, but Ire was mostly coherent. According to him they were en route, and Ire also sent the coordinates for a nearby block corner where they'd stop.

Less than a hundred yards away.

I oriented myself eastward and ran, huffing as the greenery blew by, trying to run straight and keeping my head on a swivel for threats that might have been lurking behind the large trunks of nearby trees. Heavy footsteps crunched through the asphalt behind me, gaining ground as I catapulted through the urban forest, eyes set on the white glow of the tree line until I broke through, tripping and awkwardly stumbling, trying to find my balance without dropping my sister.

My eyes slowly panned up to the intersection.

This was larger scale than I'd realized. The monsters looked less like monsters in the clear light of day. There weren't many of them, but the warped human faces mounted on monstrous bodies, and the sheer deadliness of those bodies, ensured no one would take them lightly. A few fights had already broken out.

And the pavement, where Grit and Ire were meant to arrive, was empty.

"Someone throw me a fucking bone here," I snarled, summoning my system-Prius and loading Iris into it. My sister scrambled into the passenger seat, leaning back, her eyes wild. "It's going to be okay," I told her, only to be cut off by an overhead screech.

The ravens from before had found us.

A giant bird ahead of the pack was diving straight down at me on a collision course, its talons outstretched.

<Page's Quickdraw> shot my hand crossbow's butt into my palm and I focused on the raven's middle eye, my wrist automatically adjusting to correct the shot.

The twang of a bow matched my trigger pull.

The raven spiraled from the twin impacts, one of them exploding, plummeting off course and spiraling downward, caving in the roof of a nearby car with considerable force.

A few slabs of sidewalk away from me, an archer stood from a kneeling position. The recent addition of a floating cowl that flowed behind him beside the thickly weaved body armor, green eyes, and tightly coiffed blond hair made his visage almost nauseatingly picturesque.

Fed turned Prince Charming.

"Nice shot, kid," Miles said, nocking another arrow.

CHAPTER THREE

Miles picked off two more of the massive ravens with comfortable ease, scattering the remnants of the flock.

With some negotiation, Miles had spent the last few weeks paying off his bounty in service of Nychta, eliminating what she considered to be "minor pests" from her realm. That'd been a revelation to both of us at the time, that the deities that interfered with day-to-day life within the dome had realms of their own. Pocket dimensions that reflected their preferred environment. As a result, he'd been out of play for most of the month. And as the one who got him into that mess to begin with, I aided him as Myrddin to the best of my ability.

"Thought you punched out," I said, maybe a little too casually.

"Sorry to disappoint." Miles squinted and fired off another arrow into the forest. There was a resulting squeal and thump of something heavy hitting the ground. "But reports of my death were greatly exaggerated."

"Any idea what we're dealing with?" I asked.

"Necromancy. What else?"

I'd noticed the similarities and hoped I was wrong. "One hundred percent?"

"They're dropping human cores, so yeah. But... this is a cut above the usual shit." Miles squinted. "For one, they're less single-minded than I'm used to seeing. Capable of retreating and rethinking their approach." He pulled back his bowstring and fired. I felt the wind from the arrow as it slammed into the heart of a pieced-together bear wearing a woman's face, knocking it flat. "And I could be imagining it, but I'm pretty sure they're feeling out sight lines. We need to split. Now."

That was all the prompting I needed. I hopped into the driver's seat as Miles popped the trunk, hopping into the back as I started the car and stepped on the gas. He left the trunk open, giving himself wide clearance to fire from.

"What tipped you off?" Miles asked. In the rearview, I saw him reach up to grab a rear seat to steady himself as I spun the wheel, careening around a turn.

"Huh?"

"Got your message seconds before the fighting started."

That presented a grim timeline, taken altogether. I thought quickly, trying to come up with something he'd accept. Before I could answer, something in my face gave it away.

Miles' expression darkened. "It wasn't a coincidence. They're here for you. Came at you first, blew things up when it didn't stick."

"Not me. Her." I angled myself so Iris couldn't read the words. "First monster we encountered beelined for Iris and wasn't exactly pulling its punches."

Miles blinked. "You're joking."

"Do I strike you as someone with a sense of humor?"

"No." A puzzlement grew in Miles' expression. "That doesn't make any sense."

It was difficult to overstate the value of what my sister

brought to the table. She'd helped numerous other regions with rebuilding efforts since she'd awakened to her ability. Some of that was diplomacy, other times it was simply spontaneous, out of the kindness of her heart. While healers and crafters existed, they were in the severe minority, with most User abilities centering on destruction in some form or another.

"Piss anyone off lately?" Miles asked, letting the question hang.

More people than you realize, but no one who knows me as Matt.

"No." I said aloud, before I realized what he was implying. My hands tightened on the steering wheel. "You think someone's targeting her to get to me?"

"Could be trying to make some sort of example of you or piss you off as a distraction."

"Why?!"

"Dunno. Regardless, they're idiots. Because there's no unringing that bell." A tiredness permeated his expression.

"Escalation," I said, coldly.

Miles shook his head. "Again, I really hope I'm wrong. There's enough dark shit going around without people carteling the loved ones of region leaders—Ahead, twelve o'clock!"

The Prius—previously pushing forty on the crowded city road—came to a shrieking halt. I slammed against the wheel, pain radiating through my body as the horn sounded a keening wail.

Painstakingly, I pushed myself back and the honking ceased. A trickle of blood dripped down my forehead. The hood came loose in the impact and was bent straight up, blocking any visual of what I'd hit. Despite keeping an eye on the road, I hadn't seen it. I glanced back at Iris. "You okay?"

My sister was wincing in the rear seat, an abrasion and the

beginning of a bruise starting where the seat belt had bit into her shoulder. She nodded.

Behind her, Miles was already gone.

Where the hell—

My question was answered with the sound of whining metal, increasing in volume. A bloody hand gripped the hood, fingertips denting the metal as it was torn free.

Not bloody. Skinned.

The creature before me looked like Frankenstein's flayed minotaur, stitched together from countless bodies, human and animal. Its sharp teeth and open-cavity nose were lopsided, and it drew breath in rasping gasps, fogging the windshield. It left red smears wherever it touched.

"Found... you," it said, voice a low rumble.

Iris screamed.

I slammed on the gas with every intention of running it over. It clung on instead, face twisted into a rictus of anger as I swung the wheel to the right, taking it clear off the road and through an alley, pumping the gas. There wasn't an outlet to the other side, just a sheer brick wall that we smashed into, pinning it against the wall with the vibration of crumbling brick. The minotaur grunted. Slowly, it reached down and grabbed the bottom of the car, arms bulging as the front wheels lost purchase. It smiled wide, its half-melted face the stuff of nightmares.

Seemingly from nowhere, a black hand gripped its shoulder, the person it belonged to dancing away as ice raced up the minotaur's body, freezing it in place. It roared and writhed, trying to break the ice as it accumulated despite its limited mobility. For a moment, it looked like it might succeed.

Then an arrow took it in the side of the head. Its unfrozen parts slumped, leaving it half-rag dolled, half-standing as the ice encased it.

Sae was only half in disguise after she got the call. She'd managed the sunglasses, and the augmenting armor that smoothed her curves made her upper half look relatively normal, but merging into her torso were legs with too many joints that bent the wrong way. Black chitin covered her from legs to jaw.

She bent down next to the driver's side window, staring at us through dark round sunglasses. "You good, Iris? Helpline?"

"Yeah." I said, unbuckling my seatbelt and wincing from the impact. Before, this much would have probably been enough to put me under. But a couple weeks ago I'd finally buckled and raised my toughness stat.

"Thanks for the assist. Needed to hit it with something big but couldn't risk missing." Miles jogged over.

Beside the car, Sae twisted around to stare at him, her expression standoffish. "Lucky I was nearby. Or maybe not, since I live here. Got to wonder, what were you doing in the area, Miles?"

"The usual. Heard something big was going down and found myself loitering nearby. Wasn't what I expected," Miles said, stopping a few paces from her. If her appearance put him off, he didn't show it. "Now can we get him to safety, or do you want to stand around sticking fingers in each other's faces?"

Sae ignored him and lowered her voice so only I could hear. "Gemini's on their way. Nothing from Numbers, but it's early."

"It's the middle of the day."

"For him that's early. Probably sleeping off a hangover. Orders?"

I immediately understood. "Gemini" referred to the system-titled Gemini mages, Astrid and Astria. Numbers was Max, an Estranged Officer class capable of estimating probability of an endeavor within a certain range that I'd poached from Roderick's Lodge. Numbers, Gemini, and Sae formed the entirety of my strike team. *Myrddin's* strike team.

<**Matt:** Tell them to trail and provide support.>
<**Sae:** And if they ask why they're helping some random region leader?>
<**Matt:** Myrddin's orders.>

Sae accepted that, though her expression seemed to indicate that she thought my continued caginess with the strike team was unwise. At the beginning, I'd started out intending to hide my Ordinator persona from everyone. That had proved next to impossible rather quickly and I'd looped in Sae and a handful of others, which had helped. Sae would probably prefer it if I brought all the members of the strike team into a room and took my mask off. But there were already too many people in the know.

I skimmed my messages. Grit and Ire had gotten held up due to a massive outbreak of fighting on one of the center throughways.

"Roads are in a bad way, so vehicles are out." I called over to Miles, who took that as his cue to finally come closer. "Any ideas?"

Miles rubbed his chin. "I'd normally suggest taking this vertical with the flight charms, but—"

"The ravens," I said.

"Yeah. Conspicuously absent overhead since we culled the herd. Still tempted to try it. Probably would, if we weren't transporting a potential target."

"Then we're SOL and on foot."

"It's what, eight blocks from here? That's a lazy Sunday morning walk." Miles smiled, radiating confidence that read as false. He was trying to keep morale up, but something about this situation had unsettled him.

There was a resonant crack of breaking ice.

CHAPTER FOUR

Despite being pinned between a brick wall and a ton of vehicle, the arrow still planted firmly in its half-destroyed head, and frost covering its entire body, the minotaur was *moving*.

"What the fuck!"

I drew my hand crossbow at the waist and fired through the windshield. The bolt landed lower than I'd intended, surprise throwing off my aim, bolt stabbing through the creature's neck instead of its head. Black ichor spewed from the wound, the rainbow dark of oil covering the windshield and dripping through the spiderwebbing puncture.

Without hesitating, Sae slammed a studded, enchanted metal stick into its forehead like the bases were loaded and there was a pair of wet thumps as its head recoiled from the impact, bouncing against the brick and slamming down into the engine block.

Miles fired an arrow into its incapacitated head, then another. When he lowered the bow, his satisfied smirk from before was nowhere to be seen.

"I thought you killed it?" Sae snapped. She stepped backward shakily.

"*Should* be dead. Necromancer creation or not." Miles frowned. "Ability packs the impact of a 50 cal. Even if it didn't do enough immediate damage to the brain to put it out of commission, the connecting vertebrae should be toast."

There was motion in the rear-view. Iris had curled up into a ball, her knees flush to her chest, breaths coming in quick gasps again, hands on her head, shielding her view.

Before I knew what I was doing, I stepped out of the car and withdrew a new acquisition from my inventory, a rare quality serrated blade I'd picked up mainly for gathering and harvesting valuable ingredients. <Jaded Eye> warned me I was on the outer fringes of socially acceptable actions and my current course might tip my hand to Miles.

But when I looked at Iris again, traumatized and terrified in the backseat, I found that—at least at that moment—I didn't care.

"Keep an eye on the road?" I asked Miles, my voice cold.

"... Yeah," Miles said slowly, sensing what I intended from the blade in my hand, walking backward a few steps before he turned to keep watch. "Don't take too long."

"Take Iris?" I said to Sae.

Sae nodded grimly, pulling the passenger seat open and fishing my sister out, angling her head from the downed minotaur.

I gripped **<Blade of Woe>**, looking for weak points. At first I thought it wasn't working, as nothing in the creature lit up at all, until I saw Sae's nearby vitals light up like a Christmas tree.

Is it... actually dead?

Not trusting the info, I fired off **<Suggestion>** next. It was the most subtle of my mind-influencing abilities and served as a litmus test for whether the stronger abilities would work. And if this second death stuck, I'd get no feedback whatsoever.

There was a spark of awareness still burning within the

darkness of the creature's mind. It was still alive. When I exerted influence and attempted to lull it back into unconsciousness, my connection was violently severed.

For a moment I reeled from the snapback, weathering the psychic storm. Then stared down at its motionless form, grimacing in distaste.

"Okay."

Hard way then.

I decapitated it first, carving through the muscular neck and dense spine. I'd used the rare-classification blade to great effect on tough-to-carve-through materials, but it still took longer than I expected, and I was thoroughly winded by the time the blade finally cleaved through. If the neck was any indication, completely dismembering the thing would take all day, so next I settled for severing as many tendons as I could, carving into sections of muscle that would most hamper its mobility.

From the outside, it might seem a little macabre, maybe even like a waste of time. But in theory, the worst thing you could do with a regenerator was leave it be after you spent the effort and resources to bring it down.

There were really only two viable options.

1. Figure out its critical weakness.

Or B. Inflict catastrophic damage that would take too long to repair.

1. Would be ideal, but I didn't have time. So I settled for B.

All throughout, I could feel Sae watching the process, her stare unflinching. She'd taken her system transformation hard —a penalty for being in a trial after it closed—and she'd come out the other side a harder, colder person. We had a lot of history but were on shaky ground of late due to the temporary alliance with the suits. They'd played a role in what happened to her, and I suspected the only thing stopping her from attempting to march straight into the Summit and spill Aaron's brains all over the table was that most of the strike-team's activities involved hunting, capturing, or otherwise eliminating members of Sunny's faction.

Sae still wasn't happy about cooperating with the group in any capacity, but seeing how Sunny was the one who botched Nick's recruitment which led to the series of events that trapped her in the trial and led to her transformation, I hoped eventually serving her his head on a platter would function as a stopgap.

No, not literally.

Miles whistled low from the mouth of an alley, catching our attention. He spoke in a low voice. "That's the bell. Scalpels down, kids, biology class is over."

"Chimeras?" Sae asked.

Listening while they conversed, I picked up the pace. Grabbed a canvas bag from the Prius's trunk and unceremoniously shoved the minotaur's head until it was mostly inside, save one curved horn sticking out from beneath the tie off. His body had been relatively motionless and I hadn't felt another spark from his mind yet, but I wasn't taking any chances.

I also wasn't done.

From what little we understood, the inventory the system gave everyone inside the dome was essentially a small pocket dimension. In theory, it could store anything from the leaf of a plant to a mid-sized vehicle. Any ingredients placed inside—no matter their shelf-life—wouldn't spoil until they were withdrawn, their biological timers essentially paused.

It was unfortunately inconsistent. System vehicles, for

example, could be stored easily, while non-system vehicles could not. And despite the obvious potential utility for live capture of small monsters and other specimens, it didn't work that way. Any creature had to be unconscious to be stored and came out flatlined.

The latter was what I was banking on.

There was almost a tangible relief when I successfully inventoried the skinned creature's head.

Miles peeked around the corner and turned back. "Four of them now, heading this way, moving with purpose. Not as fuck-you big as nightmare-fuel over there, but big enough to be a problem."

"They see you?" Sae asked, rubbing Iris's back with one hand.

"No. But smart money says they know where we are. Could be using the ravens to scout."

Sae chucked her thumb toward the dead-end back of the alley. "No outlet. Need to make a break for it before they close the distance."

"Even if one of us stays behind to stall them, too high of a chance they'll ignore us and rush straight for him."

I looked up at a series of spiraling ladders, extending upward in ascending rectangles. "Fire escape? Buildings are close together. Not great with the birds, but maybe we go up and climb down to the next street over."

Miles nodded. "That'll work. I'll take the car and run inter-ference. Might buy us time if they think you're still in it. Just try not to be up there for too long."

While Miles busied himself with the car, I climbed on top of a dumpster, then leapt up to the bottom platform of the fire escape, seizing the ladder in both fists and hoisting myself up. Sae followed in the same path and lifted Iris above her head.

"Miles," I called out.

"Yep?"

"Thank you."

Miles nodded, slipped into the driver's side, and started the car.

Before long we were running across the rooftops, my damaged Prius chugging the opposite way on the road below, directly toward our pursuers.

CHAPTER FIVE

The gaps between the first few buildings were close enough that most Users even partially specced into agility could have covered the gaps easily. This last one, however, was significantly longer. I'd had Audrey—my flowerfang summon—fashion a makeshift harness for Iris, using her mostly thornless mobility vines. My sister had fallen silent since the minotaur-chimeras interception, and despite a reasonable fear of heights, hadn't reacted to any of it.

I pinwheeled on the loose gravel of a rooftop, balance returning to me. Then turned, ready to catch Sae as she leapt across.

Sae cleared the gap easily. She'd put too much energy into the jump if anything, and I grunted as she clung onto my forearm to steady herself, feet sliding across the gravel roofing. Her eyebrows shot up, her mouth set as she saw something behind me. "Bird!"

I spun. The raven shot upward, attempting to hover out of reach. Its wings and oversized body weren't built for that, so the result was an awkward climb. Still, that climb placed it out of the effective area for my hand crossbow.

There was a chance I could still draw my bow and make the shot, but if Miles was right that they were communicating, any second now it would broadcast our location to the rest and we'd be overrun.

No choice.

I didn't have time to feel it out or test the waters for its reaction to my influence. And as much as I didn't enjoy using the ability as an answer for everything, nothing else was fast enough.

<Subjugate>

As of now, I am your favorite human. Do everything you can to help me and mine.

A wave of exhaustion tugged at my eyelids as nearly half my mana drained away. But none of the mental pain from a failed attempt. It'd come down to a wager on whether all the necromancer's creations had psychic protections, and I'd guessed correctly that the birds would be more simple than their human counterparts.

The bird swooped down and landed.

It hopped frantically on the gravel and cawed at us angrily, flapping its wings and kicking up dust. For a moment I thought it had shrugged off the effects of the spell, or that it had some sort of resistance that kicked in, before I realized it was pushing us toward the roof access structure.

"Matt? Is it about to peck our eyes out, or do you have it?" Sae yelled.

"Got it. Get inside!" I shouted, twisting the push down handle and throwing my shoulder into the door. It swung open, and we both made it in a second before a handful of massive shadows flitted over the rooftops.

The raven I'd subjugated was too big to enter, but it pressed itself against the open door, shielding us from view. After the danger passed, it stuck its considerable head through the door and stared at us with all five eyes. Then tapped its beak on the concrete with a considerable click.

When no one reacted, it tapped its beak again. Then spoke aloud, its voice hoarse and raspy. "Treat."

What?

It tapped its beak again, and I could have sworn I detected a trace of sass. "Good bird. *Treat.*"

Interesting. It'd been trained with traditional positive rein-forcement, either before or after it was super-sized and sprouted extra eyeballs. That added to the likelihood its necro-mancer master was a User rather than system created.

Technically, I didn't have to give it anything. The Raven was caught in the thrall of subjugation, so it would listen and imple-ment anything I said and take it as gospel. Even if I told the monster it no longer desired treats, or to forget how to fly. Under the effect of **<Subjugation>** any creature or person would follow my commands to the letter for the next day, with all the capacity for potential misuse that implied.

Whether it was a monster or a human, I didn't want to go that route.

Instead, I pulled one of the many filets I kept on hand in my inventory out and tossed it to the creature. And another. Then one for Audrey when she started whining about the "Stupid bird eating my meat."

The raven snatched the steak from the ground and turned its head upward, gobbling it down and chortling with pleasure, clearly enjoying the meal.

Mindful of my younger sister strapped to my back, I reached out to the Raven with **<Suggestion>**, more to communicate than to influence. It had a sharp mind for an animal, and as I'd suspected, it wasn't enslaved. It was trained.

In exactly a day, the influence I hold over you will fade. You will regain your faculties and your will. And naturally, you'll be angry. However, I want you to remember this moment. You attacked me first. Yet I saved you from the consequences of that. Rewarded you for your help, despite your transgressions. And if you enjoy the deliciousness of the reward as much as you appear to be, perhaps you should contrast your experience here with what would have happened if your master was in my place. And know, that if you choose to serve me, there are many rewards yet to come.

I'd used a version of this on a handful of human and monster test cases and received positive results. The additional prompting I was doing had to be more subtle on a human, but I found more direct language helped. **<Suggestion>** would translate my words into an amalgam of thoughts and ideas the target was more likely to understand, but it couldn't guarantee that understanding.

It stopped mid-chew of the second filet, swallowing. Its intelligent eyes seemed troubled. Then the moment passed and it tapped its beak again.

I tossed it a third slab of meat, then withdrew a fourth, much to Audrey's dismay. I withheld the final slab, tearing raw pieces off as I went.

"How many are there?"

The raven leaned backward, doing something unseen, then placing a pile of gravel. It used large pieces as markers, counting to nine until it shoved a pile of gravel in from the roof.

A lot.

"Any chance you can speak your master's name?"

The raven huffed.

That's a no.

I ran through a few more questions with mixed results until I came to the final query.

"We have some ground to cover. This is a lot to ask, but now that we've bonded, any chance you can provide oversight? Help protect us from threats on the ground and steer the other flocks away before they see us?"

A hesitation.

"More... treats?" It turned its head to either side, listening carefully for an answer.

"Oh, yes."

A confident squawk gave me my answer.

CHAPTER SIX

The tide was already turning.

I caught glances of it in the vertical windows that lined the building's stairway. Groups of armored and armed Users, strategically picking apart chimeras.

Whoever the necromancer was, they didn't have much of a plan B. They'd doubled down on plan A, hiding a few dozen powerful—and undoubtedly expensive to produce—chimeras in our region to sow chaos and cover the assassination attempt. The remaining chimeras had more or less accomplished that initial objective. Problem was, even on an ordinary day, Region 14 belonged to the cross categorization of well-defended and not to be fucked with. And assuming that the members of the Order fighting alongside Adventurers' Guild mainstays meant the deal had gone through, that listing had just been bolded and under-lined.

I took time to re-summon Talia before Astrid and Astria met us at the base of the stairs.

As they shared the same half-shaved light hair and ensemble down to the golden-wood wands and dark mages' robes, it was almost impossible to tell them apart at a glance.

Astrid stood with her back straight and was acerbic, the clear leader, while Astria lurked in the background, meek and lilting. But they both looked and acted more alike than they once had —Astrid losing some of her innate confidence and Astria finding some to speak of.

"Sorry. Lot of stuff to wade through out there," Astria said, her voice low and shy.

"Don't apologize to them! We're the ones out here risking our butts for some spoiled asshole." Astrid's eyes locked on mine as she barred the door.

Sae snorted and elbowed me. "Second part anyone would agree with, but spoiled? Girl's gotta recalibrate her people senses."

It was amusing, seeing this side of them.

You'd never know it, witnessing the headless-chicken hustle to secure the perimeter, but the girls were stone-cold hitters. Some of the best I'd worked with.

I'd found them for the second time in the sewers. Nick and I were chasing down a lead—our resident deity directed us there hoping to lock down the Queen, one of the five remaining members of the Order's Court, a key piece in Hastur's win condition. Why we'd find royalty mixed in with sewage and shit he never answered. Never found her either.

What we had found, huddled together inside a makeshift lean-to cobbled together in one of the many maintenance runoffs, were the twins.

The two of them had been lying low ever since the events of the Transposition, unsure of whom to trust—understandable, given the confusing detonation at the end—and had been operating mostly on their own, exploring the sprawling subterranean sections of the city and delving into dungeons that appeared there. Which, apparently, were not infrequent.

Nick encountered them first, and they'd almost immediately run him off, sporting a battered ego.

When I followed up as Myrddin later, I'd received a much warmer greeting. Astrid had apparently connected with me over the events of the Transposition. From her account, what had happened to me was apparently an influence in their ongoing refusal to sign with any large guild. I got the feeling they wouldn't have anyway. Aligning with any large group went against a core tenant of the transient code.

Trust individuals. Never institutions.

I owed them both. And even if I hadn't, they were too powerful to leave on their own. My solution to Astrid's problem was the strike team. It was, functionally, a small group of Users with varying alliances and backgrounds that took on contract work I was mostly self-funding. Myrddin provided access to the Merchants' Guild site at the Allied Guild discount, sniffed out jobs, and the strike team carried them out.

Astria glanced at Sae. "Do you want to say the thing, or—"

"Right." Sae cleared her throat. "Report."

"Not fucking good," Astrid said. She grunted as she finished the barricading, stumbling back as something slammed against the door hard enough to leave an imprint.

"Bunch of lizard people chased us here. We thought about diverting to lead them away—"

"—and that we'd go at least another decade without muttering about lizard people, but with the way you were hollering, Exo, figured we should just push through," Astrid finished.

Sae bristled at the tag, doing her best to ignore it and nodding. It was an unfortunate nickname, mercifully limited to the strike team, more unfortunate that it was accurate enough to stick. Whatever she said went when Myrddin wasn't present, and well...

She had an exoskeleton.

"Thought it was clearing up out there," Sae said, perturbed.

"It… was," Astria said. She hesitated. "The ones clawing at the door were being pushed back by a larger group, then they spotted us and peeled off. Just dropped what they were doing."

"That doesn't make sense." Sae's brow furrowed. "Were you the only mages in the area?"

"Not even close," Astrid groused. "There was several levitating in the group they abandoned."

Icy fingers tightened around my spine as I realized why the twins had been targeted. They were both female, and despite their power, diminutive. Closer in size to a child than an adult. Just around Iris's height.

The necromancer hadn't bothered with a detailed description for his rank-and-file. Judging from Sae's grimace, she'd reached the same conclusion.

Whoever you are? Congratulations. You've cemented yourself at the top of my to-do list.

Sae glanced at my back, where my sister was still silent and restless, then back to the twin mages. "For now, just assume that these things are going to act like idiot magnets and plan accordingly."

Astria angled her head toward Astrid. "Is she just calling names as usual or giving genuine advice?"

"Yes," Astrid said.

"So, what now?" Sae elbowed me. "Back up to the second floor so we can recon and kick out a window?"

Maybe I'd recognized the civilians most likely to be targeted if we bypassed these things. Maybe I was just pissed. Either way, I didn't feel like taking a detour.

"Mages pack a punch?"

Sae chewed her lip, probably annoyed at me for asking

questions I already knew the answer to. "When they need to, yes."

"Why bother finding a way around when they're all grouped up and vulnerable?" I said. All heads slowly turned to look at me.

"Claiming this region must have fucked up your—ow." Astrid cut-off mid-sentence as Astria smacked her upside the head.

Instead of squabbling with her sister, Astria waited, watching Sae attentively. "Orders?"

Sae thought about it. "Depends. Got anything heavy and directable that'll blast through but won't bring the building down around us?"

"Boreas' embrace?" Astria looked over to Astrid.

Astrid raised an eyebrow. "High profile... but it'll work. Mana's about equal between us. Prep or incantation?"

"Prep. You're the better shot."

"Yeah. That's why. Nothing to do with being nervous you'll miss."

"Hush."

Though I'd seen it before and was too distracted to properly appreciate the moment, it was great to see how far they'd come as a duo. When I'd met them, between Astrid's hovering and her own social anxiety, Astria had barely strung together sentences. She'd hidden in her sister's shadow to the point she almost faded into the background entirely. Some of that still lingered, but for the most part she was far better at taking initiative.

We moved toward the rear of the stairwell, as far back as we could go without pressing our backs against it. Sae took the stairs two at a time, checking windows on the second floor, and confirmed it was clear of anything beyond monsters.

Astria knelt, reaching down with glowing hands and

pressing against the concrete. Two curving lines extended from beneath her gloves, forming a perfect circle so bright it was difficult to look at. The longer she maintained it, the more complicated it became, a mess of undecipherable runes scrawled within smaller circles. Two imprints formed in the center, one slightly in front of the other, oblong and asymmetrical compared to the rest of the circle until Astrid stepped directly onto them, obscuring them from view.

I shifted Iris to my front.

Astrid raised her wand, pointing it at the door. It had dented inward enough that we could hear the scrabbling of the chimeras on the other side, which were picking up the pace now that they were making progress, scaled fingers and flicking tongues pushing inward, trying to widen the gap.

Shatter.

Astrid mouthed the word, and all the considerable mana from the circle drained into her, leaving only dull etchings and the imprint of a circle on the ground. She floated upward around a foot, braced her wand with both hands, and loosed.

CHAPTER SEVEN

The skull-shattering explosion mimicked the echo of a howitzer cannon. I lost presence for a moment and stumbled to the side, trembling hand reaching up toward a wetness on my cheek. My left ear, closest to the explosion, was bleeding. I grimaced and quaffed a health potion, making my way toward the twins alongside Sae.

"Got 'em?" Sae was leaning on Astrid, squinting through the gaping hole that yawned open where the door used to be, beyond masked by enough dust to pass as a sandstorm.

As the dust receded, scaly corpses came into view, chunks of their bodies missing, cleanly cut through by the laser. "Think so," Astrid huffed, breathing hard but otherwise undeterred. Considering the scale of what she'd just managed, the lack of tiredness was off-putting.

And a little disturbing.

The twins were strong, to be sure, but they hardly dominated the competition.

It was a reminder that every User still alive had been continually getting stronger, driven toward progression by the impending threat of another Transposition event. Magic stood out because it was flashy and could cause catastrophic damage from a distance, but many melee Users were advancing far beyond the realm of human potential in both defensive and offensive capacities.

I was at a higher level than most. The combination of the Allfather's backing, stumbling upon the adaptive dungeon, and early access to Kinsley's store had allowed me to get an early head start, one I'd capitalized on to the best of my ability. Subsequently, the string of misfortunes and contentious paths that led me here helped widen the gap. Between pushing higher up the tower and clashing with problem members of the Order, I'd tried to continue that trend.

But there was an uncanny sense, lately, that the gap was closing.

If I needed to deal with a User like Astrid—powerful, but lower level than me—the methodology was simple. Create enough of an opening to force **<Subjugation>** through and either direct them to turn their wand or weapon on themselves, or use them against their allies.

But if the User was equal to my level or higher?

That was a problem. In an ideal environment with plenty of space and places to hide, I could punch far above my weight class. But this was the real world. You didn't always get to pick your battles. If the wrong Users ambushed me at the wrong time, I was in a world of trouble.

Especially with family in the mix.

My eyes trailed to my sister, still ashen in Sae's arms. "We need to get going."

We darted across the street in loose formation, keeping me and Iris in the center to shield us from view as we circumvented the small groups of Users pushing back monsters, slowly making our way through back allies and side roads until our destination loomed in the distance, less than a half mile away.

Sae nearly took a step before her eyes glazed over, and she swiped a finger across her invisible UI. "Max is on comms and in range. Better late than never, I guess."

"Max?" I asked dumbly, giving Sae a pointed look.

Minor mistakes could easily sum to disaster. Though the strike team didn't require my presence to function, I spearheaded things often enough that the five of us had a working chemistry. Sae—the only person present who knew Myrddin and Matt were the same person—had to take special care.

She startled and glanced over at the twins. To their credit, they were too preoccupied with our surroundings to notice the slip. "Ops guy. Can hold his own in combat but has advanced reconnaissance feats."

Switching gears, I played the role of an annoyed VIP whose life was in danger. "There are no freaks in sight. Whatever the hell the attack was about, they obviously focused on the outskirts. It's right there." I pointed at the building. "Quick jog and we're home free."

"Confident enough to bet your sister on that?" Sae challenged. When I scowled and didn't answer, she continued. "Just sit tight for a second. Max will get back to me, and we'll—"

Her eyes flicked to her UI and Sae's expression froze, the already light skin around her chitinous material paled ghostly white.

The private message came a second later.

<Sae: Max is giving us a one.>
<Matt: What was the query?>
<Sae: The chance of all five of us making it to the tower.>

Icy fingers gripped my spine. Max's estimations were useful, but you couldn't always trust them. A positive rating—fifteen being the maximum—only factored in elements that were currently present. A fifteen could easily change to a three if some sort of threat beyond its range entered the fray. But for him to give us a one?

There was something insidious in play. A massive ambush, or something just as devastating.

<Sae: What the fuck do we do?>

I considered our surroundings. The alley didn't have any defenses, anything we could barricade save two large dumpsters with rusted wheels and a small mound of trash. The dumpsters could provide some cover in a pinch, though not much—especially under any heavy sustained fire. My instinct was to move, get the hell out, and find a place to hide. But if we moved before we knew where the danger was coming from, it'd be all too easy to run into it.

<Matt: Hold until he narrows down the query.>

Astria had noticed the lapse and tracked back to us. "Something wrong?"

Sae nodded, her mouth tight. "Serious threat. Waiting on Max's cooldown for more info."

A flit of shadows from above broke up the light, and there was a warning cry from the massive raven. It circled overhead, calling repeatedly each time it reached the left side of its circle, the call increasing in urgency.

"GUUUUUUU BAAAAAAAAAAH"

Something *roared*. Everyone present immediately covered their ears and winced. Beyond the deafening volume of the scream, it was strange. For one, it was guttural and raw, as if the creature who made it was malformed or injured. Second, it was broken up in the middle. In abstract, it almost sounded like two unintelligible words, the phonetics lost in pure, unbridled fury.

An oscillating *whoosh* followed, not unlike helicopter blades. Seconds later, a long pole with a bright yellow triangle on one end that was spinning almost too quickly to make out smashed into the raven, sending it crashing onto the building below.

In the wake of the impact, the decapitated minotaur staggered into view on the street beyond. It hadn't completely regenerated, and considering the damage to its ligaments and muscles, I had no idea how it was still standing. Headless and bleeding, it came to a standstill and pointed a gnarled finger at me.

"*Guuuh Baaaaaah.*"

"*Give it back.*"

Well, fuck.

Beyond cutting off the head and taking it with me, I'd done an astronomical amount of damage to the creature's body after it was down for the count. Hard to imagine I was worried about overkill when this was the result. The fact that it was still standing at all bothered the shit out of me. Sure, it was probably the product of a necromancer and undead creatures tended to flaunt the rules, but come on. It had a gaping hole where its neck should be. It was down three senses and still managed to track me—

I stepped to the side and its body shifted slightly, staying on target. That shouldn't be possible unless it was being directly controlled. And it was still communicating, still showing personality. Unless...

It's following the head.

I began to back away. The minotaur advanced toward me with lumbering footsteps, paying no mind to the others. Astrid charged up a spell, Astria supporting from behind.

"Tell them to stop," I murmured.

Sae's head snapped back toward me. "What?"

"The mage twins. Stop them."

"Gemini, hold," Sae said, using their official callsign.

"What, so furless-furry dullahan can roll us over?" Astrid snapped.

"It probably can't see you. And even if it can, its priorities have changed," I said, projecting as much confidence as I could considering the circumstances. It'd taken out the bird, but only because the raven was actively hindering it, and I got the feeling these things could sense each other. "Crack open the manhole and take the girls down into the sewer. Give me a minute to lead him away, then scorch concrete."

She stared at me. "I don't care how good you think you are. That thing will tear you to shreds."

"It's gotta catch me first."

"Matt—"

"Get Iris to the Adventurers' Guild. Make sure Tyler knows what's happening. Send as many people my way as you can. I'll keep the pins coming."

Max gave us a near-zero chance of making it to the tower together. If I wanted to get Iris clear, that meant improvising. I had the beginnings of a plan. Hard to say if it was a good one, but it was better than nothing.

Sae took Iris and helped her and the twins into the sewer. Memory guided me as I flew through the UI, pulling up Kinsley's store and making a very specific purchase. I spammed through the invasive warnings and prompts letting me know my purchase had been logged and selecting "construction" in the reason field. Considering that you had to be on the approved list—generally a non-fledgling member of a respected guild or vouched for by one—to make purchases on this section of the site, the warnings were probably unnecessary. But better safe than sorry.

<Forty thousand Selve withdrawn.>
<Your new acquisition will be delivered to your inventory
after the waiting period.>

Twenty minutes.

No small ask, when the battlefield had a way of turning minutes into eternity. I withdrew the bag from my inventory and fished out the contents. Considering how alive the body was, I half-expected the head to animate, maybe even speak to me. But compared to the body, it wasn't looking so hot. The once-red tissue was dull burgundy, the texture hypoxic and prune-like, eyes rolled up into the back of its head. With any luck, that meant most of its intelligence and higher reasoning were out of commission.

Ahead, the minotaur was still advancing slowly, hand held out.

"Looking for this?" I hefted the minotaur's head by the base of the skull. Then reached up with my free-hand, cocked my middle finger behind my thumb, and delivered a meaty flick to its nose.

The reaction was immediate. The creature roared, warbled voice full of rage and hatred. And rushed forward.

CHAPTER EIGHT

My pursuer was having trouble navigating. Pre-headless status, I would have placed him in the annoyingly "crafty" brute camp, high on the shortlist of foes I generally prioritized avoiding direct conflict with. Post-headless, he ran full tilt and barreled into and or over anything in his way. Considering his ample mass and speed potential, he still wasn't a joke. If I panicked, or got stupid enough to run in a straight, unobstructed line long enough for him to get his massive hands on me, that would probably be the end of it.

But my ability to panic was more or less a dead nerve. It'd been beaten out of me, time and time again, diminishing with every instance I was forced to take something ridiculous in stride.

It still happened—typically when someone I cared about was under threat. If Iris was still in danger, I wouldn't have been nearly as clear-headed.

But I trusted Sae. And I was pretty sure Headless was the reason for Max's disturbingly low evaluation. Now that he was fixated on me, Sae could take her time getting my sister to safety, using Max's ability to make sure the way ahead was safe.

"GUURAAAAAAAW."

Here he comes.

I slowed and pressed my back to the passenger side of an over-sized gas-guzzling SUV parked on the side of the street, facing down the overgrown monster speeding toward me. Despite the juddering gait and awkwardness of his ruined legs, he was still unbelievably fast.

At the last second, with *perception* screaming for me to move, Audrey's vines shot from my sleeve, anchoring on a distant light pole and launching me out of the way.

Every pound of Headless's considerable bulk slammed into the sedan, shattering windows and crumpling the frame, pushing it up on two wheels. The trunk and engine block were bent inward, leaving him thrashing and half-stuck.

"So close," I called behind me, feeling grim satisfaction when the mockery was met with an angry roar.

I kept running, making as much distance as I could before Headless could free himself. The first five minutes had been deceptively easy, effectively playing matador with a blind bull. But slowly—almost too gradually to notice—my pursuer had been growing more coordinated. He was either regenerating faster than I could hurt him, or getting better at wringing efficiency from his injured state.

Neither was good for me.

At this rate, he'll run me down before we get to the reservoir. Need to keep him on the back foot.

It'd be easy to ditch him if I wanted to. I could toss the head, but that meant taking the risk he'd revert to previous orders. Or I could zigzag across the region until he lost me. But he could just follow the head and find me again. So it was a question of keeping his attention, maintaining enough distance that I could lead him to the reservoir, and buying time for my purchase to arrive.

A small cluster of monsters raced toward me from the opposite side. Goblinoids with long ears and wings too short to function. Cutting them down would take too long, so I didn't bother. Instead, I cast **<Probability Cascade>** on the four front runners, stoking their ire and ensuring they'd arrive simultaneously. Then threaded the needle, sliding between two stinking bodies and past them. They smashed into each other and snarled, lashing out with claws, biting, fervor replaced with confusion when they realized they were fighting each other.

The back line was hesitant, confused by why the leaders were fighting. I shot a crossbow bolt through a goblin's ankle, then grabbed the leader, a goblin about a foot taller than the rest, by the forehead and covered his eyes with my palm, using the second of surprise to knock his sword hand aside and slit his throat, spinning him in a mockery of a dance. The arterial blood spray of their once-leader covered them, and the warlike growls turned to craven shrieks.

They ran.

I reached out with **<Suggestion>** this time, guiding the forerunners to retreat directly into Headless. He battered them aside, sending their broken bodies careening over the pavement. From a glance, he was more annoyed than waylaid, but the sudden interference had slowed him down.

There's more than I thought.

The influx of monsters wasn't slowing down. If anything, there were more of them now that I was farther from the center. Few casualties on our end, from what I could see, thanks mainly to their disorganized movement and lack of coherence, serving as fodder while the real mission was carried out. No matter how I looked at it, the flagrancy with which resources were expended scared me more than anything else. *Everyone* was hoarding whatever—Selve, items, favors—in anticipation for what came next. I had more money than I'd ever had, especially by pre-dome standards and, despite that, was hesitant to spend. Because there was no forecast for when the tornado was going to hit. When *this,* or the second Transposition was going to happen, and people we cared about would be thrown into chaos. The reasonable, albeit primal response was to hunker down, scan the tree line for any potential threats, and stockpile until we had the misfortune of discovering exactly what disaster we were preparing for.

Even if the mystery necromancer had more capital than god, this was an enormous waste. There were easier ways to get at me, far easier ways to get at my sister.

More to that point, if this was a strike at me, it was concerning. Matt had fewer potential enemies, less willing to escalate the ongoing tensions between regions and guilds to targeting connected innocents. But if it was someone who knew I was Myrddin, almost anyone capable would take a shot at me. Considering what they'd thought I'd done and the bounty on my head, there was plenty of motivation.

If the neck-breather didn't rip me to shreds, I needed to get aggressive. Narrow down possibilities on Matt's side as quickly as possible before I went nuclear.

<Nick: So, I know you said not to leave Aaron and Tyler alone for any reason or in any circumstance, but...>
<Matt: Negative. I have it under control.>
<Nick: Leanin out the window, man, and g2b honest. That's not what it looks like.>
<Matt: Do not leave them unsupervised. Do not fuck this up. You dip and one of them bites it, we're blown. Month of work out the window.>
<Nick: Relax. Kumbayas are already sung, there's a confirmed agreement. Best way to make them safe would be to ensafen yourself.>

<Matt: That's not even a fucking word.>
<**Nick:** Pretty sure it's an African Hymn, but w/e. Now that
negotiations are over they're joining the teams on route to you.
Coords if you please.>

I swore, jerking out of the way as the minotaur's thundering
footsteps gained ground, belatedly realizing I'd zoned out on a
straight away. Curving misstep, I mantled over a car and behind
a light pole, flinching at the clang and shudder of metal, tucking
my shoulder and ending up on my back. Above, the battered
light pole swayed precariously, whining metal and cracking
asphalt teetering toward me.

No.

As **<Probability Cascade>** landed from my fingertips, the
pole swung back the other way, teetering toward the road. The
tortured bolts at the base tore free and the pole plunged down,
landing directly on Headless and pinning him flat. He struggled,
pushing against the concrete with both hands, trying to shove
the pole off of him. It barely moved, but from the strength he'd
showed, that could be shock. It wouldn't be long until he got
it off.

I staggered to my feet, preparing to run again before I
glanced at the time. It was half past noon. I'd barely run this
thing for half of the cooldown and it was already nipping at my
heels. It was tempting to cobble him somehow, turn the tables
in my favor so I could time this properly, but if I went overboard
that would risk immobilizing him. And to make a serious
impact, I needed to get up close, putting me in range of his
bulging arms. Unless I got creative.

I blasted a piece of recently emancipated concrete about
half the size of my fist with **<Probability Cascade>**, wedged the
toe of my boot beneath it, and sent it skittering toward where

the minotaur's head would be, rock curving with perfect accuracy.

There was a hollow thunk, and instantaneously the guttural growling and snarling ceased.

The brief silence that followed was immediately shattered as the minotaur frantically clawed at his throat in a desperate attempt to clear his airway.

Come find me once you handle that.

I moved at a brisk jog, putting a more reasonable distance between us now, giving myself room to maneuver. By the time he caught up to me at the reservoir, it was already too late.

<System Notification: your purchase has arrived.>

CHAPTER NINE

There were dozens of them, milling around the upward slope that overlooked the reservoir. Odd, malformed chimeras with twisted limbs and human faces bumped into each other, as if whatever commanding presence that directed them until that point had suddenly severed the connection, leaving them stranded and agitated.

It probably had.

I cocked my head and listened. There was the minotaur's pounding footsteps growing closer, nearly loud enough to drown out everything beyond them. After a moment, *perception* prevailed. Human shouts and war cries, drawing closer. Keening squeals followed by explosions marked casters in the mix. From the sound of it, it was a decent-sized group making their way down the main road, and barring some significant obstacle they'd have eyes on me in under a minute. More than likely, the group that contained Aaron, Tyler, and Nick.

Which meant I needed to work quickly.

Matt had the misfortune of being perceived as a teenager. This worked to my purposes most of the time and allowed me to slip beneath the radar, but an unfortunate byproduct was that doing anything exceptional would raise eyebrows. I'd already shined a spotlight on Matt once in the wake of the first event, and while saving this region had afforded me certain advantages and a staggering amount of goodwill from the locals, it also meant I'd effectively lost my anonymous status and become a conundrum.

And when you're an enigma, people start watching. Questioning your every move, critiquing every loss, win, and stroke luck that comes your way. It didn't matter that most of them were amateurs. With enough would-be detectives, conspiracy theorists, and meddlers in the cheap seats, eventually someone's going to get it right.

I could deal with the minotaur. The landslide of battery, mockery, and frustration I'd subjected him to practically guaranteed he'd be both desperate and spitting mad—possibly the best state of mind for an opponent to be in.

But the decisive blow would be too ostentatious to hide. I needed to frame it in a way that made me look like I was on my last leg, disguise the coup de grâce as a Hail Mary.

"*Go.*"

Relief from constriction I'd barely even noticed washed over me as Audrey released the makeshift harness from beneath my hoodie and flung herself through the crowd of chimeras, lashing out freely with her attack vines as her mobility vines worked overtime to keep the fragile plant summon out of their reach. Snarls and clawed hands reached for her, but she was too nimble and crafty as she baited them in, letting them almost touch her before she danced away to another part of the crowd.

Simultaneously, I made a break for the reservoir, curving around the crowd and pumping asphalt until I reached the railing. Fifty feet to the water, nothing but concrete on the way down. Once there, I withdrew the bag that held the minotaur's head, along with my most recent purchase. The object was smaller than I thought, a black brick that felt solid and cold to the touch, the only hint to its significance a small line of three capacitors on the top left side.

Just holding it made me nervous. I wiped a damp hand on my shirt and pressed my thumb to the base. A spiderweb of blue circuitry that looked half-magic, half-tech, lit up on the surface.

Only then did I allow myself to look for the minotaur. He was still coming, his limp all but gone.

Exactly what I was worried about. Shrugged off that light pole like it was nothing. Outhealing the damage.

Audrey arrived with a panicked plop and scrambled to hang onto my leg. "Angry. Very very angry."

The chimeras loomed. Some of them started toward us, pausing only when they saw the headless minotaur stomping his way toward the summit.

Either way, it looked like I'd been cornered. Best I could do in so little time. If anyone perceptive stopped before entering the fray and evaluated the situation, they might surmise that something was off. I made a show of looking over the edge as if I was considering jumping, using the moment my back was turned to slip the device into the bag, then turned and faced the minotaur.

I held the bag up, giving it a casual spin. He stopped mid-stride, maintaining a charge posture, the surrounding air tense and charged with violence.

"Guuuh Baaa."

"What, so you can tear my arms off after I hand it over?" I gave the bag another practice swing. "No deal."

He took a threatening step forward.

I held out a hand. Before I could speak, I noticed a flash of movement. The combined rescue force had arrived. Mostly members of the Adventurers' Guild, but I recognized more than a few faces from the Order of Parcae. As I'd hoped, they were playing this smart, using the standoff and the fact that every chimera present was facing away from them to get into position. Their rogues and stealthy types were up front, creeping into striking distance, and several mages were already waiting on rooftops behind the tanks.

I bought them time. "It didn't have to be this way. Your master—whoever he is—could have just pranced over the region line, sauntered into the Adventurers' Guild, and said hello. We could have talked, discussed terms. Maybe even consolidated power. But instead he pulled..." I made a dismissive gesture toward the gathering. "Whatever the hell this shit is."

For the first time, the minotaur didn't repeat the same two words he'd been chanting like a mantra. Instead, a low, repetitive huff came from his neck. Almost like he was choking, or...

Laughing.

My smile was all teeth. "Oh. You come into my house, fuck with *my people.* And you think it's funny."

The minotaur continued to chortle.

I moved on, undeterred. "Whoever your master is, it's obvious he cares about you. From what I've seen, most of these freaks have the survival instinct of a lemming, but you? The second I hacked your head off and stuffed it into a pocket dimension, your goals changed. Shifted to self-preservation in a way that is almost human."

His laughter died as I put my arm into it and the bag spun faster. "Guessing he let you keep that because you're not exactly cheap to engineer and he wanted to protect his investment. Still, it's something we have in common. Wanting to live and whatnot. This is how we both get what we want. There's a device in this bag that's about to open up a portal to a realm of Flauros. A random realm. The portal will stay open for exactly five seconds. Being at the center of this portal, this bag and naturally, your *head,* will be the first objects sucked in. Maybe I'm underestimating your abilities and your awareness works across realms."

The creature shivered. Whether it was out of fear or anger didn't matter. I was getting to him.

My smile turned to a smirk. "But I'm willing to bet it doesn't. And if that's the case... I'd really, *really* try to catch this before it lands."

Before he could react, I flung the bag off to the side and over the edge of the reservoir. And like a dog after a frisbee, the minotaur charged after it, powerful hooved legs propelling him up and over the railing that housed the overlook. He sailed through the air, almost perfectly on target, and grabbed the bag with both arms before he lost forward momentum and plunged downward.

I hit the deck and covered my head.

Even fully shielded from the blast, the teeth-rattling shock-wave of the detonation rocked me to my core.

CHAPTER TEN

I reeled in the aftermath of **<Temporal Flare>**. Despite the whimsical name, the crafted explosive device's posting including a list of specifications as long as my arm. It was supposed to be a low-yield payload with a limited radius, using a mix of "temporal reiteration" and straight-up blast power to obliterate anything in a tight circumference. Its effective area was so contained and small that I doubted it would work as a car bomb—it could absolutely ruin the day of the people in either the front or back seats, or annihilate an engine block, but you'd need multiple to achieve all three simultaneously, which was both inefficient and something of a relief.

History, as always, was prone to repeating itself. With independent crafters on the rise, it was a growing area of argument and discourse among the regions at large. Some wanted to restrict the production and sale of explosives completely for obvious reasons, while the opposition argued that they flattened the playing field and allowed both low-tier Users and civilians to defend themselves against the sort of high-level threats that were commonplace during the Transposition.

My opinion was mixed. A capable mage like Astrid or Astria was more than capable of creating large-scale destruction that equaled or sometimes exceeded a run-of-the-mill explosive, so in some ways it felt like a moot point. Simultaneously, the idea of placing access to explosives at the fingertips of every gun-toting, propaganda-spouting fringe dweller in the dome—of which there were many—made me uneasy.

If I'm being honest, I wanted that access. Current circumstances served as a suitable example. I'd found myself in a situation where I needed to do more damage than I was capable of. I'd done my due diligence, identified an ideal staging ground, and, hopefully, reduced my regenerating attacker to dust.

I just wasn't sure I wanted to see what happened if everyone else had it.

Even my use hadn't been perfect. I wasn't physically hurt and had taken no damage from the blast, but just being on the edges of it had scrambled my senses. As I pushed myself up, I nearly slipped, fighting the misfiring neurons and ruined equilibrium that made me feel as if I was constantly growing closer to the ground.

The sound of conflict reached my ears as my hearing returned. More than a few of the chimeras Audrey had angered were still advancing on us, but most of them were turning to face the onslaught of their joint attackers. Mages hurled spells off of rooftops, while an aggressive and well-equipped forward line cut them down in droves. Their attention was split. Still, now that they were under attack, the creatures were putting up a more consolidated resistance, forcing back the adventurers who strayed too far forward with savage ambushes from the side. I'd disregarded them as stupid, which in retrospect was a poor estimation. They were lacking in general intelligence, but their instincts, the way they fought, gave the impression they were bred for war.

And considering the tide of the battle, they probably would not make it in time.

A snake-like chimera twice the size of the rest slithered toward me, ahead of the pack, forked tongue slipping out from human lips that were stretched too far back its arrowhead face to be called human anymore. I tried to pull my crossbow, watching helplessly as the targeting bead drifted over the snake's head.

Can't aim for shit with the shell shock.

Turned around as I was, a blade wasn't going to be much better. I growled, knowing that the only option I had left would likely kill my poor summon, but extended my arm and gave a mental command. Audrey sprung off my shoulder, vines biting into my sleeve as she launched herself from it like a cannon ball, landing on the base of the snake-chimera's neck and wrapping her vines around it, riding it as it flailed and tried to throw her off.

That would give me more than enough time to pop the flight charm and escape, but it would mean abandoning the narrative I'd crafted. Not to mention, with the size differential, the snake would kill Audrey before she made a dent.

On some level, I knew that using my summons this way was logical. If I died, they would also cease to exist. If they died, I could resurrect them once I had the mana to spare. My continuance meant their continuance. Still, I didn't like it. Maybe I was anthropomorphizing them, conflating loyalty with duty, but ever since Hastur messed with my head, it was harder and harder to not see them as people. They'd all stuck their necks out for me, risen far above what was required. Expecting them to do that as a matter of course just seemed...

Shitty.

"Hold on, buddy!" The shout was audible, even over the din of battle. I looked up, half-expecting to see Nick. Surprisingly, the man sailing over a half-dozen monsters directly toward the snake-chimera *wasn't* my friend. I was reasonably certain I'd never seen him before. Short-cropped hair, styled to perfection despite the circumstances. He was wearing the same light-weight variety of armor as me, which looked more like Kevlar-composite and was prohibitively expensive. There was a saber on his hip, undrawn, leaving his hands free.

He landed on the snake's head in an almost gymnastic display of dexterity, pressed his palms together, and slapped them down over the serpent's eyes. Audrey got clear just in time, releasing the snake and skittering across the pavement to me as fire raged beneath the newcomer's palms.

The snake bucked in its death throes, launching the man high in the air. He sailed backward, head plummeting toward the pavement before he tucked his knees, completing the back-flip and instinctually raising his arms in a salute for balance, a dead giveaway that he probably *was* a gymnast.

He snapped out of it just as quickly, sprinting back and forth between me and the oncoming chimeras, holding out his left hand and snapping his fingers, creating a collapsing radius of orange diamonds that radiated brightly.

A chimera that drew too close was immediately engulfed in flames, and the others drew back, staring at the minefield with cautious eyes.

"We always meet in the strangest places." Saber guy grinned at me, far too happy considering the circumstances. Now that he was closer, something about him was familiar, but I couldn't place it.

I spared a glance to the side when another of the orange mines went off. They were testing the range but not drawing any closer, then looked back to the newcomer. "Who... are you?"

Along the side of his neck, I spotted a tattoo of a human

face, so faded and poorly penned it was almost indistinguish-able. "Oh, sorry. Rolled in with the Adventurers' Guild to help out." He pointed to Audrey. "But I was talking to my friend."

CHAPTER ELEVEN

"M—me?!" Audrey stuttered. I felt a wave of panic resonating from where the plant summon sat on my shoulder. Ironically, more than when she'd kamikaze charged the snake. She was strange that way. Rarely, in niche situations, I'd use my summons to speak for me. Either to communicate over long distances or speak to people in situations where discretion was required.

"Your... friend?" I said slowly.

Even as I said it, I finally placed the face with a name. Brett. I'd found him in the early days, held hostage by a den of monsters on one of the early floors of the adaptive dungeon. As a naturally suspicious person with the only key to the dungeon in my possession, I'd assumed he was a dungeon construct, same as the monsters, drummed up to create a sense of urgency. When that was proved wrong, it created something of a conundrum because I didn't have the mask back then, and my side objective to not reveal myself to other Users was already in effect. Instead of playing along and being forced into a scenario where I either had to aid Brett directly or let him die, I'd gone an alternate route. Used Audrey to communicate and aided from the shadows while she appeared to save Brett single-handedly.

It was such a minor event amid so many cataclysms that I'd nearly forgotten it. Clearly, he hadn't.

"She came to my aid while I was running for my life. Unexpected, but I'm not the type to turn down help in a crisis. I take it you know each other," I said.

"Classic." Brett grinned. "Back when everything kicked off, this petaled lady pulled my ass outta the fire. Even told me about the Adventurers' Guild. God knows where I'd have ended up without her help." His smile faded. "Do you... not remember me?"

I shifted my shoulder slightly, jostling Audrey.

"WHAT DO I SAY?" Audrey's voice echoed loudly in my mind.

"You remember him, right?" I asked.

"YES."

"Then stop yelling and start there. Beyond that, it's up to you. He's your friend."

"I—uh. Yes. You... um... let me have all the meat. Very tasty once I learned to skin them and did not have to worry about the fur. Yum," Audrey said.

I suppressed a groan as Brett rubbed the back of his neck awkwardly.

"There's an image I was trying to get out of my head." He shifted his head from side to side. "But who cares. And if you're helping out this guy, I'm guessing you're doing well, mate. Good on ya."

"Thanks?" Audrey said.

"Tell you what," Brett walked along the perimeter, refreshing the fire mines, simultaneously talking over his shoulder, "stick around after the battle. I've gone back and forth on ways to pay you back if I ever saw you again, and I think you'll like what I came up with." He grinned, then seemed to remember himself. "If you can spare her."

I shrugged noncommittally and Brett took that as a yes, giving an enthusiastic thumbs up before he waded back into the fray. My eyes narrowed at that. He was either beyond confident, or he knew something I didn't.

Almost as soon as the thought crossed my mind, twin comets of plate armor landed with considerable impact, scattering the surrounding chimeras in a shockwave.

The first was Tyler, the massive leader of the Adventurers' Guild. And the second was Nick. Tyler looked the same as he always had. A good-natured grin split his lips as he spotted me, intact and whole. "Sorry for the delay."

"You good, Matt?" Nick called over.

With a single-handed sweep, his massive blade—really more greatsword than longsword, but he insisted on wielding it with one hand—carved through three chimeras, bisecting them diagonally in a shower of gore. His golden aura burned most of it away before it hit the ground. Even under siege, surrounded by countless foes, he looked every bit the hero.

I nodded. "Caught the tail end of an explosion, but nothing permanent. Where's—"

"Iris—Lipreader is at AG headquarters with Sae and your mom."

"Safe?" Last I'd seen her, she'd been borderline catatonic.

"Shaken, but yeah. And before you ask, Aaron's over there," Nick finished, pointing over his shoulder.

My jaw dropped before I could rip Nick a new one for abandoning him on the battlefield. An unarmed figure in five-hundred-dollar shoes, slacks, and a button-up shirt was walking through the throng unimpeded, hands in his pocket. Other than the fact that he looked like he jumped straight off the cover of Forbes, there was little noteworthy from this distance. Until I noticed the barely transparent bubble shielding him from harm.

"That's new," I said numbly. Up to this point, I'd believed Aaron was a civilian. That he held the helm of the Order through guile and planning alone. "Since when was he a User?"

"Not sure that he is." Nick lowered his voice, leaning dangerously close to a row of mines. "Still reads as a civilian in the group screen. But if he was keeping his status on the down-low, I think it's safe to say he's not hiding anymore."

We both knew a person's status in a system screen was anything but ironclad. Which meant Nick was basing that assumption off of something else, something he'd likely tell me later.

"No fuckery in the negotiations?" I asked.

"Smooth as silk," Nick confirmed, bashing a bear-chimera in the head with his shield hard enough that its skull cracked and it fell to the ground. "Twenty-six!" he yelled at Tyler.

"Thirty!" Tyler yelled back, smiling wide. He heaved his massive berserk-style blade in a half-circle, obliterating a half-dozen chimeras. "Gonna need a bigger sword if you want to keep up, kid."

"Size doesn't matter, you bastard!" Nick hollered back, redoubling his efforts.

It was insane how quickly they'd found rapport.

Tyler was a close ally, but he'd always regarded me with a certain degree of caution. Between his now mostly defunct truth-sight ability and uncanny judgment of character, there were likely more red flags in the mix than he was comfortable with. He saw my value, and appreciated what I'd done, but he'd always held me at arm's length. I suppressed a flash of jealousy at the ease with which Nick had slid into the guild leader's good graces and focused my irritation where it was actually due.

Aaron continued through the throng, approaching the

center, maintaining the same casual gait. The force field that surrounded him was unlike any I'd ever seen. More offensive. Instead of simply passively repelling attacks, the chimeras that approached him were seized by invisible hands and uplifted, their limbs, necks, and even tails twisted mercilessly until the creature was broken and discarded, writhing on the asphalt.

Since the dome came down, I'd seen plenty of high-level magic. But nothing quite like that.

Aaron came to a stop at the center of the melee. When he locked eyes with me, it felt like staring a shark in the face. Slowly, he nodded in appreciation.

He knows.

It was jarring, and more than a little alarming. I was used to my machinations slipping by under the radar. Making plays no one would notice, tweaking things in the background so they came to an ideal outcome while everyone else was none the wiser.

But Aaron saw the play. And I had a strong feeling he was about to make himself the star of the show.

When he spoke, his voice emanated from everywhere and nowhere, booming, unyielding.

"This region is now under the joint protection of the Adventurers' Guild and the Order of Parcae. Hastur's will be done. *Begone.*"

As his voice rumbled, the chimeras alone trembled, as if the earth beneath them was shuddering. And collapsed into piles of gore.

CHAPTER TWELVE

Power.

The thought pervaded above all else as the chimeras' gory remains spattered to the ground in a collective squelch that echoed across buildings. It was too loud, too pronounced. Either he'd use some sort of magic to amplify the aftermath, or the effect extended over the entire region. Probably the latter, considering the absence of any sign of battle. There was still yelling in the distance, some more alarmed than others, but lacking the roars, persistent clanging of metal, and shrieking of high-tier spell casts.

"Showoff," Nick muttered, just loud enough that I could hear.

I had to agree.

Almost awkwardly, the hundreds of Users shifted their attention from fallen foes reduced to fleshy puddles on the ground to the man still pushing his way through them, making a beeline toward me.

I couldn't help but raise an eyebrow as he approached. Aaron had irreversibly outed himself. It started this morning, when he'd resigned from his position on the relief council and revealed his role as a guild leader for the Order. But this was on a different level. *Everyone* would look at him differently after word of what happened here spread, both within the Order and beyond it. He'd have a lot more attention focused on him now, which I knew from personal experience could be more curse than blessing.

Tyler recovered first, sheathing the massive blade on his back and stepping forward, all smiles and diplomacy. He reached out a hand, and Aaron shook it warmly. "Our alliance is already bearing fruit. Sorry to pull you and yours off the bench so quickly."

"It's nothing." Aaron smiled. "Still game for darts later?"

"Can't see why not." Tyler grinned.

"Though that does raise the question of where." Aaron glanced at me as he spoke. "We'll need to decide the venue. Ordinarily, I'd suggest somewhere nearby, but... I wouldn't want to infringe."

This was the play. I'd harangued him in the meeting, going so far as to air out some of our pre-dome dirty laundry and serving as a heel. I hadn't gone overboard or made myself appear irrational, but what I had said made it clear our working relationship wouldn't exactly be cordial.

I looked around at the aftermath, stone-faced. "Quite the display for a civilian."

Aaron followed my gaze. "Perhaps. This wasn't something I wanted to be public knowledge, but the circumstances forced my hand."

"So you *are* a User," I pressed, dialing back the hostility of the accusation.

"Not as you know them." Aaron waved a hand, his expression thoughtful. "I can't engage with the system as you and the others do. But I'm not altogether lacking in the power that stems from it. It'd be more accurate to call me a divine conduit."

Great.

"Hastur's prophet," I translated.

"Of sorts." He stared at me with that blank, alien stare. It was probably the same look he used to bully clients and employees into submission at the hedge fund my mother worked at, before the firm's extracurriculars got her indicted. "I hope with this I've demonstrated our value as allies. A value that is perhaps worth the unpleasant ask of letting bygones be bygones." There was a tinge of distortion to his voice, indicating that he was amplifying his voice loud enough that everyone nearby could hear it, most without realizing magic was involved.

I had to suppress a smile at the ease with which he was coordinating the stage, moving everyone in it into a clearly defined role. Aaron knew I didn't oppose the alliance, just like he knew I'd used the chaos to create a scenario in which I needed the order to save me. None of this was pre-planned, yet he took it in stride, playing off my efforts to further his agenda.

Terrifying as always.

There was a moment of tense silence as Aaron reached out a hand. Out of the corner of my eye, Tyler actually held his breath.

I smirked inwardly. After all the buildup, it'd be amusing to deny Aaron here. Create some trumped-up subtext to slap his olive branch away. But that was little more than an intrusive thought. In reality, doing so would be as pointlessly obstructionist as it was short-sighted. Eventually—almost inevitably —we'd probably find ourselves on opposing sides again. And when that happened, I needed him to not see it coming.

Begrudgingly, I shook his hand. Tyler breathed a sigh of relief, and before I realized what was happening, Aaron swept me into a hug. My ears popped as the outside sound dulled, muffling sound from the city and isolating us.

"Rein in your dog," Aaron whispered, voice low and furious.

For a bizarre moment I thought he was talking about Talia, before I realized what he really meant.

"Myrddin?" I asked, smiling thinly. "You're the one who let him off the leash."

"I cannot run a guild if its members are constantly terrified and jumping at shadows. And there will not *be* a guild left to run if he continues at his current pace."

Aaron was mostly exaggerating. It was true that I'd been heavy-handed with Sunny's people, but they were generally loyalists who wouldn't have crossed the aisle to Aaron's side anyway. The few who hadn't been staunchly aligned were problems in other ways. As slick and enigmatic as it appeared from the outside, the Order of Parcae was mostly ex-cons, dishonorable discharges, and other undesirables. In a way, I could understand it, even respect it. Even with the world turned upside down, second chances were scarce. I'd be a massive hypocrite if I judged them all based on background alone.

But there were some things even I couldn't look past.

Still, the fact he was coming to me with this instead of approaching Myrddin directly was interesting. It wasn't as if Myrddin never showed face at the Order's headquarters. He was there fairly often. If Aaron didn't want to approach him publicly, he could have used a third party to summon him to his private quarters. Instead he was here, burning a chit of leverage to negotiate with me.

Was he perceptive, or afraid?

"Might be overestimating the sort of pull I have with our friendly neighborhood Ordinator," I hedged. "He doesn't exactly come to me for approval before he does something."

"Don't be stupid," Aaron snapped.

Fear, then.

He recovered from the lapse almost immediately, tempering

the anger. "We both know you'd never surrender an asset you couldn't control. Especially to me."

"Maybe I'm losing my edge."

Aaron snorted.

After deciding I'd put up enough token resistance, I rolled my eyes. "If I can spare the time, I'll talk with him."

Aaron's grip on me tightened. "Oh? Some other more *pressing* priority?"

"Yeah. Finding the necromancer who just took a swing at my sister," I growled.

All at once, Aaron's grip loosened, and he relaxed as he realized what, exactly, I was negotiating for. "Necromancers are a problem for all of us. A destructive blight on an otherwise fresh new dawn. One capable of this level of incursion is an even bigger threat. You'll have as much support as you need."

"Good. Considering that, I'll talk to Myrddin as soon as I can."

Just before we parted, I forced a series of images to mind and amplified the emotion that accompanied them.

Dead dog. First pet, a corgi with bowel problems and a worse back.

Dead summons.

Dead sister.

Dead dad.

My vision watered, and a single tear rolled down my cheek as Aaron stepped away. He stared at me, slightly taken aback as I shook his hand again in front of everyone.

"*Thank you*, Aaron. For everything," I said, voice warbling with genuine emotion.

Aaron bowed his head. "This was nothing. I look forward to the fruits of our future endeavors."

Tyler nodded, discreetly giving me a thumbs up, while off to the side Nick couldn't help but shake his head in distaste. Aaron nodded, shooting me a coy smirk as he turned to address the collective group of Users, amping up his energy and voice. "Victory is ours!"

Go ahead, play to the cheap seats.

A raucous cheer went up, only subsiding as he held his hands out to calm them so Tyler could address the group, his voice authoritative and proud. "Alright, folks. See a healer if you're injured and help others to safety if you're not. The rest of you, spread out and secure the region. Good job, people. This could have been a helluva lot worse."

There was a bustle of motion as the Users broke away, following orders. Only Nick didn't move; his arm was up, hovering frozen in mid-motion. His face was pale.

"What is it?" I asked, dreading the answer. Among the departing Users, more than a few had stopped in place, their faces drawn. Someone moaned, the sound guttural and raw.

"Pull up your UI," Nick answered quietly.

I snapped it open. And stared at the recent addition.

<13:23:59:49>

"Shit."

CHAPTER THIRTEEN

The bustle of motion that followed the chimeras' defeat was chaotic at best. Ellison still wasn't responding to messages. That could be a bad sign, but it could also be nothing. Communication wasn't his forte these days. Iris was fine. Fine, of course, being relative. She'd apparently fallen asleep, and considering how bad things were going to get in the coming days, I wanted her to get all the rest she could.

Shortly after the timer appeared, Aaron and Tyler had paired off, probably to discuss how to best manage the inevitable panic.

<13:23:44:49>

The second Transposition event. We always knew it was coming. Guess now we know when.

I forced myself to close the UI and stood on the far edge of the reservoir, watching as a mix of civilians and Kinsley's mercenaries recovered the minotaur's remains. The bomb had done its job, and other than a few large chunks, the rest of him was more or less well-dispersed oatmeal. *Sticky* oatmeal. One particularly gruff-looking man in dark fatigues was balancing on his tactical knee pads on the off-white concrete, reflective light from an honest-to-god spatula bouncing as he scraped a particularly tough sample off the ground and placed it into a vial.

"You sure this is the best use of our time?" Kinsley said. She'd come down to check on me because she was worried, and after seeing the bloodied state of my clothes, was standing a few extra feet away. "I get that he was regenerating but... he looks very dead. Super, extra dead."

I sympathized. The store was probably getting traffic from everyone who noticed the timer, yet she had people out here on cleanup detail. Still, this was important.

"I decapitated him, Kins."

She blinked. "Before you blew him up?"

"More sawed. But yeah." I peered at her. "Then, despite the fact that would dissuade most things from existing, he chased me down to lodge a complaint."

Kinsley absorbed that stoically. After a moment, she called out to her people. "Make sure you're keeping the samples separated."

Steinbeck, a gruff man with a cheery disposition, took a break from whatever he was scraping up and knelt upright, broadcasting to the rest. "You heard the boss. Handle with care. Wouldn't want to get thrown out a window."

A dark chuckle rippled through the mercenaries and civilians. At first, I took it as a generic joke coloring Kinsley as some power-hungry mob boss, but she shifted from side to side, lips pulling down in a scowl.

"Did—Did you actually throw someone out a window?"

"*No.*" Kinsley's mouth set in irritation. "He jumped."

I waited a beat. "Like actually jumped, or was 'assisted'—"

"Yes! *Actually* jumped." She sighed. "I've been meaning to

tell you that the satellite science team finished up their research, but it's been something of a busy morning."

That was the truth. The series of close calls still rattled me, so much so that with the sudden change of subject it took a second to place what exactly she was talking about.

"Hastur's potion," I realized. The reward he'd offered me as incentive. Either out of coyness or a twisted personality, he'd refused to say what it did, alleging I wouldn't believe him.

"As much as I hate to admit it, you were right. Keeping the research team under guard felt wrong, but it probably saved our asses. On that topic, I highly, *highly* recommend you don't hold onto it and use it as soon as possible."

Slowly, I connected the dots. "It's that valuable?"

Kinsley's expression was dead serious. "I mean, *Jesus Christ*, Matt, you're the best friend I have in the world and *I'm* tempted to steal it just to auction it off."

"You have more money than god," I reminded her dryly.

"Yep." Kinsley nodded. "And with upkeep, new acquisitions, paying these idiots decent wages, I'm breaking even until the dust settles. If I auctioned that potion, I'd have more money than the whole chicken-fucking pantheon."

Suddenly, I put it together. Kinsley wasn't being coy or dramatic by withholding what the potion did. More accurately, it legitimately spooked her enough that she didn't want to say whatever it did out loud.

What the hell is it?

"So the guy you threw out the window was a researcher—"

"I told you he jumped. And he wasn't just any researcher," Kinsley said glumly. "*Head* researcher. Rare vocation, sharp as hell, and had a jar of Dum-Dum pops in his office. Gave me one every time I came by. Very well compensated. But despite that he got greedy, inventoried the potion, and when the guard team cut him off at the stairwell..." Kinsley clapped her hands with a loud snap. "Dove through a window and ended up like a strawberry on the pavement. Five-story fall. No idea how the moron thought he could survive that."

I absorbed that and waited. "Send me the description."

<**Item Name:** Asura's Tears>
<**Rarity:** Legendary>
<**Item Description:** The residual tears of a false god, collected from her final prison in the aftermath of a failed insurrection. A universal palliative. Cures all lingering status effects, diseases, pre-existing injuries, impairments, or defects regardless of age, mental conditions, and unwanted alterations, so long as the recipient is still alive. Once imbibed, the secondary boon—
Asura's Gift—is received.>

What?

Barely processing what I was reading, I focused in on the highlighted square that covered **Asura's Gift.**

<**Asura's Gift:** Once this boon is attained, the recipient claims an aspect of the divine. Base kit immunity to all curses, status effects, and diseases is exponentially bolstered. Resistance to all damage types is amplified. Existing lifespan is extended by a magnitude of five. Permanent XP multiplier of 2x. Additional class utility for specific classes. Divine Aspect.>

"Jesus fucking christ." I slowly turned to look at Kinsley. Her typical devil-may-care expression was nowhere to be seen, overtaken by an overcast glumness. "If this gets out—"

"Yeah. I've already taken precautions," Kinsley said. She hesitated. "To be honest, I'm not sure if they're enough."

I understood completely. This wasn't just a cure-all. It was effectively a potion of immortality. Perhaps that was less valuable here in the dome, where any given day could potentially dish out more trouble than the average person could survive, but even so, there was the XP modifier, class utility, and amped-up resistance.

It wasn't just valuable. It was *priceless.*

The only way to guarantee something like this stayed secret would be executing the research team almost immediately after the potion's value was revealed.

Kinsley watched me, her expression grim. "Other than the head researcher, the rest of my team has done nothing wrong. They're quiet, freaked out, but generally loyal. Maybe to the paycheck, but still. Plenty of people turned up their noses when they saw how young I was, regardless of what I was paying. I'd rather not make ones who didn't regret it."

"Of course."

"I mean it, Matt."

I stared at her. "I'm not going to go after your people just because they have knowledge I'd prefer they didn't. Even if I was willing to do that, word spreads. It's probably already too late."

She looked away. "Okay."

I read through the description, making sure I hadn't missed any fine print or serious downside. The system didn't always provide an itemized list of potential downfalls, but it often hinted. Yet, there was no hint as far as I could see. If the description was accurate, the tears were as powerful as they appeared to be.

"Wait," I said, suddenly. "When he gave it to me, Hastur claimed that once I figured out what it did, I'd realize I needed more than one. And that he'd give me the second later once I'd helped him."

Kinsley said nothing, just waited. She didn't seem surprised.

The first had an obvious use case. Sae's insectile transformation weighed heavily on her. While it provided incredible speed and strength, the more... monstrous... aspects of her appearance were a constant drain on her psyche and severely restricted her ability to move freely in the open. All of which were near-direct consequences of my mistakes. I'd been too full of myself to see how sloppy I was being in the early days, and while the role I'd played in what happened was indirect, Sae had still suffered for it.

If I was reading it correctly, this potion could undo those effects.

Giving it to her was only fair.

"Cures all injuries or defects regardless of age," Kinsley echoed.

Oh. Oh shit.

Iris.

I resented the term defect. And wanted to push back against the idea that my sister had some "issue" in need of correcting. If this was the old world, I might have done exactly that. Mom wasn't supposed to play favorites, of course, but Ellison had taken to saying that Iris was "the best of us" long before the dome came down. And for the most part, I believed he was right. My sister had an essential kindness in her that almost everyone around her lacked. She was always the first to lend a helping hand, to put herself out to aid someone else even to her own disadvantage. There just weren't that many people like that left in the world. Part of me thought she'd eventually grow out of it. The rest of me hoped she didn't.

There was *nothing* wrong with her. In any reasonable, civilized setting she was more than capable of working around her own physical disadvantages and excelling.

An image of a dark shape sliding down the slide behind her replayed in my mind, and I closed my eyes.

With danger everywhere and the possibility of a second event looming in the distance, I had to be purely rational about this. And as much as I hated it, the conclusion was obvious. No matter how protected she was, or how many safeguards I put into play, people who could hear the thunder coming had a higher chance of living through the oncoming storms than people who couldn't. The potion had plenty of secondary effects that further empowered that equation—damage and status effect resistance alone factored astronomically.

Of course, ignoring the minor downside that if Iris lived through the dome, she'd outlive everyone she loved.

Fucking Darwin.

I rubbed the bridge of my nose. "Is it stored somewhere safe?"

"Safe as it can be," Kinsley said, not looking confident. "But I'll still feel better when it's nothing more than an empty bottle."

Kinsley was smart enough not to say it out loud, but I could guess. She'd probably stashed the potion in her sanctuary. Even if she was under duress, she couldn't retrieve the potion without entering her sanctuary first. Once inside, she'd be able to forcibly eject anyone who accompanied her, and would have multiple points within a several-mile radius to escape from back into the city.

Still, we were living in a time of unlimited possibilities. There was probably a way to get the potion out of her sanctuary we simply didn't know about. Which meant I needed to decide. And soon.

"I'll need to talk to Sae."

"Look, giving it to Iris makes sense," Kinsley said. From the way she was looking at me, I could tell she'd already guessed how this would go. "Sae may even see it that way. What happened to her is horrible, but there's no question her... issue...

makes her more capable than if she'd remained an ordinary User. But as soon as you tell her, it *will* give Hastur leverage over you. He'll be able to string you along until he gives you the second potion."

"I know."

"Then why tell her at all?" Kinsley asked. She crossed her arms. "We both know it's only a matter of time before the Order turns on us. Pretty sure you'd never agree to work with Aaron if you truly believed he was planning to make good on his terms. God knows I wouldn't, considering what those fuckers did to me. What they're *still* doing to my dad."

I struggled to answer. Because at the beginning of all this, I probably would have agreed.

"Too many people know what the potion does. If Iris miraculously regains her hearing, it might be possible to explain it away as some class affect or ability. But if Sae hears about the potion after the fact and connects the dots... it'd put us in vice."

Of course, that was just the rational explanation, the one Kinsley would accept. The truth was more complicated. While everything I'd said was accurate, what was really sticking in my gut was that I didn't want to lie to Sae. Not about something like this. After all the shit we'd been through together, she deserved to know the truth. Even if it sucked. Even if it made her hate me.

Still, the small quirk at the side of her mouth told me Kinsley wasn't buying it. "You're probably right. And even if you weren't, it kind of makes me feel better."

"Why?" I glanced at her curiously.

"Nothing. Just a reminder that you're still you. Part of my role is collecting information," Kinsley hedged, working her jaw. "And I've been hearing a lot about our mutual friend over the last few weeks that's... worrying."

Mutual friend being Myrddin.

"Like?"

"Nothing specific you need to worry about," Kinsley continued without answering, giving me a lingering side-eye. "But people fear him. And not just existentially, like before."

I rolled my eyes. "Courtesy of the Overseer, our mutual friend is both bogeyman and scapegoat. Someone trips and falls down the stairs, they'd probably find a way to blame him for it."

Kinsley inclined her head. "Maybe. But we both know most rumors carry a grain of truth."

I stuck my hands in my hoodie pockets and started to disengage. "You got it from here?"

"Uh, yeah I guess." Kinsley grimaced, watching as one of her people picked up a long viscous strand of meat from the pavement with a pair of tongs and stuffed it into a large glass jar. Her people were working slow, only partially because they were being thorough. From the way they kept sneaking peeks to the side, seemingly at nothing, it was obvious they were checking the timer on their UI. "Headed to the tower?"

I considered it, then shook my head. As much as I wanted to attempt to bullshit my way and rush through the remaining floors so Nick could claim **<Excalibur>**, we'd already tried that, and it had failed. What was required to make it through the upper floors was a coordinated group effort, and there'd already been too much chaos today. There were plenty of injuries, and with the reveal of the timer, everyone was scared. I suspected the impulse to rush was at least partially why we'd received such an advanced warning. The previous "game" had been divided by regions. There was at least a baseline assumption that the system established the regions for a reason, and whatever the event pertained to would probably include them.

But there was no guarantee it would shake out that way.

And most of us knew it.

So inevitably people would panic and wear themselves out

so much getting ready for whatever was about to happen that when and if it did, the populace as a whole would be on edge, primed to make plenty of mistakes, playing right into the system's hands.

As much as the necromancer attack and sudden reveal of the timer made me want to run around in a panic, I needed to resist that urge. Matt, specifically, needed to project calm. Like it or not, with the way things had gone down after the last event, the people in my region looked up to me. And the calmer my region was, the easier it would be to get things done in the long run, and the better we'd do in the second event if Nick and I failed to stop it.

"Not today, but soon." I pointed at her. "Make sure you keep that potion secure. And send some dummy quests when you can? Stuff that should be easily achievable in the tower. Not exactly low on Selve at the moment, but with the way things are going I'll probably need more."

"Easy enough." Kinsley nodded, watching me curiously. "But now you've got me wondering. What *are* you doing today?"

"Need to check on Iris. Lock in a level. Show face with the wounded. Then, after the dust settles, make sure everyone who's watching knows I'm not particularly worried about the second event or what happened today." I squinted, passing out of the shadow of the reservoir and into the sunlight.

"How?" Kinsley called after me.

"How else?" I shrugged. "By finally going on that date."

Somehow I managed to ignore the excited squawking that followed, echoing after me as I reached the ladder that led to the upper platform and beyond.

CHAPTER FOURTEEN

It was a relief to find that my previous evaluation of the attack was correct. We'd taken light casualties, nothing particularly unexpected. There were perhaps twenty or so people injured, and only three people had died.

I spent the afternoon visiting the families and loved ones of the fallen, making sure they were cared for, offering words of comfort that felt alien on my lips but seemed accepted and appreciated. The first two were more or less taken care of, with close ties to the Adventurers' Guild or other friends or family members positioned to look after them. Only one family had lost their primary User—a father with a Defender class—and I spent perhaps more time than I should have ensuring they were settled and connected with other parties who could help them.

Now, I was situated in Iris's dark room adjacent to my mother's flat, running my hands through her hair as I reviewed my character sheet. Iris herself was non responsive, laying on her side and facing the wall, either asleep or pretending to be. I'd been tempted to tell her about the potion, but given what she'd just been through she wasn't remotely ready for that discussion.

And to be honest, neither was I.

Instead, I tried to take comfort in the silence. Let my mind wander as I reviewed my character screen.

Matt
Level 24 Ordinator
Identity: Myrddin, Level 24 ???
Strength: 6
Toughness: 12
Agility: 33+
Intelligence: 20+
Perception: 14
Will: 21
Companionship: 3
Active Title: Jaded Eye
Feats: Double-Blind, Ordinator's Guile II, Ordinator's Emulation, Stealth II, Awareness I, Harrowing Anticipation, Page's Quickdraw, Squelch, Acclimation, Hinder, Escalating Fire, Assassin II, Mind Spike, Decisive Action.
Skills: Probability Cascade, LVL 18. Suggestion, LVL 27. Command, LVL 15. One-handed, LVL 30. Negotiation, LVL 25. Unsparing Fang (Emulated), Level 19. Bow Adept, LVL 12. Twilight's Nocturne, LVL 15. Subjugation, LVL 30. Riposte, LVL 10.
Boons: Nychta's Veil, Eldritch Favor, Ordinator's Implements, Retainer's Guiding Hand
Summons: Audrey — Flowerfang Hybrid, Bond LVL 10. Talia — Eidolon Wolf, Bond LVL 12. Azure — Abrogated Lithid, Bond LVL 20.

The last month had been nothing but grind, and despite running myself ragged, I couldn't help but feel that I had precious little to show for it. That wasn't necessarily true.

Reality was, leveling slowed down exponentially for everyone in the twenties. Compared to the average high-level User, I was practically sprinting through advancement, probably closing the gap with the top outliers.

But it still didn't feel like enough.

I pinched the ability section and widened my fingers, zooming in.

My primary stats were still intelligence and agility, though somewhat ironically, I was starting to doubt the practicality of the former. Early on, every point I assigned had a clear and definitive impact. I could recall memories long since forgotten, going all the way back to childhood. It was common knowledge that after a certain point, dumping points into stats led to diminishing returns, but the fact that I could no longer directly feel the difference was frustrating.

Still needed to raise it, of course. **<Subjugation>** worked far better when my intelligence dwarfed my target's, as well as a handful of other Ordinator abilities. But level mattered far more. Probably would have raised intelligence higher if Nick hadn't kept harping on me for my low toughness after a near one-shot in the tower.

And unlike intelligence, every point put into perception gave an obvious advantage, amplifying **<Jaded Eye's>** natural trap-detection and ambush awareness.

I'd made significantly more progress in terms of feats. Like the adaptive dungeon, the Gilded Tower handed out feat points like candy, especially if you were among the first to clear a floor. The second tier of **<Ordinator's Guile>** not only reduced the draw of the class-exclusive mana-hungry abilities and extended the effective range of my summons, but also increased the rate of my mana regeneration in general.

<Stealth II>, combined with my sky-high agility, made it all too easy to be invisible when I needed to be. Paired with both levels of **<Assassin II>**—which functioned like **<Blade of Woe>** on overdrive specifically on human enemies, providing a constant stream of information about their weak points and vulnerabilities I could exploit—made dropping rogue Users far easier than it used to be.

Though I wanted to avoid that whenever possible.

Nevertheless, in terms of stealth-build, I was almost set. All I was really lacking for my use case was a practical way to disappear when stealth failed me, which I was using a mix of items to compensate for.

In terms of direct combat... eh. That was a little more meager. I could scrap moderately well, and the combined psychological warfare I could reign down and bullshit I could throw out with my Ordinator abilities made me hell to deal with in a one-on-one fight with no interference, but that was in ideal circumstances. If I was outnumbered and surrounded, things were likely to get dire.

There was an ongoing attempt to rectify that weakness. **<Decisive Action>** was a Page feat that gave me several basic combat skills I'd be desperately lacking, starting with **<Riposte>**, which was effectively a counter. Counterattacks were already a priority for me before I'd received the skill, now they just hit harder. And once the skill hit 25, **<Decisive Action>** would bestow another. I'd continued to train **<Twilight's Nocturne>**, the fighting style Nychta gifted me, whenever I could. It wasn't flashy, but it was efficient and brutal. The problem was, it required me to be in some degree of flow-state. If pressed or surprised, I still had a recurring habit of falling back on **<Unsparing Fang>**. That was still working for now. The style was exotic and relatively unknown, but eventually I was going to need to branch out more. It just wasn't hitting the same way it used to, especially against monsters and Users with high defense.

Last time I was caught skulking around a hostile region by a tough-as-nails bruiser with uncommonly high perception, I'd spent nearly half an hour trying to bring him down before I caved and used my most recent acquisition, **<Command>**. He politely did as I asked and jumped off the roof, only the fall hadn't killed him, and considering the racket he was making at the bottom, his buddies had gotten to him before I could.

Yeah. I needed something else. Sooner, rather than later.

Though **<Command>** was endlessly useful, it was definitely situational. I'd picked the ability at level twenty, assuming that after I had it, **<Suggestion>** would take a back seat as a method of mental communication and subtle nudging. At first, second, and third glance, they seemed more or less linked. Suggestion allowed me to put thoughts in the minds of others, hopefully resulting in action. Command skipped the hope and forced that action.

There were quite a few differences in practice.

To use an extreme example, if I painstakingly convinced someone they could fly with **<Suggestion>**, the thought would probably persist. They'd keep thinking they could fly even after they were proven wrong. Depending on personality and, frankly, how stupid they were, they might even climb to the top of something high and try again. **<Command>** didn't persist the same way. Nor did it fill in the blanks and try to justify the action to the target like **<Subjugation>**. The target simply felt a compulsion to do as asked, and after they carried the command out, the compulsion faded.

Which meant Perceptive Bruiser spent the next few days screaming about how the mystery intruder "forced" him to jump before I could get to him and edit his memories with **<Suggestion>**. My only saving grace was that they hadn't connected me to Myrddin. In his mind, I was just a random stranger.

The longer I could keep people from realizing Myrddin had powers of compulsion, the better.

And of course, the only recent addition to my boons was **<Retainer's Guiding Hand>**. I knew precious little about it, beyond that it was a gift from Hastur. It had no dropdown text, which made me think it fell into the "unregulated" system category.

Beyond my existing build, I didn't really have a plan for twenty-five. I think, on some level, I was hoping there'd be a skill evolution, something to help me even the playing field. But if there wasn't, I needed to come up with an alternative.

After a few hours spent scrolling through feats and not coming up with anything definitive, I received a message that filled me with dread.

<Tara: Alright, I'm finally off. Meet in the lobby.**>**

CHAPTER FIFTEEN

It should have been easy. After all, I'd spent plenty of time people watching, and it took only a cursory familiarity with modern day media to get the general gist of what you were *supposed* to do. It helped that the basics weren't entirely alien to me.

Have a plan.

Be consistent.

Make conversation, but don't talk too much. Show the capacity to be a good listener, but make sure to add something to the conversation.

Be amicable. Friendliness and banter goes a long way to deescalating tension.

And of course, don't be creepy.

Sae hammered the importance of the last point home. She seemed to enjoy her self-appointed role as my relationship coach a little too much, ever since I'd made the mistake of consulting her on a series of texts. The downside of that being the fact that her idea of teaching was repetition, and she seemed to fully expect this to blow up in my face. Which made me nervous.

<Sae: Remember, ratchet the intensity *way* down.>
<Matt: Yep.>
<Sae: And don't interrogate her!>
<Matt: I won't. Christ.>

I swiped my messages away in annoyance, then checked myself in the mirror. A simple suit jacket over the top of my hoodie, white button-up underneath. Jeans, brown loafers. Couldn't do anything about the dark bags under my eyes, but for the most part, I was satisfied with the ensemble. It was more layers than I'd consider wearing in the dead of winter, but I could put up with it for a few hours. Despite my earlier commitment to not rush, in the back of my mind I couldn't escape the feeling that this was a waste of time. That all I was doing was spinning my wheels when I needed to be doing something else, anything else. The feeling of problems piling up, a never-ending collection of spinning plates, was only exacerbated by the timer. Too much to do and too little time.

Another message came in, and I nearly ignored it before pulling up my UI.

<Sae: Probably bad timing, but since I know you'd raise hell if I didn't mention it, Max has a line on Sunny.>

I stopped mid-step.

<Matt: Where?>

Sunny—the more violent, less predictable co-leader of the suits—had been in the wind for weeks now. With his loyalists consistently disappearing or meeting with unfortunate accidents, he'd put two and two together and split. Dallas was a big city, but it was still only one city. There were only so many places for him to hide with User powers in play. With that in mind, I'd cheated. Sent Max to scout likely hiding places, narrowing the search by factoring in Sunny's known associates from Mile's fed intel. When that didn't work, I had Max more or less searching a grid, using his evaluation ability to ascertain the likelihood of finding Sunny within potential hiding places.

I hadn't really expected it to work. If we could get to Sunny, that'd go a long way to removing one of the more problematic plates from my collection, one that'd been bothering me for some time.

It'd be one thing if I thought his hiatus would stick. That it was a full-blown retreat, rather than a tactical one. Sure, he'd threatened me, threatened my family, but I could be practical. If my problems were willing to eliminate themselves, I was more than happy to let that happen.

But I had a feeling Sunny wasn't hiding. He was biding his time, lying in wait. And in isolation, he'd have all the time in the world to review who his enemies were and narrow down the undoubtedly long list of who could possibly want him gone. He was one of the few people living who could connect me to Myrddin. In a way, he was even more likely to do that.

<**Sae:** Galleria.>

<**Matt:** Fuck. Max is sure he's actually inside, not in any of the surrounding buildings?>

<**Sae:** Yep. Spent a few hours circling the area, using his power to confirm. Sunny's in there.>

It wasn't great. The once-grand Galleria, a massive three-story mall, first ravaged by the rise of Amazon and other online retailers, was practically derelict before everything kicked off. The few shops that remained were looted in short order after the dome appeared. Now it was a honeycombed husk of closed-down retail stores and broken glass, populated by nothing but ghosts and the homeless.

To further complicate matters, the Galleria straddled the border of Region 19 and Region 20, slightly more on the 19 side. If the rest of us were living in some weird System dystopia, suffice it to say that 19 and 20 were living in *Mad Max*. Significantly more guns, unhinged Users, and pissed-off civilians than practically anywhere else. The only thing that'd stopped them from becoming more of a collective problem was that ever since the first Transposition event they seemed to hate each other more than the rest of their neighbors and were perpetually at war with them. Said neighbors stopped engaging with them once they started driving around in system vehicles augmented with very much non-system firearms.

<Matt: Screw it. Message the others. We're taking him down before he disappears again.>
<Sae: Today? What about your date?>
<Matt: I'll reschedule.>
<Sae: Okay, no. How about we not do that. Let's do our due diligence first, make sure we know what we're getting into before we jump the gun and get ourselves killed. Plus, how many times have you already rescheduled on this poor girl?>

I hesitated, not entirely sure of the answer.

<Matt: Uh. A few.>

More than a few. Practically every week since I'd rescued Nick. It wasn't like I was avoiding her intentionally. There was just always something coming up, something critical I couldn't ignore. Realistically, given the clear scheduling issues, I wasn't sure why she was still interested.

Come to think of it, that really was strange.

<Sae: Look here, asshole. I know how you operate, and that even if you abandoned your plan and headed over to the FOB, we probably wouldn't move on Sunny until after midnight. Ignoring the possibility that the date goes swimmingly well—because, let's face it, it won't—I'll get everyone ready and start working on a plan. We'll be ready to go by the time you're done.>
<Matt: Fuck. Fine. I should probably message Greg first anyway, see if he knows anyone in the region, and he takes forever to message back.>
<Sae: Who the hell is Greg?>

I closed the message with a dismissive wave and headed out the door.

————

Had to hand it to the cleaning staff, the lobby was as sparkling as ever. The marble floors were reflective enough to be mirrors, and you had to look close to notice a few deep gouges in the wooden panels and impact craters no amount of polishing could hide. Beyond those, and a few short Corinthian columns absent busts, there was little evidence that the violence that occurred in the city at large had spilled over here.

I walked past a woman in a golden dress, probably a half-inch taller than me, looking for Tara, finding the lobby mostly unoccupied other than a man at the front desk and a few people moving in and out of the front-facing restaurant Tara worked as a waitress at.

I nearly moved that way, guessing she may have gone over to check in before a voice called out from behind me.

"Matt?"

As it turned out, the woman in the golden dress *was* Tara. I'd only ever seen her in her work clothes, but what had really thrown me off was the makeup. Either she didn't usually wear it, or her makeup for work was of the lighter, more "natural" variety. Not to call her current makeup heavy, but with careful contouring on her cheeks and *something* she'd done to her eyebrows to make them darker, in contrast with her curly blonde hair, gave her a distinctively fresh look. It must have taken hours. Paired with the designer heels and light pink clutch, she was dressed to the nines. She offered me a small smile, smokey makeup crinkling around her brown eyes.

Oh, no, **<Jaded Eye>** murmured

Oh, no, I agreed.

"Oh... no?" she repeated, confused.

God dammit. Of course I said that out loud.

"Uh, sorry. Underdressed. Just gotta go back upstairs and change," I muttered, overwhelmed with a sudden desire to run away.

"No, you don't." She grabbed my left arm in both of hers, wheeling me back around toward the door. "Relax, you look cute." Then, lower, almost whispered, "And if I let you get on that elevator, I'm guessing I may never see you again."

I forced an awkward chuckle and escorted her outside.

The drive to the restaurant, while still somewhat awkward, was less harrowing than it could have been. Tara was skilled at filling silence, regaling me with personal details and stories about her life. It wasn't the inane chatter of a narcissist, or someone with a hyper-inflated self-image. There were plenty of pauses, for me to either confirm I'd heard what she said or offer a comment of my own. She was unexpectedly upfront, and in being so gave me a much better idea of who I was dealing with before we even reached our destination.

A&M, public relations major until she put that on hold on account of her brother Ethan. Details got a little cagey there, but I gathered that their home life was far from the best, seeing how Ethan emancipated. Regardless of why, he wanted to live with her, and for the state to recognize her as a conservator she had to hold a full-time job.

So Tara dropped out of college and made it happen.

They had an uncle in Austin they were friendly with, but they didn't see him much. Mainly on holidays or whenever Tara could get weekend consecutive days off work.

By the time we reached the restaurant, I was mildly disappointed. But not for any of the reasons I'd expected. Ever since Hastur screwed with my head, it'd been harder to be cold, more difficult to do the more... unpleasant things I needed to do. Most of the time I just did them anyway. This was supposed to be a farce. A fake, superficial relationship drummed up to conflict with Miles's alarmingly accurate profile. Tara was perfect for it. She lived in my building, she'd pursued me first to save me the time, and she didn't quit easily. She was also stunning and would easily draw attention away from me.

I just wasn't sure I could follow through.

There were enough markers, enough similarities, that I could recognize the trappings of a young adult who, forced to act as a parent because the people who were supposed to fill that role, failed.

I knew that life. I'd lived it. And it was hard enough without some schmuck coming around and wasting your time.

So, as the hostess escorted us to our table next to the window, I resigned myself to calling it. If dinner went well and I didn't get the sense that she was playing a part, I'd do what I could to help her, connect her either to Kinsley or people in the Adventurers' Guild who could offer her a better position. If I was right, she'd work her ass off. And it was the least I could do for wasting her time.

We sat across from each other, easing into our chairs as the waiter poured our water and lit the candle in the center, leaving while we perused our orders.

Throat dry, I picked up my cup and tilted it to my lips.

"So," Tara ran her fingertip across the rim of her glass, crystal emitting a pitched hum. "How long have you been living a secret life?"

CHAPTER SIXTEEN

Slowly, I swallowed and placed the glass back onto the table.

"Aw, no spit-take?" Tara pouted. "Thought I'd timed that perfectly."

At a quick mental prompt, Azure took form in my shadow, creeping down and crawling beneath the tablecloth.

"Find out what she knows."

"Your wish is my command!" Azure replied cheerily.

He wouldn't be as strong here, in the city. If we were in a realm of Flauros, like a dungeon or trial, given enough time he could have told me almost everything about Tara, from what she'd had for breakfast to her deepest, darkest secret. In the real world, he'd be limited to surface-level thoughts, which shouldn't be a problem, seeing as how she broached the topic herself.

I smiled, baring my teeth. "Interesting ice breaker."

Tara nodded. "I get told I'm interesting a lot. Mainly by men though. So I've never really been able to piece together if I'm actually interesting or if interesting is just code for 'nice C-cup.'"

By some small miracle, I ignored the bait and kept my gaze

at eye level, using **<Awareness>** to scan the room without appearing to do so. No one else looked out of place. Nothing in the parking lot had set off **<Jaded Eye>**.

If this was an ambush, she was the only one springing it.

"Depends. Where are they looking?" I asked.

"Usually at my chest."

"Then it's a mystery, I suppose."

Tara squinted at me. "Huh. You're catty, I didn't figure you for catty."

"We all make mistakes," I said blandly, doing my best to buy time for Azure. The conversation lulled as the waiter brought out bread and butter, and Azure returned with good news and bad. The good news was that she had nothing concrete. She was irritated at how long I'd made her wait, but more curious about what she'd seen. The bad news was that she was observant, savvy, and had an eye for detail, and she'd been snooping around more than I'd realized. Tempering that slightly, Azure was fairly sure she hadn't talked to anyone about her observations.

"You always start out first dates with an accusation?" I asked, smoothing the napkin over my lap once the waiter was clear.

"Nope. Really wildin' out right now." Tara rested her chin on her palm. "First date is usually buttoned up, conservative, calm." She made finger-quotes. "'Non-offensive.' The nosy, meddling side of me rarely comes out until date three."

"So you've expedited the process."

"More like you Byzantined the process." She stared at me like I was slow. "First, I see you around the building. Not usually my type, but my type tends to be fluid, so I try not to draw that conclusion too early. Eventually, I put together from context that you're the guy who got hibachi'd to keep this place from going full-on *Hunger Games* that me and my brother would have inevitably been slaughtered in, and hey, suddenly you're one-hundred percent my type. I keep my fingers crossed and my eyes open. And now—now I'm probably talking too much." She stopped at that, her expression glum.

"No, keep going, I'm enjoying this." As soon as I said it, it shocked me to realize that I was. Though my guard was still up, with all the cloak-and-dagger in my life as of late, it was refreshing to hear someone be so straightforward.

She carried on as if she'd never stopped. "So I'm there, working the seven-to-three, fingers crossed and eyes open, when you finally come in. Unfortunately, you're not alone. *Fortunately,* you have a kid brother. One who's clearly too-cool-for-school that you seem to be earnestly trying to connect with. Score. Suddenly we have common ground."

I grimaced, knowing what was coming.

"Only, it's not going so hot." Tara shook her head, her expression sympathetic. "God, I wasn't even trying to listen and I could tell that kid was ripping you a new asshole. Just tearing you to shreds."

"Trying for a blowout," I agreed quietly, without even real-izing I was talking. There was no harm in confirming that much. She'd seen it. "Easier to keep someone out of your busi-ness if they want nothing to do with you."

"But you didn't give it to him. The blowout. Though from what little I heard, that would have been more than justified. He gave you a royal beat down, and you just sat there and let him vent. Like, how do you even do that?" She sat back hard, cocking her head at me.

"Tension at home?" I guessed

Tara rolled her eyes, then nodded. "Yeah. Yeah. Ethan and I... we were always copacetic, you know? Like there isn't that much to fight over when you're just trying to keep the lights on and everyone understands that. But..." she extended a hand toward the roof. "After the first event, he was one of the civil-ians elevated to User status and I... stayed a waitress."

"Started getting ideas about who needed to take care of who."

"Oh, did he." Tara chuckled. "'No worries, sis, I'll just throw myself into danger so we can have more money.' Like that's not the last thing I would ever want for him."

"Like you're just supposed to forget how young he is. All the mistakes you had to cover for. Because fucking up in the old world, that's recoverable. Hard, sometimes, but part of growing up." I filled in the blanks easily with thoughts I'd had countless times myself.

"But now, if you fuck up out there..." she slid a finger across her throat. "Several types of dead. Easily. In a second." Suddenly, her expression went from aloof to stern. "Stop being so understanding and making me like you more. I'm trying to set the scene here."

I held my hands up in mock surrender, mildly amused. "Are you always this radically honest?"

"Definitely not." She cringed a little, offering a half-smile. "Considering how I almost died last time, I guess the timer and whole second-event-on-the-horizon-thing is driving me to be a little bolder. Which is probably stupid, because in my experi-ence guys hate that."

"I'm not like the other boys," I said, layering the statement in as much irony as I could muster.

"Gross." Tara rolled her eyes again. "Anyway. I see this pick-me—"

"—Hey—"

"—get absolutely obliterated by his brother. My first instinct is to shut it all down. He's having a bad day, probably not the best time to talk to him. But then..." Tara tapped her cheek. "I get an idea. A way to my flag my interest and maybe make his day a bit better. So I write my full name down—"

"With a heart over Strickland."

She pointed at me again. She pointed a lot. "Exactly. Hoping he'll get the message. Then, after a lot of wondering if he just wadded up the receipt and threw it into the trashcan—"

I winced preemptively.

"—he finally hits me up. Only it's late at night. He's smart enough not to go straight for the kill, starts out by asking about getting coffee, but I'm getting serious booty-call vibes." Her smile faded a little. "Tested the waters, and he went for it. Little disappointing, but I figure, that's fine. He's cute, probably saved my life, and since he lives in the same building and will inevitably want a repeat performance, this might be a convenient way to blow off steam."

"And then the fucker immediately flakes on you."

"*Exactly.*" She drew the word out in disbelief. "So I'm curious, and more than a little annoyed. Still, maybe it's legitimate, maybe he has a good reason. I'm half-expecting a hungover apology in the morning, but that never happens. Naturally, I assume he has a girlfriend, had a moment of weakness and gave into temptation. Shitty, but it happens. I keep an eye out, for my own voyeuristic satisfaction if nothing else. No girlfriend. A few nights later, I spot him leaving, alone. But I never see him come back. What I do see is him, coming into the restaurant in the mornings, dark bags under his eyes, absolutely beat to shit, nursing injuries. He hides them well, but I see it in the way he cringes when he moves wrong. Off doing User things, has to be. I catch him leaving a few more times, but again, I never see him until the mornings. So I have to wonder, where the hell is he going, and if he's taking that much of a beating every night, why does a region leader never bring anyone with him?"

Azure was right. She didn't have anything. Nothing more than a series of coincidences. But if she mentioned those coincidences to the wrong person, it could make my life considerably more difficult. And if she was as perceptive as Azure thought she was, it was better to avoid a direct lie. Stay as close to the truth as possible.

I smoothed the tablecloth. "It's... how I started. Working alone. I imagine the same way as a lot of other people, in the early days. Like you, I'm used to being the only person my siblings can rely on. That's all a little different, ever since the first event." I looked out the window for emphasis. "They have a village now."

"Your life has changed." Tara nodded along.

"For the better. But, there's a part of me that misses being self-reliant. There's a certain solace in it, when your life is the only one you're responsible for. And that's a far cry from the way things are now," I said, not having to fake the wistfulness in my voice. "Sure, I could probably tap a few people from the Adventurers' or Merchants' Guilds to tag along. That would probably be safer. But if I'm being honest, going out there, exploring, looking for realms of Flauros..."

"It's your way to recharge. You're an introvert, and it's the only time of the day you aren't around people or responsible for something." She bought it, hook, line, and sinker.

"Exactly," I smiled, then let the smile ebb. "Maybe it's reckless. It's not meant to be, it's just..."

Tara shook her head. "You don't have to explain yourself to me. I get it."

We both jumped as the waiter appeared, seemingly out of nowhere. "A complimentary bottle for the table." He placed a bucket of ice on the table, removing a green bottle and filling a glass. I nearly opted out before Tara stopped me with a quick shake of her head. Begrudgingly, I sat back and waited as he finished and left the bottle to the side. "What will we be having this evening?"

Christ, I hadn't even glanced at my menu. Didn't help that every dish was written in Italian, and other than spaghetti, the rest was Greek to me.

Tara carried on, nonplussed. "I think I'll have... the osso buco—is that garnished with gremolata?" When the waiter confirmed that it was, she nodded. "Perfect. And he'll have the spaghetti alla chitarra con polpette di vitello."

I relaxed, giving her a look, to which she stuck out the tip of her tongue.

Before the waiter left, he clapped me on the shoulder and leaned down with a wide-smile. "We deeply appreciate everything you've done." Then disappeared just as quickly.

I waited a few seconds, then asked, "What the hell did you just order me?"

"Spaghetti and veal." She blinked. "You said earlier you wanted spaghetti, and I know you like veal from the restaurant."

She wasn't wrong.

"What did you get?"

"Veal."

"Then why are none of the words the same?" I wondered.

"Dunno. I speak fine dining, not Italian." She peered at my bubbling glass. "Are you straight-edge?"

"Complicated."

"Obviously, but I was referring to the champagne."

Again, I felt a strange compulsion to be honest with her. I carefully took stock, mentally reciting memorized information, making sure there wasn't some sort of spell or skill affect screwing with me. Nothing. Neither **\<Jaded Eye\>** or **\<Ordinator's Emulation\>** picked up on anything being cast.

If anything, all my inner voices were quieter around her.

And I didn't know what to think about that.

"There's an alcoholic in the family," I admitted. When Tara immediately paled, I waved a hand. "It doesn't bother me on a fundamental level. Don't mind being around other people drinking either."

"Cost-benefit analysis."

"Hm?"

"The decision to not drink," Tara said, taking a long pull of champagne, staring at me over the rim. "Whatever short-term jollies you get from a trip to vodka—no, wait, not enough self-loathing—well-whiskey land isn't worth risking the chance you have the gene."

Azure's read was perfectly on the mark. She *was* dangerous.

"Partial credit." Had to give her that.

Her eyebrow shot up. "Got it wrong?"

"Not entirely." A small voice stopped me. This wasn't the sort of thing I usually shared. Yet, despite that, I shared it anyway. "The alcoholic gene factors, but it's not that I won't, or that I don't want to. It's that I can't."

"Very vague. Enigmatic. If that's what you're going for—"

"There's no headroom. No accounting for errors. If I fuck up, things go bad in a second. It's always been that way. Sometimes it doesn't matter and things go to hell beyond my control. And when that happens, I need to be ready. So naturally, I'm constantly expecting the worst and preparing for it. Given that, most of the time I clutch it out." I thought about the tunnel. "But sometimes I don't. And it's hard enough to deal with the fallout of failure when I didn't voluntarily do anything to impair my judgment."

Well, that was a mood-killer and a half. From my understanding of how these things went, this was probably the point where she'd go quiet, we'd finish our awkward dinner in silence, and never talk to each other again.

Only she wasn't looking away. Her expression was coy, almost playful. "How would you change my outfit, given the chance?"

What? "What?"

"Answer the question. Come on, I want your opinion."

I looked her over, keeping my expression neutral, careful not to linger. From the golden dress, to the matching earrings and perfectly coiffed hair, I had no notes. She clearly had a far better grasp of fashion than I did.

"Do you have boots or sneakers in your inventory?"

She half-shrugged, smoothly swapping our glasses so it appeared like I'd partaken of the champagne. "Flats, in my bag."

"Then nothing."

No way she was running in those heels if everything went to hell, but of course, she had a backup plan. I wasn't attracted to her. But that was hardly her fault. It'd be fair to say I'd never really been attracted to anyone. But I could appreciate the presentation, the effort she'd put in, and the attributes that inevitably made her attractive to others. Museum rules. I enjoyed looking, even if I had no desire to touch. In some ways she felt like a kindred spirit, similar to me, yet entirely different.

"Okay, fine, I'll bite. Why the fashion consult?" I asked.

"Guess I was curious." Tara took another long pull, evening out our glasses. "If you're a controlling asshole with unreasonably high expectations of everyone around you, or really just that hard on yourself." She glanced out the window thoughtfully. "Come to think of it, if you're that disciplined, I'm guessing you're not even here for me. Centrally located restaurant, window seats. That's all intentional, isn't it? You're showing me off. Or at the very least, making a public demonstration that you're not worried about the timer."

Feeling slightly guilty, I channeled Nick. "What sane person wouldn't want to show you off?"

Her eyes went dark, glittering with challenge. "Fair warning. Don't give me the hot-cold treatment unless you want me to drag you to the bathroom, right fucking now."

I stopped channeling Nick and shut the fuck up. Then spent an inordinate amount of time mentally reviewing the restaurant's possible escape routes.

Suddenly, Tara laughed until she was tearing up.

I bristled. "*Great* joke."

"No, no. Trust me. That wasn't a joke." She wiped a tear from her eye. "I'm laughing at how quick on the draw you are with the poker face. One second you're—you know—vibing, quietly enjoying yourself." She raised a flat hand and drew it downward, expression transitioning to deadly serious as her hand passed. Her voice took on an alarmingly accurate depiction of my deadpan. "Then you're about to make me an offer I can't refuse."

I took a deep breath, allowing myself to relax. "Considering how reserved you are at work compared to now, something's pot and kettle."

"Finally." Tara leaned forward. "Come on. Hit me."

"What makes you think I have anything to say?"

"Other than that infuriating smirk on your lips and the fact that we've already established you're catty?" Tara folded her hands and rested her chin on them. "I've been poking at you for the last half hour. It's only fair play."

"You're not going to like it," I warned her.

"Don't tell me what I will and won't like."

Whatever this was, whatever she thought she felt toward me, the only justifiable reason was that she didn't know me. And I had a feeling, based on our encounter so far, that if I didn't give her a genuine answer, she was just going to keep pushing. Maybe it was better this way. I wouldn't give her everything, not enough to send her running, simply enough to ensure any reasonable person would lose interest.

"Fine." I drained my water glass, placing it on the table with a clink, then leaned forward and studied her. "You dropped out for Ethan, but he's not why you didn't finish your degree."

Tara's smile vanished.

I kept going. "You didn't ditch PR. You're too passionate about it. It wasn't a loss of motivation or being overworked. With night classes or online courses, you could have easily finished it with the time you had, probably tacked on a master's while you were at it. Not to say you were stagnant. Anything but. I'm guessing you kept up your studies independently, read what you could when you could, and at some point realized finishing your degree academically was pointless. You found a mark, some under-tapped market that the archaic monoliths of corporate PR weren't reaching. And in that vacuum, you found opportunity. Smart money says you were networking, trying to form the connections to get that particular effort off the ground."

Tara's mouth opened slightly, as if to say something, but no words came out.

"Not at any fault of your own. Dome surprised everyone, fucked up more plans than god. You kept your head down, kept working at the same place. You're a hard worker. Not exactly a deep insight, anyone who sets foot in the restaurant can see that, but I still think it deserves mention—because you perfectly suppress your true personality, and the professional mask is so good I didn't catch a hint of it. Which is saying something. But it takes a toll. You're—" I stopped, noticing the glassiness in her eyes.

"Keep going," Tara whispered. "I'm enjoying this."

Okay.

"You're..." I swallowed. "Sexual. Possibly hyper-sexual, not that it's anyone's business other than yours, but you asked. I'm guessing having to stay so strait-laced at work aggravates that, but there's something else. A note of thrill-seeking to it. You were willing to hook up with a guy you knew practically nothing about and had never held a conversation with, and I'm not egotistical enough to believe there-was-just-something-about-me. You've done this before."

"So I'm a whore." Her expression was cold.

I shook my head. "No. Semantics aside, it may not even be about the sex. Unless I'm completely wrong, I'm guessing risk-taking is part of your coping mechanism. The way you deal. Not knowing what you're walking into amps up the risk factor, and therefore the enjoyment. Same reason you confronted me so openly about my 'secret life.' Willingly exposing yourself to risk and chaos helps make the stringent control you have to enact more bearable."

There was a long, tense silence. Tense enough that when the waiter arrived with our steaming plates and placed them on the table, he delivered them wordlessly and retreated. I was almost entirely certain I'd said too much.

This is where she tells me to fuck off.

Tara shifted, the strap of her dress slipping down one shoulder. Her warm breath washed over me as she whispered, "I'm wet."

I swallowed.

"I'm... ace."

The spell was broken. Almost immediately Tara leaned as far back in the chair as she could, her eyes wide. "What."

My words came out in a rush. "I mean, I probably am, I don't know, it's never really been relevant until now—"

"Stop." She pinched the bridge of her nose. "So, the bootycall—"

"—was entirely accidental," I admitted.

"And this isn't a 'I always thought I was asexual until I met you, Tara,' situation?"

"Pretty sure it doesn't work that way."

She blinked several times, holding a hand out to one side in confusion. "Was I imagining it? Do we not have chemistry? Because I've been on a lot of first dates, and this is the first time it's felt like we're in danger of setting the place on fire."

I snorted. More of that trademark honesty, even in the face of rejection. "You weren't imagining it."

"So you felt it too."

"Yes."

"Just not in a way that involves taking me back to your penthouse and tearing my clothes off," she confirmed.

"Yeah." I sighed.

"Fuuuuuuuuuuuuck."

"This has been a waste of your time."

Tara scoffed. "Hardly. Ignoring the possibility you get all weird and start avoiding me because of the awkwardness of me thirsting over you at dinner, I'm pretty sure I made a friend." She eyed me. "And you got a chance to confirm something pretty crucial about yourself. That's hardly a waste of time, even if we're all monster food two weeks from now."

I drummed my fingers on the table. She was being magnanimous, but the scales still didn't feel even. "About Ethan."

"Uh-huh."

"This isn't exactly common knowledge. I know you can keep a secret—"

"And how do you know that?" Tara asked, amused. "If anything, I've probably given the impression I'm a blabbermouth."

I fought the instinct to glance away, remembering what Azure had told me. She'd seen more than enough to gossip, yet she'd kept her mouth shut. And that was before she even knew me. Maybe I was giving her too much credit because I liked her. That concept was almost entirely new to me. But it felt right, and this was more of an open secret than anything else. "Call it a hunch. Tyler's been working on a program for kids and teens with User status."

Tara raised an eyebrow. "Tyler, as in leader of the Adventurers' Guild Tyler."

"Got it in one. Anyway, your situation isn't unique, even within this region. There's no small number of kids with combat classes who are either orphaned or suddenly have a newly strained relationship with their civilian guardians. More whose parents are too busy or too scared to teach them. Plenty of them ranging out into dungeons on their own, and we both know how many people died during the last event, children included. Tyler thinks the best course is to get the kids used to their classes and powers, as well as combat, in a semi-safe setting."

"Semi-safe," Tara repeated, unsure.

"Right." My eyes slid to the side. "No one's died. Most of it is giving them easy quests on the surface and sparring with each other. But nothing can really prepare you for live combat but live combat, so there is occasionally some danger involved. Every couple weeks, the adults scout a low-level dungeon, either confirm that there are no problematic monsters or clear those monsters out, then supervise as the kids go through it. They're compensated for any work they do, and they keep the loot they find. They're also, for all intents and purposes, considered full-fledged members of the Adventurers' Guild."

"Given that, how would they be deployed?" Tara asked cautiously.

"They're considered reserves. Tyler has a bigger soft spot for kids than I do. In all likelihood, the only reason they'd be deployed would be in dire straits, if there was a good chance of the entire region getting wiped out. And they'd be augmenting the adult squads, not deployed on their own. Anyway, it's not perfect, but it's something." I shrugged.

"Safe to say, I'm very fucking interested. Ethan would go for that in a second." Tara brushed her chin with her thumb. A light flicked on behind her eyes. "The reason this isn't common knowledge is that the Adventurers' Guild doesn't want the other regions to think they're training child soldiers."

I nodded. She caught on quick. "Tyler's still working on how to spin it."

In truth, I wasn't sure there was a good way to spin it. Regardless of what our intentions were, it was effectively what we were doing.

Tara's eyes flicked back as she chewed on her bottom lip. "What about the other regions?"

"Hm?"

"You said my situation wasn't unique."

"It's not."

"Then we're not the only regions dealing with it," Tara mused. "If Tyler was willing to open up this program to children in the same situation in other regions, it would dissuade suspicions, especially if you were willing to take on teachers from those regions."

"Unaffiliated with the Adventurers' Guild."

"Exactly. Beyond the obvious advantages of helping kids who need it, it'd be a chance to bridge the divide, encourage unity across the regions," she continued, growing more animated.

And open us up to spies large and small. Naïve.

Tara's expression turned sinister. "Imagine the pipelines that would open. Not to mention a mountain of good will. They'd have to limit the outsiders' exposure to our region, of course, no reason to give away information for free. And kids talk, so it'd probably be better to keep the outsiders in a separate group from the local kids. But think about it. If you have the option of attacking the region that's been helping keep your kid alive or turning on the other guy, how exactly do you think that's going to go?"

It was insidious, beautiful, and just a little bit evil, all wrapped in the package of doing something that was legitimately good. Something Tyler would one-hundred percent go for. It wasn't something I'd broach to him until after the second event was over or avoided—inviting the children of other regions over just before the Transposition was *guaranteed* to be a bad look—but after? It had a hell of a lot of merit.

The gears in my mind turned. I'd been shirking my duties as region leader. In no small part because I worked better from the outside. As support, rather than the star of the show. At first, I'd believed it to be little more than a title that occasionally made a decision. But the longer I stayed here, the clearer it was that these people, regardless of their history, looked up to me for saving them.

And the only thing more surprising than that was that I didn't want to let them down.

I'd been thinking too long, evidenced by the crestfallen look on Tara's face. "That's... probably a little stupid and unethical—"

"Do you want a job?" I asked suddenly.

/////

We spent the next hour ironing out the details. Tara would work for me and Kinsley, effectively doing what she'd always wanted to do. Running PR. Coming up with ways I could help my region and helping me work on my image. I'd all but discarded the idea of using her as a beard before—to my utter shock—she brought it up herself, on the basis that she'd go a long way to softening the "almost-literal-chip-on-my-shoulder" and staving off unwanted attention. We'd meet once a week as a "date" in somewhere public. I tested the water, asking if she'd be willing to undergo something like a geas, and she was surprisingly fine with the idea, citing that it wasn't all that different from an NDA, something public relations types typically signed as a basic matter of course.

Yet, I couldn't shake the shadow of a doubt that I was missing something. It wasn't something Tara herself had done, it was something else, something in the negative spaces I couldn't quite define. I was used to fighting tooth and nail to get what I wanted, tapping into every reserve I had to cinch out an ideal outcome. Yet with Tara, things had gone smoother than I could have possibly dreamed.

"It doesn't have to be a bad thing. Maybe your luck's finally changing," Azure said.

I ignored him and walked Tara to the curb. Evening was fast approaching, and Sunny's number was finally up. But I found, to my abject surprise, that the anticipation and bloodlust that would typically accompany that thought simply wasn't there.

Tara balanced on the curb and looked back at me in a daze, her once-perfect hair askew in the breeze. "This has been... a lot."

"More than I bargained for as well." I glanced down the road. The white shuttles served as public transport around the region, now that the diesel-chuffing buses of old were more or less out of commission. "Sure you don't want me to drive you?"

"No." She brushed a strand of loose hair behind her ear and shivered. "I've taken up enough of your time. And you sort of just changed my whole life, so, I kinda want to be alone and process."

As the shuttle approached, Tara opened her bag and swapped her heels for flats, balancing easily on the curb as she did so. Then winked. "Just in case something happens and I need to run."

"Your wisdom knows no bounds."

She climbed the steps, paused to wave, and then she was gone, shuttle headed back toward our complex. Her absence left me with a strange feeling, and a lingering unease I couldn't put my fingers on.

Absentmindedly, I pulled up my UI and scrolled through my messages.

<Nick: Heard down the grapevine our boy might become a man tonight—>

Next.

<Sae: Still prepping for the mall. On schedule so far. How's it going?>
<Sae: Helpline.>
<Sae: Answer me bitch—>

Next.

<Greg: Hey Man! I Would Be Happy To Help! You Don't Gotta Pay Me But It's Always Appreciated.>

Perfect. Only he was messaging me as Matt, which made this tricky. I hit him back, asking if he'd be willing to help out a friend and confirmed payment, then passed along Sae's contact details. She'd be the only connection to me, keeping Myrddin out of it.

<Kinsley: I hope you're being nice to her.>

I paused on Kinsley's message, wavering in indecision. In the distance I saw the brake lights of Tara's shuttle as it stopped, picking up another few passengers before the brake lights faded and the shuttle took off again.

Finally, I tapped the call button and swiped the UI away, watching as the shuttle disappeared around a distant city-block corner.

"If it isn't my broodiest, least responsive employee," she chirped.

"Ha ha."

"Date didn't go well?" she asked.

I shook my head. "The opposite."

"You're shitting me."

I rubbed the ever-deepening lines of my forehead. "I need a favor."

CHAPTER SEVENTEEN

The strike team operated out of the same abandoned warehouse I'd plucked a merchant girl out of what felt like a lifetime ago. We had a few other meeting places and fallbacks, but this had—once again—become something of a second home over the last few months.

When Kinsley was here, she hadn't spruced the place up much. Something about the concussions and her father's kidnapping put a real damper on her aesthetic preferences. The whole time the two of us worked out of this place, it stayed spartan.

It looked completely different now. I'd told Astrid and Astria it was temporary, but that hadn't stopped them from decorating, putting up posters, bizarre and unconnected art pieces, lamps, a dark-brown pullout couch, and several reclining chairs. And, of course, a "high-learning" sized white board, which was currently pushed to the corner of the room, half concealed beneath a curtain. I honestly should have come down on them harder for the constant ornamenting—the entire point of using this place was that it *looked* abandoned—but the truth was I didn't have the heart.

Especially considering how Astrid couldn't stop gushing about how nice it was to stay in one place.

Another reminder that I was getting soft.

Then again, I had to remember that Gemini was the star of the show here. The twins brought more collective firepower to the team than Max, me, and even Sae could leverage collectively at any given time. Maybe letting them liven the place up was a perk that came with the territory.

Max was doing basic maintenance on his crossbows in the corner. I turned him toward them. Beyond his previous association with Roderick, his background was a mystery, but he was one of many frustrated Users who had extensive pre-dome experience with firearms and found themselves unable to leverage that skill. That frustration was doubled when you factored that Max's Estranged Officer class was almost purely informational. His evaluation power was invaluable, but he didn't have many combat skills. And as someone in almost the same exact situation, I knew crossbows would translate well. Took him a week to get a solid feel for them, and after that he'd been upgraded from pure scout to auxiliary ranged.

Sae and Astrid were quietly discussing something in the corner and didn't appear to be arguing. That in and of itself was uncommon, as outside the field their aggressive personalities tended to set each other off, and it took a measure of discipline not to send Azure to listen in. There was no reason to breach their privacy. If it was important enough, Sae would bring it to me later.

Astria was talking my ear off, per usual. She got nervous pre-mission, and unlike her sister, seemed to place a lot of faith and trust in me, given our history.

"—taking dual-cast at level seventeen is the obvious choice," she continued in a stream-of-consciousness that barely required my input.

"Mhm," I said. We'd already talked about this.

"How... is dual-cast different from what the two of you usually do?" Talia—currently manifested in her darker, shadow form—lifted her head and asked.

"When we cast together, we're magnifying the same spell. Dual-cast would allow us to do the same thing with either the same spell or two different spells, quadrupling the firepower." Astria's eyes twinkled. "And that's not even getting into the reactions we could set off if we mixed different elements. Super-heated steam, maybe even lava if we do it right."

"Seems like a wise investment." Talia nodded approvingly.

"How close are you to leveling?" I asked, trying to re-engage with the conversation and ignore Sae and Astrid.

"Close. We should both tip over tonight if this one's worth as much XP as the last one," Astria said, then her enthusiasm waned. "Won't matter though. Not if I can't talk Astrid into it."

That was surprising. For as long as I'd known them, the twins had been more or less of one mind. Besides the day we'd met, this was the first hint at internal tension I'd gotten from either of them. "Astrid wants something different?"

Astria chuckled nervously, pointedly not looking at me and playing with her hair. "It's no big deal. She's just dragging her feet a little."

I waited.

Talia looked between us in confusion. "I do not understand how this matter involves feet."

"Figure of speech, Tal," I murmured, keeping my focus on Astria. "Means her sister isn't picking up what she's putting down."

"Shouldn't the person who put it down pick it back up?" Talia blinked.

"She thinks we're focusing too much on offense," Astria admitted, seeming disproportionally uncomfortable with the statement from the way she shifted and refused to make eye contact.

I shifted the mask on my face, feeling a degree of responsibility. "If the counterargument is she wants to boost your defensive spells, Astrid may be onto something. The way the strike team fights is perfect for taking out isolated, high-level targets—"

"—assassinations," Astria chirped.

"Or abductions," I said, cringing slightly at her wording. "Anyway, ninety percent of what we do is location and timing. The remaining ten percent is unloading as much focused power as we can in a short time."

"Move quick, hit hard, get out." Astria repeated what had become the strike team's mantra.

"It's worked for us so far." I nodded. Even I was surprised at how successful we'd been without a tank, and it'd been my decision to go without. "But it's a niche strategy. If you go up against numbers or end up in a prolonged, sustained conflict— which will happen eventually—there's a good chance of burning up your mana reserves before the fight's over."

Astria nodded. "Maybe we can put dual-casting off for the next level then."

I wanted to inquire further. If Astrid's hesitancy wasn't limited to their combat balance. She'd been letting Astria take the lead more, which on the surface seemed like a good thing. Astria was far more useful now that she was taking a varying degree of initiative than when she'd been following her sister around like a ghost. But what if there was more to it?

"Myrddin." Max had twisted at the waist and called across the room, still caught up with his equipment.

"What's up?"

"Got the special payloads mostly figured out, but with what we know about this guy, I'm struggling a bit." He held up two different bolts. One was dark green and splotchy, the color of mud-speckled jade, thick tip forming a variation of the classic bodkin point shape. The second was bright silver with a hollow mechanical tip. On impact, the broadhead would expand, increasing the wound channel.

It was a relatable problem, one I'd been toying with in every hypothetical that involved Sunny. The only time I'd seen him in the field—the night of the tunnel—he'd been wearing plate. Given that, the armor-piercing lowhil bolts should have been the natural choice. The issue was he moved *fast*, faster than a man in heavy armor should have been able to move, and I wasn't confident the AP bolts could punch through whatever expensive, probably magic-reinforced attire he was using. I'd be more comfortable walking into this if my commission from the Order's blacksmith was ready, but they were still days away from that.

I opened my mouth.

Max interjected preemptively. "Before you say it, I'm already planning on bringing both. The question is, which do I load?"

I closed my mouth and considered that. Most basic system crossbows worked similarly to their real-world counterparts, sole difference being that the string would mechanically auto-draw. Only the lowest-level, garbage-tier crossbows required the foot-in-stirrup routine. Advanced, higher-level crossbows varied a great deal more. Single-fire, internal chambers, even a few cartridge variants. I knew—because I picked it for him— that Max's crossbow used a rotating internal chamber. It couldn't blow through ammo as quickly as a semi-automatic firearm, but it could get bolts down range faster and more accurately than the average sightless bow.

The downside, of course, was reloading. Bolts had to be seated into slots in the internal cylinder one at a time, not unlike a shotgun, and there was no fast way to switch projectile types. They had to be manually unloaded the same way they were loaded.

"How's your accuracy coming along?" I asked, leaving Astria behind and crossing over the room to his workbench. Last outing I hadn't seen him miss much, but I wanted to know what he thought of it.

Max shrugged. "Still internalizing the lead and drop at different ranges, which makes hitting a moving target harder than it should be, but in general? Pretty damn on the dot, if I do say so myself."

I picked up one of the heftier lowhil bolts and spun it on my thumb, extending the fletching side toward him. "Load the armor-piercing. I'll run broads out the gate, so we'll start with all our bases covered."

"Fair enough." Max loaded five bolts, then set his crossbow on the bench, turning to massage the shoulders of the young man sitting in Kinsley's old computer chair. "And I'm sure Renato here will warn us if we've got the wrong idea before shit hits the fan, now that he's finally decided to show up." Max jostled the younger man as Renato glowered at him through dark eyes. "Isn't that right, Renato?"

Renato was our eyes in the sky. Like Max, his ability was informational, though we'd kept the nature of it vague. He was able to monitor events through magical means and give us moment to moment updates during combat.

Or at least that was how I'd pitched him to the group.

In reality, Renato was Azure, my shapeshifting summon. I wasn't keen on repeating past mistakes, and underutilizing my summons in order to hide connections between me and Myrddin had been a big one. Azure couldn't just take on any face. He'd gone to great pains to stabilize this human version of himself outside a realm of Flauros, and until I reached a higher level, couldn't change aspects of it easily. His current form was vaguely Hispanic, and like me he had dark hair and dark eyes. None of his features were particularly striking, keeping him intentionally nondescript as possible.

The downside was he insisted on keeping the worst aspects of my personality.

"Excuse me." Renato drug his eyes away from the screen, staring down Max with a withering stare. "I had a thing I couldn't get away from and already pre-cleared it with Myrddin."

The "thing" in question of course was taking over as Myrddin, showing face at the meeting between Aaron and Tyler, fielding Tyler's, Kinsley's, and my many questions about what happened at the tail end of the event. I didn't have to use him as an alibi nearly as often now that enough people had seen us in different places simultaneously, the earlier morning being a rare exception.

Renato continued. "At least I didn't party too hard and show up to a mission I was supposed to be at late, with a hangover."

"Whatever you say, porcupine." Max laughed awkwardly, probably squeezing Renato's shoulders more than strictly necessary before he turned and retreated to his equipment.

"Greg's on his way," Sae announced suddenly, shuffling into the overcoat that hid her more insectile features. "We're rolling out in two minutes."

"That's the contact getting us into the Galleria?" Astrid asked.

"Uhuh," Sae confirmed. "Friend of a friend, so be friendly."

"Should I pull the van around?" Renato spun around, and I spotted a barely perceptible gleam in his eye. For whatever reason, Azure really liked to drive.

Sae shook her head. "Stay put. Astrid will teleport us to the subway stairwell. We'll meet him on the road."

I coughed. "Greg's driving?"

"Yep. Said they know his car."

I didn't argue, but I wasn't sure what to think. It made sense Greg had a car. Relatively, it was probably a lot easier for him to make money in the dome than it had been in the world before. And even if he hadn't bought it, there was no end to the number of abandoned vehicles that littered the side of the road. It was more having witnessed the manic abandon with which he frequently bombed downhill on a shopping cart that was putting me ill at ease.

There hadn't been a suitable moment to break the news to Sae. Not just that there was a cure for her condition, but that someone else needed it more and it would likely be some time before we laid hands on the second. Telling her now risked distracting her before the mission, a risk I wasn't willing to take. Still, I needed to tell her tonight if possible.

"Hey, Myrddin," Sae called out to me, glancing at the wall. "Sidebar?"

I followed her out of earshot of the others.

"You ready to get this fucker?" she asked as I leaned against the wall beside her.

"Been a long time coming," I said.

"Are..." Sae hesitated, some of the sharpness in her expression blunting. "Are we sure Nick shouldn't be here, for this?"

I shook my head.

Sae lowered her voice further. "It's just stuck in my head. We all lost something in that tunnel. But Nick loved her. Like, really loved her."

"So did you," I pointed out.

"In my own bitchy, cunty way, I guess." Sae huffed a laugh and wiped her nose. "Still, we're the survivors, you know? The three of us. It feels weird to not have him here."

She wasn't wrong. For the longest time, I'd believed Sunny's involvement was limited to poor management. That he'd simply failed to keep his people in line at a critical moment. But the more distance I put between myself and that event, the less likely it seemed. It wasn't that I'd learned more about Sunny and how he operated, though that was also true. More that I'd gained life experience.

I could say definitively that the best way to break a group like ours had been was to create the same exact outcome he'd "accidentally" achieved. Swiftly and brutally killing an auxiliary member to your target when you had the numbers advantage was a perfectly efficient manner of breaking morale.

It was something I planned to ask him about, if he surrendered before he stopped breathing.

"I get it," I reached out to brace her arm. "Then again, it's not gonna bother me. If all goes well tonight, I'm gonna go home and probably sleep better than I have in weeks. And considering I the barrage of colorful ideas I had to talk you out of if we had a chance to interrogate him, I'm guessing it's not gonna bother you either."

"Probably," Sae admitted.

"Nick isn't like that. We bring him along tonight, and that shit will haunt him. He deserves the chance to move on with his life. Leave Sunny's clusterfuck in the rear-view."

Sae breathed out, then nodded. "Can't be the wisecracking hero if you're buried in self-doubt." She looked past me to where Astria was completing a runic circle that glowed blue. "Teleport ready?"

"Now it is." Astria stepped back, reviewing her handiwork before she grinned. "All aboard!"

I stepped into the teleport circle first. And the world swirled away.

CHAPTER EIGHTEEN

We were in the field now. The van was deathly quiet, pumping AC and struggling engine drowning out most noise. None of the witty banter, or nervous tittering that pervaded my first team. Even Astria was mostly silent, humming an atonal repetitive melody that was barely audible even with enhanced hearing.

I glanced in the rear-view from my seat in the passenger side.

Sae and Max sat in the two pilot seats in the center row. Max's face was scrunched up, fingers tapping quietly on his knee while he stared at his UI, waiting for his evaluation ability to come off cooldown. Beside him, Sae sat cross-legged, her chitinous ankles hanging off either side of the worn fabric of the seat, her hands relaxed and palms upward, eyes closed. Behind them, the twins sat on either size of a bench seat sized for three, if the person sitting in the center was a hobbit.

The way they were sitting seemed off. Not their body language or mannerisms exactly, but that there was a space between them at all. They'd always been closely knit. Almost clingy. This was anything but. Astria's legs were angled toward the center of the isle, as if she wanted to close the gap. Astrid's, comparatively, were pressed against the door.

The saying had been repeated so much that it was almost trite, but that didn't stop it from being true. A person's legs and feet generally pointed in the direction they wanted to go.

Which, for Astrid, was out the fucking door.

Again, I was tempted to ask Sae about it. And again, I resisted. Whether it was prayer, or meditation, or silently and maliciously manifesting harm upon the people who wronged her, I'd seen her do this often enough to understand that it was her version of a high-performing athlete's pre-game ritual.

She of all people would have told me if something was seriously wrong.

More realistically, Astrid was probably tired. The new dawn of recovery and health potions meant, barring a severe injury, we could be back on our feet the day after a mission and ready to go by evening. But they did nothing for the mind.

Fatigue was inevitable.

For the moment, I dropped it, giving them one last look before I rested my head back against the seat. An unfamiliar sense of pride washed over me. They were a good team. We'd been through a hell of a lot of shit together in a relatively short period of time. Most of them had doubled their levels since they started, putting them miles ahead of the pack. They weren't cheery or high-energy—the nature and stress of the work didn't allow for that—but they were effective. And there were no egos to get in the way, no irritating edge cases that would inevitably spin out of control.

Which left me with conflicting emotions. Waging war on Sunny's sector of the Order was tireless, sometimes terrifying work. People in his orbit seemed to have a propensity for pulling the most hair-raising bullshit out of their ass. That was the part I was more than happy to finally put to bed. It meant I could stop playing nightmare Batman and go back to fighting monsters for a change.

Put all my efforts into helping Nick and company climb the tower.

It was possible that some or even all of them would stick around. Sae obviously would, but Gemini and Max I wasn't so sure of. If they did, I intended to give them smaller assignments adjacent to what Nick and I were doing in the tower. Keep them active and continue pushing leveling opportunities their way.

<**Max:** Possibility of intercept, one.>
<**Myrddin:** Good. Road clear?>
<**Renato:** Yup. No blind spots or conspicuous debris. Not even a car pulled off to the side. System must have worked overtime to clean up the highways after the last Transposition.>
<**Myrddin:** Likely to change as we get closer. Regions in question aren't exactly focused on cleanup.>
<**Max:** Really want to ask how you're tapping into traffic cameras wirelessly connected to servers housed in buildings that no one in their right mind would pay to power these days, but I know you're just going to say magic.>
<**Renato:** Look! It's learning!>

I closed the three-way chat before my summon and scout inevitably started sniping at each other.

A bit of carpet caught the edge of my boot as I shifted in my seat, and as I looked down to smooth it, I noticed debris, the usual crumbs that adorned a minivan floor. It wouldn't have stood out to me at all if the middle wasn't immaculate.

He vacuumed.

"Nice ride," I said, keeping it casual.

Greg jumped, stealing glances, probably looking for

sarcasm. When he found none, he smiled widely for the first time since he picked us up. "You think?"

"Sure. Plenty of seats, plenty of space, milage that doesn't want to make you gouge your eyes out. What's not to like?"

"Ain't had a car for a long time. Long, long time. With all the tooth and claw going around, figured I'd invest. Had options, you know. Plenty of 'em. People throwin' around money like it grows on trees, System giving out money for pattin' your own ass. With all the green, could have bought something fancier from mini-miss-bezos but, I don't know. Probably silliness."

There was a lot of truth to that. The system would kill you in a second and laugh about it, but it never stopped seeding opportunity. Even for civilians.

Greg's car was a pre-system navy blue dodge minivan, at least ten years old.

I weighed the wisdom of continuing this line of questioning, weighed the chances of me giving myself away, then decided it couldn't hurt. I wanted to know how he'd been holding up. Greg was a regular presence in my old region, long before it had that designation. And more to the point, he seemed nervous. "I mean it's practical. But why'd you pick this specifically?"

"Silliness. Like I said." Greg's expression turned nostalgic. "But if you really want to know, I was hoofing it in uptown. Moving quick, cause the fuzz around there gets real staticky if you make the economical choice of pushing your shit around in a basket. So I'm looking out, head on a swivel. Valet line for Fyre is already around the block. Audi, three-hundy, Audi, Range Rover, Audi, *Lambo*... you get it."

"Bunch of rich bastards queueing up to pay two hundred bucks a plate."

Greg laughed. "Yeah, you get it." He paused. "You local?"

"Transplant," I lied.

"But you been here long enough to get a feel for the place."

I nodded.

"Anyway, at the front of the line—and despite me desperately needing to get up out of there—is this dusty minivan." Greg squinted, gesturing with one hand. "And this bougie-ass, America's-Next-Top-Model-ass, woman gets her and her Prada bag out the car. Hands her keys to the skinny valet, ignores the way he's wrinkling his nose, and struts inside. It stuck in my head a little."

"Because of the dichotomy," I filled in.

"Crazy. Weird thing was though, the more I thought about it, the more it made sense. It was old, but it wasn't a beater. Plenty of trunk space and seats for whatever she might need them for. But she could have parked that thing packed full of one-hundred-dollar bills in the middle of stop-six and nobody woulda looked at it twice. Figure even though I finally got some value to my name, if I go too flashy, someone'll just find a way to take it away from me. This though?" He smacked the dashboard. "If it was good enough for her high-society tomfoolery, it's good enough for me."

It was a good story. But I'd spent enough time talking to Greg without the mask to know he was leading up to something. I let him simmer, his eyes glued to the road.

He spoke without looking at me. "Yall a quiet group. Serious."

"Tired, more than anything. It was a busy day."

Greg continued as if he hadn't heard me, exiting the freeway. "The Galleria boys are alright. We go back a ways. Crashed with some of em for a few months, had a little spot under I-45. Nothing too big. Few scuffles in the night, but we kept it down. And kept a thumb on the loud ones so they didn't call down hell."

"Sounds nice. Communal." A memory sparked, something I couldn't quite put my finger on.

Greg shook his head. "Yeah... but hell has a way of coming, whether you call or not. City came in, hosed us down, took our shit and threw it away. Most of us rabbited before it got bad. Then the boys in blue beat the ever-loving piss out of the ones who didn't."

I winced. The over-funded cleanup was what I was remembering. At least one person died.

"You think they'll see us as a threat?" I asked.

"Are you a threat?" Greg asked, his eyes flicking toward me.

"No." I repeated the previous line. "We're here for a bounty, nothing more. Guy's a sick bastard. And the Galleria settlement will be safer once he's gone."

Greg's hands tightened on the steering wheel. "If any of 'em catch a stray, they'll blame me."

"That won't happen." I'd make sure of it. If we did this right, Sunny wouldn't know what hit him.

Gradually, the roads began to fracture, flecked with detritus and potholes. We drove slower, partially to give Azure more time to look for threats in the ruined streets and bombed-out buildings, partially because Greg didn't want to ruin his ride. Once it came into view, the Galleria was surrounded by a wall that looked to be made of every material in existence. An amalgam of metal, plywood, and dirt, topped with a chain iron-fence topped with spiraling barbwire that ran the length of the top. Despite the messy aesthetic, it must have been a massive undertaking.

Greg came to a stop at an enormous sliding fence on what used to be the Galleria's southernmost exit. A spotter on a rickety looking platform hollered behind him, and after a few tense seconds the gate slid open.

"Any last words of advice?" I asked Greg, suddenly feeling out of my depth.

"Don't go barefoot." Greg half-smiled. Then his expression grew serious. "I guess, just remember, this is the most a lot of these folks have ever had. If you treat them well, they'll remember. But in our heads, we're still waiting for the hoses. If you take from them? They won't ever forget it."

Greg accelerated, maneuvering the minivan inside slowly as the gates slid shut behind us.

CHAPTER NINETEEN

We were ushered into a shipping warehouse attached to the east side of the Galleria at gunpoint. Sae, Astrid, Astria, and Max wore simple white masks with cutouts that allowed them to see, leaving me as the only person appearing to show my face.

More eyes followed us than I'd prefer, both our escort and the myriad of people around—ideally, we would have snuck in without consulting with leadership at all, but the new reality of the Galleria didn't much allow for that. *Everyone* was heavily armed, with more automatic weaponry than I'd seen in a single area that wasn't waving a certain flag. There were less Users than expected, but they made up for it with heavily armed civilians. None of them were dressed poorly. For the most part, their clothes and gear were either new or in good shape. Their backgrounds were betrayed only by the plethora of worn visages and windburned complexions.

Come to think of it, they were likely this well-armed because they had to be, considering their choice of settlement lay between two aggressive, warring regions. The Galleria straddled both and therefore represented an overwhelming tactical advantage to whichever side took it first.

And the fact that it was still independent of both was a statement of its own.

In the car on the way over, Greg confirmed some things I'd only heard rumors of. A man referred to ubiquitously as The Steward led the settlement. He'd been something of a street legend before the dome. If you were homeless—especially newly homeless—the first piece of advice you'd receive from the more experienced individuals who shared your situation was to find The Steward. According to Greg, he'd show you the ropes, teach you both how to survive and be invisible in an otherwise hostile environment. He'd also give you a crash course in what you could and couldn't scavenge and differentiate between the gray-legal ventures that were lucrative, and the too-good-to-be-true sort that would rain hell down on your head.

From the way it sounded, he was reasonable before the dome. But I knew all too well that just because a person was reasonable before the system didn't mean they'd stay that way.

So, with caution in mind, I took a seat in a metal folding chair across from The Steward. The rest of my team hung back, and after Max confirmed that the chance of an ambush was low, tried to force myself to relax and take in the man sitting across from me.

For all the hype, he wasn't what I expected, but that was probably the point. In line with what Greg told me, he had the sort of presence that could blend in almost anywhere. If I had to guess, from the male-pattern baldness and salt-and-pepper, I would have put him around advanced middle age, though stress and exposure to the elements could make the homeless appear far older than they were. A trench coat with the arms cut off adorned his slight shoulders, and he was wearing a faded

Black Sabbath t-shirt over what appeared to be considerable armor that covered his vitals. A twelve o'clock shadow shrouded his jaw in bristles, and he appeared to be studying me just as intently as I was observing him.

"Shall I take a peek in his head?" Azure asked.

I considered it before sending my summon a mental negative.

"He's a region leader in everything but name. There was no bull-shitting, no posturing, no time-wasting attempt to make us wait to reinforce the power dynamic. Whatever's in his back pocket, he's confident."

"Or he wants something," Azure countered.

Both were probably true. Either way, I didn't want to risk a potentially beneficial connection on the off-chance Azure's surface level reading was detected.

Still, the silence was killing me. I used silence as Myrddin far more than I ever had in negotiations as Matt, as the uncanniness of the mask tended to get under people's skin after a while. But I got the feeling it wouldn't work on The Steward—who I mentally dubbed Stuart, simply because the preceding "The" was bothersome.

I was about to speak first before Stuart pulled an arm from beneath the table, presenting a deck of worn red-backed bicycle cards. "Do you gamble?"

Russian immigrant. He's suppressing the accent, but it's there.

"Not when I can help it," I answered.

The crow's feet around his eyes crinkled at that. "A wise answer." He shuffled the deck, cards blurring in a cascade of clicks, then ruffling as he bridged them. Despite his gnarled fingers, the movement was practiced and easy. Which created the first note of warning in the back of my mind. Because, in my father's words, a good shuffler was often the first sign of an experienced hustler. "Do you know why it is wise?"

It had the sound of a hypothetical, so I shook my head.

He continued to manipulate the cards in varying types of shuffles, some I'd never seen before. "Gambling is ruinous by nature. It has been the undoing of many a man beneath my purview. Gamble long enough, and your undoing is all but guaranteed." He placed the deck to the side and steepled his fingers. "But we cannot live without taking considerable risks. They can be mitigated, but are never truly gone. We are left with a paradox. We should not gamble. Yet we must."

I had to hand it to him. It took a special kind of person to project this much gravitas with almost no presentation. The leader of Roderick's Lodge had styled himself as a king, going so far as to secure a crown and castle, and he held perhaps a fraction of this man's regal aura. A man who—again—was wearing a Black Sabbath t-shirt.

I allowed a small smile. "Like how—despite having never met us—you allowed me and my team to keep our weapons."

Stuart scowled. "That is a risk I've come to realize cannot be mitigated."

"Oh?"

"Inventories. Pocket dimensions. Bags that transform dangerous items into seemingly harmless utensils until they are drawn out again. The god-damned market delivery." He waved a hand in frustration. "It is an area where prevention is simply unsustainable. It is better to simply trust those who are proven. Isn't that right, Greg?" Stuart cold gaze shifted toward where Greg stood, nervously in the corner.

"Y-y-yes, Steward," Greg stammered, stumbling over the words as his voice echoed over the concrete. "Friend who asked for the connect's a good one. Even let me hide out on his couch a few times when the asphalt was boiling or my shit got stolen. Wouldn't do us no harm."

"So you've said. Yet you've refused to give this mysterious third party a name."

Greg visibly struggled. "He's... a private person. Wouldn't like it if I was throwin' his name out and about."

Damn. Greg's taking more of a risk with the referral than I realized.

It made sense. We knew each other in the way you can only know someone who's lived in the same sphere as you for years. I'd done him a number of favors over the years, many of which he'd returned, but this was by far the biggest. I had to be careful here. Make sure I didn't put Greg in more of a bind than Stuart already had him in.

"Normally, that would be enough." Stuart nodded regretfully. "But ever since you crossed our threshold, the—" he hesitated, considered his next words carefully, "—let us say, angel, on my shoulder has been disproportionally concerned."

"Angel," I echoed, my mouth going dry.

Deity. Has to be.

There was always a risk that region leaders—even unofficial ones—had some sort of patron. After all, I was one of them. The combined effects of **<Double-Blind>**, **<Nychta's Veil>**, and the Ordinator's mask were more than enough to shroud me from direct identification as the Ordinator by the wandering gaze of any deity. But if that deity were to look closer, I had to guess the absence of certain information would create a question of negative space.

I paused long enough to check in with Max and make sure nothing had changed. The likelihood of ambush or apprehension had increased by a single point, from two to three. It wasn't nothing, but it was still small enough to be a rounding error.

"By threshold, you mean..." I cocked my head.

"When your vehicle passed through our gates," Stuart answered.

"Then I guess, I have to wonder why I'm sitting here." I leaned back, resting my hands on my lap. "There were multiple points after our arrival that this meeting could have been aborted. You could have turned the car away, used your numbers to detain us."

"Perhaps these things did not occur to me."

I cracked a smile. "*Please.* You don't hold the most tenuous position in the city by being incompetent. And I'm guessing this," I knocked lightly on the felt table, "isn't just here for the sake of a metaphor."

Finally, the side of Stuart's mouth quirked upward. "Correct. On both counts. The angel on my shoulder is generous, but when it comes to personal judgements, she can be a bit... how to say... hasty. Often, my instincts align with hers. When they do not, I find it better to resort to more primitive methods."

"What's the game?"

"To ascertain what kind of man you are."

"I meant, what are we playing?"

"The game of your people, of course."

"Colonialism?"

"Hold 'em."

I nodded. In theory, I'd have more control in something like Five-card or Black Jack, but there was still plenty of opportunity there.

"And what's the buy-in?" I asked.

He pointed the deck at me and smiled. "The second most important question. I'm thinking we throw in something tangible. You will either be paid up to ten thousand Selve to join our guild as a restricted member, or pay up to that same number depending on the way the chips land."

That it was a ten-thousand Selve bet arbitraged through the

system was the obvious part. The part I was supposed to notice. What was less obvious was the fact that both outcomes ended with me joining his guild. A restricted guild member was often temporary and could see little to nothing about the guild or members. Meanwhile, guild leaders could see almost everything about a restricted member.

My feats covered my ass in that regard. If that was what he was gunning for, he was headed for disappointment.

"—In addition, if you win, I will allow you entry into our home. If you lose..." he paused, examining me, "... then you will take off this mask my angel says you wear."

Fuck.

CHAPTER TWENTY

It wasn't going well. In the sense that it wasn't going quickly. The Steward was an extremely cautious player who rarely bet on the first round. And while I did my best to affect the shuffles, there was a limit to how specific I could be. After the shuffle ended and the first three cards flopped, I'd find mixed results in my favor and be more or less confident in how the rest of the round would go. Even if he only bet the minimum, the results were inevitable.

If it was just a question of winning, it was already in the bag.

The problem was I was pretty sure it wasn't about who won. The Steward had hinted that gambling was a method of getting a gauge on a person. It made sense. You could gauge a far more authentic picture of what someone was like when they had money on the line. Caution, greed, ability to evaluate risk, performance under pressure. He was looking for something, and I wasn't sure what.

That he'd not-so-casually presented the information that he had a patron—or at least something that functioned as a patron—begged more questions than it answered. Possibly a bluff to dissuade his opponent from cheating or a distraction from something else. I decided early to not use Azure to cheat—between **<Probability Cascade>** and the low action happening early in the rounds, it was better not to risk it. Especially with a potential patron in play. Instead, he was lurking in the shadows of The Steward's surrounding men, making sure none of them were paying disproportionate attention to anything problematic.

He wasn't running **<Squelch>**, so there was a real possibility of cross-talk and outside interference.

Of course, Occam's razor said he simply wasn't aware. **<Squelch>** was a feat that was more beneficial the less well known it was. Miles told me about it during the Transposition, and I'd told a handful of others. Considering how often I ran into it passing through other regions, it was safe to assume it was a known factor in most leadership circles around the city. But it was rarely discussed openly and well-hidden in a proverbial mountain of perks. If these people were as isolated as they seemed, it was entirely possible that no one had stumbled across it.

Which meant they'd gotten to this point—holding a sizable chunk of territory—entirely without it. More than impressive. Even if it was hard to picture. And it presented an irresistible opportunity.

He folded and I collected the pot, netting a measly two hundred Selve. At this rate, Sunny could leisurely walk out of the settlement and be long gone by the time we finished.

After the reset, I bent back the corner of my cards. Two of diamonds, five of spades. No existing pair or possibility of a strait or flush.

Dogwater hand.

"Found the spotter," Azure communicated excitedly, *voice*

unusually high. *"Guy's directly behind you, staying out of the others' peripheral."*

I tilted my head, trying to get a look at the guy without giving it away. Dreadlocks framed a craggy face masked in focus. His thumbs were hooked into his belt. And he was all but openly ogling my side of the table.

I bet well over the minimum before the flop, testing Azure's theory.

And The Steward raised, all but confirming it.

"How are they communicating?" I asked my summon, keeping my expression neutral.

"Hand signals."

Old school.

That The Steward was cheating was disappointing, but not surprising. After all, we were both cheating. It made sense. Only a fool would wager giving a stranger access to his region over a mere card game.

However, this revelation complicated the way forward with his so-called judgment of character. With the spotter, he could see my cards even when he folded. Winning would take forever and out me as a cheater, the sort of hands I was regularly pulling with **<Probability Cascade>** being statistically unlikely, if not borderline impossible.

I needed to incentivize keeping his word. And I had a good idea how.

"Leave The Steward alone. Otherwise, gloves are off. Surface scans on everyone in the room. Go invasive if there's something worthwhile. Don't get detected."

"What am I looking for?"

"Anything about their situation, their relationship with Regions 19 and 20, resources. Anything and everything they're afraid of. Then summarize it."

"And the spotter?" Azure asked.

I considered that. *"What's his int?"*

"Not an idiot, but nothing to write home about."

"Leave him for now."

Needed to play the minimum for a while, give Azure time to work. I glanced over my cards, sighed, and folded. The Steward wordlessly collected the chips and cards and shuffled.

"How am I holding up?" I asked.

"Hm?" Now that the game was underway, he seemed annoyed by any attempt at conversation.

"Guess I'm curious if you've gleaned any insights through the tao of Texas Hold 'em."

"Mock all you like. It does not matter. While I cannot yet make a definitive ruling, one thing is certain." Stuart almost chewed the words. "I trust you less than when we started."

Because you're losing. Naturally, I didn't say it out loud. Not that he was a sore loser, more with the combination of cautious play and cheating, he *should* have been winning. And he wasn't.

"Just out of curiosity," I started, tossing five-hundred Selve worth of chips on the table and raising the pot. "If you wanted to make sure no one in this room was tossing messages back and forth, how would you do that?"

"Are you tossing messages back and forth?" Stuart asked, point blank. He called, evening out the pot.

"No. Not the point. The question is, how would you stop it?"

His expression was impassive. But not without the slightest glimmer of perplexity, as if I'd asked how one might invert gravity if they were so inclined.

"I do not have this concern. But in an increasingly complex situation, the simplest solution is best."

"Meaning?"

"Limiting variables. To start, I would send everyone but the two of us out of this room." He drummed his fingers on the table. "And instate a timer to increase the tempo of the game.

Naturally, this carries with it other risks." Stuart grimaced. "Not to mention questions of intention."

Like why a person who wasn't cheating would bring up counter-measures during a card game.

"Okay, I've got plenty to work with." Azure returned, a slight imprint in the shadow at my feet.

Regions 19 and 20 had been fighting since the Transposition. 19 ripped the other region off, potentially screwing them in the late hours, only for 20 to almost immediately make a comeback. The resource Region 19 "won" for completion was titanslate, a rare metal with a high mana resonance that could hold significantly more potent enchantments than something like steel, seeded within the naturally occurring realms of Flauros within the region.

Of course, it wasn't that simple. If the forge fire ran too cool, the metal wouldn't melt, and a forge fire that ran too hot would obliterate the magical properties that made it desirable. The difference between the two was only a matter of degrees.

There was only one reliable method for stabilizing the forge fire at a perfect temperature. Kolbor. A substance which, to the knowledge of everyone present, only existed within Region 20.

Cue the ensuing clusterfuck. Which was, coincidentally, the only thing allowing the Galleria to remain untouched. They were an entrenched, otherwise unaffiliated third party. Neither Region 19 or 20 could afford to commit to an extended engagement with them, for fear of creating an opening for the opposing region to swoop in. Not that they hadn't tried. Both regions had sent envoys to the Galleria, all of which were politely but firmly turned away. An utterly prudent decision, if you didn't have a manner of controlling the flow of information.

The Steward and his people existed in a perilous balance.

Of course, none of this was my problem. But in a vacuum, I

was more inclined to help these people than either of the surrounding regions. Both 19 and 20 had turned their regions into wastelands out of little more than short-sighted greed.

The Galleria folk, by contrast, just wanted to exist.

I increased the tempo of play, slowly but surely draining Stuart of his chips through the blinds. He maintained stoicism better than most, but after a while his irritation shone through.

"I have a proposition," I said, finally sensing the desperation I was looking for.

"What sort of proposition?" There was a growl in his throat.

I lowered my voice. "I have no desire to embarrass you in front of your men. But it's obvious where this is going. In less than an hour, the game will be over. And you will have nothing to show for it."

"The money is not the point."

"Sure," I leaned forward. "It's about evaluation. So, evaluate. I'm in a hurry, so next hand, after the flop, I'm going to raise my bet. If you win, it will be enough for you to break even and then some. If you lose, you keep the remaining chips. We never agreed to play until one of us was out, correct?"

He nodded slowly. "So. That would be the last hand?"

"Exactly."

"This proposal is slanted. The onus of time is on you. I have no such constraints, and if I wait, the cards may turn."

"Fair enough. Then I propose we make a side-bet. One that will be invalidated if you don't call." I smiled. "Win or lose, I'll give you a key piece of information that will make your current situation far easier to manage. If you don't find that information useful, then you may consider this agreement invalidated."

Interest sparked in his eyes. "That is a lot of power to leave in my hands."

"Let's just call it a demonstration of trust."

The Steward didn't seem to like that framing, but it wasn't

an offer he could realistically ignore. A completely unscrupulous person could simply absorb the information, deem it unworthy, and call the game off on a technicality. With the terms I'd set, a more scrupulous person could still evaluate the cards they were holding after the flop and back out if they had nothing. And a person in-between, with a spotter, held almost no risk at all.

He held a stack in his hand, flipping a chip from the bottom to top mindlessly. "The longer we sit across from each other, the more I am inclined to believe you are the devil my angel suspects you to be."

Damn patrons.

I leaned back, feigning disinterest. "Maybe. Purely geographically, you're surrounded by devils. How many of them offer unconditional aid?"

As he reshuffled the cards and dealt, he didn't respond. But the doubt in his eyes spoke for him. If I did this right, when the time came, he'd make the bet.

It was already over.

CHAPTER TWENTY-ONE

I pulled up the corner of my freshly dealt cards slightly higher than necessary, flashing a two-seven nothing to the spotter. Or at least, that was what Azure made him see. Off-suite, it was possibly the worst hand a person could have in a game of Hold 'em. To dissuade any notions of too-good-to-be-true, I paired them as double-diamonds, opening up the possibility of a flush.

"This would be a lot more interesting if I understood what was happening," Talia grumbled in my mind. *"From my perspective, the two of you are doing little more than shoving clay circles and throwing uniform pieces of parchment around."*

"Even if you understand the rules, that's what they're doing," Azure pitched in.

"Cut the chatter. I need to focus,." I quieted them.

Across the table, Stuart looked at me with something approaching sympathy. My temporary hesitation and his knowledge of my cards probably made for a sad sight.

Doubly so when we reached the flop.

An ace of spades, a four of hearts, and a jack of clubs.

"Before we continue, I will allow you to walk back your bet, if you wish," Stuart said. From anyone else, that would have been trash-talk, or goading, but he seemed to have an authentic sense of honor about the whole thing. An honorable cheat. I could respect it, even if the rationale behind it was beyond my understanding.

I let the silence ring. Recalling a childhood memory of a talent show I was forced to perform in on repeat, focusing on the most uncomfortable, agonizing aspects until a bead of sweat dripped from my forehead.

Instead of answering, I shoved a pile of chips forward. Enough that The Steward would end in the lead if he won the hand without forcing him to commit everything he had left.

Disappointment flashed in his expression. "To this point, you have played a cautious game. More cautious than most. It would be unfortunate to see this ethos you've presented tossed away at the last possible moment, for the sake petty of haste."

I brought a hand down on the table with an audible thump. "Little late to talk trash."

His mouth worked. "I was not—"

"Then call. Or fold. Do *something,* for fuck's sake." I let full-fledged irritation into my voice.

The Steward's eyes hardened, and the finger that idly tapped on his face-down cards grew still. If I was right, I'd just crossed the threshold from an odd stranger to a fool who needed to be taught a lesson.

Carefully and methodically, he collected chips into uniform columns and pushed them into the center. "I look forward to uncovering the face you are so committed to hiding that it is obscured from even the gods themselves."

I crossed my arms and waited, tapping the table to signal no further bets as The Steward dealt the last two cards—internally breathing a sigh of relief as he did not raise the pot further. The fourth card was a king of hearts, and the ultimate card a five of spades. To his credit, he didn't so much as twitch when the card dropped, waiting until I tapped my last check, officiating the end of the round.

A satisfied expression broke the stoicism on his face as he revealed his cards face up. A two and a three, giving him a straight. "Let this be a lesson. No matter how clever one might be, it is impossible to bullshit through every obstacle."

I sighed, steepling my hands beneath my chin. "Disappointing."

Stuart did a double-take. "You're taking this well."

"It's fine. Just seems anti-climactic. All that build up..." I flipped my cards, revealing an identical hand. "To end it with a draw."

The table jostled as Stuart stood upright, bashing his thigh against the table and sending piles of neatly stacked chips clinking into an orderless mess. "How did—" his anger faded quickly as he realized the situation he was in. He knew, definitively, that I had cheated. But voicing that accusation would be the same as admitting he'd done the same. The Steward fell back into his chair and looked at me. Now that he was over the initial shock, bemusement had taken its place.

Why cheat a tie, when you could cheat a win?

Other than the clinking of chips, his already quiet men grew quieter as we divided up the winnings. There was a sense of tension that grew more palpable as we tallied the total.

I held my breath as Stuart recounted his total, murmuring to himself with a frown. Then counted them again.

A boisterous belly laugh ripped out of him, honest as it was deafening, startling everyone in the room. He laughed until there were tears in his eyes. "It appears that I have lost." He exploded in another fit of laughter, then scowled, waving away what I assumed was his patron. "Help is no longer needed in this matter. Begone."

I sent The Steward an in-depth description of **<Squelch>**

and where in the feat list most classes could find it. His eyebrows shot up, and he whistled. "This will solve... many problems for us."

He fiddled with his UI and a prompt popped up on my screen.

<The Steward has invited you to join the Driftless on a trial basis.>
<You have been offered a recruitment stipend.>
<Recruitment Stipend: 1 Selve.>

"Now, I would advise you to be careful," He leaned forward conspiratorially. "This is not technically arbitrage, but if you leave the guild within a month, the system will consider it so, your bounty void."

"Perish the thought," I said.

The Steward nodded. "And should you leave and return, I could not offer you another stipend."

Damn. This was the closest I'd come to a loophole for the "Gifting Selve" restriction. Good to know, but a shame it was so limited.

"Interesting." I smiled. "And your judgment?"

"You are a good man to know, and a terrible one to play cards with." He cocked his head. "And while I cannot not definitively speak to where in our home your quarry lives, I can certainly guess. Though this feels a bit... uneven... as you will absolve problems for me as well."

I shrugged. "If it's that much of a bother, I'm already a temporary member of the guild. Just make a quest only for experience."

It would also allow The Steward to set parameters for our stay within his walls, a fact that surely wasn't lost on him.

Soon enough, the quest was created and accepted. The

Steward assigned us an armed escort, and as they directed us toward the Galleria proper, my mind was miles away, reliving memories of a bloodstained tunnel. A long-burning ember within me caught fire. He'd threatened my family. Killed a teammate. Kidnapped my friend.

No matter what happened, if Sunny was here, he'd finally pay for it. In full.

Tonight.

CHAPTER TWENTY-TWO

Taking a little extra time to develop new contacts is rarely wasted effort. At worst, you end up with a much better idea of the person you're dealing with and the world they live in. And at best, you end up with a helluva lot more support than you would have had otherwise.

This was the latter. The Steward was so delighted with the discovery of **<Squelch>** that he offered to assign a few of his men to use in our favor. I let Azure loose, finally, and allowed him to take a peek inside The Steward's mind, as that set of circumstances could screw us just as easily as it would screw Sunny. Other than some... unrealistic... ideas about the benefits a long-term relationship could yield, the upside being that he was thinking long term, no hints of betrayal or plans to sell us out.

The downside was, he suspected I was the Ordinator. I didn't know how other than guesswork, rumors, and whatever the hell his patron was whispering in his ear. The suspicion didn't seem to carry the usual stigma. He seemed to see it as a potential benefit and point of leverage—from the system's announcement, the Ordinator was presented as a powerful threat. But the nature of the announcement alienated him, made him a target. And pragmatically, the Steward was more interested in him as an ally than a ticket out.

Either way, I had no intention of confirming it for him. The Driftless were in deep shit, the sort of shit I couldn't afford to get mired in with everything else on my plate.

But, if things ever went cataclysmic and left me completely burned with everyone I knew either dead or gunning for me, I had a place to go.

There was a slight comfort in that.

They escorted us through the Galleria proper, finding the interior almost entirely transformed. The skeleton of the mall itself was still there, glossy floors, escalators—some of which were still working—but almost everything else was altered. On the ground floor, there was a massive communal crafting area superimposed over the wide-open space that was once a large skating rink. A few storefronts were untouched, but most were heavily modified, glass windows removed, replaced with finished wood or brick, adorned with a three-digit-number placard placed somewhere on the front.

Commercial turned residential.

And unless I was misinterpreting the purpose of the handful of tanks that towered at regular intervals, they had running water going as well.

All of it was far more elaborate, clean, and permanent looking than I'd expected. It was no wonder the Driftless were so attached to this place, clinging to it stubbornly despite the hostility of the surrounding environment.

They'd put down roots.

"Check it out." Our civilian escort grinned. The sides of his head were shaved, remaining hair curving up and bouncing as he walked like a cockatiel's crest. Went by Cisco. He pointed the muzzle of his fuck-you-very-much shotgun toward the center floor. The weblike metallic piping and spouts arranged over plots of dirt arranged directly beneath the skylights were immediately recognizable.

"Hydroponics." I raised an eyebrow.

"Are you growing weed?" Sae asked, suddenly very interested. "*Please* tell me you're growing weed." When I gave her a skeptical look, she shrugged. "What? I haven't been able to take a damn breath since this shit started."

"Hah, I wish." Cisco shook his head. "Be nice to get a proper chill on. There are some herbs and medicinal shit, but it's mostly food. We wanna be independent of the market ASAP."

"You don't trust the market?" I asked.

"Do you trust food that magically appears in your pockets after you pay for it with Monopoly money?" Cisco shot back, then seemed to hesitate. "Maybe that's unfair. Supposedly, girl who runs it did everyone a solid when she slashed the prices of healing items during the fucksposition."

"Probably saved my ass," Max admitted.

"I dunno. Just seems like a bad idea to take it for granted," Cisco continued. "The cabal of divine dingos running this show have changed the rules more than once. And from what little I know, merchants get most of their inventory from nowhere, shipped in on the sky fairy express. What if, at some point, the powers that be decide they want us a little more desperate, a little less prepared, and start limiting the merchant's inventory?"

"No more shipments on the sky fairy express," Sae said wryly.

"That's what I'm saying, sister!" Cisco exclaimed, either unaware of Sae's irony or unaffected by it.

Buried beneath a significant portion of tinfoil, he had a point. The small, unstable economies that had developed around the city at large were almost entirely dependent on merchants. If whoever was running the game disabled merchants, or hell, even hamstrung them, everything would go to shit in short order.

"Self-sustainability is the way, man," Cisco reaffirmed, talking to himself more than any of us.

Astrid—who'd been mostly silent up to this point—suddenly spoke up. "Are you taking us in circles so you have more time to spew hippie shit, or are we close?"

"Stop it," Astria hissed.

I shot Astrid a look. This confirmed we needed to have a talk after the mission. There was a serious bug up her ass, but taking that out on our hosts wasn't going to help anything.

Thankfully, Cisco didn't seem to take it personally. "It's a big mall, little girl, we're getting there. Chill." He glanced over at Sae. "Tense group."

"Why do you think I wanted weed?" Sae groused.

"Fair 'nuff."

Most of the population of the Galleria were shut up inside, given the late hour, though there were a handful out and about. Many ignored us, though I felt a handful of lingering looks.

Up ahead—

"Body." I stopped in place, immediately tensing. Up ahead, a middle-aged man in civilian clothing splayed out on the ground, one leg at an odd angle. Scarlet pooled around his head, but there was no shine to it. The blood had dried.

"Yup." Cisco said grimly. "Jumped about a week ago."

And you just left him there?

"And you just left him there?" Astrid said, aloud.

Cisco nodded slowly, smirking a bit. "Tell you what, girl boss. Walk over and see if you can figure out why we left him there."

"Astrid, hold. Proximity?" I snapped, looking to Max.

"Close." Max squinted at his UI. "But I'm getting conflicting readings."

<Max: Probability of success is oscillating between six to twelve. It's been flip-flopping since before we met The Steward.>

The difference between a coin flip and near-guaranteed success. But why?

I glowered at Cisco in the way I found made most people exceedingly uncomfortable. "Given that we're on good terms with your guild leader, it would be prudent to tell us what we're walking into."

He took a step back, holding up a hand defensively. "It's not a trap, if that's what you're thinking. It's just weird. Some sort of persistent area-of-effect. Our magic types can't hack it. No one really knows what it does, other than that it affects memory and seems to be limited to a small radius around this section of the ground floor. Can't dispel it, can't identify it."

"Be my eyes?" I asked Azure.

"You got it, boss," Azure chirped back. There was an odd sensation as I felt him take root in my mind, my vision fraying at the fringes

I approached the body.

CHAPTER TWENTY-THREE

What... was I doing?

I felt disjointed. Like my mind had gone on auto-pilot and my body had followed along. Slowly, I swiveled, looking back. Our escort, Sae, and the rest of the team were still behind me. There was nothing inherently wrong with that. I'd started walking ahead without them, scouting out the area immediately in front of us. They were holding, waiting for me to motion that it was clear.

Ashamed to say it, but I nearly did. Until I spotted the body, somewhere around fifteen feet behind me. The man with a broken leg and a scarlet halo.

Right.

I hadn't just been walking ahead, I was walking *toward* him.

"What the hell happened?" I asked my summon.

"Hm? Nothing happened. You glanced over the body and kept walking—Ooooh. Wasn't what you intended to do?"

"Not even a little."

"Let me out, I'll take a peek under the hood."

I did as he asked, extending my arm and ignoring the sensation of oil trickling down my wrist as he slipped into my shadow. Considering illusions and misdirections were Azure's specialty, him not picking up on the effect was downright unsettling.

"Everything alright?" Sae called over, shifting uncertainly, about to take a step forward.

"Stay put," I called back. A shadow, almost imperceptible to the eye, flitted across the walkway, and back, and across again.

"How... delightfully insidious," Azure mused. *"Whatever it is, it doesn't affect me as strongly, but it's definitely there. Compulsion. One that forces the belief that there is absolutely nothing interesting here and to keep moving. Can't even stay in the center for long without subconsciously drifting to either side. It's kind of amazing they noticed this at all."*

If there wasn't a body, they probably wouldn't have. *"Can you trace the origin point?"*

"If it functions the same as the average ward—stronger at the center—then somewhere in the center of the walkway."

I absorbed that. "Is it permanent?"

The shadow flitted back and forth a few times, then circled. "Probably not. Permanent wards are exorbitantly expensive and take time to set up, and I'm guessing this was set up in a hurry. Temporary wards are simple enough to deal with. Anchored to something physical—I'm guessing a section of the floor, possibly a specific tile. If we destroy that, the effect should dissipate."

"Then what's the problem?" I asked. Hair raised on the back of my neck. If Sunny put the ward in place, he was close. Very close. Probably hiding in one of the unoccupied storefronts within the radius of the wards.

Watching us.

"It's taking the lion's share of my concentration just to stay in the radius. I don't think I could maintain a corporeal form, and even if I could, I'd also need the strength to shatter concrete," Azure said, clearly annoyed with the situation.

I could relate. The setup posed a lot of problems for us, and a lot of advantages for Sunny. Nimrod solution was to have the twins blow up tiles from outside the radius. The area of effect wasn't that big, comprising around three-dozen tiles, far less if they focused on the center. Problem was, that was both loud and would take time. And if Sunny had a backdoor, which he almost assuredly did, he'd have more than ample time to get clear before the ward was offline.

It was a complex problem. I returned to the others, shaking off the mental effects of the ward and relaying what I'd found.

"Well, shit," Max said. He thought for a moment. "Think that's what's causing the borked read?"

"Gotta be," I agreed. "Upshot is, we take it out, our chances suddenly get a lot better."

Astria crossed her arms, considering the tiles and the surrounding storefronts. "I get we can't take them out piece-meal. But what if we just went big? Like, really big?"

"Shocker, she wants to nuke something," Astrid mocked.

"What's the point of being able to cast powerful spells if you never use them?" Astria's eyes flashed as she turned on her sister.

"Dunno. Being a reasonable human being, maybe?"

I held out a hand, stopping the argument before it got started. "Ordinarily I wouldn't have a problem with that. It's a question of collateral damage." I glanced at Cisco. "Anyone live in this section? Most of the storefronts seem intact."

He swallowed, suddenly looking out of his element. "Uh. A few did. Asked for relocation on account of, you know, the unrecoverable body. There's a lot of us on the upper floors though. And we figured out real quick that a place this large has support beams *everywhere*."

Astria deflated. "Okay, so big's a bad idea."

"Solid concept, just not what we need right now." I patted her on the shoulder. She perked up at the praise.

Sae crouched down, knocked at the tile beneath her feet. "Not to steal the mage's thunder, but I'm pretty sure I can break a bunch of these in quick succession." She peered up at me. "And the effect is isolated to this floor. What if I went up a level, jumped down, and smashed it?"

"Same problem." Max sighed. "You fuck up, hit the wrong tile, he rabbits before we have time to fix it."

"Speaking of which." I turned back to Cisco. "Let's say someone was hiding in one of the storefronts. How would they leave if they didn't want to go out the front?"

"Well." He pointed to the left side. "If they were on that side, they'd be straight-up screwed. There's a few back rooms, but nothing that connects to any sort of exit."

"And the right?"

"There's a connecting hallway that runs through most of this wing," Cisco confirmed.

"He's on that side then, gotta be," Sae realized, openly staring in that direction before she caught herself. Max seemed openly unhappy with that but kept whatever it was to himself.

The solution hit me all at once. It wasn't ideal and would take a good deal of cooperation from Sae. But if she was willing, it was doable.

I leaned in and asked her quietly, "How bad do you want to get this guy?"

"More than I've ever wanted anything." Sae stared me dead in the face. There was no lie in her expression, no hesitation.

"Whatever it takes?"

She nodded.

"Then I have a plan."

Max finally spoke up. "The right side could be a misdirect. He expects anyone who comes looking and knocks down the ward to search the stores on the right first while he slips out behind them," Max said.

"There's a difference between going for a fake out and being stupid. Choosing a tactically hamstrung option because it's unexpected would be straight up stupid," Sae argued.

"You're both right," I cut in. "Sunny's smart. But he's also unpredictable. However we come at this, we need to leave someone in the open, preferably with an upper floor vantage, ready to sound the alarm if he slips out of somewhere unpredictable."

"I'll go up," Astrid said, almost immediately. When I hesitated, she continued. "We're more independent than we used to be. Astria will have access to most of our heavy-hitting spells if I'm nearby."

"It takes a few things off the table," Astria said slowly.

"Not many," Astrid countered.

For the moment, I ignored the fact that she'd jumped to volunteer for the assignment that put her the farthest from the action. "Fine. We move in two minutes. Monitor your interface and get in position."

Astrid scampered off toward the escalator, taking the moving steps two at a time.

"Max—" I started.

"Back hallway?" he interjected, already moving toward the service door our escort pointed out.

"Yep."

That left Sae and Astria. I trusted them both, probably more than anyone else in the group. Sae had been with me from the beginning. While Astria was a more recent addition, it was clear she saw me—or Myrddin, at least—as a mentor and friend.

But some things were better kept secret.

"You okay with clearing with me and Sae once the ward comes down?" I asked Astria.

"Yep!"

"Then head to the other side of the ward."

"Coms are squelched. How will I know when it's down?" Astria asked, looking between us.

"Trust me," I said, feeling a surge of anticipation. "You won't miss it."

CHAPTER TWENTY-FOUR

Like any kid from the south, I grew up around an overpopulation of game hunters. Some were the exact redneck stereotype you'd expect. Scruffy beards, beater trucks with mounted antlers, mouthy bumper stickers haw-hawing their truth to anyone with the misfortune of being in the rearview, and more flagrant open-carry than a third world war zone. Others were less rote. Bankers, managers, government officials skipped the accouterment but, come November, would pack up their transit and join the oil-slicked expedition to Somervell County, eager to get the jump on Whitetail season.

I'd always regarded both varieties with a sort of distant caution, unable to come to any other explanation for the enthusiasm beyond a primal excitement to legally cull something.

The last month had granted perspective on the topic.

It was about so much more than the kill. It was about the anticipation. The patience. Long periods of waiting, tracking, and searching, all building up to an often terrifyingly brief window to act, where the painstaking efforts of the lead up could be lost with a single misplaced step. It was the adrenaline of landing the final blow, and the internal satisfaction that came with knowing that in order to get here, you did *everything* right.

There was still a part of me that resisted. Recognized that Hastur and the Order put me in this position. Of the Users in Sunny's faction we'd hunted, I'd spared who I could. Naturally, a person backed into a corner would do or say anything to keep breathing, which made Azure a priceless resource when it came to evaluating them on a case-by-case basis. The psychopaths, predators, and truly loyal we put down. The rest were remanded to Kinsley's custody. I told myself that I wasn't beyond the pale. That I was just doing what needed doing, and once it was done, I could bury it and pretend it hadn't happened, just like before.

I hoped that was true.

Even a floor above the hideout and out of range, I could feel the tug, the insistent reminder that there was nothing there and I was better suited moving on. It was getting easier to identify and ignore, but the strength of the enchantment had me worried.

Because Sunny didn't seem like the type to cast it himself. He was a combination of speed and brutal strength that typically required sacrificing all avenues of arcane development. Either he'd somehow stashed and spent an astronomical number of spells on a magic item capable of casting the enchantment—unlikely, given how swiftly and decisively he'd been cut off from his resources—or there was an unknown third party who just happened to be a powerful mage.

Neither felt right. We'd been methodical in isolating him from contacts and allies. If there was someone else in there, they were completely unknown by the rest of Sunny's people, and unless we'd missed something huge, they weren't with the order.

So who the hell are they?

I watched from above the abandoned walkway as Sae traveled through the affected area, eyes blank, and tensed, fingers gripping the railing tightly.

Almost exactly in the center, with no warning, Sae stopped a couple stores down from me. I moved further down the walkway, lining myself up a little off to the center of where she was standing. Once I was in position, Sae slowly turned. Her insectile eyes refracted red behind her mask, and her mouth split in a wicked smile that was all Azure.

Crack.

Sae dropped to one knee, a blurring fist shattering the tile beneath her feet. The feeling of forced disinterest dissipated, and I vaulted over the railing and down, twisting in midair to face the storefront as Azure released her from his possession, leaping from shadow to shadow until he was inside.

Practically emanating spite, Sae took a step forward.

Trap! Azure screamed, his mental voice commingling with an alert from **<Jaded Eye>**. I dropped, scissor kicking Sae's legs out from under her and sending us both to the ground just as the glass display windows exploded, screeching tinnitus overtaking almost everything else. Sae grasped my forearm and hurled me clear of the opening with superhuman strength, glass shards skittering beneath her as she scrambled into cover after.

"Thanks." She grunted.

"Yep."

"Was that a fucking shotgun?"

"Shotguns. Spread was too wide for just one."

Astria slid in beside us. Her wand was shaking, but I knew from past experience the nerves would subside as soon as the fighting began in earnest. "Inside doesn't look too big, but there are a lot of obstacles. Could freeze them out?"

I nearly agreed. Gemini's frost spells were devastating. A

low tier blizzard spell limited to the interior of the store could easily trigger or otherwise disable any remaining traps, allowing safe passage. With such a small contained area, the temperature would drop dangerously low quickly, potentially severely injuring or even killing anyone inside. But I couldn't shake the feeling that my earlier instinct was right. There was someone else besides Sunny in there, potentially independent of the order. Razing the place without knowing that variable didn't feel right.

It took a monumental amount of effort to shake my head. "Wait for recon."

Precious seconds ticked by. Azure called out the traps right off the bat and had been uncharacteristically silent ever since. I still felt his presence, so he wasn't dead—but with the gap in time, he was either waylaid or tied up with someone.

Need to make a call.

"Flash and breach," I said. I drew my dagger and a handful of crossbow bolts, extended the metal edges toward Sae. With a wave of her hand, they glowed sickly green, noxious fumes. The poison wouldn't last long, so we needed to move quickly.

Astria muttered something unintelligible. A breeze swept through her hair, motes of light forming around her and drawing inward toward the wand clutched at her chest, illuminating the silver rod gold. Once the spell was charged to max power, she pushed against the wall, exposing as little of herself as possible and dipping the wand toward the opening.

Instinctively, both me and Sae covered our ears and braced.

The resulting scream was hair-raising as always, and even facing away from it, I opened my eyes to numerous purple blotches, leaned around the corner, threw **<Blade of Woe>** with a flick of my wrist, low-trajectory landing the blade between two racks of women's clothes. Talia emerged snarling in a cloud of smoke, triggering two more shotgun traps and darting into the darkness. There was a low hiss of escaping gas, followed by a yelp.

"There's something—the bastards blinded me!" her voice resonated in my mind, pained and enraged.

"Return." I recalled the blade as Talia shifted back, snatching the hilt out of the air, breathing deeply, then turning the corner, bringing my crossbow to bear.

No movement. Nothing but darkness and silhouettes. With my tainted vision, every outward-facing piece of metal and cylinder shape looked like the barrel of a shotgun. I pushed further in, relying on **<Awareness>** and **<Jaded Eye>** to highlight any actual threats, ignoring the surging thrill that tempted throwing caution to the wind.

Toward the back of the store, behind the counter, a rectangle of light shot open.

Door.

Sunny's panicked face came into focus for a half-second.

I fired.

There was an audible grunt, then a metal clang as the door slammed shut.

From outside, the distinctive *thwip* of a crossbow fired twice more, undercutting the sound of heavy boots pounding down the hallway

"Runner!" Max screamed out.

Sae blasted by, tucking her head and lowering her shoulder like a linebacker. She slammed into the back door, chitin impacting metal as she knocked it clean off its hinges, pausing for only a second before she disappeared through the door frame and around the corner, running at an Olympic sprint. She was faster than me, but only just, and I followed closely, seconds away from the exit.

He said runner. Singular.

The hair on the back of my neck raised, and I dropped into a roll, smelling ozone. A fiery red gash cut through the sidewall, exactly on my left. Somehow, it hadn't triggered perception. I whirled, training my crossbow on the obvious origin point—behind the counter.

A boy, no older than twelve, awkwardly holding a staff stared defiantly back at me.

CHAPTER TWENTY-FIVE

My finger tightened on the trigger. "Put it down."

"Fuck you," the kid said, all spite and vitriol. His face was flushed red, and he was wearing civilian clothes. A t-shirt and cargo shorts, both ratty. From the gauntness of his cheeks, he hadn't eaten in a while. Hunger always looked the same.

"I don't want to hurt you."

His hand trembled, green gem at the top of his staff swaying, constantly on the verge of moving off target. He looked angry, tired.

Dangerous.

I called out to my summon. "Could really use your help here, Azure."

"Short stack's got... some serious... firepower. His illusions... blocked our communication. Trying to take control."

More serious than the fire laser? The spell that nearly skewered me had gone off instantly, without enough lead time for **<Perception>** to trigger. If that was the cheap seats in his arsenal, I didn't want to see the VIP.

Mana shifted as the green gem crowning the staff glowed.

God dammit, I don't have time for this.

"Last chance," I said, putting as much menace in my voice as I could muster. "Put the staff down."

The safe option would have been to fire. This sort of thing was inevitable. Both my brother and sister were evidence that the system didn't exactly discern by age. And like the firearms of the previous age, magic was the great equalizer of this one. It was only a matter of time before a kid with power ended up on the wrong side with more guts than sense.

"Please," I tried.

His expression shifted to something I recognized. The moment of resolve transformed to action.

Shit.

There was a burst of light, and a bludgeon of energy curved from behind me, slamming into the boy's chest. He grunted, the staff in his hand spinning away as he slammed backward against a shelf, knocking a plastic display case of knock-off jewelry free and tumbling to the ground.

Behind me, Astria gaped, her chest heaving from the exertion. "Why—Why is there a kid here?"

"Dunno," I shook my head, then started moving toward the door. "Eye-in-the-sky says he's powerful. Make sure he stays down?"

"I'll keep watch." Astria nodded, her focus returning as she shrugged off the residual shock.

The kid murmured something barely intelligible. Almost impossible to make out.

Almost sounded like, "Don't hurt him."

I took off down the hallway, moving at a dead sprint. There was no sign of Astrid, Sae, or Max, and no way to check in with them as the Galleria folk were still running **<Squelch>**. Multiple lockers and doors had been thrown open, probably Sunny trying to throw obstacles in the pursuer's path. I followed the trail, falling deeper into the mask, suppressing the ramping anxiety.

I was pretty sure I'd hit him with a poisoned, armor-piercing bolt. While Sae's poison wasn't generally lethal to Users, it was a debilitating paralytic. After a matter of minutes, he'd have trouble moving. After ten, he wouldn't be able to walk. If Sunny was as clever as he acted, he'd figure that out in short order.

And he'd make a move.

As it turned out, Sunny hadn't made it far. His once perfectly coiffed salt-and-pepper hair was wild. Both Sae and Max had backed off, given him space. For good reason. The most likely scenario played out in my mind. Sae and Max had chased him from behind, while Astria—hearing the callout— had circled around to flank. Either she'd frozen, or miscalculated how quickly Sunny would close the distance.

Now he had an arm around her throat, steel barrel of a 1911 pressed to her head. "Where's the fucking bogeyman? Come on, bring him out."

Astria whimpered.

I went cold. In that moment, the day of the tunnel played on repeat in my mind, over and over. Only now, I could see him for exactly what he was.

A throwing knife twitched in Sae's hand, charged and green. Max had a crossbow trained at Sunny's head.

I crept up, sticking to the wall, using Max's frame to obscure my approach.

"Let's just take it down a notch." Max subtly angled, trying to get a shot.

"Landing a bounty isn't going to help you get out of this," Sae added. Her voice was casual, but from the tension in her shoulders, the way every muscle was poised to spring forward, I could tell she was feeling the same weight.

"Riiiight. I look stupid to you?" Sunny spat, shifting his human shield erratically, making it next to impossible for either of them to find an opening.

"File I read said you're a great fighter. A genuine threat with a sword. All the leveling and questing... be a shame if it all went to waste because you wanted to play hostage negotiation." Max heard me approaching out of the corner of his eye and held a hand behind his back, splaying out five fingers.

Low chances we save her as things stand.

"Put the gun down, let the girl go. She'll sit this out. Big guy like yourself can handle a two-on-one." Max dialed up the accent and smiled, shrugging toward Sae. "She's most of the firepower here anyway. So really it'd be more of a one-and-a-half on one."

"Where's the bogeyman?" Sunny's voice escalated into a shout. "Come on out, fuckface. I know you're here." He sounded unhinged. Off his god damned rocker. And I didn't think he was faking it.

I could appreciate what Max was going for. But it wasn't going to work, not with the state Sunny was in. Once upon a time, I would have questioned the wisdom of using my powers here. It was the best way to subvert Max's reading, but all three of them were too close not to realize there was fuckery at play.

But we were far past that. The strike team had gotten me this far, and to their credit, they were all decent people despite our business. Astrid and Astria were just trying to survive, level up, and amass the power necessary to make it through the next event. Max was the kind of guy who knew how to shut the hell up when he had a line on a good thing. And Sae already knew everything.

I was done hiding. I reached into his mind with **<Suggestion>**, amplifying his fear, stabilizing his hand.

"Picked apart. Pinned down with nowhere to go. How does it feel?" My voice reverberated down the hallway, echoing.

Sunny stiffened, then crouched lower, his expression a twisted sneer. "There he is. The conquering hero. Figured you had to be the one going through my crew like tissue paper. Everything's gone to shit since the day I met you."

It took a moment to connect that he was talking about the day I'd invited himself into the backseat of his car and chatted him up about joining the Transposition, not the incident outside the trial.

"In fact—" he continued.

"—Just, uh, who's the kid?" I cut him off, glancing back the way I came. "The one you left behind." Unstable as he was, I'd picked up in the tunnel that Sunny was a seasoned negotiator. And the best way to deal with that kind of person was never letting them get their footing.

There was a long silence as Sunny glowered with a look that could kill. "He alive?"

"For now." I smiled. "Who is he?"

"Nobody. Just some street trash I paid for the wards." From the blank expression, to the apathetic tone, the lie was supremely convincing. Without context, it might have passed. But even if the kid hadn't been worried enough to potentially throw his life away, Sunny had fucked up when he asked after his well-being.

Family. I'd put money on it.

"Uhuh." I stared at him blankly. "Look, whoever he is to you, I really don't care. Things don't have to get nasty. The way I see it, you have one of mine and I have one of yours. There's potential for an even trade. We'll call this a draw and you can go on your way."

To his minor credit, for a moment he seemed to seriously consider it. Then his expression hardened. "So you and yours can regroup later and pick us off on our way out, once this poison cuts my legs out from under me? Nah. We're not gonna play it that way. I don't give a shit what you do to the kid. I'm gonna walk away with the girl. If I see a single tail, she's done. And if I don't, maybe you get her back." He smiled cruelly. So confident he held all the cards.

If I was the same person I was when we clashed in the tunnel, that might have been true. I might have let him go. But we were long, *long* past that. The truth was, I didn't need to threaten the kid, or buy time. Because the longer Sunny ran his mouth, the more opportunities he was giving me for cast after cast of **\<Probability Cascade\>**, cementing his fate.

"You know what?" I tilted my head. "I would have negotiated. But I was *really* hoping you'd say no."

CHAPTER TWENTY-SIX

Some part of me was disappointed Sunny was such a mess. He made a habit of preying on the weak. Pressing others into the corner, threatening them, forcing impossible decisions upon people whose lives simply hadn't equipped them to handle it. Given that, you'd think he'd at least have a theoretical idea of what to do if the tables were turned.

I'd built him up in my mind as some scenery chewing villain. I'd expected him to shift into a higher gear, be invigorated, perhaps even elated as he rose to the challenge.

Instead, he just ran.

By grabbing Astria, engaging in this pointless stalling tactic, all he'd done was give himself the illusion he was in control.

Azure cut off his supply of adrenaline while I strummed the whispers of sleep in his mind, amplifying them into a symphony. Easy enough. He was already exhausted, on the tail end of weeks on the run and what I guessed was several days awake. Probably hadn't managed a full night of sleep since the body fell at his doorstep. Even now, his eyelids drooped and his weapon wavered, signaling to me I'd done enough in that regard.

Specks of dust, glimmering in the haze, were drawn to his face and nose like moths to a lamp.

Several applications of **<Probability Cascade>** on hammer, trigger, and slide, insured the handgun would never fire again. Redundant, perhaps, but contingencies paid dividends here.

His focus slipped. For perhaps a fraction of a second, sleep took him, and his vice-like grip on the small mage loosened.

TWANG.

A bolt from Max took Sunny in the shoulder of his gun arm. He dropped the 1911 with a pained grunt and stumbled backward, pinwheeling at the loss of balance, his face twisting in disbelief. I watched as—as if in slow motion—his heel caught the floor at an odd angle and he twisted to catch himself. Only he twisted the wrong way. A bone in his leg snapped with an audible crack.

Sae reached out, ushering a stricken and sobbing Astria behind us before she pulled her throwing arm back.

Not yet.

There were still questions that needed to be answered. I caught her arm and shook my head. "Give him a minute."

With difficulty, Sunny climbed to his feet. He turned his back and began to limp away, reaching out to steady himself. But he just couldn't seem to keep a good grasp on anything. The wall was too slick. And when his hand slipped off that, the table he reached out for toppled, thumping against his thigh and sending him back to the ground in a tangled heap.

"Jesus." Max breathed. "We didn't even have to come."

"Hm?" Sae murmured.

"All that build up and this asshole's already dead." Max shook his head. "Good-fuckin-riddance."

His observation was unexpectedly cutthroat for someone typically jovial and good-natured, but I shouldn't have been surprised. The one piece of scant information I'd shared with him about the Order was that our ultimate target was behind the soul-harvesting operation during the last Transposition. They'd been ambushing entire convoys of Users trying to secure their regions, killing them wholesale. Max had lost nearly his entire squad to the effort, with only half of them returning home alive after the rescue.

With the target neutralized, I checked on Astria. She'd retreated a small distance down the hallway and gasped for breath, hand clutched to her chest. "You good?" I asked.

"Yeah." Astria straightened up slightly. "Careful. I just... blinked... and he rushed me down."

"His rushing days are over."

"Myrddin," Sae snapped.

I turned, half-expecting to see Sunny on his feet, sprinting down the hallway, defying all expectations. But no. He was on his stomach, having apparently giving up on walking. But he was crawling, and seemed to be doing so with a destination in mind, trailing diagonally toward the right side of the hallway. All the exits were at the far end or to the left, through the stores. Instead, he seemed to be making his way toward a door marked "Utility Closet."

"What's the plan, Sunny?" I circled around him at a leisurely pace and paused at the door, waiting for **<Jaded Eye>** to warn me. It didn't. "Rigged to blow?" I pulled the door open. "Guess not. Is there a portal back to the order? Something stashed in here?"

"Last one got a reaction," Azure informed me.

"Well." I dragged him inside by the back of his armor, pushing him up against the wall in a sitting position. "Not sure what'll give you a chance in hell at this point, but better safe than sorry. Where is it?"

He looked at me, his gaze radiating hate.

"Here?" I pointed to the left side of the room.

No reaction.

"Maybe here?" I pointed to a cluster of dirty mops, stacked in the corner.

Not even a flicker.

"That's alright, we've got time." I paused dramatically. "Please tell me you didn't hide it behind the power cabinet."

Despair filtered into his expression.

Bingo.

Behind the cabinet, beneath a layer of torn-up insulation and covered in a layer of dirt and dust, was a forest-green duffle bag. Again, I waited, half-expecting a title warning not to touch it. When none came, I pulled it out.

Casting something—

I spun, pulling my crossbow and firing. My aim was dead-on, but the bolt impacted with a fuzzy thud, bouncing off his head and falling to the ground. In its wake, he was covered with a dull red glow.

"Trouble?" Sae did a double-take when she saw Sunny. "What the hell?"

Sunny laughed. For the first time, he seemed calm, more like his old self. "Better get moving, asshole. You and yours haven't exactly been quiet. In case you missed it on the way in, the subhuman trash running this place are jumpy and well-armed. With all the noise, I'm guessing they're gonna have questions."

Ah. So there was a plan. Just not a good one. He'd come here without informing the residents and assumed we'd do the same. Like me, it probably wasn't his first choice, but if plan A through plan-whatever-the-fuck fell through, he could raise a ruckus and pop whatever this ability was. He'd be captured and interrogated, but with his charisma, talking his way out of it was a real possibility.

"Sorry. Didn't even think, he just went for it," Azure said.

"*What is it?*"

"*Adrenaline got going again, so he's a little harder to read but... it's a shield spell. Like Nick's Sanctuary. Temporary impermeability.*"

"*How temporary we talking?*"

"*Depends on how much mana he poured into it... but... I'm getting ten minutes, tops.*"

"Eh, I'd rather look through the bag, thanks." I unzipped the duffel and started rifling through the contents, feeling Sunny's incredulous gaze.

A shitton of healing potions, status potions, couple throwables, cracked smartphone, and... what are you?

There was a rectangle rubber-backed zip case with a cloth exterior and black and gray crosshatching. It had a decidedly modern feel, like something from before. I opened it up and paused, sizing up the unexpected contents. It was a handheld gaming console with pink and green siding. For curiosity's sake, I pressed the power button. The screen stayed black, with nothing but the reflection of the mask staring back at me.

I tilted it toward him. "Not yours, I take it."

"Are you delusional?" Sunny tried again. "They'll be here any minute."

"They're not coming."

"What... do you mean?"

I left him to ponder that and returned to the doorway, where the others were looking in. "Good news, he doesn't have shit. Bad news, we're gonna have to hold tight for a while."

There was relief in their faces, but also discomfort at the idea of staying in one place. We generally didn't, and that strategy had worked out for us so far.

"Sure we're not gonna have a third party problem?" Max asked warily.

I shook my head. "The Steward wants this problem off his

doorstep. He won't order anyone to interfere, but that doesn't mean one of our new friends isn't gonna get curious."

Out of the corner of my vision, I saw Sunny deflate.

"Got it. I'll keep the voyeurs away," Max confirmed. "Do what you gotta do."

Beside him, Astria was shivering violently, clinging to the sleeves of her robes. I discarded my previous order and softened my voice. "Check on your other half. Make sure we don't have a containment issue."

She searched Sunny up and down, teeth chattering. "H-h-he's not going anywhere?"

"It's over," I reassured her.

It was only half true. By the time I locked the door, pulled over a stool, and settled in, Sae cross-legged beside me, I got the feeling that Sunny knew exactly how dire his straits were. His body had gone slack during the exchange, his visage meek and blank as a pious martyr. Saint Sebastian, tied to the execution post.

"It's late, and I have a long day tomorrow. Wanna take the shield down, save us all some time?"

"Ask," Sunny said.

"Hm?" I cocked my head and cupped an ear.

"You aren't stupid enough to gloat. I'm still breathing…" he wheezed, "because there's an itch you can't scratch. Either you've got something to say or a question to ask."

"Wasting a lot of breath for a guy who doesn't have much to spare," Sae growled.

"No, he's right." I'd gone back and forth on whether engaging him at all was worth it. I'd bought my way out from underneath the geas, but Sunny hadn't. There was a limit to what he could tell me. And the question I had, the one that kept me awake, made me sick… didn't strictly matter. It wouldn't change the end result. And it wouldn't buy him more time.

I asked anyway. "A while back, you and a couple crackpots ambushed a much smaller group." His brows knitted together. "A confrontation that led to a kidnapping—right, probably doesn't narrow it down. Lot of kidnapping going on in the Order. But maybe this does." I leaned forward. "A mage died. Freaked out at the unexpected confrontation, tried to fight back. Took a bolt in the throat for her trouble. Bled out in seconds. Ringing any bells now?"

His jaw worked silently. As the reality set in, I could almost see him searching for a lifeline, looking for any angle he could use to leverage his way out of the situation.

Finding none.

When he had no objection, I continued. "The thing I couldn't get out of my head was how damn unprofessional it seemed. Clearly your group was experienced, nobody there batted an eye at the violence, and other than that one, monumental slip-up, you ran a tight ship. Maybe it came down to the individual, and considering what a miserable conniving fuck you are, I have to imagine you're also not the sort of guy who keeps one token idiot on your team. Meant to ask the shooter myself—ah fuck, what was his name?" I looked to Sae. "Dean? Dan?"

"Darren," Sunny rumbled, the word coming out in a gravelly sigh.

I snapped my fingers. "Right. That's it. Only when we set out to interview Darren on his dire absence of trigger discipline, he declined."

"Made toast in the bathtub. Enjoyed it so much he'd stayed in for days by the time we found him," Sae added.

"Wait." Sunny frowned. "That wasn't you?"

"It wasn't you?" I asked. When he shook his head, I smiled thinly. "Well, he wouldn't be the first in the dome to sign off that way. Must have caved to the stress. Or the guilt."

"Of course he takes the coward's way out. Always was a pussy." Sunny's lip curled.

"Sometimes there's wisdom in being a coward." I gestured to him and the surrounding room. "Take your situation, for example. This is the end of the road for you. The finale. Terminus. All that's up for negotiation is how cleanly you shuffle off this mortal coil. Given the circumstances, the brave thing would probably be to clam up and take whatever you have coming on the chin." I glanced at Sae warily. "Considering my friend's *ample* motivation to make that as unpleasant as possible, it would be braver than answering."

Disbelief shadowed his face as I took off my mask.

"The question is, how wise do you want to be?"

CHAPTER TWENTY-SEVEN

"You," Sunny exhaled, staring openly.

Me.

For a moment, I let the silence hang. The look on his face oscillated from anger, to bewilderment, to despair, unable to settle on anything for longer than a few seconds before it finally settled on rage.

"I *spared* you," he snapped, flecks of spit peppering the inside of his shield.

"Cut the shit. If Daphne hadn't stepped in, we both know how it would have gone."

"That's where you're wrong. It was my call," he argued, insistent. "Aaron's whelp stuck her nose in, but leaving you alive was my decision alone. Could have slit your throat and walked away, and aside from her, no one would have cared."

"So you let me go out of what?" I mocked. "The kindness of your heart?"

"Out of *respect,*" Sunny growled. "Your entire party was losing their shit—including the so-called Ceaseless Knight—and there you were in the middle trying to cut a deal. Earnestly.

Felt wrong to flatline someone so rational just for falling in with subpar people."

Subpar?

A chill of rage traveled down my spine, barely suppressed. "And *Jinny* wasn't worthy of respect?"

"Doesn't matter what she was worthy of. We had background on you guys. Not a lot. But enough to know the girl was dying."

"We're all *fucking dying,* Sunny, I'm gonna need a little more. How does that factor in ordering your redheaded stepchild to *murder her?*"

Another sigh. "Just... think it through. We need people in his position to be solid. Stable. With the goal of eventually giving them autonomy. Our shrinks and psych-freaks are good at the brainwashing shit, but they aren't miracle workers."

A wave of nausea rocked me.

"What? I don't understand." Sae looked between us, more confused than angry. "How does that even make sense?"

"Nick's a Knight in their fucked-up Court. Not the highest possible position, but critical for securing the upper echelon." I filled in coldly, gesturing to Sunny. "Go on. Tell her the rest."

Despite the prompting, Sunny stayed focused on me. It was like he wanted to convince me that what he was hinting at wasn't monstrous, like if he could just put the right spin on it, it would all make sense. "It's easier to rebuild someone who's broken than convince them to abandon a dying loved one. The girl was a ticking time bomb. She starts to check out, at best he completely loses focus, at worst we lose him. Better to make it look like an accident and tear the Band-Aid off early. If anything, we did him a favor—"

Sunny's shield picked that exact moment to drop. In a blur of motion, before I could even rise from my stool, Sae moved before I could, slamming a fist into the side of his head, toppling him to the ground.

I turned, clenching my fist and staring at the wall, listening to the heavy impacts. Part of me—and not a small part—didn't want to interfere. Just let things take their natural order. Cause and effect.

Only rely on your ruthlessness when you know, beyond a shadow of a doubt, it is needed.

"Stop," I said.

There was a hesitation, followed by one more painful thud, before Sae stepped away.

"The fuck even is she?" Sunny hissed.

I retook my seat on the stool in front of him. His face was bloodied, bruises already forming from the impact. A slight crater where a prominent cheekbone used to be. "The *other* casualty of your decision that night."

He rubbed his face, then put it together. "You're her. The girl who slipped back into the trial before it collapsed. Jeeeesus Christ, heard you got worked over, but that wasn't the half—"

"—Matt?" Sae snapped over him.

"—Yup."

I couldn't help but wince as the brutal haymaker landed right on his chin, slamming Sunny into near-unconsciousness. He groaned, then slowly pushed himself back up to a sitting position. There was a long pause. "You look great." He coughed. "Really."

Sae looked at me again. This time, I shook my head.

"Are..." Sunny swallowed, struggling to stay lucid, "are all my people dead?"

"You care?"

He managed a nod.

"Some. The real monsters, anyway." I shrugged.

"And the others?"

"They've thoroughly forgotten the oaths they took and moved on to more productive things."

He stretched his mouth, jaw emitting a painful click. "Clever. No reason to waste good talent. Thank you for that." His once-winning smile looked slightly cockeyed. "You know, this doesn't have to be a one-way street. If you did that for them, you could do it for me."

I stared at him. "And why the hell would I do that?"

"Because you're smart. And anyone with a pair of eyes and an IQ higher than their shoe size can piece together that no matter how bad I am, Aaron is just as bad, if not worse. Don't pretend you're his lapdog." He pointed a finger at me. "All this is the start of something, not the end. You're planning to turn on him, eventually. It won't be easy. If you make me forget, same as my people, I could help you. I know so much more than he believes."

"Only if I did, you wouldn't remember it. That's kind of how forgetting works."

That stumped him, but only for a moment. He raised a hand and waved it dismissively. "Even still. I hated him for a long time before the world went to shit. A long, long time." A half-laugh, half-moan escaped his lips. "Hell, could probably forget the alphabet and still remember how much I hate that back-stabbing bastard." His motions were sluggish as he reached out, pointing toward the center of the room. "My... phone?"

"Why?" I asked, wondering exactly how far gone he was. The towers had been down for months. If there wasn't cranial hemorrhaging from the beating, he at least had the mother of all concussions.

"... pictures."

Begrudgingly, I fished the iPhone out of his duffel. "Code?" I prompted, after holding it in front of him for Face ID didn't work, and punched it in when he gave it to me. The phone unlocked, and I pressed the photo button on the home screen. I had to scroll through several pictures of badly mangled bodies before finding one that stood out. Sunny and the kid from earlier. Sunny wore overalls and a straw hat, while the kid holding a pitchfork was dressed as a scarecrow. Both were trying to keep a straight face, the pose a play on American Gothic. Instead of handing it over, I placed it on the ground in front of him.

Sunny smiled, then all at once seemed to panic, remembering the lie he was supposed to be sticking to.

"No one's gonna hurt your kid."

As pissed off as I was that he'd threatened my family, that was a line I wasn't willing to cross. Not out of spite. Not ever.

It spoke to his state that he immediately relaxed, seeming to believe me without a second thought. "Decent. Rules help to keep it together. Keep you alive. I had rules, once." He squinted, staring at the picture for a long time before he spoke again. "You know why I didn't want to kill you, Matt?"

"Why?"

"Because we come from the—"

THUNK.

Blood spattered the phone. Sunny reached up in confusion, tips of his fingers gingerly brushing the bolt in his neck.

I released my finger from the trigger.

And then he was gone.

CHAPTER TWENTY-EIGHT

There was a hollowness to it. Not in the traditional cliche sense —there was no part of me that regretted what we did to Sunny, and regarding the act itself, I felt nothing but satisfaction. It was good that he was gone. Right, even. Nothing he could offer us as a prisoner mitigated the risk of keeping him alive. And now that he was gone, I was all but certain I would sleep better.

It was the way he went that felt anti-climactic. No actual plan, no sudden, unexpected-yet-brilliant strategy to prolong his life. It almost felt like he'd been hoping we'd just... forget about it all. Move on in lieu of a greater threat.

Only we hadn't.

All throughout the trek back through the Galleria, I expected a wrinkle. Some buzzer beater complication to throw us back into the shit. For the Driftless to turn or simply for The Steward to suddenly require more payment for the hunting license.

None of that happened. I got the sense that unlike a lot of guilds operating in the city currently, the Galleria folk simply didn't have the energy to start shit. They were stuck on defense, between two camps of assholes that wanted them gone. I came in with a team, solved a problem cleanly, and left The Steward confident he'd made a friend. Realistically, he had.

I was starting to owe too many people favors.

Greg had already left, so we drove the spare SUV Sae kept in her inventory out. At Astrid's prompting, we paused a few blocks away, pulling into the drive-through of a now-derelict food chain. She and Max got out alongside me while the others waited.

"Sorry." Astrid winced, one eye half-closed, and reached out to steady herself on the bumper. "Whatever he's doing in there, it's sapping my mana. If he's doing it on purpose, he *clearly* doesn't realize that me running out of mana means him running out of air."

"Guessing he missed that fine print." Max stuck his hands in his pockets.

I scanned the night, looking for the odd passerby or faces peering through windows. Finding nothing. "Bring him out. We'll keep **<Squelch>** up and put him in the trunk." The main reason we'd relied on Astrid's pocket dimension spell in the first place was to obscure the kid altogether. No matter how flexible they were being about their human infestation, anyone would ask questions if you were carting a kid away.

"He's gonna remember her car," Max warned.

"Doesn't matter. Sae keeps this one around for a reason. It's disposable."

He sighed reluctantly. "Maybe we should consider other options."

"No, we really shouldn't—"

Before I could finish, Astrid rounded on Max, shoving him hard. "What the *fuck* are you talking about? No really, what are you suggesting?"

Max held his hands up defensively, backing up in a circle as Astrid advanced on him. "Look, I like kids as much as the next guy. Got a couple myself. But that's not a kid you've got locked up in the shadow realm. That's a child soldier. One almost guaranteed to have a fucked-up childhood with plenty of motivation to hate us."

"He didn't see our faces," I said, trying to keep things low-key.

Which clearly didn't work, as Astrid rounded on me next, hands clenched into fists at her side. "And if he had, then what?"

"Hypotheticals are pointless. We were careful. We did it right, and he didn't see shit. Let it go."

Astrid crossed her arms. "I want to hear it. What would you have done if he saw our faces, Myrddin? Because up to this point, your go-to response to inconvenient problems hasn't exactly been pacifism."

Max rolled his eyes. "Girl joins hit squad. Is shocked when there's hitting involved."

"You fu—"

"*Enough.*" They both jumped at my tone, Astrid frozen with a finger planted on Max's chest. I stared down Max first. "The rest of you are more or less anonymous. Sure, he saw your height and build, but that's all he's got. Sunny was running scared for weeks. I'm the bogeyman in this scenario. If the kid's gunning for anyone, he'll be gunning for me first."

Max grimaced. "This isn't just self-preservation. I've worked for a lot of guys. You pay better than most and never treated us like we were expendable. Pulled my ass out of the fire more than once. So I'd be a shithead to not point out what might be a fatal mistake, just because it's unpleasant."

"Okay. But you agree that I'm right?" I held his gaze. "That I'm holding the lion's share of risk here?"

"From the kid, maybe," Astrid muttered.

"Yeah," Max said, his voice clipped. "I suppose you are."

I stared at Astrid next, resisting a subtle temptation to use **<Suggestion>** on her. Not to lie, just to ensure she believed my next words as truth. Most mages with high int would be able to shrug it off, but Astrid was deeply unsettled, and the ability worked better on elated emotional states. Especially when I was familiar with the person in question.

But that was a slippery slope, and I knew it.

"If he saw our faces, I couldn't just let him go." I started with an admission. "But I'd come up with something. A safe place to keep him within my circle of trust."

"A prison cell." Astrid stated with obvious distaste.

"No. Somewhere humane, a place where he could contribute and have some semblance of a life while managing the potential threat."

"And if he takes advantage of that compassion to come after you?" Max prompted.

I locked eyes with him. "Then that's my problem to deal with."

"Whatever. Just trying to keep you alive, chief." Max waved over his shoulder. After a couple of seconds, I heard the hum of the low radio as the door opened and shut.

With Max gone, I turned to Astrid. "Satisfied?"

The van shifted slightly as she sat down, fight draining out of her, leaving her drawn and pale. "I'm all fucked up."

"Why?"

She wiped her face, fingertips cloying at the sides of her eyes. "It's just... I always knew the world was a scary place. Like I knew that, even before. Astria and I wouldn't have survived if we were that naïve."

"You've had to be strong for a long time," I filled in, almost automatically falling into therapy mode. In truth, it was far easier to empathize with Astrid and Astria than most people simply because of their history. Like me, they'd grown up fast out of necessity, been left with the lifetime's worth of baggage that went hand in hand with accelerated growth and now weren't really sure where they fit in the world. "We've seen some shit. Some real monsters too. And while it might be scary to see that firsthand—"

"You told us once that we could quit. Step away for any reason." Astrid's voice was quiet.

"Of course. Though that's a little beyond the point, considering."

"Because we're done now."

"Yes."

"And if I said I don't want to stay on retainer?"

At first, I said nothing. I'd been open with the strike team about what we were setting out to do. Maybe it would have been wiser to obscure that. But I thought it was important that they knew there was an end in sight, and even more vital, that there was something for them when they were done. Sae I didn't have to worry about—she was already a member of the Merchants' Guild. Max had a cushy consulting position waiting at the Adventurers' Guild, with a third party ready to make the introduction.

The twins didn't like big groups, so hooking them up with a guild was out. Instead, I'd come up with the idea of keeping everyone on the strike team on retainer. They'd get a monthly payout in the form of easily achievable quests, and I'd have an emergency resource if the situation called for it.

But I knew *why* she was asking like this. While she held something potentially problematic for me in her pocket dimension, it was leverage.

Astrid was afraid of me.

"Have I caused you any hurt, or frightened you somehow?" I asked.

"No." She shook her head, then shook it again. "No, you've been great to us. God knows Astria really looks up to you."

"Then can I ask why?"

Astrid wiped her eyes again. "If it's about firepower, Astria will stay on retainer. Probably couldn't talk her out of it if I tried. I don't think you're going to come after me. It's not about that. Before the strike team, I thought I was a realist. Like I knew how temporary life was. How quickly it could all be over."

"But knowing and seeing are two different things," I filled in.

"Yeah. Guess they are."

It was difficult to stay rational. At the end of the Transposition, when the less appetizing actions I'd had to take to fill the receptacle came to light, Astrid and Miles were the only two people who'd gone to bat for me. I'd helped her first, but it cost me nothing, while she'd burned her entire guild telling Rodrick to back off.

"Okay."

If taking her off retainer was what she wanted, I'd abide by that. But I would not use her reticence as an excuse to ignore my debt and let her twist in the wind. I'd give Astria her share, doubling the remaining member of Gemini's payout, which would trickle down as resources for Astrid one way or another.

"What, that's it? Just okay?" Astrid blinked several times.

"That's it. If we have to part ways, I'd much rather do so amicably. On one condition."

She braced, setting her jaw as she waited for the other shoe to drop.

"Don't be a stranger, stupid." I lightly swatted the back of her head and smiled as she scowled back at me. "Regardless of how you feel, I see you as a friend. And I owe you. If you're ever in over your head, you have my contact info. Just shoot me a line. I'll be there."

With that, Astrid managed a smile, and all the weight she'd been carrying melted away. "Astria trusts you a lot. The way she used to trust me."

I thought of Ellison. "It's probably just a rebellious phase. That tension will fade."

Probably.

"If you do end up calling her in for something, I'll stand by so she can use the whole mana pool. Just take care of her, alright?"

I nodded and put a hand on the trunk. "Ready?"

When she confirmed she was, I opened the bottom compartment of the SUV. It was a secondary storage space large enough to hold two spare tires, a lot of gear, or an average-sized person. The sound proofing and carbon reinforcement were obviously after market. Astrid cast a spell, removing the kid from her pocket dimension directly into the compartment. He seemed hazy, out of it somehow, until his eyes locked on me.

The hatred in his gaze as we closed the compartment stuck with me long after I dropped the others off and they went their separate ways. I'd intended to talk to Sae about the potion that night, but by the time we got to the exit point she was fading, barely awake.

Still, I couldn't just leave it. I'd talk to her tomorrow, barring some greater disaster or unexpected bullshit. Actually, probably better to just commit to having that conversation tomorrow, regardless. If I kept procrastinating every time life threw me a curveball, I'd never get anything done. Max gave me a knowing glance as he left. He was more used to this line of work than Astrid and probably assumed that regardless of what was stated, I was going to be professional and make sure there were no loose ends.

It bothered me because he was right. Blood had been spilled. The sort of blood this kid would never forget. Reality wasn't fiction though. There was no guarantee he'd go the Monte Cristo route. It was far more likely he'd either die the same way dozens of Users died every day in the dungeons, or simply be too occupied with surviving the chaos of the system to do anything else.

But I was all too keenly aware that there was a lesser chance I was making the same mistake Sunny made in the tunnel. The grave misstep of showing mercy to the wrong person.

Do the kid.

The voice from a distant memory left an unpleasant taste in my mouth as I drove mindlessly, looking for an isolated spot. No. No matter how bad it got, there had to be rules. And no matter how inconvenient his existence was, the kid was an innocent.

Were you an innocent?

I ignored **<Jaded Eye's>** commentary as I drove up to the top floor of an abandoned parking ramp overlooking a park. Belatedly, I realized this was the first place I'd spoken to Sunny, when I was still looking for a way into the Order. Less than six months ago, but it felt a lifetime away now.

"Done," Azure told me. *"Didn't take much to calm him down. I think whatever Sunny told him must have scared the shit out of him. He seems genuinely shocked he's still alive."*

"Let's get this over with."

I left the engine going and killed the lights, got out, and popped the trunk.

CHAPTER TWENTY-NINE

Within weeks of the asteroid hit, most places lost power. There were backups, of course, but cut off from the outside and isolated as we were, the emergency power was routed to critical infrastructure first, leaving the once-vibrant skyline filled with perpetually dark monoliths jutting up toward the sky.

The light was returning now, albeit a glimmer of what it once was. The skyscrapers of now-derelict multi-billion-dollar companies were repopulated with smaller businesses, guilds, and crafters. Several regions—specifically 3 and 9—acquired methods of ample power generation gleaned as rewards for their performance in the Transposition. They couldn't be paid directly in Selve for their power, instead leveraging the resource for alliances and trade. The recent addition—the Gilded Tower —emitted no light of its own but never stopped glimmering.

I tried not to think about how I'd be there in less than three hours and returned to more pressing matters.

The kid was quiet. My intention was to take him some-where open and unconfined, but I couldn't help but wonder if he was worried that if he made a scene I'd throw him off. He squinted slightly, then placed a pair of glasses on his nose, removing them to wipe them on his shirt before replacing them on his nose. They sat slightly crooked. With the set jaw and dark eyes, he reminded me of Sunny.

Maybe it was cruel, but I said nothing. Just sat beside him and waited.

"What's wrong with my magic?" He finally broke the silence.

I reached over to point at the manacles on his wrists, and when he flinched, pulled my hand away. "The bracelets dampen and drain your mana pool to almost nothing. Easier to talk without lasers burning ozone. You get it."

The slightest tip of his head. "And what happens to me now?"

"That depends." I mused. "Do you have people? A place you can go?"

I already knew the answer. Sunny didn't have any close friends or family, so far as I could tell. However, his ex-wife did. She had plenty of relatives who lived around the metroplex, and several within Dallas itself. Despite hating Sunny with a passion, several of them were friendly enough with the kid to take him in. Assuming they were still alive.

The kid didn't answer.

"If not, there's a few groups that'd be willing to take in a stray mage—"

"I have somewhere I can go," the kid said quickly.

I jingled the key, showing it to him. "Then we take in the scenery for a bit, have a chat, then I take those off and go our separate ways."

His eyebrow raised, and he seemed unsure. "Okay."

"What's your name?" Again, I asked a question I already knew the answer to.

"David."

"Sorry we had to meet this way, David."

I really was.

"Is he dead?" David asked. Something in his tone seemed off. Almost resigned.

"He's gone."

"*Fuck.*"

The silence lingered, accented by distant sirens and the sound of traffic dozens of floors below. There was nothing I could say to help him through this. Any words of comfort or support I offered would be seen as condescending at best, cruel at worst.

Tears formed, receded, then formed again, threatening to spill down toward white lips pressed tightly together, trembling with rage. "Of course. He... he..." David frowned. "Why can't I remember your name? Dad said it. I'm sure he said it. He wouldn't shut up about you. What the hell?" He sounded confused, rather than accusatory.

The name "Myrddin" was the one thing I let Azure take from him. Tragic as it was, losing a parent is a formative experience. You're simply not the same person after as you were before. From my experience with memory edits, tearing the entire memory away would be like bringing a hammer down on his psyche. He'd be unable to function, his intelligence would be hamstrung if not outright obliterated, and even if he survived with minimal damage, he'd never be able to escape the feeling that he'd lost something integral. So Azure removed my name from his memories of Sunny, otherwise doing nothing more than blunting the harder-to-stomach aspects.

He'd already lost enough.

"Suppressed memories are the mind's way of protecting a person from trauma," I told him. "It may come back to you. But if it doesn't, that's probably for the best. Some things are better left forgotten."

He shook his head. "Why would I remember everything else other than that?"

"It doesn't always make sense."

For that matter, he didn't remember everything. Azure was pretty sure he'd overheard the beating. Listened to it happen. Yet when my summon had poked around looking for the memory, he'd found it as neatly packed away as if he'd suppressed it himself.

The mind was an unknowable thing.

David didn't accept the explanation but didn't seem to know what to make of it otherwise. I sat quietly as he cycled between rage and depression, and back again, the cycle of grief alternating frames in a film wheel.

"It's okay if you want to scream. Tell me to go fuck myself."

Whatever you need for closure.

David shook his head. "He wasn't... a good dad. I was always getting in his way, you know? Always inconveniencing him. We hated each other. Some days less than others."

"He hit you?"

"No. Just... screamed at me sometimes. But I gave as good as I got."

I hesitated, torn on whether to reveal more. "He tried to protect you, in the end."

David's head snapped around. "What?"

"Claimed he didn't know you. That you were some street kid he picked up for the runes. Didn't want us to take the sins of the father out on his son."

"Why would you tell me that?"

"Because in your place I would want to know. Even if he wasn't the best father. He tried to do something selfless in the end."

"What—what the fuck even is this?" David snapped,

leaning in, all but spitting poison. "You coddle the families of everyone you murder?"

Damn.

Gently, I put a hand on his chest and pushed him back. "Easy."

His face screwed up, and I felt the beginning of a tirade.

I cut him off before he got there. "You have the right to be livid. This was not the result of anything you've done. This should not have happened to you."

"So tell me why? Why?! What the hell did he do?!"

I paused, deciding whether or not to address the thought Azure found in his head. "There was nothing wrong with the rune. It was cleverly placed, and the central tile was objectively the best spot you could have anchored it to. Just like the only reason you missed me in the store was because I flinched. Sunny didn't need one mage running his defenses, he needed twenty. It wasn't your fault—"

The kid let out a cry and threw himself at me, bashing his forehead into my chin, nearly unseating the mask.

"Okay, fair." I grunted, sitting him back down with a little more force than necessary, hoping he'd stay there. He did. "That was your free shot."

I expected him to bite back. But he just sat there seething, taking big heaving breaths. Most people—especially kids his age—would have been completely irrational. He'd handled himself exceptionally well up to this point, even with whatever brain chemical cocktail Azure had served up to keep him calm. I stood up, leaving him alone in the trunk of the SUV, standing directly in front of him while still giving him distance.

Probably time to make my exit.

"Now I'm going to say some things. And it's important you listen."

He glared but held his silence.

I continued. "First. If you go back to the grind, Sol Mages have a branching path at level fifteen. I know this because I'm friends with one. The branching path essentially forces you to choose between a significant boost in power and passive regeneration. It'll be tempting to take the power boost, but you'll want to take the regeneration path, because the passive regeneration *scales*. There's an entire laundry list of upper-level spells you'll be unable to utilize properly if you forgo the regen for a short-term power boost. We're talking magnitudes of difference in the endgame, depending on which path you take. Verify what I'm telling you with someone. Don't ignore it out of spite."

"What—"

I held up two fingers. "Second. You don't have to believe me. You can hate me for saying it, but I need to be clear here. Sunny had it coming. He got a lot of people killed, both directly and indirectly." The kid's face screwed up in obvious pain and I softened my voice. "If that's not good enough and you decide you can't live without hearing all the gory details, come find me."

"How am I supposed to find you when I don't even know your name?" the kid snapped.

I ignored him and approached with the key. David flinched but didn't do more as I freed his arms and stowed the manacles in my inventory. "Last thing, then we're done. I'm letting you go. No conditions. You'll find your things as well as Sunny's in the bag beside you." He glanced at the bag. When he looked back, I tossed him his wand.

He stared down at it as if I'd just handed him a loaded gun.

I basically had.

"My recommendation is to bunker down, protect yourself and anyone left in the city you care about, focus on leveling, and try to forget this ever happened. But I'm aware my recommendation doesn't mean jack shit right now. So if instead you somehow manage to track me down? Great. You'll have another choice. Come to me in good faith and I'll answer every question you have about what your father did. I owe you that. But don't mistake my mercy for weakness," I stepped away. "The shot in the trunk was free. The next one will cost you."

With that, I turned and walked toward the rear stairwell, fighting every instinct I had to look back. The SUV's suspension squeaked behind me.

"He's aiming at you," Azure warned.

"I know."

"You're just gonna stroll away at wand point?"

"He has to make a choice."

"Why?" Azure sounded mystified.

"If he doesn't do something now, every time he reconsiders, he'll remember that he chose to let me go."

"And if he fires?"

"Shouldn't have enough mana for the bullshit beams from before. Anything else—we'll cross that bridge when we come to it."

"You're just... gonna leave your car here?" David called after me, a slight warble of tension betraying him. I smiled, despite myself. It was clever. If I stopped in place, it'd make me an easier target for an inexperienced mage. He was using the car as an excuse to get me to stand still and turn around. Give him more time to work the nerve up.

I didn't stop. "Key fob's in the passenger seat. Take it."

"Hey! Asshole!" David yelled after me. I kept an unhurried pace, waiting for hell to break loose. But he didn't fire off a spell. Didn't give chase.

Good. He was smarter than Sunny.

Smarter than me.

I walked past the door and hopped up on the concrete median, then plunged downward, activating the flight charm halfway to the ground, and flew into the night.

CHAPTER THIRTY

The Gilded Tower had an annoying tendency of relying on themes. If this was a traditional game, its variety would be lauded. From the cabana-esque vibes of the first floor, to the crypt where Ellison and his attaché fought the Nosferatu. What annoyed me was there didn't seem to be any consistency from floor to floor. We went from the over-saturated sheen of a silver city, complete with eldritch-touched horsemen spouting tendrils, to the current setting.

Which was ants.

A giant ant mound filled with ants.

Come the fuck on.

And while the inherent ridiculousness of this place paled in comparison to the pastel murder-unicorn floor, it still carried forward the same problem—the average User didn't take them seriously. The murder-unicorns, which held the collective talents of being fast and carrying a sharp armor-piercing horn on their heads, had still managed to seriously wound Nick.

Yes, it only happened because he tried to ride them.

Yes, it worked out exactly the same way you'd expect.

The difference between Nick and the others was that Nick

learned. Quickly. When we'd run into a forest colony of anthropomorphic bears on a later floor, he'd been wary. And when their invitations for porridge turned violent, he'd been ready.

Trouble was, we now had to convince a mix of strong personalities who had never worked together that they needed to progress slowly and not judge the monsters based on appearance, and needed to take the colony of ants seriously rather than turning this floor into a competitive pissing contest. As a result, I'd barely be able to speak with him since I'd shown up as Matt.

At the moment, he was helping two inexperienced members of the Adventurers' Guild, the bodies of dog-sized ants strewn around them. Only one had been stung severely, skin turning black around his abdomen, while the other had a handful of bruises and scrapes from mandibles.

Nick shifted away to flick the bug guts off his sword, sheathed it with a flourish, then helped them both up.

"Thanks," Scrapes said, rubbing the back of his neck sheepishly.

"They just piled up out of nowhere," Bite complained.

"Anytime." Nick held onto Bite's arm, pausing before he released it. "But this is why we recommended sticking in groups of four. Come on—if you're local, you've seen your share of ants. They swarm."

Both rescued Users glanced away in obvious guilt.

Scrapes—who I was guessing had heard of Nick—seemed to be trying to put his best foot forward. "We'll head back to base camp, see if we can pick up any stragglers."

"No. You won't," I interjected.

Both of them stiffened. Scrapes puffed himself up, trying for a macho put-upon. "I understand that you're a region leader. But we're not in your region. We're members of the Adventurers' Guild on a field mission—meaning the only person who can bench us is someone with guild authority."

Technically, Tyler told me I had authority to order around practically any of the rank and file if the need arose. But this guy didn't know that, and jumping through the hoops to prove it would be inefficient at best.

I took a deep breath and stepped into Scrapes' personal space. He was a head taller than me.

"Uh oh," Nick muttered, taking a step away.

I stuck a finger in his chest. "Look here, motherfucker. I don't give a shit what you do. Go back to base camp and pick up some aphids to fill out the spots on your team for all I care. Not my business, not my problem." Without breaking eye contact I pointed at the other User. "But you're gonna need at least three, because he's not leaving camp."

"I'm fine," Bite argued, wincing slightly as he shifted on his feet. "Just jabbed me a few times. It burns, but I can keep going."

"He's fine," Scrapes repeated, using his height to loom over me.

I didn't back down. "We don't know what the bites do yet. If you'd listened during the briefing, you'd already know that. What I can say after seeing them up close is they look a lot like fire ants. What do you know about fire ant venom, big guy?"

To his credit, he listened as I went through a perhaps too explicit description of what the necrotizing alkaloids common in fire ants would do in drastically higher quantities to living flesh. By the time I was finished he seemed shaken, though not entirely ready to swallow his pride and drop it.

"Uh. Craig?" Bite interjected, drawing Scrapes' attention. "I want a cut of the loot as much as the next guy, but I'm also not crazy about the idea of rotting holes in my torso."

"Smart man," Nick said, nodding sagely. "Chicks dig scars, but rotting holes? Not saying you couldn't find someone who'd be into that, but uh, they might be *into that*, if you catch my drift."

"*Craig!*"

"Thanks for your help, Ceaseless Knight," Craig said smoothly, nodding to Nick as he took Bite by the shoulders and escorted him away. He paused next to me long enough for a withering stare uttering the word "Page" before he walked away.

We watched them go.

"The fuck did I do?" I asked after they were out of earshot.

"Slapped down his pointless-bravado peen with your epic-knowledge peen."

I rolled my eyes. "If I'm right, it may save his friend's life. And for the love of christ, stop saying peen. You're supposed to be doing a rousing imitation of a heroic leader, not a twelve-year-old."

Nick smirked. "And now I'm being assailed with your half-hearted-decorum peen."

"Ugh."

As intentionally annoying as Nick could be, I wouldn't trade his presence for anything. I'd almost lost him a little more than a month prior. His charisma and easy-going nature were tempered somewhat by the trials he'd endured, but in exchange he was more driven, and the combination of charisma and drive drew people to him with a magnetic pull that might have been even stronger than before.

Since we discovered the prophecy in the tower, we'd more or less stuck to the rules of operation. Nick as the figurehead, me operating in relative secrecy, cleaning up the unpleasant, ambiguous problems, keeping his head clear and his hands clean. It worked surprisingly well. For the most part, Nick was smart enough not to ask about my moonlighting as Myrddin, and I knew better than to tell him.

Though the events of the previous night, I'd decided, should be an exception.

"It's done," I told him.

Nick stopped mid-stride, trying to ascertain my meaning. "So... he's gone, then?"

"Along with anyone who would have created an obstacle to the Order's current agenda of cooperation."

On the rare occasion I reported to him, this was typically as far as it went. He'd absorb the end result, acknowledge my efforts, and move on without asking for more details.

Which was why it surprised me when he stopped, leaning against a root-strewn wall. "How... did he pass?"

"Sure you want to know?"

Nick nodded, looking ashen.

"The same way she did."

I half-expected him to judge me for it. Hell, I judged me for it. There was no question that what happened last night had been a violation of my code. I didn't kill if I had the resources and ability to detain. If the risk could be justified. And if the risk couldn't be justified, I tied off the problem as quickly and humanely as possible.

My mind replayed the moment I shot him. The split second in time I'd aimed for his eye, intending to euthanize him instantly. Only for the bolt to strike him in the neck instead and leave him bleeding all over the ground.

In the grand scheme of things, it barely mattered. A difference of ten seconds, if that.

"Well, first of all, thank you. Seriously. Can't even describe what a relief it is," Nick said, eyes darting back and forth as he processed the information. I got it. It'd been a relief for me, and unlike me, he'd known Jinny for most of his teenage years. His mouth tightened, as if a thought had suddenly occurred to him. "Wasn't exactly thinking clearly at the time, but in retrospect, it's weird that he kept the shooter around. Never saw his leadership in action, but from the rumors, he was a one-strike-and-you're-out kind of guy. Did he... say anything?"

"About that night?" I stalled.

Nick deserved the truth. But it was my job to protect him.

"Yeah," Nick said, waiting expectantly.

I looked Nick dead in the face, long enough to sell it without going overboard. "No. We got in, did what we came for, and left. Not a lot of room for a confessional."

He chuckled nervously. "Pretty cold, bro."

"Next time I'll bring a priest and a hallmark card."

"Easy. I'm just asking."

"Yeah." I hesitated, squinting and forcing my vision to focus. "Sorry. Didn't sleep much. Got knives in my eyes."

"Do you regret it?"

"No," I said, the statement almost a reflex. "It needed to be done."

Just maybe not the way I did it.

He took me by both shoulders and stared me dead in the face. "Don't play it down. It's not like it was when you were alone. Yeah, sure, we're on a timetable and paid vacation's gone the way of the dodo, but you have me. Not to mention a handful of other reliable people to lean on. If it gets to be too much—be that quantity or quality—whatever, just let me know. I can sub-in whenever you need."

I shrugged him off. "I'm fine."

"You're not." Nick chuckled and looked down. "But you'll land okay."

"Always do."

It sounded more dismissive than I wanted. If I'm honest, the check-in meant something. Letting him take over even a portion of my side of things would be almost as disastrous as me trying to take his place as the charismatic hero. It just wasn't realistic. But knowing he was willing to try, and maybe more importantly offer a non-judgmental ear, made all the difference in the world.

"Heard anything from Vernon?" Nick asked, anxiety peeking through his otherwise calm facade.

"About our mutual project?"

"Yeah."

I shook my head. The last time I'd spoken with the necromancer, the man hadn't seemed optimistic. Admittedly, I hoped it was temporary. His work speed had taken a serious hit ever since he found out his daughter Kinsley was still alive. "He's at a progression wall. Having some trouble breaking through. If he figures it out soon and continues at his previous pace, we should have an answer."

Nick chewed his lip. "It's gonna suck if it turns out we enabled a necromancer for nothing."

I offered the only words of reassurance I could. "If there's a way to bring her back, we'll make it happen."

A long silence passed between us.

"What if she doesn't want to come back?" Nick asked. The question blindsided me.

"Why wouldn't she?"

"Dunno."

Nick wasn't going to say it, but I could guess. Jinny had been diagnosed with a terminal illness in her teens, and it had been implied—though never directly stated—that her home life left much to be desired. Even back then, the world she'd left was already cruel. But it was a far darker place now, one that irreversibly tainted those struggling to survive in its grasp. Even the cores I turned over to fuel Vernon's research almost without thinking would probably give her pause.

"Jinny wanted to make a difference in the world, before she left it. Maybe she'll succeed. Maybe not. But the least we can do is give her the chance."

"Yeah. Yeah. I know you're right." Nick rubbed his eyes. "And even if Vernon comes up dry, we have a backup now."

"A backup?"

"The moron who threw a barrel of nasties at your region. Gotta be high level, and I'm guessing it's only a matter of time before you find them."

Right. The other necromancer. I'd put out feelers, and even now Miles was already kicking down doors, but the unfortunate reality of the matter was that hunting a necromancer was a waiting game. We had to find the correct trail of bodies, and bodies weren't in short supply. "I'll let you know if I need the muscle."

Nick coughed awkwardly. Then coughed again.

"Fucking—what?"

"It's unrelated. You're gonna tell me to fuck off."

"I'm about to do that anyway."

"Well..." he waggled his eyebrows. "Any chance you'll spill the tea on your *other* conquest of the evening?"

"Fuck off."

"Who could have seen that coming?" Nick elbowed me. "Come on, dude. Meeting and approving your homie's girl is a sacred tenet of the bro-code."

This was so not what I needed right now.

"One, she's not my girl. Two, I don't need your approval. Three, the fucking second Transposition is in thirteen days, which doesn't leave us much time to live out your Judd Apatow buddy-movie fantasies."

"Maaaaaatt," Nick whined.

I rolled my eyes. "You'll probably meet her at some point.

She lives nearby, and Kinsley's putting her on the Merchants' Guild payroll."

Nick stiffened and stared at me in disbelief. "Dude. You're not supposed to *pay* them."

"For services unrelated, goddammit."

"Uh-huh."

"She has a unique skill set—actually, just shut up."

"Copy that." Nick waggled his eyebrows. "Definitely need to stop by now though. Make sure everything's on the up-and-up. Ready for your Court debut?"

Nick, along with the rest of the Court, was saving his strength for the boss. We'd been making our way toward the base camp set up at the return elevator, and other than a few of the Knights, most of the Court would be there. I'd met a few of them already as Myrddin, but Myrddin's reputation blew up any chance of a copacetic relationship. Matt, Nick's politically well-positioned Page, was much more innocuous.

I breathed out through my teeth. "Hopefully it goes better than last time."

CHAPTER THIRTY-ONE

A new game meant new players. And new players meant unknown quantities.

When I'd first considered how to approach members of the Court, I resolved to treat them with a modicum of goodwill. Unlike the rest of the Order, most weren't there because they chose to be. They'd all been aggressively recruited. Some more forcefully than others, as Nick stood in clear evidence of.

Still, that was only how they started. Post recruitment, they were elevated, informed of their status, and treated as nobility with all the luxuries and kid gloves that implied. From what I understood, most of them hadn't set foot outside during the last Transposition, let alone contributed to the efforts.

In short, they were coddled.

Case in point: the base camp.

There were the usual trappings for an extended dungeon crawl—medical tents, cots, crafters, and quartermasters for both guilds. But past them was the court lounge.

Their servants—and yes, of course they had servants—had only just finished hauling up a ridiculous assortment of furniture, luxuries, and a banquet spread arranged in the center atop patterned lavish rugs in garish purples and deep reds. They had personal tents, glittering gear, and countless attaches running about. It occurred to me that the Order had—either intentionally or unintentionally—created an almost bizarro version of the Stanford prison experiment, only the "prisoners" in this case believed themselves the ruling class, forming a Costco-brand lottery bourgeoisie. To be fair, the efficacy of this varied person to person. Some stayed grounded, took their luck for what it was, and were trying to make the best of their circumstances.

Others were so deep in the fantasy Kool-Aid that they couldn't separate the food coloring from the cyanide.

A scattered cheer went up as Nick strode into the lounge, back straight, armor clanking in a steady march as he cranked his gigawatt smile to nigh-unbearable levels and waved to the handful of heads that turned to greet him as they passed.

Only a few of them noticed me, fewer still for longer than scant seconds before they returned to their business. In a sense, being Nick's shadow wasn't so different from wearing the mask. Prime difference being, if I screwed up and brought suspicion on myself, they'd remember it.

Without breaking stride, Nick threw back both flaps of the central tent and entered. I caught the covering before it could hit me in the face and followed him.

There were five sitting around the table, one pointing emphatically at a map in the center. Nearly half of the Court had shown up for this—which was more than I'd expected, less than I'd prefer. The pointer was a redheaded guy in his early twenties, sporting expensive-looking light armor and glaring at the rest. "I'm telling you, the boss room *has* to be here."

Julian. The Prince.

"Sure." The gruff response came from an older man in his thirties sitting near the back. He had a muscular build and somehow seemed simultaneously focused on the conversation and bored. HONOR danced on the knuckles of his right hand, tattooed letters cascading as he tapped his fingers on the table. "Thing is though, we don't have confirmation. No recon whatsoever, beyond your guesswork, Julian. A schoolboy hunch. This is our first official joint op with these people—you really want to go out on a limb and be wrong?"

Nathanial. The Duskblade Knight.

"Perhaps a compromise is in order?" a girl said. She was wearing skull-themed mage's robes, interwoven with platinum thread in complex patterning, her hair and eyes both dark, accented by goth-adjacent makeup. "A scouting party, lightly armed and armored, small enough to slip through one of the narrower passages undetected. They could stick their heads in—confirm a high-level entity—and disengage."

Charlotte. Princess of Malediction.

There was a loud scoff as an unshaven man who clearly thought he was the smartest person in the room pushed horn-rimmed glasses up the bridge of his nose. "And you'll what, cast something on the poor bastards so the door doesn't slam shut behind them? Oh, that's right—you only do curses."

Somehow Charlotte kept her cool, though her mouth turned downward at the edges. "Denigrating as always. My repertoire has only grown. For that matter, this floor is an anthill. From my limited knowledge, there are few doors to speak of."

"Then the tunnel will cave in behind them, or they'll be cut off by a force field, or some 'glorious' deity will slam their big swinging dick down and block the passage. Whatever. If there's a boss, most dungeons find a method to trap whoever goes in first. Why don't you let the grown-ups talk and go grab us all a platter?" He chucked his thumb at the door.

Lucas. Heedful Knight. Subclassed in asshole.

"I have as much of a right to be here as you do," Charlotte said, clearly seething.

Beside her, a wrinkly old man stared down at the table, holding on to his gnarled staff for support. "I will beseech Hastur for his guidance this day. And should he deign not to answer... I will atone."

Paul. Priest of Thorns.

Julian rocked back on his heels, looking skyward at the crowning canvas. "Appreciate that. But let's remember that our patron wants us to be self-reliant. Guardians to the city. He can't be expected to make every decision for us. Just, please, for the love of god, stop whipping yourself."

"It is *for* the love of God that I worship lash to flesh. His score on my temple."

"Is it really a legitimate mea culpa if that mark arbitrarily disappears when you... heal yourself after the fact?" Lucas asked, shrugging when the others glared at him. "Just saying."

Paul's eyes flew open. "Oh. Hm. Perhaps there is wisdom in—"

"Enough." A regal voice boomed out from the back, cutting the chatter immediately. The source was a woman, pushing six feet tall. The many braids in her long blonde hair made her look more Norse than Arthurian, and with what seemed like near-zero effort, she slammed one side of her double-headed axe into the table, burying it to the haft.

Everyone jumped.

"Shit," someone grumbled.

"Seriously? We just had that patched."

"Silence." She scanned the group with a fierce glare, and this time they stayed quiet. "With all this chirping and chattering you forget yourselves. Your place. Julian is the heir apparent. You will all treat him with the fealty and respect he is owed."

Regarding delusion among the Court, Queen Mari was

patient zero. I'd asked Azure to look into her, convinced the grandstanding LARP had to be an act, relatively certain her intelligence would be low enough that he could do so unimpeded.

I'd been right on the second count, wrong on the first. In the short time he perused her mind, Azure found that the Queen of the Court believed in her charter, mission, and authority *completely.* There was no part of her that questioned the system or the circumstances that led to her ascent. The padded walls that came before, the orderlies that forced medication down her throat, the electrodes clamped to wet sponges against her scalp, the endless days that stretched on like lesser eternities staring out the window while figures dressed in white shambled in and out of her vision: *that* was the delusion. She had almost no memories from before, no present family or life to speak of. From what I could tell from Azure's findings before she ejected him through pure willpower alone, she suffered from paranoid schizophrenia, the sort of fringe extreme that seldom manifested.

After the meteor, her title kicked in and cured the most severe symptoms. She, a blank slate, no longer forcefully detached from reality but only loosely tethered by it. Until Hastur spoke to her. She was the only member of the Court who had sought Aaron out rather than the other way around.

She was a true believer.

And in my experience, true believers were as rare as they were dangerous.

"Until the King is either found or made, I am the reigning authority. My son speaks with my voice, and you will treat him with respect." She scanned the table, as if waiting for rebuttal. None came.

Not that cured. Still thinks Julian's her son, and they can't be more than ten years apart.

More of note was that other than a quiet sigh, Julian didn't challenge her at all.

"Ceaseless Knight." Queen Mari lifted her eyes to where Nick stood.

Right on cue, he gallantly dropped to one knee in a respectful bow. "Your Grace."

I nearly followed him but decided not to. They hadn't noticed me or didn't care enough to, but either way it was better not to draw unnecessary attention to myself.

"It's a relief to see you returned to the fold. I missed you." There was a tenderness to the statement that disappeared just as quickly. "You heard our conversation, yes?"

"Only the last of it."

"What would you advise?"

"Yes, let's consult the favorite," Lucas muttered, cutting off in a grunt as someone kicked him beneath the table.

"Well," Nick said, turning back to look at me.

What the hell are you—

"As it happens, my Page is an *excellent* tactician." And with that as an introduction and a giant grin, he rose to his feet, placed a hand on my back, and shoved me forward.

You actual bastard.

CHAPTER THIRTY-TWO

They'd missed the early briefing, so as far as I knew, this was the first time they saw me in person.

There was a considerable silence as the group took me in. At best, a few of them—Julian, Charlotte, and Lucas—seemed politely interested. Paul and the Queen were less engaged but willing to hear me out.

Nathanial, though? The grizzled knight was pissed. He was making some effort to hide it behind cold rationality, but all the signs were there. He'd been leaning back in his chair this whole time, barely engaging with the others. Now he was sitting with his back ramrod straight, piercing gray eyes lancing through me.

He spoke to Nick, never shifting his gaze. "This... is your Page?"

"Yup." Nick grinned obliviously. "Ask him whatever. He's wicked smaht."

I'm not a genie, asshole.

"Sorry." Nathaniel rested his chin on his thumbs, still staring me down. "I'm the old man in the room, so maybe I'm just slow or missing something here. Isn't your Page also the leader of Region 14?"

"That's him," Nick affirmed, completely walking into it before I could stop him.

"Right." Nathaniel nodded, unimpressed. "And on an unrelated note, didn't the leader of that region directly oppose the guild alliance?"

A wave of realization rippled through the group, ambivalence shifting to caution and even distaste.

"Uh." Nick stalled, probably realizing how badly he'd flubbed the introduction but otherwise unsure how to salvage it. "He came around?"

The air of skepticism grew. I couldn't even blame them for it. If Kinsley brought a random stranger into the Merchant Guild's inner circle with that weak of an explanation, I'd be looking for my first chance to get them out of the room so we could have a conversation about proper vetting. Unfortunately, passive-follower-Matt—the role I'd intended to maintain—wasn't going to work now. It would look like I was a trojan horse, doing what they wanted in the short term until I gathered what I needed to break up the alliance.

Better to play it aggressively.

"I didn't." I stared them down in distaste.

"Oppose the guild alliance?" Nathanial asked, raising an eyebrow, preparing to catch me in a lie.

"Come around," I corrected testily, glancing at Nick with an annoyance that was all too real before addressing them again. "I still think this is a stupid idea. Instating a court and king and establishing a class system we collectively left behind centuries ago. Aaron pulling my region's ass out of the fire didn't change that."

I let that linger, watching until I was sure I was about to be thrown out of the room.

"*However,* I spoke to Hastur. And that experience... widened my perspective."

"Bullshit," Nathanial countered.

Charlotte seemed to agree. "Not to be rude, but our patron doesn't speak to outsiders often. As far as I know, he never has. Even as one of his chosen, it takes a considerable effort and a multi-step process to contact him at all."

"Fair." I made a show of considering that. "If only there was someone here with a more direct line of communication with management. So you could verify my claim."

There was a long silence before Lucas sighed and elbowed the doddering old man. "He means you, dumbass."

"Oooh." Paul straightened. He appeared—for lack of a better word—senile most of the time, but as soon as he was called on to engage with the gods, he seemed to gain some clarity. Some percentage of the doddering was an act. The question was, how much? Paul raised his staff upward and everyone else seemed to cringe. I had half a second to wonder if there was a loud noise or other unpleasant magic effects involved before Paul brought the staff down, striking something beneath the table with a meaty thump. Most likely his foot. His eyes literally clouded, a cumulus gray-white rolling over both pupil and iris, and a bead of sweat formed on his forehead while his free hand gripped at his chest.

"Is he okay?" I asked. Given the amount of stress contacting the other side seemed to cause and the man's advanced age, it wouldn't be surprising if he'd had a heart attack.

"He's fine," Nathaniel said. Short. Clipped. Making it clear he didn't trust me.

When I didn't seem satisfied with that, the Queen strode over to the Priest and pulled a handkerchief from her inventory and used it to wipe his brow. "It takes more effort to speak to any patron within the bounds of the tower. We don't understand why. Paul can do it. He is Hastur's ordained chosen. But it takes considerable effort—"

She stopped mid-sentence, caught flat-footed as Paul took the handkerchief from her. His eyes were still clouded over and nothing physical had changed, but his entire demeanor had shifted. The shaking, half-there old man from before suddenly seemed alert but relaxed. He dabbed at his forehead with a practiced motion, far smoother than before. All at once, a dense weight seemed to manifest, pushing my shoulders and neck down until I gripped the rounded table in a forced bow. Several members of the Court knelt, while others remained seated, holding onto their cushioned armrests for dear life.

"Now, now." Paul chuckled, but I had a strong suspicion it wasn't really *Paul* anymore. He reached down and patted Mari's head. "Rise. No need for kowtowing amongst friends."

Hastur.

The presence seemed to ease some. Beside him, the Queen rose first, expression stricken with adoration and gratitude. "I am unworthy."

Nathanial—to my surprise—seemed almost as affected. He rose from his kneeling position, all attention shifted off of me and onto Hastur. "We did not intend to summon you, my lord. We only sought confirmation."

"I was aware of that," Hastur assured him, then winked at me. "But a father doesn't need an excuse to visit his children. Forgive my self-indulgence."

Several heads turned back toward me once they realized I was being included in the statement, and I inwardly sighed. While I appreciated the backup, this was drawing far too much attention, potentially solving one problem by creating another. The more people were aware of me, the harder it was to operate in any meaningful capacity. And if Aaron ended up catching wind of this, I wasn't sure what conclusions he would draw.

"How are you, Matthias?" Hastur addressed me directly.

I allowed a small smile, if only to cover up the internal screaming. "Odd question, from the omniscient."

"My nature allows for great insight, not unlike yours. But we're both aware that's hardly a replacement for hearing it from the source." He tapped a spot on the table to his right. "Come. Speak with me."

Fuck. I didn't know how to play this. He wasn't giving me anything to go off of. While part of me was terrified he might say something to out me as Myrddin, I knew refusing him here in full view of the Court would be beyond stupid. Begrudgingly, I approached and leaned against the table beside him. When he stared at me blankly, I realized he was still waiting for an answer to his previous question.

Fine. If he won't give me anything else to go off of, may as well be honest.

I was all too mindful of the eyes on the back of my head as I answered. "Stressed. Conflicted."

Hastur gave me a proud smile. "Yet you performed admirably, regardless." There was an undercurrent of pained sympathy in the statement.

"I only did what was required."

"And that was no small matter." He looked past me, addressing the room now. "Matthias had his doubts about our institution. Doubts that were entirely justified, given a history I will not share out of respect. But this is a new age. One where it is unnecessary to label skeptics as heretics. More importantly, he holds the same spark of potential within him as the rest of you. I sought him out after the assault on his holdings, we conversed, and in the wake of our recent intervention I asked him for something incredibly difficult. Something only he could do. And he came through. While he may not be a member of the Order on paper, make no mistake. He is one of us."

Just like that, Hastur was gone, leaving a bleary, disoriented old man blinking in his wake.

I turned, facing the rest. They were still stunned and flat-footed from their patron's sudden appearance, and I needed to strike before they recovered. "Again, I have my doubts. But same as the rest of you, I still have people living in the dome who I care for, people I don't want to see put through another event." From the way their expressions darkened, they understood. "A tenth of us died during the first event, and if the trajectory of the game is anything to go on, the second will be worse. Stopping it is all I care about. And despite my position, there's not a political bone in my body. So long as we're inside the tower, I'm not here as the leader of Region 14." I inclined my head toward Nick. "I'm here as Nick's attendant. A Page of the Court."

It was a big swing, putting myself in the same boat as them. Risky enough that I wouldn't have dared to do so, if Hastur hadn't interfered directly.

For a long time, no one spoke. The inside of the tent was deadly quiet.

Mari broke the silence. "Perhaps a simple test. To establish if you are as capable as the Gilded Knight believes you to be."

"Go ahead," I said, half-expecting the giant of a woman to challenge me to a duel, right then and there.

"You heard our earlier discussion." She tapped the round table. "The issues broached and solutions given. With that in mind, what is the best path forward?"

Arbitrary as it was, *unearned* as it was, these people obviously cared about rank. I declined to answer and stared down at the floor. "As an attendant, it is not my place to say."

"And if it was?"

Well, you asked.

Dropping the faux modesty, I looked over to Charlotte. "What sort of curses can you cast?"

CHAPTER THIRTY-THREE

I tapped my foot impatiently just outside the tent. Inside, the Court was still arguing, voices only partially dampened through the tent's thick canvas. It sounded like a few were in favor of my plan, others more vehemently opposed. It wasn't surprising. The strategy I'd cobbled together was unorthodox and required a certain flexibility and willingness to put one's self in danger.

I'd studied up on curses out of diligence after learning from the Adventurers' Guild doctor the Witch class existed, mainly because they were one of the few forms of magic I couldn't directly counter or affect with **<Probability Cascade>**. In short, they were a pain in the ass for both caster and target. They took forever to deploy and had a heinous number of difficult-to-fulfill requirements that varied depending on the curse—sometimes requiring hair, skin cells, in more extreme cases blood or even teeth. They also required line of sight. Casting without the target present was possible, but high enough level that the Witches I spoke to seemed to think of it more as a pipe dream than a realistic goal.

But if you managed to get the curse off and the requisite time passed without the target seeking the services of a Priest, the possibilities were terrifying. Temporary and permanent polymorph, blindness, cancer, liquefaction of organs. Even death—though the death hex was high level and required so many components from the target that if you died that way, you probably had it coming for ignoring the old woman cackling over the boiling cauldron.

The less alarming options were more interesting. Along with lower requirements, they created situations that were still distressing to the target but had curious and often practical side effects. Obvious examples included causing the target's skin to harden into a shell-like form, or sprout gills, or grow a tail.

And while few people would sign up to be a turtle-fish-monkey hybrid, the alterations always functioned. The tail would be strong enough to support their weight and prehensile, the gills would allow them to breathe underwater, and the shell—while bulky and hideous to look at—would provide some protection.

Hell, I'd probably ask Charlotte for permanent gills if it didn't mean struggling for air every time I wasn't out of water. It just seemed too useful to pass up.

Most Witches ignored these options for obvious reasons. They were already barely a support class—they couldn't afford to waste their development and feat points on curses that wouldn't pack a punch.

But, given her position as a member of the Court and the fact that Charlotte *only* had access to curses, I'd guessed that she had something we could use.

And I was right.

The tent flap opened. I half-expected it to be Nick calling me back in, or Nathanial telling me to shove off. Instead, Julian emerged from the tent, nodded to me, and pulled a small gray square from his pocket, holding it to his lips. The light at the bottom illuminated green as he breathed in, breathing out a puff of vapor.

He saw me looking and held it out in a silent offer.

I considered saying no, then realized I had no real reason to decline and took a pull. The nicotine went straight to my head, a temporary buzz taking the edge off the stress headache gnawing at my temples since early morning.

"Strawberry?"

"Strawberry milk," Julian confirmed. "Very princely."

I took another pull—entirely aware I was trading mental clarity for the possibility of an unnecessary addiction—and passed it back to him. "Thanks."

"Sure."

The voices from the tent lost focus as I prepared for him to try to work me. But he didn't. No side eye, no sudden observation to pry information out of me. He just stood on the other side of the tent flap and puffed.

"Something you want?" I asked, giving him a lead-in. Being social wasn't in my blood, but Julian was an unknown quantity I needed to get familiar with as soon as possible.

Julian nodded. "A break from the noise."

I frowned. He was among the members of the Court most interested in my plan. Having him out here seemed less than ideal. "They don't need you in there?"

"Hah. No." He waved me off. "Already made my case. Now it's 'Mother' and Nathanial's turn to argue it into the ground."

"Queen for, Nathanial against?"

"Yep." He blew out a puff of vapor. "You don't miss much. She likes it because it's ballsy and interesting and new. Nathanial hates it for the same reasons. It's Charlotte's chance to shine, so she's obviously hugely in favor, which almost automatically means Lucas is against it, but that doesn't matter much. Nathaniel and Mari's opinions hold the most weight."

"Paul?" I couldn't imagine him as a tiebreaker.

"Nah. Paul goes with the majority. Barring that, he'll throw his lot in with Mari. They're... on similar wavelengths." Julian smiled apologetically.

Out of their minds.

I'd already gathered most of what he'd told me, but it was good to have their dynamics confirmed. Julian was being oddly open, and I was tempted to exploit that, but people with authority were often more sensitive to that sort of thing.

"Gotta wonder," I said finally.

"What?"

"How Lucas isn't covered in sores or transformed into a toad by now."

Julian coughed out a laugh. He cleared his throat and bared a tired smile. "Same. Honestly, I think the only thing keeping him out of the crosshairs of a voodoo doll is Charlotte's astronomical self-control. Keeps trying though. Everything short of straight up asking for it."

"Playing with fire."

"He's just a contrarian. And an asshole. Socially, he's miserable to be around, but he snaps into shape when shit hits the fan."

Absent-mindedly, I pulled up my messages to Ellison. There was nothing new since my message this morning, checking for what had to be the tenth time if there was any sign of life. "My little brother is kind of like that. More contrarian, less asshole."

"Most of the time?" Julian asked knowingly.

"Most of the time."

"Is he... still with us?"

The question startled me. It was presented carefully, almost compassionately. But I could count the number of people I'd told about Ellison's disappearance on one hand.

"Sorry." Julian winced, seeming to kick himself. "Just... I

dealt with something similar when I lost my grandparents. The whole past-present tense confusion thing. Wasn't trying to stick my nose in."

I ran back the conversation in my head. I was certain I hadn't said "was." But I'd hesitated slightly on the "is." It was either more obvious than I recalled, or Julian was an empath. Still, I couldn't walk it back now. Not with him paying that much attention. He'd either suspect the lie or catch it outright. The whole point of meeting the court was to build trust.

"He's still alive. Just... missing."

"For how long?"

"Since the attack on my region." When Julian jolted and stared at me, I shook my head. "Unrelated. He was elsewhere when it all went to shit."

"You're sure?"

"Positive. Plus, he kind of has a history of disappearing for extended periods of time and then popping up out of the blue. That's probably all it is."

"So you're not sure."

Again with the read. Getting too reliant on the mask covering my reactions.

"No," I answered.

"Well..." Julian stretched as my mood grew darker with thoughts of Ellison. "Assuming we're not all about to get rolled over by giant ants, I know some quality trackers. People outside the order. I can call in some favors. Maybe even help with the search."

Of all the things I'd expected a Prince of the Court to say, that wasn't it. It was so far out of my realm of expectations the confusion must have shown on my face, because Julian snorted and looked away.

"Funny," I finally said.

"Not a joke. Days are pretty packed, but my nights are free. Don't sleep much anymore."

"Me neither."

With the strike team retired, barring the occasional Myrddin outing my evenings were also free. I already intended to budget at least a portion of that time to search for Ellison, but I had no clue where to start. I'd thought about asking Nick for help, but by the time he was finished with the tower for the day he was usually one long blink away from passing out. I couldn't ask him to extend himself more, especially when Ellison might just show up one day, with no explanation for the absence.

"Why help me?"

Again, Julian shrugged. "Hastur says you're a member of the Court, which puts you under its—and by extension my—purview. You have missing family, which kind of speaks to me personally. Not to mention we're united in our dislike for Lucas. Explanation enough?"

Not even close.

"Don't you have more princely things to attend to?"

"Please." Julian rolled his eyes. "They keep me cooped up most of the time unless I have a reason to go out and be a glorified adornment. You'd be doing me a favor."

Out of every other member of the Court, Julian was the person I needed to have a handle on. Because when Nick reported the prophecy to the Court, he'd left out a key detail: that he was the one who'd pull the sword out of the stone. As the person holding the Prince class, Julian was the "legitimate" heir. Which in a very real way made Nick the usurper.

Of course, Nick was convinced Julian was a good guy. That he didn't really buy into the Court and had no interest in being King. But Nick often thought too highly of people. And if Julian turned out to be unhappy with the sudden shift of power and became a threat?

I needed to be ready.

"I'll talk to your trackers, at least. See if they can offer any resource I don't already have," I said.

"Great!" Julian seemed oddly happy at the idea of another responsibility. "I'll send you my contact—"

There was a rustle of fabric, and Julien jumped as Nathanial thrust his head through the flaps with a blatant scowl. "Perhaps it would be wise not to ignore your duty in favor of a smoke break, Your Highness."

"Whatever you say, Elder Knight," Julian muttered, giving me an apologetic look and returning within.

Nathanial stared at me for a moment, sides of his mouth turning upward in a subtle smirk. "Well. Come on then, new-blood. Let's get you cursed."

CHAPTER THIRTY-FOUR

Compared to some of the other shit I'd pulled in recent weeks, this was a simple ploy, a solution to the original problem. If the Court sent in core muscle and got stomped, it made them look weak. Alternatively, if they sent in a scouting team that got locked in the boss room and torn to pieces, it made them look stupid.

It helped that we were up against monsters rather than humans, which was a refreshing change of pace. The monsters of Flauros could be nightmares, sure. A single lapse of attention during combat or scouting could spell instant death. What made them easier to deal with was their single-mindedness and uniformity. Every type of monster was different, but once you understood their core objective and mandated behaviors, it was easy enough to predict what they could do.

Not so much with humans.

The greater issue was, we didn't know shit about the ants. They had plenty of familiar Old World analogues to extrapolate from—the ones we'd seen behaved identically to fire ants—but making an assumption of a system monster based on the creature its inspiration stemmed from was a potentially fatal mistake.

Charlotte gave us an avenue of better observation and simultaneously pulled back the veil on what she could do.

<**System Notification:** Due to either your perception or a voluntary alert from the caster, you have detected a malediction placed on your person.>
<**System Notification:** You have been afflicted with Hex – Indespectus.>

Linking chains of mana loosened with an ethereal rattle as they fell away from my face and shuffled off the rest of me, landing with a clatter on the floor. Now that the chains were off and the curse was cast, I felt different. More apathetic. The closest comparison was probably when I first wore the mask. Nothing new, but what was far more interesting was how the curse affected my perception of myself.

I held up my hand, studying the results. It looked more or less the same, minus a few scars and blemishes. The swelled knuckle of my thumb that had persisted ever since it healed after a break had receded. It didn't feel like my hand. More like someone else's had been attached to mine, yet that fact struck me as utterly disinteresting. Which made it all the more significant.

"How does it look?" I asked Nick. Chiefly because despite going first, his appearance didn't seem to change much. Some of the more striking aspects of his features had dulled, but beneath the lack of polish he was still clearly the same person. Either the curse was less effective than I'd hoped, or one of my feats was allowing me to see straight through it.

"Who are you again?" Nick asked, scrunching up his face comically.

"Hilarious."

Beside him, Julian whistled, looking me up and down. "Unbelievable."

"Look alive, Matt, Prince Charming's making a move," Nick whispered conspiratorially, then grunted as Julien shoved him lightly.

"Nick just can't handle the rare occasion he's not the center of attention." I shrugged, ignoring Nick and focusing on Julien.

"Hey!" Nick complained.

Unperturbed, Julien circled around me, hands behind his back. "It's uncanny. You're so... unassuming. Like a person I'd pass on the street and glance at out of the corner of my eye, only to never give them a second thought. The only reason I know who you are is because of context."

It was like he was describing the person I used to be, before I accidentally staked my claim on a region.

"How do I look?" Lucas asked.

"Exactly the same as you always do," Julien said, not missing a beat.

Before Lucas could rise to the bait, Charlotte stepped in. "This curse is unique because it tailors itself to the observer." She put a hand to her chin, surveying her handiwork. "If Julian and a hexed monster were standing side by side—you'd see a human, while the monster sees another monster."

"Hard rule?" I asked.

"Haven't had a chance to test it extensively, though from what I've seen? Yes."

"What about solitary hunters? Predators that avoid or prey on their own kind?"

The question stopped Charlotte short. From the way she cocked her head, she hadn't considered the possibility before. Not surprising, considering how many curses she'd probably accumulated by this point. Charlotte pulled up her UI, sifting through the description before coming back with an answer. "Unclear. Dammit. The descriptions are always so oblique."

"You've never used this on a boss before?"

Charlotte scrunched up her face. "There was a group of gnolls—which from a distance appeared to have some sort of dominance hierarchy—"

"—They do," I confirmed.

She nodded thoughtfully. "I hexed their chieftain. Once he was hexed, the pack ignored him. Not right away, of course, but the longer the curse stayed in place, the less deference the pack showed him."

Julien's eyes widened. "That's what you just cast on us? That hex from the barrens?" When Charlotte confirmed it was, he grimaced. "A little warning would have been nice."

I'd gotten the sense that Charlotte was hiding something when she'd excitedly explained how the Indespectus curse functioned. Because from the way she told it, it had nothing but benefits. I'd intended to push her on the topic once we were locked in, but from the looks of it, Nick and Julien would do that for me.

Nick blinked several times as he looked between the Princess and Prince. "He's freaking out. I've heard you guys talk about the barrens." He pointed to still slack-jawed Julien, then pivoted to Charlotte, who was grimacing. "You look like you just got your hand caught in the non-vegan cookie jar."

"I'm vegetarian. Not vegan," Charlotte argued, in the way people argue over something unrelated to belabor a point.

"Same difference." Nick waved her off. "Problem is, all I know about the barrens is that they're a terrible place for people with coulrophobia, and that mentioning them is a great way to get the two of you to shut down." He shifted toward Charlotte and took a single step into her personal space, his expression friendly. "And if it's all the same to you, I'd like to go into this with as much sense of the situation as possible."

I had to respect it. I almost always pushed too hard when there was a possibility of critical information at play. While this approach worked to keep the subject off balance, it often created a hostile environment difficult to deescalate from. Nick's aw-shucks mentality allowed him to achieve the same results with minimal enmity. Not realistically achievable for me, but something I could learn from.

Charlotte blushed furiously at Nick's proximity, glancing everywhere but directly at him as he waited patiently.

Definitely not something I could achieve.

The Princess swallowed. "I wasn't—uh—hiding anything. Assuming the scouting is done in less than six hours, which realistically it should be, the floor isn't that large, there shouldn't be any problems."

Nick smiled, nodding acknowledgement. "Great. Maybe I'm just anal-retentive or it's this guy's influence," he chucked a thumb at me, "but I like to know what sort of timetable I'm working with. It's really helpful."

"Definitely a luxury these days," I added.

"I don't get a lot of chances to contribute," Charlotte breathed. "Curses work slowly, and so far, at least, we've steamrolled over almost everything really fast. I'm just trying to help."

With a motion that was almost obscenely suave, Nick reached out and gently tipped Charlotte's head upward, prompting her to look at him. Nauseating, but from the star-struck expression and red cheeks, clearly not to her. "You're a *big* help. Your specialization is better suited to large-scale threats, the really scary shit. Makes me feel better just knowing we have you on our side." He grew serious, still maintaining the charming facade. "But power is a double-edged sword. We have to wield it responsibly."

Way, way too much. Jesus Christ, Nick. You're going to kill her.

I'd identified Charlotte as kin almost immediately. A fellow studious introvert. As such, she was not prepared for the sort of nuclear shit Nick was throwing her way. If cartoon-style steam started pouring out of her ears, it wouldn't be a surprise.

To Charlotte's credit, she didn't short circuit as I'd expected. Instead, she took a step back and seemed to take a deep breath, steadying herself. "Uh. Okay, it won't apply to this situation—again I wasn't hiding it—but I get wanting to know all the details. So, the barrens. It was supposed to be a routine clear. In line with the sort of softballs the order was tossing us early on to help the Court level with minimal risk. The report from the survey team counted twenty gnolls. A few captains and some special mobs, but nothing particularly powerful, and despite fewer numbers the initial team cleared the dungeon with no incident and okayed it for Court assignment."

"Guessing it didn't go down that way?" I prompted, giving Charlotte an escape from Nick's perpetual smolder.

She shook her head, grateful to have someone else to focus on. "No, it really didn't. System barred the door behind us by the time we realized the count was closer to fifty. Far more organized than the reports implied. To make matters worse, they all reported to a chieftain, one apparently strong enough that even our assigned reconnaissance specialist couldn't see his level."

I frowned. "One hell of a disparity."

"To this day, we're still not sure what happened," Julien added. "The Order questioned the survey team after the fact, and despite considerable pressure, they swore they were thorough and that original reports were accurate." He paused thoughtfully. "It's almost like the dungeon just... changed."

I weighed the pros and cons of filling in the blank for them. On one hand, even acknowledging the existence of the adaptive dungeon increased the likelihood that someone else would find it. On the other, I had the only key, and considering what happened on my last foray, had very little interest in returning. After a moment, I decided the risks were minimal and sharing would only raise my perceived value.

"I've heard from a reputable source that there's a variant of dungeon that scales."

Julien's head whipped around. "Wait, *what?*"

"Scales based on level, or number of Users?" Charlotte asked, leaning forward.

"Both. It adjusts initially, based on party count and level, tailoring the rewards. Resets after. Sounds like you might have encountered something similar," I said, trying to bring the attention back to them.

"Suppose so." Julien mused. "Either that, or the system was intentionally out to screw us."

"Also completely possible," Nick muttered.

Julien shuddered again. "Like Charlotte said. She hexed the chieftain, and for a while it worked great. We kept an eye on him as he ran from scruffy a to scruffy z, trying to get anyone to listen to him, acknowledge his authority and presence, whatever. And then things got weird."

"Weird how?" I asked.

Charlotte breathed out a long breath. "Keep in mind this was over the period of several days. Before we went in, I think we all still had a sense of things. That there was a gnoll chieftain, and we needed to monitor and avoid. By the time we started to clear, we could barely remember what he looked like. But after we'd completed it, all we could remember were... the signs."

"Scrawling on the wall in a language we couldn't understand," Julien filled in grimly. "First using the sort of tribal paint they wore on their faces, and later... written with other substances. And the writing wasn't the end. We found a gnoll with his throat slit, destroyed rooms. Eventually the chieftain must have lost his mind, because he started throwing shit. Tossing around furniture, buckets, even a few swords."

Nick and I shared a glance. If I'd known all the details— well, I probably still would have signed up for it. There were risks to be sure. As long as Charlotte remained safe and safe-guarded, the hex gave us a serious advantage. The fact that she'd withheld the details, though, and that she was still with-holding them, gave us a point of leverage we simply hadn't had before. As much as I wanted to hand-wave the slight away and act like it was no big deal, that simply wasn't the play here.

"Jesus *Christ*." I pressed a palm to my forehead and walked a few steps away.

"It'll be fine," Nick said, assuring Charlotte more than me.

"Yeah," I hissed. "That's what you always say."

I used the awkward silence to think through my next steps. If I'm honest, I didn't have a problem with the deceit or the potential downside of the spell. What I had a problem with was that Charlotte seemed like the wrong sort of person to hold the only key to undo the hex. She'd hidden the downsides out of a lack of self-worth and desperation to contribute. Even now, out of the corner of my eye, I could see the way a hand clenched at the front of her robe, bunching up the fabric violently.

It occurred to me now, seeing them in this context, that I'd been thinking about the Court all wrong. In my mind they were the system's version of children of privilege, handed the keys to the kingdom with little care or oversight simply because of who they were.

In reality, they were closer to the golden goose. Show

animals held in cushioned captivity. And no matter how you sliced it, a gilded pen was still a cage.

I waited.

Come on. Give me what I need to trust you with this. Show a spine.

Charlotte approached, though she maintained a respectful distance. "Reversing the hex is easy. It's—"

Sensing she was about to give me an out—the opposite of what I wanted—I interrupted, intentionally misinterpreting her words. "And if something goes terribly wrong here at camp while we're gone and it ends up taking you out of play?"

Charlotte winced, almost shrinking away before her expression hardened. "Look around." She gestured to the bulk of the Users in the center. The bulk of the Order's and Adventurers' Guild Users were milling around. There was a sense of camaraderie among the group. It didn't surprise me that the Adventurers' Guild had warmed up to the Order, what was unexpected was that it appeared to be mutual. Everyone liked heroes, and everyone enjoyed the experience of being a hero, even if you were only following orders. Maybe that was all it was. No matter what the agenda or underlying motivations were, what the Order had done in my region was undeniably heroic.

Beyond the friendliness on display, the collective gear they wore was undeniably high tier. Just from where I was standing, there were dozens of sheathed weapons and worn armors that emitted a soft glow or odd sheen, a mark of Epic rarity or above.

With the Order's shady head start and the Adventurers' Guild's connection to Kinsley, I was probably looking at the best equipped Users in the dome.

Slowly, I crossed my arms and faced her. "Yeah. They're a tough bunch. Camp is probably safe. None of that matters if the only person who can undo this shit gets bored and wanders off."

"Hey." Charlotte moved, circling until she stood directly in front of me. "For one thing, I've been caught flatfooted one too many times to be the wandering-off type. And even if I was, I take this responsibility seriously."

There it is.

"Okay."

"And for that matter—wait, what?"

"Sidebar." I switched gears and moved out of earshot of the rest of the group, not giving her time to backpedal. "Hold anything back when we went over your curses?"

Charlotte blinked. "Some of the trivial and less powerful. Nothing of note. Why?"

Because of the way her nose was perfectly in proportion with her face. How everyone besides Julian was walking around with a full set of luggage under their optics, and Charlotte didn't even have a shadow. The swell and natural glisten of her lips. All without a single blemish, frown line, freckle, or mole. She was an LA 10 and a Dallas-does-not-exist. No matter how you looked at her, the beauty was uncanny. Maybe that was a side effect of being a member of the Court. But judging from the Dusk Knight's grizzled visage, I was inclined to believe otherwise.

And the more I thought about it, the less comfortable it felt leaving Sae's fate up to Hastur's whims. After everything she'd been through, everything she'd contributed, I couldn't just come back to her empty-handed. She deserved better than that.

"Anything cosmetic?"

The reaction and confirmation were instantaneous. Charlotte looked down, cheeks flushing in embarrassment. "I overdid it."

She had, but only slightly.

"Not really. Just gathered from context."

"Huh?"

I chucked a thumb at the rest of the room. "Most of us are out here looking like the walking dead, while you could have walked off the set of some CW network post-apocalypse." When she said nothing in response, I tried to soften the commentary. "Just seeing the group with fresh eyes. Guessing no one else has noticed."

"And what do you intend to do with that information?"

No matter how tactful I tried to be in negotiations, people always ended up zeroing in on the blackmail conclusion. "Find out more and make a business arrangement, if possible. Assuming the hex isn't fleetingly temporary or exclusively self-cast."

"For you?" She looked up curiously.

"God no. Not my bag." I chuckled self-deprecatingly. My looks and appearance even post-system changes were decidedly average, and despite that I was still getting far more attention than I wanted. "Rather not talk details out in the open, but... a friend of mine has an ongoing dysphoria thing. I owe her a lot, so..."

Charlotte chewed her lip. "Sculpere could work for that. But a hex is still a curse by nature. It takes multiple applications to get right and... the process is painful."

I paused. "Like, break every finger one at a time painful, or could drive a person insane painful?"

"Depends on the extent of the changes."

Realistically, it wasn't a full replacement for Hastur's potion then. But I was pretty sure Sae wouldn't mind if we did this piecemeal.

"And if the changes were focused around the face?"

Couldn't say for certain, but I was pretty sure it was the compound eyes that gave Sae the most trouble. Mandibles being a close second. With Iris's more recent, functional adjustments, Sae's chitinous body held a convincing human form and could easily pass as slick armor. But the eyes made sunglasses in public entirely mandatory. And while that worked in a pinch, it was a ticking clock until they got unseated in a critical moment.

"Should be manageable," Charlotte confirmed. Then, hesitantly. "And if I do this..."

The groan was reflexive. For once, I didn't bother holding it in. "What, I won't out you for being the most attractive person in the room? Just—If you help my friend out, I'm going to pay you. If you don't, I won't."

"Oh."

"Uh-huh."

"It would be nice to have a legitimate excuse to get away from the Court. Especially legitimate, because I'd be making inroads with a new ally," Charlotte mused. "It'll probably take a few hours at least. Factoring in the time and components, knocking off a bit because it seems to be for a good cause... twenty-five thousand Selve?"

It took all the self-control in the world to not immediately jump on the offer. Weird as it was to say considering where I came from, twenty-five-k was nothing to me, even less to the Merchants' Guild. I was all but certain Kinsley spent at least that on her monthly allotment of white truffle lobster mac-and-cheese. It was an extreme lowball, and I was pretty sure Charlotte was only offering the service at that price because she was relieved not to have another foot on her neck. If she had any self-awareness at all, she'd realize that eventually, which created space for resentment to grow.

"Make it fifty thousand and we have a deal."

"Done," Charlotte said automatically. Then paused, confused. "Wait—"

"It's a complicated case, and I don't want you to feel like I fleeced you after the fact." I stuck my hands in my pockets and turned back toward the group.

"Just, off-record for a second," Charlotte called out to me. More than anything else, she looked ashamed.

"What, too low?"

"No. The offer is more than generous. But... you really don't judge me for wasting slots on something as trivial as appearance?"

"The fact you did works out great for me. Why would I?"

Only from the downtrodden expression that wasn't what Charlotte wanted to hear. From what she'd implied, she'd used the hex on herself extensively. Extrapolating the introvert energy and lack of confidence, it was a safe bet she was less than thrilled with her previous appearance and still adjusting to the new one. And now she was looking for absolution from the one person who knew the truth.

It's like despite being the most fucked-up person here, I'm the only one who actually went to therapy.

I sighed, running a hand through my hair. "For one thing, my thoughts and judgments shouldn't matter. I'm a guy. Relatively speaking, the only real societal expectation we have and can't do anything about is being six feet tall. Compared to the pressure you and yours get on a daily basis, that's a drop in the bucket."

"You're not *that* short."

"Thanks."

"Sorry."

"Point being, I can't know what it's like." I mused, trying to strike a balance between dismissive and thoughtful. "But self-doubt, self-loathing? The way the intrusive thoughts tend to crop up at the worst possible time? Those are things I can speak on definitively." I glanced at her. "Any of that get better after your... adjustments?"

Charlotte nodded.

"Then it was worth it."

I genuinely believed it was. Maybe speccing for vanity wasn't exactly optimal, but eliminating anything that could distract you in the heat of the moment, even for a second, absolutely was. Charlotte would be a far better ally, teammate, and potentially friend, if she wasn't regularly splitting her focus outward and inward. That, at least, I could relate to.

She paused for a long moment and swiped at her eyes, then peered at me curiously. "So, you really think I'm the most attractive person here?"

"I have a girlfriend."

Leaving Charlotte behind in an awkward retreat, I returned to Julien, Nick, and Lucas. From Nick's shit-eating grin, he'd overheard my parting words at least. "My *boy,* melting the ice princess—" He grunted at my drive-by elbow in his gut.

"Let's get this over with before we disappear."

"Fucking finally." Lucas rolled his eyes.

CHAPTER THIRTY-FIVE

Talia padded alongside Nick, ears up, nostrils flaring. She was manifested in her true form, white and gold fur rippling as she kept pace at his thigh. The two of them together made a picture straight off the cover of a fantasy novel: The Ceaseless Knight and his elegant talking animal companion.

Other than Nick and Talia, the rest of us maintained a single-file marching order, not unlike the ants we supposedly mimicked, trying to match behavior to appearance. Lucas took up the middle in front of Julien, while I brought up the rear.

I watched mutely as a small trail of ants passed by us, each approximately waist height. So far, at least, between the hex and the marching order, our precautionary measures seemed to be working. The invertebrates were oddly scarce and for the most part paid little attention to us.

It was odd, though. Because despite the honeycombing network of passageways and tunnels, there didn't seem to be nearly enough of them. Part of me wondered if this was nothing more than my own bad habit of looking a gift horse in the mouth, but every time I was about to disregard the notion, there was a slight buzzing from **<Jaded Eye>**. Not enough to sound the alarm, but from my prior experience with the title, I kept my guard up.

For the most part, the team we'd put together seemed competent. Julien and Lucas both had no issue with following Nick's cues.

The only problem—and I hesitate to call it a problem—was that Lucas seemed dissatisfied with the lack of action and couldn't seem to stop running his mouth.

Once the most recent ants were far in the rearview, he started up again, like clockwork. "As usual, Charlotte's 'help' was completely unnecessary. These tunnels are a ghost town."

From behind, I saw Julien's fist clench at his side.

"Whole point of prep is it's better to need it and not have it, then have it and not need it." Nick shrugged.

"And we may still need it," Julien agreed. "Not exactly a bug expert, but I'm guessing we'll see the most resistance closest to the queen."

"Dunno, big guy," Lucas elbowed Julien, "could definitely see you as an insectologist."

"Entomologist," Nick corrected, at the same moment I said "Myrmecologist."

I shrugged. "Same difference, tighter category."

"Fuck me, I'm surrounded by nerds," Lucas groaned.

"One in every group."

"Huh?"

"Nothing."

The jab at Lucas was unnecessary, but if I was honest, he was wearing on my nerves as well. I knew what he was. The sort of person who agreed to a difficult task almost exclusively because it gave them something to complain about. Harmless. But that didn't make it any less annoying.

Lucas walked backward, doing his best to stare me down. "Got a problem, Page?"

I snorted. "The second Transposition event is a problem. Organizing the regions before said event hits is a problem. *You* are not a problem."

From the way his face darkened, Lucas didn't like that. He was about to say as much before Nick interrupted. "Speaking from experience, I can confidently advise *not* starting an argument with the guy who runs practice LSAT questions to pass the time."

"Whatever." Lucas turned his back to me. "It's always the smartasses that crumble fastest when the action hits."

No self-awareness whatsoever. It's honestly kind of impressive.

Julien slowed, staring down a side passage. Further down the tunnel was the silhouette of an ant, roaming in panicked meandering circles. It wasn't the first time we'd seen this behavior, but the queer feeling of wrongness washed over me just the same.

"Another off the trail. How many does that make now?" Julien asked.

"Four," I answered. "Thirteen, if we're counting the ones that seem sluggish and drunk."

"You kept count?"

"Yeah."

He nodded in approval, lips quirked in concern. "It's a little weird, right?"

"Maybe." I wanted to say more, but for the moment all I had was a gut feeling with little evidence to speak of. "If there're hundreds, it might not be that strange for that many to have a screw loose. Odd that we keep seeing them, though our sample size is in the low fifties, so we may not have an accurate picture."

"So, bide our time and assume system fuckery."

I raised an eyebrow. Having thoroughly learned my lesson about keeping my paranoia to myself, I'd been on the verge of voicing something similar. Julien kept hitting all the right notes, like he wasn't even trying. Suspicious. But not unwelcome.

"Exactly."

For once, Lucas had nothing pithy to say. Maybe the sense of uneasiness had gotten to him like the rest of us, or maybe he was just tired of the sound of his own voice. Nick froze in place and held a fist up, directing us to the cover of an upturned mound of dirt before a half-dozen ants scampered through the intersection in front of us. It took a second to identify them as the addled, scrambled variety, largely because they were moving quicker and less aimlessly.

"Okay, *that* looked organized." Nick squinted, stretching up to take another look before dropping back down.

"Something pissed them off," Julien agreed. "Or someone."

"Nobody should be this far in." I shook my head. Then waited, giving my mind time to work as I isolated a single image, no more than a flicker from the last ant to cross our paths. Like the rest, they should have only had three segments —abdomen, the lumpy, trunk-like center, and the head. But I could have sworn I'd seen four. I poked at Lucas, using the disruptive element of the group to stall while I worked through it. "Thoughts?"

"How the fuck would I know? Maybe it's aphid milking hour or something?"

I cocked my head. Despite fully expecting the verbal equiva-lent of hot garbage to come spewing out of his mouth, that wasn't the worst theory. It was wrong of course. But not half-bad.

However, Nick and Julien were both holding in laughter.

"Milk them? Like... cows?" Nick wiped a mirthful tear away as Lucas scowled.

"I'm imagining a full factory farm setup, only with aphids instead of livestock." Julien grinned.

"To be fair, some species do that. Not saying that's what's going on here, but it's possible." I spoke up despite myself. It wasn't about helping Lucas, exactly, just making sure the others weren't dunking on him when he was actually throwing out legitimate ideas.

"Ah." Julien elbowed Lucas as his eyes glazed over and he reviewed the route the Court had cooked up. "Who's the myrmecologist now?"

Lucas muttered something almost imperceptible that sounded like "fucking magic school bus."

"Well. We have two options. Follow the war party, or stay on route." Nick chewed his lip.

"Or both," Julien said, still focused on the map. "Easy detour in the direction they headed. Assuming their end destination isn't too far away, we could follow, observe, then be back on the path."

"Not gonna reveal the origins of this highly convenient map?" I pushed a little, keeping my voice casual. A route directly to the suspected boss room was one thing. But Julien seemed to have in-depth knowledge of the tunnel system. Anything I could glean about a highly placed User's abilities or class was valuable information to have. But the way Lucas visibly recoiled, I got the sense that I'd touched on something sensitive.

"Told you." Julien grinned, giving nothing away. "We have excellent trackers."

Nothing I picked up even hinted that the question bothered him. But from the way Lucas's head swiveled like a spectator on a tennis court, I decided on instinct not to press further. "Fair enough. More information is always better than less." I looked to Nick. "Let's divert—follow until we have a better idea of what they're doing and why, or it takes us too far out of the way."

We followed the train of ants from a distance, trailing, the feeling in my stomach growing more sour the longer we observed them.

"Try to relax." Julien looked over to me, pitching his voice low. When I glared at him, he shrugged. "Stress is bad for your skin."

"I'll exfoliate," I snapped back, a little more vehemently than I needed to. Still, he didn't seem to mind.

"Something about there being two distinctive groups of these things bothers you."

Hesitantly, I nodded. "Yeah."

"Care to share with the class?"

When it came to dungeons, the system didn't care about creating a realistic or viable ecosystem. Not unlike a video game, the intention was to create set-dressing convincing enough that the User clearing the floor couldn't see the matrix. Given that, it often relied on stereotypes to create a false sense of security, emphasis on false. Because there was always some sort of twist. The fact that it was telegraphing something off this early alone made me uneasy. I did my best to convey this without sounding like a crazy person, and Julien just nodded, looking troubled as he absorbed it.

Instinct, rather than logic.

"Matt, worst-case scenario?" Nick said. From the curtness in his voice, he was feeling the same thing.

"Won't be great for morale," I warned him.

"We're past that."

I blew air through my lips. "Absolute worst case? Some play on zombie ants."

"What the actual fuck?" Lucas said.

"There's a real-world basis to draw from. A type of fungus

and parasitic wasps." Almost thoughtlessly, I reached in my inventory and withdrew four antifungal philters, passing them around. Nick downed his immediately, while the other two hesitated. "Obviously, I'm leaning more towards fungus than wasps. We haven't seen any larvae, and the wasps use that to propagate. Fungus would be a serious problem, because there's no guarantee it only works on ants, and there's no guarantee the spores would be visible."

In other words, we could already be infected.

At that, both the new additions from the Court popped their philters and drank, grimacing at the taste.

My heart sank as I watched the trail of agitated ants suddenly curve, skittering legs taking them directly down a side passage.

"It's a side chamber with no outlet," Julien said, frowning at the map. "Maybe that's the end of the line?"

Emboldened, Nick approached the chamber, the rest of us following behind. There was an audible crunch that echoed down the tunnel and he cringed. We waited, listening for movement. After hearing nothing, he muttered, "Floor's different here."

Something twisted in my gut. Forgoing the marching order, I jogged up next to him, eyes glued to the ground. From far away, it looked no different than the dirt. Studying it up close, however, revealed something as alien as it was alarming. Layers upon layers of chitin, folded on top of each other to give the appearance of terrain. I could make out bits of legs, eyes, and antennae mixed in with the slurry.

I nearly lost my balance as my stomach flip-flopped, leaning against the side of the tunnel for support, a wave of nausea overtaking me as a very different memory rose from my subconscious, suppressed but never fully gone.

Nick bent down next to me and whispered, his voice barely audible. "Is it..."

Not a fungus, not even close. It's eldritch.

I forced myself forward, taking the first look inside the chamber. Despite their formerly clunky movements, the sporadic ants were organized in their efforts, forming a half circle. They surrounded a major easily three times their size. The major backed away in confusion until his abdomen pressed against the chitinous back wall.

As one, the aberrations curled their abdomens over their heads, spraying the major with a dark black gunk. The large ant in the center recoiled and turned in an immediate attempt to run, only to collapse.

Its aggressors didn't attempt to savagely pull it apart, as I'd half expected. They peppered it with a multitude of bites, but the bites were firm, held for a second and then released, not unlike the method a mother dog might use to discipline her brood.

They're trying to keep it intact

More than enough for confirmation. I gestured for the rest of them to follow back to the main path, barely keeping the nausea and terror at bay. Thanks to the Overseer's broadcast of the situation in Region 6, it didn't take long before they connected the dots.

Nick looked like someone punched him in the face, while Lucas looked as close to the verge of panic as I was.

"We have to go back. Warn everyone," Nick said, looking fully prepared to sprint all the way back to base camp.

"No. That's exactly what we need to avoid." I clenched a fist.

"This isn't the time for coy shit, Matt—"

"*Listen to me.* Word gets out before we have our ducks in a row, it's chaos. Especially the Region 6 connection. More than anything else, keep that to yourselves. Someone infected slips

down the elevator in the mayhem and the entire city is fucked."
I looked to Julien and Lucas. "You've both spent more time in
camp than I have. How many people have been injured, leaving
room for error?"

They exchanged glances. After a moment, Julien cleared his
throat. "Less than ten, on the conservative side."

"Assume *twenty*." My mind raced as I recalled the encounter
with the Adventurers' Guild Users earlier, how they'd wanted to
get back into the action immediately. "Cross-reference with the
healers. Keep in mind there's a good chance that not all injuries
were reported. Look for anyone walking in a strange way,
favoring one side or another, wincing as they move, any tell.
Lock the exit down. No one gets in or out." I started to pace.
"The Duskblade Knight and the Queen. How are they in a
crisis?"

"Their arguments suddenly disappear." Lucas rolled his
eyes.

"Will they stay put?" I rounded on him.

"If we hint how important it is, they will," Julien said.

I nodded. "Park them in front of the elevators. Out of
everyone they command the most respect, and they're the most
intimidating. We need a full accounting of everyone present
and anyone who might be missing. Any User who's received
medical care since arriving needs to be isolated, sedated, and
monitored."

"Guessing you're telling us all this here instead of back at
camp for a reason," Julien observed.

I ground my teeth. The point of going over it this way was
burying the lede, because I knew Nick wouldn't like the next
part.

Julien continued to jump ahead, understanding dawning in
his eyes. "You still want to scout the boss."

Lucas's eyes bugged out. "Are you *insane?*"

Just as expected, Nick immediately squared off with me. Trauma-fueled terror took over. "Hell no. No way we're splitting the party for a scouting op. This takes precedence."

Judging from their collective body language and the way they hesitated, it was obvious I was losing them. Best bet was to put everything on the table. "Think about how fast this thing spread. An entire region was overtaken in a matter of hours. Just because there's less right now doesn't mean it'll stay that way. I'd stake my life on that. So, no, we're not scouting the boss. We're killing it. And we have to do it *now*."

"Matt—" Nick started again. He had every right to be afraid.

It wasn't a card I wanted to pull. But I leaned in and whispered in his ear, playing it anyway. "We're out of time. Let. Me. Work."

Nick stiffened and pulled away, his mouth tight, looking vaguely hurt. He knew I was referencing our deal to combine our methods to do whatever was needed to end this before the second event. In that detached, theoretical moment, he'd agreed. Simple fact was, it was a lot more difficult in practice.

But Nick didn't argue. When he spoke, he purposely looked away from me. "Okay. Where do we go from here?"

Julien mused aloud. "More importantly, how many people do we send back?"

"Much as I hate to say this... it has to be me." Nick rubbed the back of his neck. "People in both camps listen to me. I'm already going over the order of who I need to talk to and how."

"I'll go with him." Lucas immediately volunteered, visibly sweating.

Julien rolled his eyes. "Of course. Not like we could use the extra firepower."

Talia stepped forward, giving Lucas serious side-eye as she gravitated toward the center. "As a summon, I am immune to most status effects and can simply be resummoned if I die." She looked at Nick. "May I remain with the attack team?"

Nick nearly missed the fact the question was being directed at him instead of me but recovered quickly. "That's probably for the best."

"Can you handle a boss?" I turned and asked Julien point blank. From context and some whispers I'd heard around the Order's compound, I already knew he was monstrously strong. On the upper echelon alongside Nick. But more importantly, he seemed to have a better-than-average head on his shoulders, with little ego to speak of. Given the stakes, further bolstered by the fact he appeared to be in deep thought rather than answering immediately, I'd probably get an honest answer. "If you can, I'll do everything possible to support you. I've seen Talia in action enough to know she's fairly strong, so between the two of us you won't be solo. If you can't, that's okay. My instinct is to have all four of us return together, wrangle a few other heavy hitters, and do this the hard way. But we'll lose the benefits of a stealth approach."

"... and significantly increase the group's risk of exposure. A group filled with strong Users. Fuck." He rubbed the bridge of his nose. "Uh. I feel... *uncomfortable* making that assessment."

Good.

"Realistically, there's no way for me to know." The color of his eyes was almost clear in the lighting, entirely unreadable. "Assuming the boss is a simple bump in difficulty from the floor below, then, yeah. Easy enough. But there's no guarantee it will be. And if you're right about this floor being completely over-taken in a short time, whether we throw twenty people at it or two people and a summon, this is our only shot." He cocked his head. "It's a question of harm reduction now. And, being frank, if the three of us can't handle it together, I'm not sure throwing more people at the problem would do anything other than increase our casualties and put both groups in a worse position for the second event. I think we go for it. Do or die."

This was the outcome I'd wanted. But something about it made my mouth go dry.

"Then we need to move," I said.

Julien nodded.

He'd repeated my reasoning almost verbatim. Between an anti-eldritch summon, the Ordinator, and a high-ranking member of the Court, I was pretty sure we had this. But Julien shouldn't have known any of that. To him I was just a low-ranking member of the Court, and Talia was a magical wolf. I thought back over our interactions, reviewing everything I'd said and done since our first encounter, finding nothing he could have possibly drawn the conclusion from.

Maybe he really was just that confident in his abilities and had included me and Talia in the estimation to be polite.

It was either that, or we had a serious fucking problem.

CHAPTER THIRTY-SIX

Tunnel after tunnel blurred by. We were moving faster now, less concerned with being detected than getting back to camp.

I was concerned anyway. Julian seemed to be having the time of his life. He'd been edgy, uncertain until we had a plan in place. But now he seemed to revel in the moment, smiling to himself. He was approaching a level of speed that was making it far more difficult to justify my supposedly lower-level self keeping pace. This was something I'd never had to worry about with Nick. Despite the two of them sharing similar energy—infuriatingly good-natured and positive—Nick's high-pressure sports background and subsequent injury meant I never had to worry about him screwing up when shit hit the fan. As long as no one close to him was dead or dying, Nick locked the fuck in. Julien, on the other hand, was an unknown quantity.

At least he wasn't paying attention to me—

"Dex build, huh? Nice!" Still making distance at a ridiculous rate, Julien craned his neck back to look at me and grinned.

"If I wasn't, you would have left me in the dust by now," I answered dryly.

"Sorry. Gotta prioritize killing the boss with or without you. Lives at stake and all."

"Less talking, more running."

At a reasonable pace. So you don't remember this late at night and start wondering how the latecomer had so much agility, I added silently.

As if he was simultaneously psychic and antagonistic, Julien lowered his head and picked up speed, only slowing once he reached the next cross tunnel, boots skidding across the earth as he dropped to a knee and checked the corners. I made a show of cutting speed a few seconds early and catching up to him, panting slightly.

"Clear?" I pitched my voice low.

"Few normal drones heading that way, looks... pretty clear." His brows furrowed as he stared at the passage ahead. It widened gradually, leading into a large circular chamber that was inundated with boulders that resembled pebbles in everything but scale and bits of bark larger than me. "For now. That's gotta be it, right?"

"Seems too easy."

"We did kind of cheat."

"Still." I stared into the room, trying to suss out exactly what was putting me off. Then it hit me. So far, the Gilded Tower had shown a strong tendency toward single-target bosses. There'd been a few duos and even a melee trio, but only one other floor that had lower-level minions active during the boss encounter. Generally, dungeons were as unpredictable as they were dangerous, but if you looked closely, certain patterns emerged. For one, the boss was *always* on theme. If there were werewolves, you'd probably be fighting either a werewolf or a human with the capacity to shift. And considering how the enemies on this floor were comprised of ants and the red eldritch corruption that plagued Region 6 controlling those ants...

No way there weren't ants, right?

"Any scents?" I murmured to Talia. When she shook her head, I gestured for her to move closer. She crept forward, nose low to the ground, until the swishing of her tail suddenly ceased. She slowly raised her head and backed away, a growl deep in her throat when she returned.

"Not sure how you knew, but yes. There are nine creatures lying in wait that smell similar to the infected hexapods. Both their aura and smell are subdued, but they are there."

Not good. The bark scattered across the floor created a lot of hiding places for something not-quite-human-sized. If they were just normal monsters that was one thing. But if Talia was right and the bugs were infected, that put us in a rough spot. Because a single hit could be lethal.

I slipped across the hallway, studying the passage. At first it looked exactly like the rest of the smoothed-out tunnels. But the longer I stared at the earth, the more subtle cracks and fissures stood out to me.

"Shockingly, your friend was right about something," I told Julien.

"What?"

"The second we go through, the tunnel will cave in."

"Shit." He thumbed the hilt of his sword nervously. "Look, when I told you I could handle a boss I meant it, but..."

"Maybe not with a small horde of ankle-biters peeling the flesh off your shins?" I said.

He nodded, his eyes flicking back and forth before they finally closed and he put a hand on his forehead. "Okay. Okay. Like you said earlier, the more contact we have with this floor, the higher chance the corruption will spread. We have to clear this now. There's no choice."

"You're going to get bit if you just charge in."

"I'll charge in, brute-force my way through everything. If I make it through unscathed, great. It's possible even if I get bit, I can shrug it off. If I don't, I'll take care of it. But I need you to stay behind until it's over."

"Why?"

"Because I need you to make sure I'm dead if they get me." He stared at me, as if it was the most obvious thing in the world. "Can you do that?"

A mental flash played in my mind of Jinny stepping off the bridge.

"Fucking altruists." I pinched the bridge of my nose.

"Almost right."

"How about we skip the noble-sacrifice part and just get through this?"

———

Julien watched, quiet for a change, as I set things up, removing twenty firebombs from my inventory and placing them in a pile. It was around half the supply I'd obtained from an earlier boss, a fire wyrm that Nick and I had struggled with and ultimately brought down. Chastity typically charged an exorbitant rate for her work, though in this case she'd given me a discount due to the pleasure of working with such a rare material. The result was a round sphere bisected in the center, silver liquid on one side and a lava-like substance on the other. They were impact grenades, which simultaneously made the setup harder and the payoff easier.

"Be careful to make any use of power seem ordinary. He is observing you closely," Talia warned me.

"Got it."

This was a task that was easy enough to pass off as simple

human dexterity. System grenades varied a great deal. Even if he identified them as an impact variant, he didn't know the material and wouldn't realize they should be breaking when they weren't.

Ambush pile first.

I used an area cast of **<Probability Cascade>** on the pile to avoid any possibility of accidental discharge, held my breath, then rolled one underhand. It rotated in a blur, traveling across ground and slowing to a stop around six feet into the opening. I would have preferred a little farther, but my abilities rarely gave me exactly what I wanted.

Now that I had a focal point, it was easier. Nine more joined the first, forming a neat pile in the center. I paused, listening for movement.

Nothing.

A bead of sweat trickled down my forehead as I rolled the rest, each coming to a stop adjacent to a piece of bark large enough to serve as a hiding place. With the initial ambush pile in place, I was prepared to prematurely start the encounter. Instead, it went smoothly. So smoothly that I wondered if **<Jaded Eye>** was wrong and the corrupted monsters were pulling the classic "hide beneath the floor" trick.

As I rose, Julian and Talia took their places. Julian stood beside me with his sword at the ready, while Talia prowled further back, claiming a spot in clear view of the boss room.

"Sure you can hit those?" Julian leaned over and asked quietly.

I fought the urge to scoff. With a hand crossbow and **<Probability Cascade>** paired with my quick draw ability, hitting every single impact grenade—even the ones that had rolled farthest on either side of the room—would be trivial. However, Julian was watching me closely. He passed it off as idle curiosity. Maybe it was, but I'd spent much of my teenage years watching my brother use a similar persona to lucrative ends.

"Who am I, Hawkeye? No. We let the expert do it." I shifted my head back toward Talia.

"Maximize the glamour's effect. Picking up what you're putting down." Julien grinned at Talia, who scowled at him openly. "Alright, show us what you've got, captain."

The light show started, motes of holy fire circling around a prismatic halo that appeared around Talia's neck. As they accelerated, Julian leaned in and whispered, "Uh, heads up. Once the boss shows itself, I may do and say some stuff that won't make sense. Just need you to know I'm doing it for a reason."

"System thing?" I realized immediately.

"Almost right. And I'd appreciate it if..."

"Not my first rodeo. Or the first time I've worked around a difficult title. I'll keep it to myself," I reassured him, waiting for a denial. He showed nothing beyond plain relief. Figured. My assumption came with experience. Most classes's general abilities and skills were relatively straightforward, except for a few outliers. It was the titles that always threw a wrench into things and gave the Users quirks that ranged from debilitating to outright overpowered.

The first projectile loosed, smashing an impact grenade and setting the nearby ground ablaze. And the screeching began.

CHAPTER THIRTY-SEVEN

I barely heard the insectile whining keen before Talia's other projectiles hit, each emitting a sound similar to a bottle rocket with far more devastating effect. Flaming segmented bodies, some far larger than others, scrambled out in a squealing dash, mandibles clicking, feet skittering as they raced toward the only visible source.

Talia fired projectile after projectile, moving more than necessary to hold their attention, while Julian and I pressed ourselves against the walls.

A *BOOM* and subsequent rush of heat escaped from the boss room as Talia detonated the ambush stockpile. Flaming ants heavy with pheromones and chemical scents brushed against us as they passed, unsettling Julian and nearly knocking me over. Either the glamour worked, or they were too angry and unsettled to notice the two lesser threats holding up either side of the tunnel.

"Now," I snapped.

I leapt over a flaming ant as Julien shoved it aside and dashed through the doorway. This time he actually kept pace with me, and we entered the boss chamber at the same time.

There was a deep rumble and a cascade of falling rock and soil crashed down behind us, crushing most of the ants. A few probably still made it through. But in smaller numbers and away from prying eyes, Talia could handle anything Eldritch in nature easily.

Julian evaluated the cave-in behind us, taking a step back. "That worked *way* too well."

"Twelve o'clock, hanging upside down from the indentation of rock," I spat out tersely, my bow at the ready.

A praying mantis clung to the ceiling, pinprick eyes barely visible with its rock- and soil-colored camouflage. It swayed slightly, mimicking a leaf in the breeze. Tendrils of oozing red were wreathed around its body, digging into its limbs and carapace.

I sighted its head. It was a plausibly easy shot from here with the thing being so large. "Let's get this started."

Julian put a hand on my bow, pushing it down.

"What the fuck—"

"My thing, remember?"

I fell quiet, annoyed at the interruption. A system quirk that forced you to fight differently was one thing. Losing the benefit of surprise when it was the only advantage we had was an entirely different level of irritation.

After waiting until he was confident I wasn't going to fire, Julian raised himself up and approached the mantis. "Are you intelligent?"

A set of human teeth clicked impatiently. Its voice was a harsh noise, forced out through a throat clearly not designed for it. "I am a servant of the disruptor. There is no me. Just as there is no you. Merely the wills and ideals we are driven by."

As if that was somehow satisfactory, Julian sheathed his sword.

What the hell are you doing, idiot?

I nearly said something inflammatory but didn't want to draw more attention to the opening. **<Ordinator's Emulation>** suddenly proc'd, informing me that Julian was using a skill. But there was no further sign of one. "You're intelligent enough to speak eloquently, and can grasp abstract concepts such as the erosion of self. Surely you must hold some sort of belief of your own accord. Some will."

The creature chortled. "All willing springs from lack, from deficiency, and thus from suffering. Fulfillment brings this to an end; yet for one wish that is fulfilled there remain at least ten that are denied. Further, the desire lasts long, and demands are infinite; the fulfillment is short and rarely measured out."

The statement gave me a chill. The added context of what this thing was—or rather, what it was controlled by—made it worse.

Julian chuckled back, as if the creature had just told nothing more than a clever joke. "That's a direct quote. Schopenhauer, right?" He frowned. "Though I suppose you may or may not be aware of that. In my opinion, it overlooks a lot. Cruelty and suffering might spring from lack, but so do empathy and compassion. One side cannot exist without the other."

Are you seriously arguing philosophy right now?!

I told myself it was some sort of stalling tactic. He'd cast an ability, so he was doing something. Right?

"Which is why I'm prepared to offer clemency," he said, oddly solemn.

"You offer *us* mercy?" the mantis asked flatly.

"I do. We have an entire region of people afflicted with a similar condition. And it's possible, given your control over others and retention of self, we may be able to learn how to cure them by studying you."

Completely silent, I slowly moved, shifting counter-clockwise until I had a decent view of the mantis's side profile and gripped

<Blade of Woe's> hilt, leaving the knife in its sheath. The mantis had no obvious weak point. If it had any, they were hidden beneath the network of red that looked vaguely like a circulatory system. Just like the victims of Region 6, the Eldritch Infection was the only thing left the weapon's magic effect considered critical.

I was nearly to the point of abandoning any concern for Julien and striking out on my own. Starting the fight on my own terms before he got himself captured or controlled, or worse. The fact that he even thought he could reason with something clearly so malevolent and barbaric cast a permanent shadow on his potential as an ally.

"Strangely, we hear truth in your words. Had you come to us alone... perhaps we might have considered this... offer," the boss hissed, head flicking toward me with inhuman speed. "However, we suspect your companion does not harbor the same sentiment."

Julian's smile grew thin. For the first time I noticed how pale he was. The way his hands shook. He was clearly terrified.

But... not by the boss.

For the sake of the small, infinitesimal chance Julian was taking a page out of my playbook and pursuing a misdirect for the sake of an opening, I played along.

"Doesn't matter what I want. Julian's in charge here." I shifted my head toward him, making a show of acknowledging his position. "I do what he tells me."

It rotated its head until it was nearly upside down. "Because of your boon, I will make this offer only once. Leave now."

"What boon?" Julian turned to me in confusion.

"Does that apply to both of us?" I asked. Leaving it alive wasn't an option, but if it was shortsighted enough to open an exit for me to shove my misguided companion through before the fighting started, I would not turn it down.

"Only you."

Unfortunate. The old me would have jumped on the opportunity in a second. In part, I was still tempted. Julian had blown this in so many ways he'd essentially made his own bed. The cold, rational option would be to leave him here to lie in it, eventually returning with a stupid amount of firepower, casualties be damned. But there were countless ways that could come back to bite me.

"Yeah, I'm good to get out of here." I shrugged and inventoried my bow.

"Matt?" Julian called after me, his concern clear.

"Don't." I snapped at him suddenly. "Whatever you're trying to pull here, this half-assed it's-a-small-world horseshit wasn't part of the plan."

"Oh."

I ignored him as he looked down, hands still shaking, and addressed the mantis. "Where's the exit?"

It chortled as it extended an insectile leg toward the wall. "This way, kindred. Though I do wonder how many days this mercy will grant you. Not long, most likely."

I trudged through the soft dirt, all business, in the direction the mantis indicated. Disappointment swept over me as I realized where he was directing me—toward the only patch of stone-looking wall in the arena.

I kept talking. "Strange to warn me if it's true. Stranger still to threaten me if it's not."

"This is neither a warning, nor a threat. Simply an observation. The lithid's scent is strong on you." It leaned down, body proportions allowing it to simultaneously tower over me while it stared me in the face. "It will grow stronger still until one is no longer distinguishable from the other. After that? It will no longer have need of you."

My mouth tightened. "Thanks for the warning then. May I go?"

There was a grating of stone on stone and a human-sized passageway opened up. It was barely large enough for an average person to fit through. More annoyingly, the stone that surrounded it was thick and solid. Dungeon infrastructure tended to be anywhere from five to ten times as strong as its real-world equivalent to prevent sequence breaking, so it might as well have been steel.

I'd hoped getting the boss to reveal the exit would give us an avenue for retreat. Not so much. The door itself was thicker than the average support beam. We wouldn't be forcing it open in a pinch.

Realistically, abandoning Julian here wasn't an option. On the off-chance he made it out, it would create animosity between our factions. And if he died, he was too beloved and central for the people around him to not take his loss personally. Too valuable as a foothold into the Court. Those were all sound, logical reasons to help him.

That it kept me from having to take advantage of someone who was misguided and naïve was just a lucky coincidence.

If the battle went badly and I was forced to rely on Ordinator abilities in a manner that was obvious, I'd **<Subjugate>** him in a second.

"There are no traps. My kind might be devious by nature, but we do not offer boons often. Thus, in the rare situation they are encountered, we treat them seriously," the mantis said, looking between me and the tunnel, misinterpreting my hesitation.

The fight was inevitable. There weren't many angles left to play. I was well within range for something devious, but a sneak attack wouldn't mean much if there was nothing critical to target. Moreover, Julian seemed to be taking the betrayal *really* hard. Like I'd catfished his mom and kicked his dog on the way out hard. The only play I had left was turning this moment into something cathartic and stirring, something that would etch me in his mind as an ally. Wouldn't help us with the fight, but it would pay dividends if this didn't end with subjugation.

I sighed and resigned myself to channeling Nick. "Well, Mr. Prince? Hope you've legitimately got something up your sleeve, because we're not brute forcing our way out if you don't." Julian's head snapped up, and I knocked on the solid stone of the exit for emphasis.

"What... is this?" The mantises's eyes seemed to bulge, and the mandibles around its human mouth clicked nervously. "The way is open. It will not open again unless I am slain. *Leave.*"

"Hear that?" I said, discreetly stepping out of swiping distance. "Clear cut and plainly stated. Never intended to negotiate, after I left. Probably just wanted a clear shot at infecting you as a host."

When in doubt, poison the well.

Julian shook his head, his mouth pursed. "Why?" he asked me.

"If I'm honest, I don't really have a reason." I stuck my hands in my pockets, crossed the room, and returned to him, fully prepared for the boss to strike at my back. It didn't. "Maybe because you seem like a decent person. Or maybe it's just that you got under my skin back at base camp. Felt like we made a connection, but I wasn't born yesterday. Could have been nothing more than savvy maneuvering."

He blinked several times. "What? No, not at all."

"Then you treated a stranger and outsider as a friend. And I don't abandon friends."

Drawing on Nick in this moment felt so saccharine I could almost hear the stirring cinematic strings, crescendoing to a fever pitch. It was all I could do to keep my cringing internal. It felt so over the top and inauthentic I couldn't imagine *anyone* taking it seriously.

Julian grasped my shoulder, his expression stoic and serious. "I won't forget this."

Someone please kill me.

"What entertaining company." The mantis cackled. "A system-borne so earnest and straightforward it is a miracle it still lives...." One pinprick eye rotated toward Julian, while the other remained trained on me. "And another that lies as easily as it breathes." Its cackle grew louder. "Had you never wandered into my lair, I suspect the pair of you would have reached the same inevitable conclusion."

Regaining his composure somewhat, Julien stepped to the forefront. "That being?"

The mantis smiled widely, showing the dark, unhealthy looking gums that surrounded its human teeth. "Tragedy."

<Awareness> screamed milliseconds before four crimson spears buried themselves in Julian's torso.

CHAPTER THIRTY-EIGHT

Multiple attacks launching from a ridiculous number of angles. Can't dodge. Can't even see where they're coming from.

Overwhelmed by the feedback from **<Jaded Eye>**, I grabbed the flight charm in my pocket and activated it, shooting straight up. A mess of red tentacles exploded out of the now-torn-open cavity of the mantis's torso, several barely missing regardless of flight.

Julian was less fortunate. In the tunnel I would have guessed his agility was on par with mine, but the boss's initial onslaught was inescapable, and lacking a charm, he was still bound by the laws of physics. Four pulsing tentacles speared through his chest at an angle, pinning him in a kneeling position. He painfully clung to them for support, his face pale and drawn.

This was bad.

But it wasn't the first time the system had dropped the floor out from underneath me, and it probably wouldn't be the last. In a way, I expected it. It forced me to do what I'd always done. Improvise, take stock, and survive.

Barring an insane stroke of luck, Julien was infected. As good as dead if not worse, no matter what happened here.

I needed to end this quickly and efficiently to avoid exposure. Nothing else mattered.

I dismissed all of my summons, including Talia, and stayed mobile, zipping across the chamber in corkscrews and zigzags, preparing for the taxing mental process of bringing all three summons back at once. I saved the flight charm for unexpected escapes most of the time, but its utility in combat couldn't be overstated. A few tentacles gave chase, lashing out at air, but only barely. The misses were getting closer and closer to hitting their target, but the unexpected verticality presented an unusual avenue of attack. If I could just buy a second to grab an impact grenade and throw it—

Something sharp and hot pierced my calf, followed by the sensation of countless stinging barbs. I lost focus and plummeted to the ground, barely rolling with the impact. It'd only been a glancing blow, but...

<**System Warning:** You have been infected by Eldritch Miasma.>
<**System Notification:** The impending status effect has been canceled due to Eldritch Favor.>

The boon bought me breathing room. But not much. Even an indirect hit had blown through my armor and left a golf-ball-sized crater in my leg. The wound bled and twinged as I dove away from another onslaught of tentacles and pulled the entire satchel of grenades from my inventory, prepared to throw the entire thing. Even if I aimed slightly behind the mantis, the fire would likely spread and kill Julian. But we were past that. He'd asked me to wait outside the boss room to finish him if the worst happened.

In a way, doing this honored that wish.

Before I could, Julien mouthed something inaudible.

<Ordinator's Emulation> went off, despite no visible sign of a skill.

The mantis stopped, tentacles freezing where they were. I swore quietly and held the satchel by my side, prepared to throw it as soon as the fight started again.

If you actually have something in your back pocket, now is the time.

Surprisingly, the mantis seemed just as frustrated. It peered down at Julien, its expression indecipherable. "There is no point in this. Whatever power you are using to prolong your life, we can sense its nature. It will crumble shortly. And when it does, the battle is won." It shifted its tentacles, jarring the Prince slightly for emphasis and opening the wounds wider. "Are you really so craven?"

"Maybe." Julian coughed blood, raising a fist to the red that lingered on the edges of his mouth. It lowered to reveal a grim smile. "I don't want to fight you. We've never met, never even had a conversation. The only reason to kill you is fear. Fear that you'll kill me first. That you'll hurt my friends and family if you escape. If you were mindless, or incapable of reason, I'd do it. But you're intelligent enough to hold a conversation. So there's still a chance we can come to an accord."

Another flesh spear struck him through the gut. They seemed to have some sort of tensile strength, because without the support of the spears pinioning him to the ground, he likely would have fallen.

"This world does not favor mercy any more than the last. Those who cling to it will find their final moments wanting."

Julian looked up at the creature and grinned through bloody teeth. "Then why haven't you finished it?"

The mantis growled in frustration. "Because of this... inconvenience."

"The power only holds if there's something left unsaid. A desire I can grant, something that might tip the scales before drastic action is taken. Already put my cards on the table. Where are yours?"

Despite the insanity, a small part of me admired the way Julian was holding himself together. Dignity was a luxury most people lost the second they took a serious hit. He was covered in blood now and still negotiating, still clinging to his ideals.

Naïve as they were.

Yet the creature didn't deny it. The longer the stalemate went on, the more obvious it became that it wasn't letting Julian live out of cruelty or puzzlement. The mantis looked up, his pinprick pupils staring toward the ceiling but not focused, as if they were searching beyond any physical constraint.

"We wish... to see the sky."

"Is that all?" Julian forced a smile. "I was under the impression you were a hive mind. Can't you look through the eyes of a human under your control in Region 6?"

"It can't," I realized. "The Region 6 outbreak happened during the Transposition—after the sky had changed. It's back to normal for now, but if you get around the containment measures and look up from inside the region itself, it looks the same as it was back then."

"The realms of Flauros are intertwined with our nature. We have taken root in many worlds. Each time, the sky grows red and desolate long before we develop the strength to overtake a host capable of vision."

This was already a clusterfuck. Might as well gather information before I had to deal with the rest of the shitshow.

I frowned. "I've heard from the more adventurous in my circle that the hosts say things, reference events and specifics from their life before. That implies memory retention. Hard to imagine all the people you took over were chronic shut-ins."

The mantis shifted slightly, then bowed its neck in a motion that could have been a nod. "There is truth to that. It was once our way to wipe any hosts clean, producing entirely empty vessels. That turned out to be nearly as harmful as letting them keep a degree of agency. We absorb them into the fold, add their knowledge to ours. But the process is not perfect. Many extraneous details are lost."

As bad as the current situation was, I felt a long-held weight lift from my shoulders. I finally had an answer to what would have happened if the remnants of Region 6 finished their receptacle. Though it wasn't completely clear, it seemed obvious now. The vessels—the people they used to be—were gone. And no amount of Lux or Cores would have returned them to their previous state.

At the time I'd made the only choice I could. Blindly.

Now I knew the truth.

"Got any copies of *National Geographic* in your inventory?" I asked Julian, partially to keep things moving, partially to remind him how stupid this was.

"Next best." His arm stirred at his side, shedding blood from his fingertips before it went slack again. "Phone in my front satchel pocket. Grab it and pull up the photos?"

I approached, using the excuse to inspect the damage. Five perforations that were anything but small, located around his chest and abdomen. It already looked bad from a distance. After seeing how sodden his armor was and the blood pooling on the ground beneath him, it was dire. I leaned in to unzip the satchel's zipper, using the proximity to pass a message.

"Not sure how you're still coherent—the pain alone would be enough to put anyone under. Going off what I can eyeball, you're losing blood fast. Might be pushing two. Gonna lose consciousness soon. So I'll say it again. If you're going to do something, you need to do it now." He grunted, and I fished the device out of his pocket, an iPhone a few generations old.

The screen—a golden, ethereal background behind a clock that looked oddly meditative—shook as the facial unlock failed.

"Code?" I asked

"1-0-0-2-6-9."

I plugged it in, silently committing it to memory as I discreetly thumbed the screen, immediately scrolling through his pictures before he could direct me. There were a few accidental blurry shots, a couple pictures of animals in a domestic setting—either his pets or someone else's—but those made up maybe ten percent of the reel at most. The majority was... landscape shots. Sunsets, sun rises, cityscapes, some from Dallas, some from elsewhere. The absence of composition and borderline hostile rejection of the rule of thirds told me they were amateur, pictures he'd taken rather than saved. At the end of the reel, there was another selfie of him and an older woman with gray-hair with oxygen tubes in her nose, smoking a cigarette.

"What am I doing?" I asked.

"Pull up my photos. Should be a few pictures of the big blue."

A few?

I closed the photos app and opened it again, scrolling to somewhere in the middle. He'd taken a picture from one of the taller buildings in the city but angled the phone upward too much. "This work?"

"Y-" He trailed off in a fit of coughing, looking paler by the second. "...that's perfect."

I stared at the mantis coldly. "He's happy to give you what you want without bartering. Probably on account of all the blood he's lost. Unfortunately, I'm holding the goods, and I don't give things away for free. Need assurances you can sustain him in this state. Otherwise, no deal."

For a second Julian was about to argue, but his eyes lost focus, and any disagreement he might have offered went with it.

"We have rebuilt hosts from atoms. Extending one's life is a simple matter." There was a slow hiss, followed by a low, thrumming hum, and the spears fixing Julian in place glowed orange. Clarity trickled back into his expression and the bleeding slowed.

I tried not to take it as a good sign. It would still kill him as soon as whatever ability he used to force this stalemate had faded. But buying him time was all I could do.

"Great. Thanks. Maybe take the skewers out of him while you're at it."

The mantis's head swiveled, and while its expression was neutral, I could sense the distaste. "No."

I bristled. "Then go—"

"Matt, it's okay," Julian murmured weakly. "Show them."

Fine.

Not wanting to make an easier target, I bent low and tossed the phone screen up, watching in odd fascination as the mantis bent down and scrutinized the picture from inches away. "Such a grand view to be contained in something so small."

Julian chuckled between heaving breaths. "If you come with us and we find common ground, I'll make sure you get to see it for yourself."

"Impossible. Flauros is a part of us."

"Just because it's always been like that doesn't mean it has to stay that way," Julian argued. "We have scientists and researchers now who can do things they never could in the old world. When was the last time you worked with someone who wanted to help you, someone who had access to vast resources? It—"

Julian trailed off, coughing again as the orange light faded. His eyes widened, reacting to something only he could see.

"We appreciate... the gift," the mantis said slowly, almost begrudgingly. "Unfortunately, it is not enough."

"But..." Julian trembled and stared at the ground. I put a hand on his back to steady him, arm bumping the hilt of a sword—

I did a double-take. The hilt was covered in white and gold cross-hatching, and the weapon's aura buzzed at my mere proximity. He had his original blade still sheathed on the left side. More importantly, I was *certain* the second sword hadn't been there before.

"Vague promises of a future that might be better are nothing in the face of a more achievable destination," the mantis said.

"The merciless domination of the host planet," I filled in flatly.

"Our way is the only way," it agreed.

"Glad we fucking humored you."

In a manner that would have almost been funny in a less dire situation, the monster shifted uncomfortably. "This favor will not be forgotten. We will allow the Prince to keep more of his personality than most once he has joined the collective."

How generous.

All at once, Julian's demeanor changed. The desperation and weakness drained out of him, and he glared up at the creature with pure conviction. His hand stirred by the sword at his side, blood still dripping from between his fingers. "There seems to be a misunderstanding."

"Oh?" The monster's mandibles clicked. "Explain."

"If it was just me in here, things might be different. I don't have anyone depending on me. But he does." Julian shifted his head toward me. "I dragged him into this and asked for his trust. He's had multiple chances to walk away, and he hasn't." His eyes were blank, cold, as the dynamic in the room seemed to change. "So. For his sake. We are leaving this room. One way or another. Please let us. *Please.*"

The last word was more prayer than demand.

"And if we don't—"

A tentacle lashed out with a deafening snap. The attack came immediately, without warning. If it was the first time seeing it, I might have moved too slow.

But I'd been coiled like a spring since the beginning of the standoff.

<Blade of Woe> moved in confluence with my martial skill, entirely on instinct. **<Probability Cascade>** activated reflexively, amplifying my aim as I hacked through the tentacle, severing it in a gout of black, vile-looking blood that covered Julian from chest to forehead.

He didn't blink. Didn't react.

I hurled an impact grenade at the creature's face as time slowed down, watching out of the corner of my eye as Julian's mouth pulled up in a sad smile. When he spoke, his voice amplified through the room, final and authoritative.

"Be at peace."

He gripped the new sword, blood marring the white crosshatching. I only saw it for a split-second. A blade made of a material so foreign and unknowable my mind couldn't make sense of it.

There was a pop as my eardrums ruptured.

And everything went white.

CHAPTER THIRTY-NINE

My first thought upon regaining consciousness was that it shouldn't have happened. **\<Vindictive\>** was a simple skill. Clear cut. You could still sleep, be willfully or forcefully sedated, but no amount of pain, shock, or damage could put your lights out until your body or mind gave out and you died. Divine energy had struck me at the end of the last Transposition, and despite being the most agonizing experience of my life, **\<Vindictive\>** kept me lucid through it.

I wasn't even the target.

It felt wrong. I collected myself and struggled to a sitting position slowly, taking stock. We were still in the boss room, but the mantis was nowhere to be found. There was a massive crater in the back that had destroyed the sliding stone door entirely, as well as expanding the back half of the room in an amalgam of charred rubble and dust. And in the center of the room, where the boss stood previously, was a small stone structure that put a chill through me. I'd only seen one other. But it had given me the mask.

I looked down to find Julian kneeling near me. A light glow

encompassed him as he seemed to meditate, his expression slack and relaxed. Still pale. But somehow not dying.

"I'm alright," he said without opening his eyes. "Just finishing up here."

The perforations were closing slowly. There were still trace amounts of blood seeping from the wound, but far less than there should be. He was healing, or something analogous.

"Sure." I licked my lips, mouth dry and stood shakily to my feet, still gripping **<Blade of Woe>** tightly in my hand. "Take your time."

I genuinely hoped he would. Because this might be the only shot I had at containment. There was no blood, no insect legs strewn around, no goddamn trace that the boss had ever been there. It'd been vaporized. The only remaining evidence that *something* had happened was the crater in the ground and the back wall. Even the wound on my leg was closed. A display of absolute power unlike any I'd witnessed, and that was a high-fucking-bar.

And the person who held that power was infected.

That was too big of a threat to ignore, even for a second.

I gripped **<Blade of Woe>** tightly, taking audible steps to the side before circling around silently, positioning myself behind him, blade at the ready.

His vitals lit up.

"Matt?" he said.

I didn't answer, unsure of what to do. My proximity was too close to be explained away as anything other than threatening, so I held my tongue.

Julian spoke again, his expression conflicted. "There's something I want to ask. I have no right to put this on you, but there's no one else."

"Go ahead," I murmured.

He started at the sound of my voice but didn't move. "Tell Charlotte I love her. And tell her... that she was right."

I scanned his vitals again, not entirely believing what I was seeing. Pissed off, frustrated, and confused, I stalked away. "Tell her yourself, asshole. The hell's the matter with you."

With that, I started sorting through my notifications as Julian stared after me like he'd misread the room and had very little idea why.

"It got me," he said.

"It did," I agreed.

"I should definitely be infected."

"You should."

"But I'm not?" He cocked his head like Talia did when her ears caught a high frequency.

I sighed. "I have an item with an effect that highlights anatomy. Natural armor, vitals, and so on. Used it to scope out the mantis during my not-betrayal and got a solid read on what an infested creature looks like. It's not subtle. The network of—whatever—is impossible to miss. You're clean. No idea how, guessing it has something to do with the ability you cryptically hinted lets you shrug things off," I said, then looked at him pointedly. "Just consult with a healer at camp? Guessing they have better diagnostic resources than a fucking magic knife."

Annoyingly, Julian seemed chagrined. "I will. You're very cross when you're angry."

"No. I'm cross when I'm confused and have no way to process or even remotely understand what I just saw." I glared at him. "When I'm angry, it's something else."

He blinked. "I took care of the boss."

"No. You *one shot* the boss," I corrected.

If you could do that, why the hell did you wait so long and put us both at risk?

"And that makes you angry?"

"*Not* angry—you know what? Let's just skip to the contemplative, *quiet* part that comes after a battle, shall we?"

I was being shitty and I knew it. But I needed to get my head straight. Part of me—the thrumming drumbeat that always lurked beneath the surface—told me this might still be the best opportunity I had to deal with someone like Julian. Especially considering the reality that he and Nick might come into conflict over control of the Court. And if Julian ever lost his mind, hardly an impossibility if he was tearing his hair out trying to parlay with every half-sapient creature he met, the rest of us were in serious trouble.

God knows he's willing to fall on a sword at the slightest justification. Tell him you were wrong. The infection is there. It's small, so small you missed it at first. He'll accept that. Christ, he'll probably thank you for it.

I frowned, double-checking my title screen to make sure I hadn't somehow selected **<Cruel Lens>** by mistake. After a few seconds, I confirmed that I hadn't. **<Jaded Eye>** was still in place.

The annoyingly gentle sound of Julian's laughter floated through the room.

"You're definitely angry."

"Shut up."

There was a long silence before he spoke again. "There are a lot of conditions, before that..." he cringed, "*avenue* is available to me. A whole laundry list I have to work through."

I peered at him over the notification screen. "Glad to hear the tactical nuke has launch codes."

"It's not like that."

"The atoms of the boss you obliterated suggest otherwise."

I forced myself to bring it down a few notches. I didn't have any legitimate ground to stand on for keeping shit close to the vest. His power terrified me, but my power—my actual power

—would undoubtedly terrify him as well. Sniping because I didn't like the way he played this would do nothing at best, erode the goodwill I'd accumulated at worst.

I forced a smile that felt false. "We prevented a disaster. More accurately, you did. I'm a little freaked out, but I'll be fine."

Julian frowned. My answer hadn't satisfied him, likely because I was too rattled to lie well and he was too perceptive to buy it. He leaned back on his hands and gave the new altar in the center of the room a long look. "What do we do about that?"

"Fuck all."

"It's a Shrine of Elevation. Priceless. They—"

"—ascend a common-class item to something higher. I'm aware," I hedged. "And we found it in a boss room of a tower floor also containing an eldritch monster with delusions of grandeur. Guessing the deity that put it there isn't the goddess of cookies and good cheer."

Just because I had various items with eldritch resistance and matching boon didn't mean I was safe if something got through, and an eldritch deity—one with a justifiable bone to pick with me—would absolutely be capable of that.

But Julian could.

He couldn't seem to tear his eyes away from the shrine. "Assuming the tower sequesters this floor, we probably won't be the last people to come across it. Everyone knows how valuable they are. Wouldn't it be safer to use it up?"

I swiped the notification screen with a groan and thought about it. Put my biases aside. He was right that someone else would eventually use it. Whether it was the tower's staff, whatever cleanup crew they sent up to salvage this floor, or some asshole who broke in out of curiosity. Didn't like it, but Julian was, perhaps, the only person capable of depleting it safely without becoming a walking viral load.

"Look. I'm not conveniently immune," I grumbled. "So I'm not touching it."

Instead of calling me out or balking at the idea, he limped toward the shrine and circled it, studying it from all angles. "It doesn't look evil."

"That changes things then."

"Are you always this sarcastic?" He squinted, immediately moving on without waiting for an answer. "What should we, uh, elevate?"

"You're taking the risk. Your decision."

"I'm kind of geared. Nothing common on me."

I scanned my inventory, not entirely displeased with that turn of events. "Pretty loaded myself. Some consumables that are common, but that would be a waste. Usually I pick up common drops just to sell them, but I offloaded everything earlier this week and this floor was a wasteland—"

Something at the bottom of my inventory stood out, and I froze. Because I did, in fact, have a single item considered common. I'd played with adding additional weapons to my kit as a method of delivering various magical effects and debuffs. Problem was, as I lacked magic myself, someone else had to apply the effects ahead of time. And not a single person I consulted with could figure a way to make the magic last long enough for that to be practical. Surface area and weapon-type didn't seem to matter. I'd already sold a variety of knives, swords, bows, and crossbows back.

But there was a single knife left. A basic, common knife that I'd somehow missed, despite being sure I'd cleared everything out.

There it was again. That feeling that I was playing into someone else's plan.

"I have one."

CHAPTER FORTY

I retreated the equivalent of several rooms down the exit hatch. My previous experience with a Shrine of Elevation taught me to be wary of them—the last and only time I'd used one, I'd met the Allfather in person. That he happened to be my patron was a lucky break, tipped in my favor by the adaptive dungeon.

Feelings of disquiet washed over me as I imagined what may or may not be happening at base camp.

How long has it been?

An hour total. Fifteen minutes of that since I left Julian alone with the shrine.

"Jules? You dead?"

Nearly a full minute until he answered. "Uh. No."

"You done?"

"Yep." He sounded strange. Troubled. "But I think the eldritch gods might not like me too much."

I returned to the boss room, footsteps echoing on stone, half-expecting to see some corrupt abomination waiting, parroting Julian's voice.

Beyond the pale face, he looked more or less the same. He was holding a dark red karambit in both hands away from him and observing it with a mix of wonder and dread. It had no discernible aura. When he shifted it back and forth, however, the knife blurred, the way it would look if it was moving at high speeds, even though the movement itself was slight.

"Interesting," I hedged. "It completely changed form."

"Watch." He shifted it back and forth. "Faster it moves, the harder it is to see. Almost like camo, or an active cloak or something. Not that useful for my purposes, but useful."

"Huh."

I waited, and when he didn't seem keen on offering a further explanation, prompted him. "You said something about the eldritch gods?"

"Yeah." Julian stirred, his brows furrowed. "They really don't like what I did to their vessel. I think."

"You think?"

"On some level I was hoping to pick up negotiations where we left off, but it wasn't much of a conversation. They weren't speaking their own language half the time, and a lot of what I did understand was threats, insults, and more talk of conquering and consumption."

"Well, you trash-canned yet another incursion attempt, so kind of makes sense they'd be sore about it."

"I think you might have been right, about leaving it alone."

I glanced at the knife warily. "Is it dangerous?"

"Not the sort of threat you're thinking. No properties that imply it might start sprouting tentacles." His eyes widened. "Actually, this might be perfect. You're nice enough to downplay it, but the way I killed the boss shook you up." Before I could deny it, he shook his head. "I get it, I've seen that reaction before. *I* know the requirements and myself well enough to believe I don't pose a danger to everyone around me, but with the limitations of what I can explain, you'd be forced to take my word on it."

"Not sure I'm following."

"You're a knife expert, right?"

"I'm okay."

"Uh huh." Julian smiled knowingly. "Someone who's casually slicing tentacles moving at mach speed out of the air isn't just okay." He held the blade by the safe side and extended the handle toward me. I took it, curiosity winning over caution.

<**Item:** Luciana>

Description: A weapon stolen from the expansive armory of a fertility deity and reforged in the fires of malice. It loathes armor nearly as much as its original creator, and while capable of changing form, will never lose its edge. According to legend, once coated in blood, it will sing a song of insurrection, deafening and disorienting any who oppose its wielder.

Item Class: Artifact

Item Value: S???

Christ.

"A lot going on there," I observed.

"I'll say."

"Even if they were pissed, at least they didn't give you trash. Although the description making it sound semi-intelligent is a little concerning. If you let it go, you'll need to test it and make sure there's no discoverable 'quirks...' but assuming there's not? You could sell this for a *lot* of Selve."

I might even buy it.

Julian was already shaking his head when I looked up. "Not sure that's a great idea, unfortunately. Uh. Among the more general insults and inter-dimensional trash talk... I received a very specific warning from the tentacle monsters upstairs."

"Which was?"

"This knife will eventually kill me."

"The User, or you specifically?"

"Me." He paused. "Unless it meant 'feckless orphan' in a general sense, which is an odd demographic to intentionally target."

I blinked several times. "Yeah. Maybe don't sell it."

He sighed. "Keeping it on my person seems like a bad idea. And as much as I like most of the other members of the Court, none of them are really rogue types."

And you don't fully trust them. You can't. Not without knowing how things are going to shake out. You're a central foundation of a power structure that has no clue how its hierarchy or succession works.

"Which is why I want you to take it," he finished.

I did a double-take. "Excuse me?"

Julian shrugged. "You're good with a knife. I have a good feeling about you in general—which sounds stupid, but trust me when I say good feelings about people are getting harder and harder to come by. You're smart, cautious, and capable of making hard decisions. It holds intrinsic value to you, which means you're less likely to sell it. And given the level of power I just demonstrated which also can't be explained, I figure you'll be a lot more comfortable with a kill switch."

You barely know me.

Regardless, his estimation was half-right. But taking it was a bad idea if it was going to make him more paranoid around me.

"And if I said fuck the Court, might as well start with Julian?" I tested.

The brittle smile returned. "It would have been easier to just tell me I was infected."

There it was. I took the blade. There was just one last thing I needed to quash a distant possibility. Bracing myself, I pulled up my title screen and swapped into **<Cruel Lens>.** As we were out of direct danger, it did what it always did.

Oh no. Wow. Get a load of this guy. Talk about a fish out of water. He doesn't belong in this era. Doesn't belong in any era, really. He's trembling, uncertain, afraid. But not of death. He's upset because he couldn't find common ground with the eldritch hive mind freak dead set on the Borg imperative. How offensively stupid can one person be—

I forced myself to filter it out and refocused on the present. "They straight-up told you this knife would eventually kill you?"

"They did," Julian confirmed.

True. No hesitation or micro-expressions. The strange part is that he believed them. Doesn't track. Should have seemed like an idle threat, or poor sportsmanship on the part of the deity intended to deny an invaluable reward, but he bought it entirely. The only lie he's telling is one of omission. There was more to their conversation, either personal or class related. Something he intends to take to his grave.

"And you really trust me to hold onto it?"

"I do." He grinned. "Sure, maybe we haven't known each other for very long, and maybe you were just playing for the cheap seats to get a look at the escape route, but what you said really struck a chord."

He doesn't. But he hopes he can. He knows trust goes both ways and he's willing to earn it. It's only partially political. He likes the way you challenge decisions and take him to task for them. For some unknowable reason, he also seems to like your cantankerous attitude. Have to wonder if he'll ever realize how big of a mistake he's making giving it to—

Thank you, **<Cruel Lens>.** As much as I disliked the way it said things, it was telling me everything I needed to know. Julian was a bit of a fool, but even ignoring the one-shot, he brought something to the table we desperately needed. A non-merchant ability tailored around negotiation would have been invaluable during the first Transposition, and likely would be just as useful in the second if it came to that.

"Okay." I inventoried the knife for later study and looked up to find Julian swaying on his feet. "Uh..."

"Feeling a little... woozy... all of a sudden." He squinted at me, eyes losing focus. Then fainted. Somehow I caught his head before it hit the ground.

"Oh, for fuck's sake."

———

"Why do I have to carry him?" Talia grumbled, padding down the long exit hall.

"Can't carry him while he's wearing plate. Azure is generally around as strong as me physically, so he can't carry him. Audrey could, but I don't think either party would enjoy that process. This was clearly a job for a magnificent, mighty she-wolf."

She preened at the flattery until she caught me looking. "The chamber was sealed and secure. Could have just left him."

"Almost did." I inclined my head, glancing over the Prince's slack form draped over my summon. "But I want a healer to take a look at him sooner rather than later."

Occam's razor said it was a combination of blood loss and exhaustion. As a general rule, healing potions and spells could repair most physical damage, given enough time. They amplified regeneration of blood but didn't replace it immediately, meaning the body still had to do its part. The proximity of the fainting spell to his encounter with the shrine god, however, set my teeth on edge. <Blade of Woe> was still showing normal, human vitals, but it was possible something more subtle had been done to him, and I wasn't willing to roll the dice on that.

Talia's ears perked up and she stopped, straining to listen. Seconds later, an angry voice carried down the hallway. "Trouble at camp."

Now that I was listening, I heard more voices, many more, all forming a low indecipherable din of anger and fear. I started running.

And as the hidden exit unsealed, I found myself in the center of an absolute shit-show.

CHAPTER FORTY-ONE

"Let us out, you fucks!"

"The longer we're here, the more likely this thing is to spread!"

"My kid is by herself alone. Bastards can't just lock us up, there's people outside relying on us!"

Panic was spreading quickly. In a way, it was oddly nostalgic of the early days when we first discovered the dome. I spotted Nick by the elevators doing his best to hold back a small crowd of increasingly irate adventurers clustering around him. Not good.

Factoring time, they're too panicked. Did someone turn? Or—

A howl came from a closed medical tent—a man—followed by a more feminine scream from another tent that was almost blood curdling.

Now it made sense.

Most of the Court was clustered outside their accoutrement, holding defensively and doing nothing to quell the panic coming from members of the Order.

God dammit. Okay. Think. Triage. Whoever's being operated on in the tent is lowest priority. Good chance they die or they're too far gone to save. If I waste time on them first, Nick may lose control of the situation, and then we're completely fucked. Priorities are Julian's glamour, elevator, Court, tents.

I fired off **<Suggestion>** tagged with calming thoughts and images toward some of the loudest voices in the elevator crowd and waded in, simultaneously looking for Charlotte. I found her near the back, her eyes wide.

"Princess!" I waved her over. She started toward me, then froze in her tracks when she saw Julian. "He's fine. Just needs to be checked out, low prio. Better to dispel him now if you can."

"What happened?" She rushed over, pushing hair out of her face as she began to cast something.

"Took a beating and did his thing," I said, staying vague in case she was out of the loop. With the way she jerked up and looked at me, she knew. "Passed out after he healed himself."

"You *idiot.*" Charlotte hissed at Julian, then finished her casting. As soon as she was done, she reached toward me.

Wait.

"Later," I told her, making the decision immediately. "I need to get a lid on this."

"They won't recognize you—"

"I'll circle back." I paused, realizing the position I was in. With the glamour in place most people wouldn't recognize me, but Charlotte could. While the Ordinator's abilities were mostly imperceptible, if I didn't give her anything other to do than watch me from afar, she'd inevitably pick up that I was doing something to work the crowd. I looked toward the tents. Might be able to kill two birds with one stone. "Actually, do you have a muffle? Anything that could dampen sound in an area?"

"To quiet the screams," she realized, looking back and forth from the tents to me.

"The louder they are, the more people are going to feel trapped, and the more they'll panic."

"Uh, shit." She stared at an invisible screen, scrolling through. "I have an envelope hex, but that blacks out an entire area."

"Counterproductive, probably."

"Nothing." Charlotte grimaced in annoyance. "Have a few points to spend, let me check the list."

Another scream echoed out of the tent. I cringed. "Why the fuck aren't they being sedated?"

"They can't," a nearby man said. He was tanned and enormous but unarmored, smoking a tiny stub of a cigarette that seemed even tinier in his hands. From the shell-shocked look in his eyes, I immediately realized he'd been inside the tents. "Nothing they give the sick ones puts them under."

"Who are you and why are you here?" I asked him, trying to sound terse rather than rude.

"Phineas Briggs. Alchemist, crafter, and supplier extraordinaire," He said, his voice a calming baritone.

Less trustworthy than he looks. But with the gentle giant schtick, he looks very trustworthy.

"Yourself?" Phineas asked.

"Matt."

"Pleasure to make your acquaintance." He squinted in recognition. "Matt as in—"

"Found it!" Charlotte interrupted excitedly. "Creates an invisible barrier outlining an area of the caster's choosing. Filters out any vocalizations not amplified by magic."

"Perfect, you're a lifesaver." Charlotte made a selection and hurried toward the tent as I turned my attention back to Phineas. "Yes, that Matt. Got armor on you?"

Phineas hesitated. "I'm not a combatant."

"Don't need you to fight. Just need you to stand somewhere and be friendly-yet-impassable."

He barked out a laugh. "Been doing that my whole life. I got armor, yeah."

"Wanna help me out here?"

"Not to be a total piece of shit given the circumstances," Phineas said slowly, dropping the cigarette butt and stamping it out. "But what's in it for me?"

Merchants.

"Allegiance?"

"Here assisting the good ol' AG. Few friends inside that vouched, and since folks can't use the system store inside the tower, figured I'd provide my services as a stopgap."

"Then the offer is a preferential contract with the Merchants' Guild and a metric fuck-ton of goodwill," I tried.

"Done. Word is Miss Kinsley's been driving a hard bargain lately, I'd be a fool to pass that up." Phineas grinned, and his body blurred as he equipped a set of chrome armor that gave the impression it was more flashy than practical.

"Circle around," I pointed to the elevator. "Get next to the big guy with the aww-shucks face, join him from the side so it's clear you're with him, but don't push in on them. Just let him know Matt sent you."

"Present myself as a force multiplier but don't fence anyone in. Got it." Phineas waved at me and lumbered toward the elevator. I waited, creating distance and checking my surroundings and Charlotte before I pulled the **<Allfather's Mask>** out of my inventory and put it on. Immediately, it amplified my title's voice so loudly it competed with my thoughts. I waded through the crowd of twenty-something adventurers all but invisible, trying to filter out any title commentary and listen for the loudest voices.

"There's something they aren't telling us," someone

announced loudly. A middle-aged man balling meaty fists. "We're all fucked if it's airborne. That's why they're not—"

"Shut the fuck up." I hammered him with **<Suggestion>**, tagging it with a mental image of the crowd he was in the middle of trampling him in a blind panic. Sensing acceptance and little resistance, I moved on.

"My daughter is *alone*." A woman this time, mage's garbs. Not great. Mage meant high intelligence, and that could be a problem if it was higher than mine. Struggling with the mess of feedback from my abilities and title in the emotional crowd, I grabbed her shoulder to help isolate her mind from the noise.

"And you're displacing guilt because YOU left her alone. Could have left her with a friend and didn't. That was your choice, no one else's. Stop making your fuckup everyone else's problem. If you want to ensure she still has one parent around to protect her during the second Transposition, cooperate."

She jerked away from me subconsciously, her eyes wide. Then her expression hardened.

Fucking INT.

No choice. Just had to hope her stats weren't too high for the alternative.

<Subjugate>.

The woman stopped, frozen in time, slowly turning toward me as if seeing me for the first time, waiting attentively. Waiting for orders.

I gave them silently through suggestion. "You are a bastion of calm. You've always been that way, keeping your head when everyone else is losing theirs. It's a good thing you're here and willing to help keep the crowd in check, because leadership clearly can't handle it all themselves. That's why I picked you. Because you're special. I need you more than anyone else has ever needed you." The woman nodded and even smiled a bit, pleased with herself. Belatedly, I added the postscript I'd used ever since I discovered it worked when

<Subjugation> was used in a simple context. *"I may have more orders for you later."*

"Anything you want," she said aloud and winked, leaving me with a vaguely nauseous feeling.

The last, loudest voice in the crowd was both the most difficult with the worst justification. Another mage, yelling about untended experiments. His int was high enough that neither **<Suggestion>** nor **<Subjugation>** made a dent. Even worse, he seemed to notice the intrusion, looking around in alarm.

Fuck it.

I pulled the **<Mage-Bane Garrote>** out of my inventory, slipping it around his neck as discreetly as I could and holding it with one hand, keeping it tight enough for a consistent drain but not so tight he'd drop on the spot, yanking his head back so I could whisper in his ear. For once, I let **<Cruel Lens>** speak directly. "One word, one single cry of alarm or whimper of distress, and every single person in this dome will find out about the weird sex golems you have cooking in the basement."

The man went limp, completely compliant.

"Put your arms down."

He released the garrote string and stood, awkward and uncomfortable but still cooperative.

"Turn."

I guided him, still holding both sides of the garrote with one hand and walking him out of the crowd. Once we were far enough, I tightened the slack, sapping what little mana he had left until his eyes lost focus, then helped him sit down propped up against a wall. I walked away then returned, crouching in front of him and snapping my fingers, borrowing Phineas's rich baritone. "Everything alright, buddy?"

"Uh." He came to and peered around through thick glasses in confusion, hand going to his naked throat. "I'm not... really sure what happened."

"You just wandered over here out of sorts, all lost. Light-headed or somethin'?"

"Someone—I think someone just threatened me." He scanned the room suspiciously. "Did you see anything?"

"Nope." I patted his shoulder. "From a distance it just looked like you misplaced a few marbles and the mental gps lost service, but it's a high-stress situation. Bound to happen to anyone, eventually. Just glad you didn't fall or hurt yourself. Grace of god and all. Maybe don't push it and catch a breather for a while."

It took a second, but his suspicion ebbed into exhaustion. He leaned his head back against the wall. "Got any water?"

I smiled and put my thermos in his lap. "Course. Don't worry about returning it, I got others. And feel better, pal, alright?"

"Thanks," he said, clearly unhappy but too disoriented to push things further.

"Hey," I grinned back at him and winked as I walked away. "My pleasure."

With the key instigators disarmed, the crowd calmed, losing steam. I ducked into an empty tent to remove the mask and exited, approaching where Nick stood at the front. I sighed and said the passphrase.

"Thundercats."

"Woah-ah-oh." Nick returned, jerking around to look.

"Here." I stood beside him, hands in my pockets.

"Matt? You still glamoured?" he asked, squinting at my face.

"Not for long, but yeah. What the fuck happened?" I asked, my voice low.

Nick looked over to several large members of the Adventurers' Guild standing at the side. "Take over for me? I'll be back, just gotta bring someone up to speed." As we walked away, his face turned grim. "We may have screwed up a little."

"How many infected?"

"Only two, way better than it could be." Nick bit his lip. "Healers figured out this was out of their wheelhouse real quick, sent for an expert. Contacted Tyler as well. He's in a meeting with the tower folks."

"Expert being—"

"Someone with the hazmat crew working Region 6. Prim, Pam?"

I waved him off. "Good. I'll get the name later. What was the mistake?" A second later, I realized it before he told me. "You had to send someone down the elevator to get word out."

Nick winced and gazed toward the medical tents. "Yeah. Then the screaming started, which... really didn't help. Thankfully, the crowd seems to be cooling a bit."

"Lucky."

"You alright?" Nick asked. "Boss a pushover?"

"Yes... no. Need to get this glamour off and get in the med tent, more details later. Anything else pressing?"

"With all this chaos I have the irresistible urge to binge eat and not nearly enough food in my inventory to make that happen."

I stared at him dolefully, then slowly handed him the sandwich I'd packed.

"That's a start. I should probably get back to the line." Nick grinned.

"Stay safe." I paused, twisting around. "Of the two infected, who's worse off?"

"That would be tent numero uno." Nick grimaced. "The dude you dressed down. Not sure who the woman is, but she got hit way later." He hesitated. "Heads up though, Ansari's the one in there. It's spreading too fast for them to wait."

"Great."

I left Nick to hold the line and returned to Charlotte. She

started at my appearance, and I got the sense she'd been looking for me for a while.

"Ready?" she asked.

"Hit me."

The dispel acted quickly, leaving an unpleasant buzz in my fingertips as I shed my last layer of anonymity.

"Wasn't sure where you went," Charlotte fished, but her curiosity seemed innocent enough.

I rubbed the bridge of my nose. "Everywhere." Absentmindedly, I glanced at the now-silent tents. "Good fucking job Charlotte. Between the glamour and the mute, you really came in clutch today."

"Oh." She seemed surprised and thrown off. "It was nothing."

"It wasn't." I paused, glancing up at the crowd. It'd stilled and a few people had walked away, but there were still too many. "And I hate to keep asking for help, but any chance you'd be down to loop some of the Court into admin duty?"

"Sure. Most of them just aren't sure what to do, but they'll help."

I breathed out, leaning back and forth on my heels. "We need to pull people away from the elevator. I'm thinking... two tables set up in the center. First one designated for anyone who has pressing business outside that can't wait. Emergencies, dependents, so on. Write them down, note their full names and the full names of anyone pertinent, and once we have someone cleared, we'll send them down to send messages and coordinate with our people outside."

Charlotte pulled an old android phone out of her robes and jotted down notes. "And the second table?"

"Sign-up for takeout, when it arrives. Barbecue, pizza, something universal. Complimentary." I looked at her meaningfully. "For anyone who's already seen a healer, of course."

"Got it." She paused. "Okay. Just, I have to ask. What did you do before this?"

"Eleventh grade."

With that, I jogged toward the first medical tent and braced myself. Then unzipped the flap and stepped inside.

CHAPTER FORTY-TWO

A man in a blood-spattered doctor's jacket nearly bowled me over, white-knuckled hand clasped over his mouth, eyes glazed with shock as a woman's accented voice yelled all manner of colorful expletives after him.

"Come back around once the hard part is over to get scanned, you simpering fuck," Ansari yelled. Judging from her blood-soaked appearance, she'd seen better days. Her forearms bulged as she leveraged considerable strength to hold down the writhing figure on the operating table. The man was conscious but not lucid, actively fighting her as he struggled against the straps that fastened him to the gurney.

"Tighten the bindings!" she grunted at me.

I moved on instinct, seeing the issue and grabbing his leg before he slipped a foot free, fumbling with the corresponding strap beneath until I figured out what to pull to tighten it. The man on the table was in terrible shape. The surgical incision on his ribcage was a clean cut, but all his struggling had torn it open wider than intended. Despite that, he was giving as good as he got, slamming his weight from side to side—the table started to tip, and I slammed my weight down on the rising side, barely stopping it from flipping over.

"Why isn't—" he slipped out of my grip and I grunted, readjusting my hold and applying more pressure. "Why isn't he under?"

"This infection is unlike anything I've ever seen." Ansari grimaced, "*Nothing* works. My 'colleague' miscalculated and gave him enough morphine to kill a horse, and he's still conscious."

Shit.

My mind raced. "Then how do we deal with it?"

"You need to go out there and make sure no one leaves. With the noise he's making, it won't be long before people start losing their minds." Her brow furrowed.

"Already handled," I said. The healer stared at me blankly, clearly not putting much stock in my words. I was reminded again how she'd had the misfortune of healing me after the first Transposition event. Despite having no memory of it, I'd been sedated while **<Cruel Lens>** was active, and whatever I'd said in my subconscious state hadn't made a positive impression. "The crowd is contained, we're organizing short-term necessities, and there's a muffle hex on the medical tent."

Ansari blinked. "That's... a relief."

I nodded and tapped the table. "What next?"

The doctor glanced down at the man and shook her head. "Nothing good. The growths are tumorous. In ordinary circumstances it would be simple enough to operate and remove them, debriding and disinfecting along the way. The inefficacy of sedation poses a multitude of problems. Despite that, I wanted to try—until that spineless *chutiya* lost his nerve." She stared down at the man, a vein standing out on her forehead. "It was always going to be a long shot, regardless. The only humane course of action is to ease his suffering."

Seeing how the usual hospice option—stacking him with meds until he passed from natural causes—wasn't possible in this case, it wasn't hard to read between the lines.

Cracked fingernails clawed at my forearm. The adventurer stared down at me, mouth breaking a rictus of agony as he struggled to form words. "Please. *Please.* It hurts. Keep her away from me. It hurts."

Ansari already hates you. She'll be watching you closely. Anything you can do to help could raise suspicion. He didn't listen earlier, now this is the price he pays.

I shook my head, trying to ignore **<Cruel Lens>** even as part of me wondered if it was right.

"Look, Doc, I get we're not exactly friendly. Regardless of our history, I genuinely want to help here."

"Are you a medical professional, Mr. Matthias?" she mocked.

Technically no, which she probably assumed. I had an extensive repository of knowledge on the subject of anatomy and biology, but my advanced medical knowledge was entirely lacking in real-life experience. "I know enough to assist."

"How?" Ansari challenged, clearly not ready to take me at my word. "You're too young to have gone to nursing or medical school. Unless you are some sort of prodigy, which, frankly, I doubt."

The bar was already on the ground. A little honesty wouldn't make her like me more, but it might help my case here. "Not a prodigy. I—uh—I just—"

"Spit it out," Ansari snapped.

"I scored well enough on the MCAT for admission to med school."

Again, the doctor seemed surprised. Until her eyes narrowed. "And why would someone who should be more concerned with college achieve such a goal?"

"Because I needed rent and my clients were willing to pay for it."

"Cheating," she accused.

"They cheated." I scoffed. "I did it the hard way."

An awkward silence followed. This admission was a gamble. No medical professional who'd put in the all-nighters, godless amounts of study, and put up with years of skull-fucking-stress would look kindly on their fellow professional who took shortcuts, and by proxy the people who made those shortcuts possible. But it was my only move. All I could do now was hope Ansari's desperation and rationality overshadowed her pride.

"To be clear..." I added, as she was taking too long to answer. "I could never do this without you. No question. I'm not telling you this to flex, or belittle your position. Hell, I'm not even sure if what I know would be of help."

"Then why offer?" Ansari snapped.

"So you can make the call." I sighed, leaving it entirely in her hands. If she had a god complex—and to varying extents, most doctors did—she'd appreciate the deference. "I can stabilize and assist however you need, and I have a method of detecting the corruption. I'll do whatever you tell me to."

Ansari squinted, something dangerous glimmering in her eyes. "And if I tell you to get the hell out of my operating area?"

"I'll give you the detection item and fuck off." I shrugged.

For a moment, she was about to. Then the reality sunk in. Operating solo was difficult enough when the patient was unconscious. Without an extra set of hands, she simply couldn't hold him and operate at the same time. Her tone changed, rapid-fire and stoic. "Did you study the questions or the material?"

"Both."

"Switch places with me and hold him as still as possible,"

Ansari commanded. Now that she'd decided, her hostility disappeared almost instantly. I did as she asked, bracing the man's shoulders. As soon as her latex-clad fingers touched his chest he thrashed, moaning in panic.

Ansari swore. "I *cannot* help you if you keep fighting me."

From the shellshocked lack of focus and full-blown panic, he wasn't processing anything, entirely fixated on the possibility he'd soon feel pain again. Not great. But the primal state made him far more susceptible to **<Suggestion>**.

I leaned down and whispered in his ear. "Go somewhere else."

Slowly, I cycled through the usual images that often worked when I needed to impart tranquility. A library, the faceless warmth of a mother's embrace. The usual go-to's didn't work. I kept iterating, trying one after another until something stuck.

The forest at night. Light of a stone-circled campfire glowing orange, crackling, casting long shadows into trees that shelter owls and other creatures of the night. Solitude. A little cold, but with your warm jacket and its fur hood, you barely feel it. There's no ambient noise, no people, only you. No demands, no quests, no expectations or Transpositions. The purest peace. Nature is your church, and it accepts you into its silent arms, asking nothing, imparting everything.

All at once, the struggling stopped. The man's face went slack, his expression blank as he slowly surrendered reality for fantasy.

"What did you do?" Ansari asked. She was looking between me and the man on the table, scalpel held loosely in her hand.

"Talked to him," I said, forcing a smile. "I've had some practice managing panic."

She stared at me for a moment, then moved on. "Well, keep doing that. This is the most relaxed he's been since the beginning."

"Got it."

Slowly and laboriously, Dr. Ansari cut. Over time, I got the sense that she was acting as a surgeon by necessity rather than choice. After one last dubious look over the mask, she seemed to resign herself to the situation.

"Think you can handle changing the IV?"

CHAPTER FORTY-THREE

It was not a fast process. For every section of corrupted flesh that was excised and removed, another growth began. Most of my time was split, half of it spent beneath the operating table, using **<Blade of Woe's>** ability to track our progress and call out new growth before it could metastasize and spread closer to vitals that would render removal impossible, the other half spent keeping the patient entrenched in his fantasy.

Minute by minute, the auric red mass illuminated by **<Blade of Woe>** grew smaller.

The smallest splotch of red drew my attention, barely larger than a comma. "Fresh growth in the mediastinum, between the left lung and heart."

Doctor Ansari clicked her tongue, the noise muted from behind her mask. I watched the new splotch, waiting for it to disappear. It didn't.

I slid out from beneath the table. "Problem?"

"Do you have steady hands, Mr. Matthias?"

"Steady enough. Why?" I slid out from beneath the table, careful not to jostle anything with my movements as I emerged. The first thing that stood out was how exhausted Ansari looked. Beneath her beleaguered eyes, she gripped the scalpel tightly, the blooded razor trembling in the light. "Shit."

"There's a reason I went into general practice." Ansari grimaced. "The damn tremors."

God dammit. I quickly went to her bag, sifting through a countless number of bottles and tinctures, looking for the only thing I knew of that would help, sorting through an ocean of labels until I found what I was looking for "Propranolol, right?"

"Two tablets," Ansari confirmed.

I forcefully twisted the childproof lid and shook two round pills into my hand, then tossed them into Ansari's waiting open mouth. She grimaced while she chewed, then forcefully swallowed. Eyes closed, seemingly at war with herself, she paused before she spoke. "Did you learn from your studies how long it takes to work?"

"No," I said quietly. "Guessing it's not instant."

Almost nothing was.

"Correct." Ansari crunched down on the tablets. "I have an overactive metabolism, and chewing them helps. It will come on faster for me than the average person, but fast, in this case, is not nearly quick enough. Hold a hand out, palm down, if you would."

I extended my right arm as instructed, my hand level and steady. She scrutinized it and sighed. "This is not fair to ask. Realistically..." she dropped her voice, glancing at the man on the table, "It may end badly. But there are no alternatives. If we wait, he will die. If I leave this to you, it at least alters that certainty to a possibility."

My eyes were drawn to the man's open chest cavity. The once generic blotch was a dark mass, around half the size of a grape. There was blood, so much blood it set my teeth on edge, sung to the dark vestiges in the depths of my mind. "Not sure that's a great idea, Doc."

From the look on her face, she wasn't either. "As I said. It is not fair to ask."

I strapped on a cloth mask and pulled a fresh pair of nitrile gloves from a box and put them on, using the makeshift wash basin and pumped an ample helping of sanitizing foam onto my gloved hands, washing as thoroughly as I could.

The scalpel felt solid in my hand. Natural. On some level it made sense. A knife was a knife, regardless of its purpose. "What now?" I asked.

Methodically, Doctor Ansari's low voice walked me through the steps of several careful, complicated cuts. Initially, I was afraid. Scared shitless that I'd slip, or worse, that I'd *want* to slip. But as I followed her directions exactly, that fear slipped away. It felt like picking up an old habit. The motions, the movements, and their purpose made sense to me in a way few things ever had. By the time the problem splotch was nearly gone I was breathing hard, more from the mental drain than anything else. I placed the last chunk of infected tissue in the biohazard bin, on top of what had already been harvested.

Where now?

Wordlessly, Ansari pulled my arm away and took the scalpel.

I blinked. "Is something wrong?"

Ansari shook her head. "The opposite. The imminent threat is removed, and my hands have steadied."

Oh. Right.

————

When it was over, I nearly sprinted out of the tent. It was small to begin with, and that feeling only intensified into full-blown claustrophobia with the thick scent of blood and the disquieting looks the doctor kept sending my way. A heavy weariness clung to me, which was, perhaps, why I didn't realize the obvious.

Every person in the staging area immediately looked over as soon as the tent flaps opened. It tracked. We'd been in there for hours with no breaks, and while the joint group was no longer on the verge of a riot, they were all anxiously waiting for news.

Somehow, I managed my usual indifference, stuck my hands in my pockets, and made the announcement. "It'll be a long recovery. Our mutual friend isn't out of the woods yet, but thanks to Dr. Ansari, the surgery was a success."

There was a few cheers and some scattered applause, but more than anything, an almost tangible sense of relief. Without the slightest clue of what else to say, I awkwardly walked away, beelining to the nearby table and loading several slices of pizza onto a paper plate. As Charlotte had predicted, the Court members had spread out some in my absence and appeared to be helping to keep things in order, which was good. Unfortunately, they glanced my way far more often than I'd like.

Good job, idiot. You drew too much attention. Again.

As if responding to my thoughts, a gravelly voice spoke. "Julian seems to be under the impression you're some kind of badass." The Duskblade Knight said, holding up a wall a few yards away from the table.

"Julian is very generous," I said between bites. "And possibly concussed. I'd check back after he's recovered a little."

"He told us all about how you lured the little bastards out and secured the combat area."

Why is it so hard for some people to keep their mouths shut?

"Just basic strategy."

"Basic or not, it was quick thinking." Nathanial tapped his fingers, tattoos rolling with the motion. "Impressive. How'd the fight with the boss go down, anyway?"

Every single alarm bell went off in my head like a chorus. "Quickly."

"Not to sound ungrateful, but from where I'm standing, it seems like he got the piss kicked out of him while you got out more or less unscathed. That a 'strategy' too?" Nathanial asked, an audible growl in his voice.

Ah. So you're not just the surly obstructionist.

It was an elegant trap. Obvious. But elegant.

I gave Nathanial another once-over as I processed the new information. He was on edge, but not nearly as much as he was pretending to be. Nathanial didn't actually give a shit how much of a beating Julian took. The intention was to make me *think* he did, panic that my standing with the Court might be called into question and scramble to correct him, detailing exactly what happened in the boss room.

Either he was testing my ability to keep Julian's secrets, or he was fishing for information.

<Cruel Lens> was confident it was the latter. Nathanial had seen glimpses of Julian's abilities, aftermaths, results with no explanation. But like me, he had no idea how it worked.

I glared at him defensively. "It was a single-target slug fest. I peppered it with arrows from a distance while our resident Prince fought it in melee and kept its attention. Of course he'd take more hits than me."

"Anything unusual happen?" Nathanial prompted.

"Other than it being the tentacle monster version of Pandora's box instead of an ant?" I shrugged. "Not really. It attacked us. We hit it with sharp things until it died."

Nathanial snorted. "You're not much of a storyteller."

"Is that all?" I asked, "Because I really should go check in with Nick."

The older man stretched, giving me one last scowl. He didn't want to drop it—guys like him rarely did—but I'd given him no reason to be suspicious, and he was smart enough to know this wasn't the time or place to push his luck.

"Good work today," he finally said and stalked away.

You too, gramps.

/////

The rest of the already waning evening was lost in a flurry of activity. Tyler's meeting with the tower's administration was a begrudging success, and a team of Users from the tower arrived to seal off the elevator exit behind us. They seemed to take the task a little too easily in stride, which left me wondering when and why, exactly, they'd closed off a section of the tower before.

Everyone else on the floor was evaluated, and no one showed any signs of infection.

A notification popped not long after I left the tower region in the passenger seat of Nick's Charger. Every part of me wanted to talk to Nick about Julian's one-shot, but my friend didn't have much of a poker face and he spent more time with the Prince than I did, so it more made sense to keep it to myself for now. He seemed withdrawn—probably just worn out—so I pulled up my messages as we drove in silence.

There were a few updates I'd missed from Kinsley, a message from Miles, and a couple from my mother. But the one I least expected sat clearly at the top.

*<**Ansari:** Thank you for your help today, Mr. Matthias. Time is precious with the event on the horizon and you are likely faced with a great deal of responsibility, but if at all possible, I would like to sit down and speak with you beforehand. There are matters we should discuss.>*

I leaned my head back on the headrest and groaned.

"What?" Nick asked.

"I might have fucked up."

"How bad is it?"

"Two out of ten." I thought about it. The most questionable thing I'd done was the way I'd used **<Suggestion>**. From Ansari's perspective, it looked like I'd spoken to a dying man in drastic pain and somehow persuaded him to be unreasonably calm. Dodgy perhaps, but not damning.

> **<Matt:** Sure. If it's high priority we can meet first thing in the morning. Want to tell me what this is about?**>**
> **<Ansari:** Any time before the event will suffice. But not tomorrow. I am already exhausted, as I'm sure you are as well.**>**

She hadn't fully answered my question. That could have been bait, testing to see if I pushed for more info, but my title didn't trigger, meaning it probably wasn't.

> **<Matt:** Topic?**>**
> **<Ansari:** Your future.**>**

"Three out of ten," I amended unhappily. "Or she's just being vague and we're fine. Hard to tell."

"Need help?" Nick asked.

"No. Well, probably not. If Ansari comes to you and asks about a certain standardized testing business—"

"Deny it," Nick filled in automatically, then paused, puzzled.

"Actually, just corroborate," I corrected him wryly.

"Why, exactly, would the Adventurers' Guild doctor be asking about that?" He turned to look at me, aghast. "More importantly, you want me to *tell the truth?*"

"Shut up." I rolled my eyes. Then noticed for the first time where we were. "Uh, Nick. You missed a turn." Now that I was paying attention, he looked straight-up nauseous.

"You forgot." Nick grimaced. "Guess it makes sense with everything going on."

Forgot what?

The answer came to me slower than I would have liked, as did the reason Nick looked so uncomfortable. I pinched the bridge of my nose. "That's today, huh?"

"If she's there, we just give our condolences, make sure she's settled, give her some stuff and tips on where to go and what to do during the Transposition, then we leave," Nick said, reassuring himself as much as me. "Quick and easy."

"And if she's the monster Jinny said she was?"

"Jinny never called her a monster," Nick argued.

She didn't have to.

Time gets away from you, one way or another. Nick would have gone the day she died if he wasn't kidnapped, imminent Transposition be damned. But the Transposition happened, then the clash with the feds, then power struggle after power struggle. After we'd made the deal with Hastur, Nick tried to contact the mother multiple times through messages and voice calls. The lack of response meant one of two things. The woman was either dead or ignoring us.

Either way, we'd know before the night was over.

CHAPTER FORTY-FOUR

It took an argument, but Nick and I split ways not long after. I pulled off the highway and navigated my system knock-off Prius toward the curb until rubber ground concrete, then placed it into park. The slate-blue car was part of my recent initiative to further separate the identity of Matt, the low-level User, from Myrddin, the Ordinator and public enemy. In truth, I should have hammered on that venture far earlier, but there had been little downtime to speak of, as I'd been juggling crisis after crisis to the point that I'd started dropping things that weren't life-threatening but were still important.

Which was partly why I was here, in the middle of a suburban wasteland that stretched on for miles. There was evidence of quick evacuations all around me. Trampled gardens, a few homes burned to the ground, abandoned half-packed cars with the trunks still open, the gaping maws of multiple unlit garages.

By comparison, Jinny's house looked pristine. The grassy lawn had yellowed some, but there was still a sparkling pre-system SUV parked in the driveway, and from the looks of it, lights on inside.

Figures.

I sighed. The now-familiar purple light of a notification hung in the corner of my vision, and I focused on it, pulling up a slew of messages from the legend himself.

<**Nick:** Dude, are you sure you don't want me to come with you?>
<**Nick:** I feel bad. What happened was my fault. I should be there.>
<**Nick:** Fuck it. I'm on my way.>

The last message was time-stamped a minute earlier.

<**Matt:** Still outside, haven't gone in yet. Stop. Find a place to park and we'll talk. I'm not arguing with you while you're barreling through traffic.>
<**Nick:** ... I wasn't barreling through traffic.>
<**Matt:** Uh-huh.>

A few minutes later.

<**Nick:** Have I ever mentioned you creep me out sometimes?>

I rolled my eyes.

<**Matt:** Only every other day. Are you off the road?>
<**Nick:** Yeah, yeah. I'm parked. Pacing outside a 7-11.>
<**Matt:** We talked about this. We work in tandem. You handle the hero-shit, I deal with everything else. Dealing with anything likely to fuck with your mental is part of it.>
<**Nick:** Isn't applying that to this a little dramatic?>
<**Matt:** Considering what Jinny meant to you? It's really not.>

<Nick: Maybe her mom only hated me because she never met me.>

<Matt: Regardless, I'll handle it.>

<Nick: I just... feel like a coward. Not facing her.>

<Matt: It doesn't matter how you feel. What matters is there's nothing she can do or say that will hurt me. You, on the other hand, she'll have a field day with. Just because this feels small compared to what we usually deal with doesn't mean it's not important. Especially with you keeping this running smoothly with the Order. I have to take a backseat there, for obvious reasons. You, alternatively, need to be at the absolute top of your game. They're better than I thought, but there are plenty of sharks. Those sharks smell chum in the water and the Camp David Accords turn into a bloodbath.>

<Nick: God. Fine. Just... idk, let me know if you need backup or something.>

I snorted, imagining calling in backup for a surly old woman who lived alone.

<Matt: And you said I was being dramatic.>

<Nick: Bro, just... keep the mask on?>

<Matt: Which mask?>

<Nick: Seriously. Even if she's awful. It's what Jinny would have wanted.>

<Matt: Text you when it's done.>

I banished the message screen and centered myself, trying to carve through the unease and anxiety. Conveying utter confidence was the only way to get Nick to piss off, but at the moment I felt nothing of the sort. My father—a career cop—lost a partner once. Not to violence, or something as rote as a shootout. It started with a headache, then the man's speech slurred as he complained about someone burning something in the precinct kitchen right before his head hit his desk. The massive stroke finished the job before the paramedics could even load him onto a stretcher.

And as his partner, it was my father's duty to deliver the death notification. From his account, it was by far the hardest thing my father ever had to do.

"They look at you like it's your fault. And some part of you wonders if they're right. Even if it makes no sense. Obviously, I didn't give him the stroke, but the stress of the job contributed. You wonder if you could have done more, all while delivering the worst news in the world."

In a way, he'd been fortunate, my father. Because he at least had the luxury of doubt. He couldn't say, definitively, that he'd contributed to his partner's death. It was unknowable.

My case was much clearer cut. It was early days, I hadn't known what I was doing, and Jinny had paid the price for my mistakes. I hadn't pulled the trigger, or pushed her in front of the bolt, but she would be alive today if I hadn't made those mistakes.

And now I had to own it.

There'd be recompense, of course. Assurances that many of those responsible were already dealt with, the rest would be shortly, and enough Selve for a single civilian living within reasonable means to sustain themselves indefinitely.

But, having been on the other side of it, I knew the truth.

Nothing would replace the daughter she'd lost.

I stepped out of the car and climbed the steps of Jinny's suburban home, preparing to deliver the news.

———

Once I told her I had news regarding Jinny, Marjorie ushered me in.

The three-bedroom house looked like a snapshot, captured from a more modern time before Users roamed the street with swords and maces. The plants flanking either side of the door were well-watered and healthy, and the expensive-looking wood paneling was polished and untouched. This region had a wealth of strong Users, and with most of the violence occurring closer to the city center, there was a good chance Marjorie could likely hide in her home.

I shifted, glancing over the door and finding no evidence of forced entry, more or less supporting that assumption.

There was a glinting metal placard above the door inscribed with a flowery font:

Be Kind to One Another — Ephesians 4:32

Bounding, scrambling footsteps thundered across the tiled floor as two huskies with classic coloring, tall as my waist, raced over to greet me with wagging tails and lolling tongues. I reached down and let them smell me, then crouched down and scratched them both behind the ears. A third—older, judging from its cloudy eyes, raised its head balefully in greeting.

From the little time we'd spent together, I knew Jinny loved her dogs. So it was a relief to see they were intact. A bit thin, judging from the loose skin, but intact.

"You have a lovely home, Miss Stiles," I said automatically. At some point I'd shoved my hands into the kangaroo pocket of my hoodie.

"Thank you, dear." She smiled at me from behind counter, rummaging around unseen. The first thing that struck me walking in was that she was older than I'd expected. She'd given up on dying her hair and let what was once platinum blonde fade to a regal silver, accented by a plethora of gentle wrinkles and crow's feet "Tea? Or coffee?"

"That's not necessary," I said quickly, not wanting to put her out before I delivered the worst news of her life.

"None of that." She gave me a stern look. "Have a seat. It might be Disneyland outside, but some of us still care about southern hospitality."

I cut right to it. "I have bad news."

She stilled, her movements and rummaging coming to a slow stop. Her face and subsequent expression were shielded by an open cupboard. "Yes. Gathered that from the messages." There was enough bite in the words that it caught me off guard. Seconds later, her voice was back to normal, carrying the subtlest edge. "Columbian or French Roast?"

"Uh. Columbian would be lovely," I said, surrendering. Of course she'd realized that something had happened to Jinny by now. People grieved in their own way, and ritual—whether it was a funeral or pre-discussion coffee—was a simple way of expressing and managing that grief.

"Columbian it is."

As she went about the process of brewing it, even going so far as humming a tune that sounded ancient and repetitive, I felt my uneasiness grow. It was possible Marjorie was in denial. That she was expecting me to tell her that Jinny had been injured in the Transposition, or that she needed help. If that was the case, this was likely to turn explosive quickly. Jinny had hinted, though never outright stated, that she and her mother had a difficult relationship, though she'd been vague around the details.

I needed to be ready to handle this as smoothly as possible, comfort her if she cried, and be an empathetic and compassionate ear.

None of which came naturally and made me profoundly uncomfortable to even think about.

By the time she returned with small steaming cups, I was almost ready to leap out the window.

"Try it," she urged, pushing the cup closer to my mouth. "It's the perfect temperature. Won't stay that way for long."

I did as she asked and kept my expression stone-neutral as the blandest, stalest coffee I'd ever tasted washed down my throat.

"Good," I said.

She sipped from her cup and wrinkled her nose. "Beans are a bit old, but I like to think I still have the knack." She fixed me with a cool stare. "Now, what were you in such a hurry to tell me?"

I took a deep breath and launched into the version of events I'd rehearsed. Staying surface level but as close to the truth as possible and censoring critical or gory details. Jinny was a User. She was part of a small group of Users early on who undertook a trial and overcame it. I paid special attention to her achievements during the trial, how she'd done well and saved multiple lives. And grew vague again, when I described how the group was attacked on exit. Fibbing a bit when I described her death as quick and painless.

Because while it might have been quick, nothing about it was painless.

Marjorie's expression remained neutral throughout the telling. When I reached Jinny's death, I thought I saw something flash through her eyes.

Regret?

But it was gone too fast for me to identify. Slowly, Marjorie lowered her cup and placed it on the dark-wood table between the two sitting chairs, still completely composed.

"And where... is her body?" Marjorie asked, voice a million miles away.

"Gone," I said. For a brief moment, I considered mentioning the User Core before discarding the notion. She'd likely ask for it, and there was no guarantee she'd return it—especially if Vernon's necromancy research bore fruit and we told her why we needed it back. "The Users who ambushed us covered their tracks."

"Of course." Marjorie sniffled, then laughed. "Can't even put a bow on it and bury her properly." Slowly, her eyes trailed to me. "Why are you here?"

I blinked. "To... notify—"

"Not that." She held up a hand. "You specifically. For that matter, why were you with her in such a dangerous place?"

"Acting as support—"

"So you weren't the boyfriend?"

"What?"

"Were you *fucking* my daughter?" The edge in Marjorie's voice overtook her quiet demeanor.

What the hell?

I was too taken aback to do anything other than gape. Eventually, I managed to shake my head.

"Good for you," Marjorie said, staring toward the wall. "Always told her there's no charm in a trampled field. Not that she listened. Chances are you would have caught something."

It took a helluva a lot at this point to throw me this far off axis, but she'd managed it. Finally, she seemed to notice how utterly taken aback I was. "You must think poorly of me."

Yes.

Aloud, barely able to string the sentence together, I said, "We all deal with tragedy in our own way."

"Oh, I'm not grieving." Marjorie shook her head. "I've already grieved."

"Because of the illness?" I asked, trying one last time to give her the benefit of the doubt.

Marjorie rolled her eyes. "That excuse for the evil she did? No. I'd be surprised if it was even real."

"It was an *auto-immune disease*. She had *medication* for it."

"Doctors prescribe pills for anything these days," Marjorie stated, as if it was the most obvious thing in the world. "My grief was for the innocent daughter I lost. I feel nothing for the whore who took her place."

It was then that I realized two things. The first was that Jinny's mother was not the sort of person who could be reasoned with.

The second was that I needed to leave.

Now.

I sent her the pre-written contract that followed a layout one of Kinsley's researchers discovered, one that allowed the transfer of Selve from one party to another without arbitrage restrictions. "Confirm that for me, if you would."

"What's it for?"

"Transfer of assets."

After she confirmed the prompt, I withdrew a bag of fifty thousand Selve. Given physical form it was as heavy as blood money and made for a more dramatic display than I would have preferred as I lifted it with one hand and dropped it on the ground with a loud clink. "This should cover your necessities for the next few months. Half a year if you stretch it, give or take. Stay inside. Especially during the Transposition. If the current trend continues, most of the really bad shit pops up around downtown. In the meantime, don't get sick. And I'd start thinking about what you intend to do when it runs out."

She stiffened. "I don't like your tone, or your profanity. And don't need your assistance."

"I'm just the foulmouthed courier. The Selve is inheritance, courtesy of your dead daughter."

"Take your pity and get out."

"Course you think of it that way. Any sort of help is a hand-out." I stood, pushing my hands in my pockets, eyeing the stacked-up column of Charmin toilet paper next to the hall, far more than any single person could reasonably use in over a half-decade. She'd been one of the early preppers, the people snagging everything they could get off the shelves and maxing out their Amex's before the economy collapsed. I stared through her. It was so obvious, despite her airs, how small she was. "Sucker's bet you've never struggled. Never had to lift a finger for anything. Probably worked a few years out of college at most before you locked it down with a rich guy who paid off your grants—"

"—As if your generation ever worked a day in their lives—"

"He knocks you up, you cut him loose. Congratulations, you've escaped the middle-class."

White-hot rage told me I'd struck a bullseye. "He left *me*."

"Obviously."

Marjorie stood, fists clenched at her side. "You have no idea what you're talking about. And you have *no right* to judge me."

I observed her coldly. "Oh, don't get me wrong. I don't have a problem with what you did. If anything, I respect it. You played your cards well. At the end of the day, a hustle's a hustle. But I'm not the one cowering in my ivory tower calling other people *whores*."

As she simmered and shook to the point she was nearly vibrating, the small voice in my head told me this was enough. I'd made my point clearly enough that the bug in my ear would stop chittering after I'd left.

But Marjorie wasn't done. She advanced on me, all fire and

venom. "How old are you, seventeen, eighteen? You think you're tough coming in here, bullying a grieving old woman?"

"Thought you'd already grieved."

"We're *all* mourning." Her lip trembled. "As we should be. People are killing each other in the streets. The beasts of the apocalypse walk among us, and creatures from the beyond deign to tell us we are in need of *correction. Us.* God's children, created in his image. And every day we stray further from him. Not that someone as arrogant as you would give a single thought towards a power greater than himself."

It wasn't that she was religious. Speaking as a lifelong resident of the south, there were plenty of normal, well-adjusted human beings who were devout in one faith or another. The problem was that Marjorie was an extremist with no one left to burn on her pyre. And I didn't catch easy.

"Your beliefs are none of my business. And as an agnostic—"

She scoffed, "—atheist with extra steps—"

"—I've given it *plenty* of consideration," I talked over her acidly.

Images of the torment Jinny must have endured at the hands of this woman proliferated through my mind. Jinny herself was one of the kindest people I'd ever met, bordering on naïve but never quite crossing into it. And to see the naked hatred she'd endured, and the person she'd become despite it?

I twisted the knife. I had to. "Gotta wonder, have you truly thought this through?"

Marjorie took a step backward, seeing something in my expression she didn't like. "What... do you mean?"

"Guessing you've bunkered down and stayed static since this all started. Haven't networked. Few people in your old circles left, if any. Which means it's just you, a bag of money, and whatever else you squirreled away at the beginning. And six months from now, you won't even have that."

The gears in her mind turned as she looked from the bag, to me, to the bag again. "It's not my fault the world has changed."

"True."

"I never asked for this. None of us did."

"On that, we actually agree."

Her cold fingers gripped at my forearm. "That's a system car outside, isn't it? And I can't imagine my daughter was clever enough to earn all that money. Clearly you've done well for yourself."

Here's the windup.

I looked down at her hand on my arm until she removed it.

Marjorie almost scowled, but she'd had practice and the sweet, demure facade held. "Surely you have parents of your own. They must have struggled with how quickly everything moved. It's harder for older folks, dealing with drastic changes in the world."

Lady. My mother's a convicted felon and recovering alcoholic who's spent more time relapsing than breathing and hasn't held down a steady job in nearly a decade. And if I had a choice, I'd still choose her a thousand times before I chose you.

"It took her some time, but she adjusted," I said aloud.

"Because you were there for her. Now imagine what it's been like for me." She pressed a hand to her chest. "A mother whose daughter would barely speak to her before she died."

And the pitch.

"That how you see it?" I asked, unimpressed.

"You took her from me. You and the rest of her shitty little friends. You all decided to play hero and took her from me and left me with *nothing*," Marjorie raged, shifting on a dime, spittle flying from her mouth as she screamed in my face.

I didn't budge, my forehead inches from hers. "Miss Stiles, are you fishing for a handout?"

"You—"

"No one wants to work anymore. Why don't you pull yourself up by your bootstraps. Network. Put the effort in. Keep sending in resumes, eventually you'll find something. I'm sure the qualifications for most jobs these days are reasonable. Maybe even more reasonable than they were before. Hell, we have yet to see any real inflation yet, so that's one-up on the old world. Once you find a place willing to hire you, make sure you keep your nose to grindstone even if the pay sucks. If you can't afford basic cost of living, just find another job. Plenty of people work two jobs these days—"

Slippers scuffed carpet as she backed away, her eyes glazed over. "Callous. Callous and cruel." I watched emotionlessly as she wandered away from me, back to the kitchen. Her echoing tone was almost dreamlike. "I had a bout of insomnia a few years back. Better these days, but I kept the pills. Powerful stuff." She grunted and rose up to reach for something, and a plastic rattle followed. "Almost... took them all during the last event. I know it's a sin. But with all the *sounds,* and the gunfire, and the monsters lurking in our streets... I was tempted. Imagining it all happening again? And that it might not even be the last time? Maybe that was the right idea."

Tempting as it was, I wasn't going to tell her to go through with it. But I had no interest in playing this game.

Nick's voice replayed in my head.

It's what Jinny would have wanted.

The pile of leashes next to the door caught my eye. When I looked up all three huskies were splayed out on the hardwood floor, panting. They'd picked up on the elevated atmosphere but seemed more confused than stressed.

"Alright. Let's skip the back and forth and cut a deal."

There was another rattle as Marjorie placed the bottle down immediately and returned to the living room, victory in her eye. "What kind of deal?"

I crossed my arms. "I'll put you in touch with a single contact. He's highly positioned, in the process of rebuilding and rebranding, definitely needs the help."

"Sounds promising so far..." Marjorie trailed off, expecting more, because of course she did.

"The negotiation of your role and pay is entirely up to you."

She hesitated, "That's all you're willing to do?"

"That is the absolute limit of what I'm willing to do. If you want to tell me that's not good enough and take a mortal shot of Xanax out of spite, that's your prerogative. I tried."

Her eyes flicked toward the kitchen before they returned to me and she glowered, dropping the weak and feeble act. "Fine."

"Not so fast. This is a trade." I tilted my head toward the huskies. "The dogs, along with their collars, leashes, and bowls."

"They're lineage breeds. Purer than purebred. Jinny would have settled for mutts, but I insisted. They're worth far more than that," she argued.

"Any of them know a guild leader you can bum work from?"

"Bastard." She clenched her fists.

Realizing this was likely the closest we'd come to an accord, I gathered up the leashes. All three dogs wandered over, more excited by the prospect of a walk than they were concerned by the presence of a stranger.

"Check your messages. I'm sending a contact." By the time she pulled up her UI, I was already walking away. "See? Networking already."

———

I leaned against the Prius, awkwardly holding three leashes and letting the night air wash over me as the dogs ran a train on the nearby postbox. Some part of me still hated the suburbs, the astroturfed grass, the HOAs, how fake and artificial everything felt. Lately, I kind of got it. It was still normal and mundane. But normal and mundane were getting harder and harder to come by.

<**Nick:** How'd it go?>
<**Matt:** Great. We cooked s'mores over her fireplace and watched the poorly colorized version of *White Christmas*.>

The call came in immediately, and I answered. "On second thought, I might have needed backup."

"Really?" Nick prompted.

"She would have torn you apart."

"That bad, huh?"

"Worse."

There was a pause. "Did she get under your skin?"

"No." I grunted. "Yeah. A little. It takes a special kind of person to make me want to dismantle their life in minutes." Choosing my words carefully, I gave him the rundown, abridging some of the conversation and blunting Marjorie's more venomous comments.

There was a long silence. "Man, I wasn't even there and I'm boiling."

"Yeah."

"Kinda surprising you helped her at all."

"Help is a strong word. Other than Jinny's payout, which was rightfully hers if we're going by old world law, all I really did was steal the dogs and refer her to Roderick."

"Poor Roderick." Nick chuckled. "What are you going to do with them?"

I shrugged. "The lodge isn't even on my radar right now."

"Talking about the dogs, Matt."

"Oh. Still figuring that out," I admitted. "Wouldn't mind having them around the apartment, assuming Talia's fine with it. I'll prep the same meals Jinny did in bulk at the beginning of the week, and I think there's a dog park nearby. So everything they need is either order-able or in walking distance."

"Uh. Wasn't expecting the dog heist, otherwise I would have warned you. They gotta get, like, multiple hours of exercise. Daily."

"They sure as hell weren't getting that from Marjorie. I'll do my best, get someone to handle it when I can't." I wrinkled my nose. "Pretty sure she was feeding them Purina."

"Yikes." Nick groaned. "Should have checked up on them earlier. I'll sub in whenever I can, help out. It's the least I can do."

"Sae probably will too." Another silence followed. When he didn't say anything or hang up, I knew there was more. "Talk to me."

"I dunno." Nick sighed. "Keep thinking about how you're the most unflappable person I've ever met, and all it took was a single conversation to get your blood up."

"And how Jinny dealt with that every day?" A cold gust of wind chilled me, blowing hard enough that it created static on the line.

"Yeah... man. On top of all the shit she was dealing with, one thing after another, she had that demon breathing down her neck. But despite all the judgement and manipulation..."

"—not to mention psychological abuse, emotional extortion, gaslighting—" I filled in, barely making a dent.

"Despite all that, she still somehow managed to be the best person I knew. She was vulnerable, and honest, and real. No matter what life threw at her, she never gave up on trying to make the best of it. And then…"

"And then she fucking died," I finished, trying to tamp down on the anger as soon as it surfaced, only partially succeeding. "I know. I know it sucks and nothing about it is fair. But try to focus on what we *can* change. Vernon's making progress. Everything's advancing faster since he unlocked the ability to work with multiple Cores. The abilities are looking promising."

"Promise me," Nick said, his voice dead serious.

"Can't promise what I can't know, Nick."

"No—just that we'll do everything we can to bring her back. Even if it's a limited resource and the smart thing to do would be to save it. Even if it costs us. We owe her that."

"Jinny was always first in line. But. Yeah." I closed my eyes. "I promise."

CHAPTER FORTY-FIVE

The problem with being an introvert is that, short of communicating that detail explicitly, most people won't intuitively pick up that you are one. There are markers and coinciding behaviors, sure, but almost all of them can-slash-will be misinterpreted as dislike, disinterest, snobbery, or standoffishness. Before the dome my solution to this issue was simple: keep my head down, act like I'm in a hurry—in most cases, I usually was—and be polite yet short with anyone who approached me.

To some extent, that still worked. At least until the end of the last Transposition event, when I was unexpectedly thrust into a highly visible leadership role. I tried to make it clear it was the Adventurers' Guild and Merchants' Guild that were more or less calling the shots with region management. But that didn't seem to matter. People around the region would linger by my building to catch me for a quick conversation. Some wanted something. More perplexing were the ones who didn't have an agenda at all. I got the sense they were curious or simply wanted to be acknowledged by a person who seemed relatively ordinary and had some degree of control over their daily lives. It could be difficult to manage, especially after a long day when I wanted to do nothing but flop into bed and surrender to the void.

Apparently it was time to batten down the hatches. Because something I'd learned within minutes of stepping out of my Prius and heading into the building was that, even late at night, leading three goofy-looking dogs around notched the introvert setting all the way up to hard mode.

"Beautiful!" An old man ruffled the pure-white husky's face. "And such intelligent eyes as well."

"Yep."

I eyed the path to the elevator, where another woman blocked my way, petting the larger female dog, several more people crowded around behind her. "Where did these sweet babies come from?"

"Boarding them for a friend."

A father with terrible paternal instincts who carried a small child bent down so her face was inches from the largest dog, a black-tan mix that was mostly black. "Doggy!" She giggled excitedly, thrusting small fingers into the animal's nose.

When a nascent growl started in the dog's throat, I reached out to him with **<Suggestion>** immediately, sending an entreaty for calm tagged with an image of a pup awkwardly waddling around, exploring her environment. Almost immediately the growling stopped, though the dog still didn't look pleased. Instead of snapping at the child, he reached up with a paw and—surprisingly gentle—pushed the girl's arm away.

"What are the doggies' names?" the child asked, unbothered.

Uh.

If I'd known there was going to be a test, I would have studied. As it was, I settled for cheating and scanned the dogs' tags discreetly. "The white one's name is Ghee, brown-and-white is Marmalade, black is Truffle."

Thanks for that, Jinny.

With growing despair, I watched as more people emerged from the elevators with plans for the night while others returning home for the evening cut off any avenue of retreat. Even if I was as direct as possible, it was going to take hours to extricate myself from this, and I could see my fantasies of a long, uninterrupted sleep slowly slipping away. Someone stepped forward from behind, well within my personal space, and, before I could react, wrapped their arms around me. Something soft pressed against my cheek, followed by a smacking noise. "Ditching our plans to show off your new pals?"

Tara's timing was impeccable. She slipped her arm through mine with casual intimacy, looking at our many observers with bemusement and giving me the out I'd been looking for.

"Never." I squeezed her arm and smiled. "But I should get these guys settled first. They've had an exciting day."

"They're not the only ones. Heard things at the tower were rough today. Surprised you're not dead on your feet." To anyone else it sounded like an innocuous comment. But I didn't miss the way she projected slightly, ensuring her voice carried to everyone else around us.

"We should get out of your hair." The old man stopped petting Ghee and stood straight, hand on the small of his back.

"It's no bother," I assured him, hoping he ignored that for the pleasantry it was, feeling nothing but relief when he did. The crowd dwindled until there was enough of an opening that Tara could pull me away. I let her lead, quietly reviewing how easily she'd extracted me from the situation, pondering if I would have been capable of doing the same thing. I wasn't sure I could. The innate awkwardness I felt with others—especially when I didn't fully understand why they were there and what they wanted—was just something Tara didn't share. She had a way of defusing people, communicating important information without being direct or creating conflict.

I eyed her as the elevator slid shut. "Just happened to be nearby, huh?"

She's hiding something.

<Cruel Lens'> voice skewered the reverie like a spear.

Even worse, she seems to think whatever she's keeping to herself is incredibly funny. My title chuckled in the back of my mind, uncharacteristically slow to provide useful information. A slow anger started in my chest, spreading out to the rest of me until my fingers tingled. I'd been suspicious of Tara from the start, but that suspicion had faded quickly. Now it was back, alongside the realization that whatever this was, I was being played.

"Well, I got off an hour ago, figured my not-boyfriend was probably on his way home, and waited for him." She played with a lock of hair idly, giving me the same come-hither smile she'd maintained for most of our "date."

Everything she's saying is true, from a technicality standpoint. If that's her preferred way to lie, it makes sense that your other titles would have difficulty picking it up.

"And now you're following him to his suite. A more chaste person might wonder what your intentions are," I said, taking a few steps closer and narrowing our proximity until I could feel her breath on my cheek.

Instead of reacting negatively, Tara shivered. "Well, I... saved you. Don't deny it, they might not have noticed you getting ready to run out the door at a moment's notice, but I sure as hell did. Provided a service. And as I'm not officially on payroll yet, it's only right to pay me some other way."

"Like?" I raised an eyebrow.

Tara let the tension linger for just a while longer before she spoke. "I want to see your place."

"Okay. Why?"

"It helps." She glanced down at the dogs. "They're adorable by the way. Not to mention a great first step in making your public image less mercurial, but if you're serious about putting me to work as a PR consultant, it helps if I have a foundation to draw from. Need to get a better sense for who you are as a person. I could probably get that just from talking to you, eventually, but there's no better shortcut for getting to know someone than seeing how they live."

Still not entirely accurate to her motivations, according to my title, but the substance of what she'd said was dead on. Breaking into the home or quarters of a powerful User almost always provided key insights to their routine, their agenda, and their psychology. If I was hunting someone stronger than me, it was absolutely necessary.

The prospect would have worried me more if I hadn't already tangled with feds in a world that operated without warrants. *Everything* was locked down tight. Any critical records or documentation were kept off-site. I'd even arranged the place strictly according to feng shui to throw off the pseudo-science types. If anything, it was psychopathically clean, but all that could realistically be read from that was that I was a stickler.

<**Matt:** Kinsley, anything weird happening around the penthouses today?>
<**System Notification:** The designated User is either signed out of the messaging application or offline. Please try again later.>

My heart skipped a beat. *What the fuck?*

<**Matt:** Sae, you at my place or yours?>

<System Notification: The designated User is either signed out of the messaging application or offline. Please try again later.>
<Matt: Nick.>
<System Notification: The designated User is either signed out of the messaging application or offline. Please try again later.>

My pulse quickened. At first I thought my comms were being shuttered by a new, more subtle form of **<Squelch>** when I spied a new message from Roderick complaining about a woman he'd never met before harassing him for work after she name-dropped me.

I spent the rest of the elevator ride messaging everyone else that mattered, getting the same error message over and over. Regardless, I kept trying. Because if it wasn't something interfering with comms, everyone in my circle was either off-line—which I couldn't imagine any circumstance where that would happen simultaneously—

Or dead.

Out of everyone, Miles responded just as the elevator opened.

<Miles: What's up, kid?>
<Matt: Can't get Kinsley on the line. Messaging app is erroring out for a bunch of other people as well.>
<Miles: Huh. Think it's trouble?>
<Matt: What else would it be?>
<Miles: Hold on, let me try reaching out from my end.>

I stopped mid-step a few units away, staring down at the black space beneath my doorway. Because it *shouldn't* be dark. I always left the bathroom light on, and the bathroom door open. It should have been visible from beneath the door. There were any number of people who had access and could have stopped by, turned the light off, and left, but there were too many things adding up in ways that clawed at the back of my mind. I reached into my inventory and withdrew the remote, toggling the lights on.

"Something wrong?" Tara asked, noticing my hesitance and cocking her head.

"Dunno. Just... got a little dizzy." I leaned against the wall, buying time.

It was only a matter of time until this happened. A single missed camera or overlooked tail was all it took. I tried to imagine how they would do it. Put myself in their shoes. Team of four, minimum. Three if they were all heavy hitters. Question was, where to put them? There wasn't much cover in my suite. The couch on the back wall was the obvious choice and could work in a pinch, but magically enhanced bolts and arrows—which they'd expect—could penetrate it easily. They'd place a ranged User there, but they'd want others nearby to stop me from running or firing back as quickly as possible. The wide-open space in the center left two options, and if they were smart, they'd pick both. One in the bathroom, one posted up next to the door.

Three down. Now where was the fourth?

It wasn't Tara. Even if she was a special class, none of my titles, detection abilities, or even Azure had picked up the slightest suspicion that she posed a threat. No one was that airtight. Most likely, her role was to distract and deliver me. A second shooter fit the scenario better than another melee, and the only reasonable cover left beyond the couch was off to the right side, behind the kitchen island.

In any case, they'd want the lights off for this. The hallway was brightly lit, and they'd want to strike during the short transition from bright to dark, when my vision would be worse. They'd need to account for mess, which meant someone capable of creating an instance if they were thorough, a thick sheet of plastic on the floor if they lacked greater resources. Either way, any second now...

Like clockwork, the lights in my suite switched off.

I angled carefully, going down on a knee to retie my shoe, shoving **<Broken Legacy>**—and Talia, contained within it— beneath the door.

"How's it look in there?" I reached out to my summon through our mental connection.

"Matt, you alright?" Tara peered down at me. "You seem off today."

"Yeah." I made a show of looking for my key. "Just can't get something out of my head. There was this unaffiliated merchant kid Kinsley was gonna bring into the fold. James, Jim, something old school. At first everything seemed more or less copacetic. Popped up at an ideal time, had a corner on key resources Kinsley's been lacking for a while. Seemed flexible enough in negotiations, but not so flexible he was a pushover."

"Sure," Tara said, following along.

"*Then* he got desperate. Starting pushing for things to move quicker—which didn't at all make sense in context, cause, so far as we knew, he was already getting everything he wanted. So she had someone look into him and then it all fell apart."

"Talia."

Again, no answer. That was somehow more alarming than the lights.

"The kid was trying to rip her off somehow?" Tara asked.

"Sort of. Some of it was true. He was a merchant. But he wasn't at all unaffiliated. Those key resources weren't his. They were held by another group of merchants who gave Kinsley the finger, regretted it, and were planning to use the kid as an alternate pipeline for selling on the online market."

"Geez. That sucks for Kinsley. In that situation and the

greater context. Always having to question peoples' agendas when they approach you."

"Sucks for everyone," I agreed. "But especially the kid. Because Kinsley's literally been where he was, you know? A kid with shit people want to take and no way to give it without payment. It's a bad situation, and Kinsley knows that better than anyone. She probably would have brought him in even if the only thing he had stocked was toothpaste. But as he was beholden to another group—one prone to poor decisions—they put pressure on him, and because of that, instead of using his best judgment, he rushed and ended up fumbling the bag for everyone."

<**Miles:** I was able to get through to both Kinsley and Nick. Few others as well. Everyone seems fine, just mildly confused why I was reaching out. Might be some issue on your side.>

And here I thought we were making progress. It was obvious he was lying immediately before my title started crowing falsehood. Nothing about it made sense. Et tu, Miles?

"Tragic. But for how messy everything post-dome has been, the chain of events is oddly fable-like," Tara observed, smile ebbing slightly. "It even has a moral at the end."

Fuck you, I had seconds to come up with it.

Problems rarely resolved themselves. And if Tara was a problem now, almost guaranteed she'd be a problem later. But for some reason—maybe her greater hustle and sense of drive I'd connected with, maybe because she also had a kid that wasn't hers that she'd nevertheless taken responsibility for—I wanted to give her the chance to reconsider.

"Do you want to go somewhere else?" I asked, point blank.

"*Matt.* We're literally already here. And it's late, where would we even go?"

"My place is pretty bare, and I haven't cleaned in a while. Wafflehouse is always open, unless that's beneath your palate. The boba place closes at three. And if you're not hungry or thirsty... we could always go to yours," I said, knowing what that implied. Implying it anyway, because it would tempt her, even as the thought made me nauseous.

A silent communication passed between us, and Tara cocked her head as if trying to pick up an almost imperceptible frequency nested in my offer. "Not a great idea. Any other day, I'd be down. But if we go now, I'll start to wonder. What, exactly, was in Matt's suite that day he was trying so hard to keep secret?"

"Not hiding anything," I grunted.

"Maybe not. But I'd wonder," Tara insisted.

It was a solid reversal, one that effectively slapped away my olive branch and strengthened her position, narrowing my options to one. Between the contingencies scattered around my suite and my experience being on the other side of this exact sort of ambush, that even with Talia out of play, I felt confident I could handle the immediate threat. It was everything that came after that was the big, blinking question mark.

Screw it. Not happy, but not seeing any other way, I dropped the dogs' leashes—it was a closed floor, so short of someone opening the fire-escape or escorting them down the elevator, they'd be out of danger and couldn't wander far. Before Tara could react, I turned the lights back on.

Unlatched the door.

And threw it open.

CHAPTER FORTY-SIX

It was going to catch up to me, eventually.

I cut the power in the building first. In the old days it would have been harder. The local power grid was horrifically inadequate, but even that terrible system had more contingencies than the generator setups providing power now. As it was, a relatively non-destructive use of **<Probability Cascade>** bought me at least a few precious minutes to work with. The fact that I'd turned the lights on earlier—effectively blinding the would-be ambushers before they turned it off again—would help me. They'd had a minute longer than I had to adjust, but **<Stealth>** enhanced my perception in the dark, which put me one up on the rest of them.

"Matt?" Tara said, squinting at shadows, trying to pick out my silhouette.

With seconds to decide, I left the mask off. Whoever was waiting inside was waiting for Matt. And Matt was a region leader. Unfortunately, that also meant a hard breach wasn't an option. There were too many people I knew offline, too high of a chance there was a hostage.

Leaving Tara behind, I opened the door and slipped inside.

The security shutters that covered the expansive skyline view were lowered, keeping the pitch-dark interior insulated from any external light.

Still, I could sense them. A grunt toward the back of the room, quiet breathing just loud enough to make out as a slight rasp. The smell—

Were they cooking in my fucking kitchen?

Either they hadn't heard me come in, or they were slower than I'd expected. From a brief scan there was no plastic on the ground, and the best ambush point—the bathroom—was clear. Most of the noises I picked up seemed to be coming from the back of the room, behind the long couch.

Carefully, I pulled a crossbow and leveraged the dull-green dot just above the back cushion. I could see well enough now to put down the first head that popped up.

Talia's voice suddenly resounded in my head, a mix of alarm and amusement. "Do not fire. Do not use any further abilities. Put away your weapon and attempt to smile."

"Now you fucking talk."

There was a snapping buzz as the power switched back on.

"Okay, not gonna lie, my life flashed before my eyes," someone who sounded exactly like Nick said.

"Speaking from experience, jumping out at him is a terrible idea," Sae agreed, sounding equally unhappy. "We really ought to just spread out, hands on our knees, in clearly non-threatening positions."

"Really doesn't like surprises, huh?" Was that *Julian?*

"Dios mio, my knee is killing me." Abuelita's voice.

"Maybe we should just take it as a sign," Kinsley suggested. "Grams can stretch out—"

"Pendejo, I am not that old!"

Slowly, I put a hand to my face, turned around, and opened the door, allowing both a confused Tara and the dogs she'd apparently chased down and collected inside, then closed it loudly. A collective "Surprise!" rang out as an absolutely stupid number of people jumped up from behind the couch, only partially contested by Sae's "Don't shoot!"

———

Iris, Sae, and Charlotte sat cross-legged on the floor, intent on befriending the dogs. Sae and Charlotte kept shooting me apologetic glances—albeit for different reasons—while Iris seemed totally fixated on the animals, laughing as they sniffed her curiously and pushed her with their noses. Julian and Nick sat on the couch across from Professor Estrada, watching the girls awkwardly as Nick turned repeatedly to check on me, glancing away when I looked at him.

There were enough people here that I should have been angry. Most knew I was jumpy on the best of days, and today had certainly not been the best of days. But tempering that with the fact that my mother was here, the story told itself.

I leaned against the wall next to her as she prepped a tray of tacos on the counter. "So... you mad at me?"

"Of course not, sweetheart." Mom smiled thinly as she portioned chicken and distributed it. "Your eighteenth birthday was weeks ago. We had to do something special."

My birthday had always been a non-event, quietly acknowledged but rarely celebrated. It said a lot for how chaotic things had been lately that I hadn't even realized, otherwise I probably would have put it together.

"Guess I'm just wondering why you went with this format."

"Because you don't like surprises?" Mom rolled her eyes.

Yup. Her idea. Probably roped everyone else into it and insisted, and no one wants to shoot down the recovering alcoholic.

"Yeah."

Unbothered, she continued to slice the chicken. "I barely hear from you anymore, let alone see you. If I'd messaged you about it, what would you have said?"

I shrugged. "That we should do it after the Transposition deadline."

The knife came down hard enough that the poor chicken probably felt it in the afterlife. "And then there would be something else in the way. Another crisis, more problems demanding your attention at all hours of the day. Not to mention," She waved her hand toward the living room, "there's no guarantee any of these people—people who clearly love you—will be here then. You need to treasure what you have while you have it."

Pretty sure Julian and Charlotte barely knew me and had probably come by, only to be dragged into this as collateral, but realistically she wasn't really talking about them. Or anyone else for that matter.

"If you feel like I've neglected you, or taken advantage of your contributions in any way, I'm willing to have that conversation."

Suddenly changing the topic, she pointed out a tray of brownies. "I was warned not to eat those. You probably shouldn't either."

"Mom."

"It's not about me. Even if it was, a region leader is an important person. The more important you are, the more time becomes a commodity." She turned her back, continuing to prepare the food.

Tell that to the bug up your ass.

More annoyed that I didn't understand why she was doing this than that she'd done it in the first place, I pulled up my messages from her and scrolled up. Beyond the usual parental hovering and check-ins, most of which I'd responded to, I found it. A message from the night we took down Sunny.

<Mom: The reworked forum's ready to launch. I'd like you and Kinsley to look it over before it goes up, when you have time.>

Damn. I'd seen it. I'd even replied to the next unrelated message she'd sent. But I'd never acknowledged the progress. Scrolling through the screen caps—how the hell was she using the UI to send photos, anyway—it looked good. More old Reddit than IRC, but seeing how the point was creating a resource for the general public, that was a good thing.

Mom strode over and put her wrists on my shoulder, grease-glistening fingers precariously raised over the red fabric, and pushed me toward the living room. "Get out of my kitchen and enjoy the party."

"Pretty sure it's my kitchen," I complained, even as she pushed a platter of tacos into my hands and pushed me out. Eventually I gave up and sat down next to Nick and Julien, glancing toward the latter curiously.

"Sorry—" Julien started.

"Here for other reasons and got roped in by gunpoint?" I filled in.

He opened his mouth, closed it, then nodded.

"Your mother's a very persuasive woman," Charlotte added, leaning back and squinting as Marmalade lapped at her face. She chuckled. "After I was—um—*recruited,* I needed to go back to the complex to grab some ingredients, and she barely let me leave."

Nick waggled his eyebrows at me. "Always nice to have someone who bakes in the friend group, am I right?" As usual, his double-entendres veered closer to single.

I shook my head. "Are you high?"

"Nooooo," Nick lied, then grimaced, head bobbing slightly as he narrowed his eyes at Charlotte. "That really just the usual stuff? It barely tasted like anything other than chocolaty good-ness, and I am *sent* right now."

"Technically, yes," Charlotte hedged. "Warned you to eat half."

"I was hungry!"

Across from us, Abuelita was cracking into the last of what looked to be several brownies, so far entirely unaffected.

"Technically?" I asked Charlotte, more for Estrada's sake than my own.

"It's the oil. Had a... uh... questionably legal side hustle before the dome..." Charlotte trailed off, scanning faces for judgment.

"Join the club. Trust me, he doesn't care," Nick said auto-matically.

"I don't," I agreed.

"It started as a hobby. Something I just did for friends who kicked me a few bucks in return. But friends refer friends, who refer friends, and so on. When the statewide bans on the delta-alts went through, demand was at an all-time high." Charlotte shrugged. "I started making serious money and decided to actually take it seriously. Sourced better stuff, learned the whole decarbing-double-boiler-filtration process. What no one warns you is that it takes a while to dial it all in. Threw the weak batches away, and most of the dialed-in stuff I'd already used up."

So all she had left was the strong stuff. I slapped Nick on the back. "Sounds like you're fucked."

"How is she fine?" Nick complained, pointing at Estrada.

"Jódete, gilipollas." Estrada shook her head.

"Well first off, unless my Spanish is completely rusty and I'm mistranslating, I'm not sure that she is." I gave her a long look as I addressed Nick. "Second, the professor's been dealing with back issues for longer than you've been alive. Tolerance is probably way higher than yours."

Julien shifted awkwardly. "Much as your mom means well, this is obviously meant for close friends and family. If Charlie and I are at all imposing..." he trailed off, leaving it open-ended.

I fought a strong compulsion to take him up on the implicit offer to leave. Parties were uncomfortable for me. Parties where I was the focus with near-strangers in attendance were even worse. But my most recent rant to Jinny's mother on the importance of networking was still fresh in my mind. Matt needed to be able to do this—be congenial and welcoming to newcomers, meet and greets, cordial political shit that didn't come naturally to me. Somehow, irrelevant yet equally important, Iris seemed to like them.

Surrendering, I rubbed the bridge of my nose. "No, that'd be a special kind of shitty. Don't feel like you have to stay if you'd prefer to go—if that's the case we can talk about whatever you came here to talk about before you leave—but you're welcome."

"Must have made quite the impression." Sae called over, eyebrows raised over her sunglasses. "It took him weeks to warm up to me."

"Try getting a date. Month's wait minimum." Tara winked, serving herself two tacos from the platter and plopping down in the over-size armchair next to Estrada. She bit into a taco and grimaced slightly.

That was something else I needed to get used to. "You guys all meet already?" When the answer was a mixed no, I did a round of introductions, including Tara. Iris came out of her shell enough to politely greet Julien and Tara, then seemed to withdraw again, standing to the side awkwardly.

"Kiddo," I signed. "Want me to get you something to eat?"

Iris gave one quick shake of her head and signed back. "Not really hungry."

"Wanna just sit with me instead?"

A nod. I waved her over and she clambered onto my lap, settling in, seemingly content to just absorb the festivities passively.

Nick absorbed this, oddly somber for how intoxicated he was. He stared at Tara seriously. "Never thought anyone would lock Matt down. He's always been a player."

I elbowed him. "Shut up."

Undeterred, Nick crossed his arms. "I'm almost ready to give the best friend seal of approval, but before that can happen, you need to answer a very important question."

Tara set her plate on her knee and leaned forward. "Mmm. Intriguing. Go for it."

"What is the best hour of television ever filmed?"

"Subjectively or objectively?" Tara asked.

"Objectively," Nick insisted.

Sae looked between them, unimpressed by Nick's sudden posturing. "It's obviously the end of *Six Feet Under*."

"No." Nick shot that down immediately.

"It is!"

"Says you and the thirty senior citizens still alive who watched it."

"Michael C. Hall is a national treasure, you dick."

Charlotte snapped her fingers. "Oh-oh, the intervention episode of *Euphoria*."

"Weren't there multiple interventions?" Sae asked, scratching her head.

"From season one," Charlotte clarified.

"Great show. But too zoomery." Nick shook his head.

"Aw."

Tara made a show of thinking, tapping her bottom lip in amusement. Nick was joking around, but he'd put her on the spot, and she didn't have time to get a feel for the group yet.

Given that, I threw her a lifeline. "Just cold-read him. He's practically asking for it."

"Are you... sure? Most people don't enjoy that party-trick." Tara raised an eyebrow.

"He's used to it."

"What better place for a party trick than a party?" Sae shrugged, watching Tara curiously.

"Okay. Just going off of energy and limited information, so don't take anything personal, alright?"

Nick nodded.

Tara leaned forward, steepling her fingers and studying Nick. "From the zoomer comment, I think we can eliminate anything recent. You're giving 'bro too cool to like anything from his era,' but if you were too far in that direction, I can't imagine you and Matt being as close as you are. So you're masculine, likely with masculine tastes, but nothing too overboard. Even for that niche, you have an odd air of vulnerability. Almost like you make a point of it." Her eyebrows furrowed. "It's something popular, critically acclaimed, and relatively well-known, older than *Euphoria* but newer than *Six Feet Under*." She snapped her fingers and pointed at him. "But you specified episode. Not finale, not season, episode."

"It could be a finale..." Nick attempted to misdirect, looking entirely caught off guard by the depth of the analysis.

"Judging purely from that reaction, it's not. Which is interesting. A lot of shows have good seasons, some have great finales, but there's not a ton that have individual, standout episodes the typical person can call back to. From what we've already established, I think I can already narrow it down to four." Tara held up four fingers, then pulled one down. "*The Sopranos* is a little old. Even if it wasn't, the characters probably aren't to your tastes. You don't mind gray, it's the dickishness that puts you off." She closed another few fingers. "We can eliminate *Mad Men* for the same reasons. *The Wire* packs plenty of standout episodes, but it was too disjointed and emotionally divorced for your tastes."

The longer she went on, the more Nick sank into the couch, his eyes wide. He stared at me, genuinely unsettled.

Don't look at me. You started it.

Tara sat back, smiling in victory. "Which leaves us with the obvious choice. *Breaking Bad*, Season five, 'Ozymandias.' 'Boom. Done.'" She mouthed the last two words and feigned dropping a mic.

I snorted at Nick's abject shock, chuckles growing into outright laughter at how called out and exasperated he looked.

"Holy shit, she actually out pop-cultured Nick," Sae gaped.

"You coached her," Nick accused me, still reeling.

"Swear to god I didn't."

"I just... like a good puzzle." Tara pushed a bang behind her ear self-consciously. "Sorry if that was creepy."

"You're fine." Sae waved away the anxiety. "If that's the bar for creepy, Matt's creepy all the time, and we still keep him around."

"Whose birthday is this supposed to be again?" I flipped Sae the bird and she responded in kind.

"Do me next!" Charlotte said.

Tara seemed surprised—both that her so-called party-trick hadn't put anyone off, and that she had another taker. Nevertheless, she recovered quickly. "That would be *Euphoria*, season 1, episode 4."

"Aw."

"Nah nah nah," Nick leaned forward, rallying. "You're guessing what we, individually, think is best. Which is impressive. But you haven't shared your opinion."

"Well... *Breaking Bad*'s a great show..." Tara smirked.

"Uh huh..." Nick was on the edge of his seat.

"And 'Ozymandias' is a great episode."

"*Uh huh...*"

"But 'Fly' is objectively better," Tara finished. Before she'd even completed her sentence, Nick collapsed over the armrest, groaning.

"Matt. I've been mortally wounded. She likes... bottle... episodes," He croaked.

Tara absorbed his ridiculous display stoically, then looked to me. "Don't think I'm getting the seal of approval after all. We might have to break up."

"Unfortunate." I waited a beat. "I'm keeping the dogs."

"Bastard."

Beside me, Julien had been unexpectedly quiet. I watched him for a moment, wondering if he felt out of place, until I picked up on the telltale eye-flicker of motionless UI manipulation. "Trouble?"

Julien shook his head. "Shopping, actually. If I'm gonna crash a birthday party, least I can do is buy you a present."

This fucking guy.

I rolled my eyes. "You are literally the only person here who already gave me something."

"What? *Julien,*" Charlotte squawked.

Nick slugged me. "Since when do you do gifts?"

Julien frowned and lowered his voice. "It's not really a gift if it has a responsibility attached, is it?"

"If the inherent value overshadows the complexity of the responsibility? Pretty sure it's still a gift," I answered dryly.

"And it was something nice? Now I look like the asshole." Charlotte huffed, fiddling with her UI for a few moments before swiping it away in frustration. Suddenly, her eyes widened. "What if I don't charge for the glamour work? That could be my present."

"The-who-what now?" Sae's head whipped around, suddenly laser-focused on Charlotte.

Shit. With the unexpected surprise, I still hadn't had time to talk to Sae. About the glamour or the potion. "Uh—"

"It's a hex," Charlotte chirped. "Um..." She trailed off as Sae approached her, the other woman's fists clenched, body trembling. "It's... a bit like sculpting, only for... appearance and stuff. That's why I came here. To talk about the commission... oh..." Charlotte trailed off as Sae removed her sunglasses.

"Could it fix these? Make me look normal again?" Sae pointed a shaking finger at her compound eyes, almost cringing, expecting a no.

I was slower than I should have been, struggling with a sensation that felt almost like a mental lag. Finally, I managed to interject. "Sae—wait."

"Been waiting, Helpline," Sae said, eyes still locked with Charlotte's.

"There's something we need to talk about first. Another more permanent option—"

She'd picked up on my discretion but didn't seem to care much. "Is the other option available now?"

"If you answer the way I think you'll answer... no."

For how fish-out-of-water she must have felt in this situation, Charlotte caught on quickly. "It's painful at first, but the touch-ups are easy, and I'm happy to keep it intact until the more permanent option is available. Guessing... you didn't exactly sign up for that."

The sudden outburst of tears was natural. Almost expected. What was less expected was the way she hugged me. "You might be the best friend I've ever had."

"That's the brownies talking."

"It's not," Sae sniffled. "Haven't even had any brownies. Just the tacos."

Something about the way she said it, then immediately hugged Charlotte, then Nick gave me pause. I glanced down at my plate and the half-eaten taco, then glanced around. "Mom? Wait—where's Kinsley?"

"In the bathroom. Been there for a while, hope she's feeling okay."

Feeling a growing urgency, I knocked on the bathroom door twice, and when there was no response, opened it. Kinsley was prone on the bathroom floor dead asleep, snoring loudly, wadded-up towel beneath her head serving as a pillow. The water was still running from when she'd started to wash her hands and apparently decided to take an impromptu nap instead.

I turned it off and left her there for the moment—despite the tile, she looked comfortable enough—and raced into the kitchen, searching the labels and containers for something specific. "Where—What did you cook the tacos with?"

"Love." My mother chuckled at her own joke.

"No, the *oil*, Mom. What oil did you use?"

"The only one I could find." Mom passed me a bottle I'd never seen before, label handwritten in loopy feminine print. **Cooking Oil: >25 Percent. Use with caution.**

Slowly I panned the room, noting the numerous empty and half-eaten plates, including my own.

Well. Shit.

CHAPTER FORTY-SEVEN

I stared at the opening. The upside down "U" shape was perfectly cut and sanded, the interior lavishly upholstered with system-sourced vicuña wool, a small cashmere pillow with golden trim creating asymmetry. I turned it diagonally, then back again, deciding after a moment that it looked best aligned with the bedding. It was resplendent, extravagant, perfect.

And yet.

"It's a little off. Something about the roof tiles."

"I see it," Iris signed grimly and pressed her hand to the roof. The tiles rearranged themselves. "How's that?" My vision blurred, everything simultaneously bigger and smaller than it should be, and I blinked, trying to force my perspective closer to reality.

Behind us, there was a loud thud as a large wooden board hit the ground. I turned and squinted through the bright halo of effervescent light at Nick, flexing as he slapped the saw back down on Iris's worktable. "This saw is fire. I'm on fire. I'm a two-by-four machine, bro!" Utterly pleased with himself, he flexed both biceps, then his energy seemed to flag a bit. "Hot. I'm really hot. Kinda wanna take my shirt off."

"Hello? My sister's here," I snapped.

"Oh damn, my bad." Nick grinned guiltily.

"He can cool off if he needs to," Iris signed, still withdrawn but seemingly unbothered.

"Well—" Nick started.

"Not happening. He wants to cool off, he can go take a cold shower. Keep your damn shirt on," I stuck a finger at Nick.

Nick scratched his chin, then his eyebrows went up. "What about my pants?"

"Motherfucker—"

"Got shorts on underneath, bro, chill."

"Then why the hell even ask me?!"

Julien snorted, then laughed. "You guys are never gonna get three done if you keep bickering like an old married couple."

"Bruh," Nick said.

I looked back to the row of doghouses taking up the back of what was once Sae's room. "Jules, you went to college, right?"

"Yeah?"

"They teach you to count in college?"

Julien did a double-take, glancing back over the row of doghouses and blinking. "Oh no. I am *gone.*"

"Leave the man alone, Matt. Might be seeing single, but he's also making history." Nick scooped up the fallen two-by-four and stuck it out to Julien, who took it and fastened it to an ever-growing structure with expert precision.

"That's way too easy for you," I said, openly envious.

"Welp." Julien grunted, tightening a screw. "Helps that I've made a few treehouses in my time. Similar concept, different setting."

"It's shaking a lot," Tara called down. "If I get tragically paralyzed from installing an intercom into a prototype before it's even built, I'm suing you, Julien."

"I promise it's stable!" Julien replied, giving the center pylon a quick shake, grimacing as Tara yelped, then adding on another supporting beam.

Nick snorted. "Don't worry, Tara. If that happens, Matt'll call a bunch of friends over, get everyone high, and remodel the entire apartment to be wheelchair friendly."

"Isn't it already wheelchair friendly?" Iris signed, showing a ghost of a smile.

"It is. And bitch, this was your idea," I snapped at Nick, turning back to Iris's work after warning Tara to be careful.

"Like I said it, sure, then you deadass started buying shit wholesale off the marketplace."

"Yeah, yeah, yeah."

There was a knock. We'd closed the room off for the dogs' safety more than anything else. "Boys? We need a second opinion."

I caught Nick's eye and mouthed, "No matter how it looks, be supportive."

He mouthed something back that looked like, "I'm always supportive, you mothering bastard." Or potentially "I'm always providing motherless bastards," but I was mostly sure it was the first.

"Come in."

Charlotte threw open the door, cheeks tinged from exertion. Then she saw the state of the room and her eyes widened. "Holy shit, you guys work fast."

"Kinsley still doing okay?" I asked.

"Yup." Charlotte nodded. "Still sleeping like a rock in the living room, but she only had a bite. Breathing and pulse are normal. She'll sleep it off."

"And be cranky she missed the party," Nick laughed.

Charlotte turned to the tall, meandering spiral structure Julien had already started putting rails on. "Uh, Julien? What is that?"

"Greetings, Charlotte," Julien said, his voice over-serious and seductive. "What you see before you is the result of what happens when three brave, upstanding men of the Court—and one little sister—identify a grave injustice."

"Jules, you are gone," Charlotte put a hand over her mouth, trying not to laugh.

"That's what he said," Nick added helpfully.

Julien shook his head vehemently, squaring his stance and putting a hand to his chest. "What is gone, Charlotte, are the hopes and dreams of the canine ancestors that came before. We domesticated them. Then betrayed them. And today, we will finally right that wrong. No longer will dogs be forced to observe the bourgeoise trappings of their feline antagonists with envy. No longer will Fido, or Prince, or Wheatley live out their days in the dust, deprived of any hint of altitude or verticality."

"Really stirring for the subject matter," I noted dryly.

"Kinda tearing up a little," Nick agreed.

Julian grinned and extended his arm toward the structure, then finished in a solemn voice. "I present to you the first ever canine arboreal relaxation station. The Dog-Tree."

"Here, here!" Nick raised his giant water bottle.

"It's looking great, Jules, it really is," Charlotte bit her lip.

"Everything alright?" I asked, fighting a sudden upsurge of paranoia.

"Right. Sorry, you said you needed an opinion," Julien said, dropping the noble prince act.

"We really fucking do," Sae's voice announced from outside the room. Trying for the same harshness as usual, but overcompensating. In my addled state, I might have been overthinking it, but Sae sounded terrified.

Charlotte's smile drooped a bit. "Keep in mind we're not done. This is like the sketch before we fill everything else in. It might have been smarter to wait until I was no longer... ahem... chemically altered but..."

"She insisted," Nick said, waving the worry away. "It's alright. No worries. This is a place for friends. Judgment-free zone. Right?" He looked at me.

"Judgment is suspended until everyone is sober," I agreed. "Come on, Sae, let's see it."

"Bring her in, bring her in, bring her—Jesus Christ," Nick's jaw dropped as a beautiful stranger walked around the door frame. Someone who looked so completely different from either version of Sae I knew that my mind was having trouble keeping up.

The stranger scowled and immediately turned around and walked out.

"No, Sae, that was a good Jesus Christ," I raised my voice, glaring at Nick—who still looked completely flabbergasted.

Far more tentative than before, Sae returned with her arms crossed. As long as I'd known her, she'd always been eye-catching, but this was something else. From the neck up, the insectile features were entirely gone. Thick, shining hair framed full lips, high cheekbones, and a slender jaw line, the compound eyes she'd loathed traded for a dark, captivating stare.

"Hot-diggity-damn," Nick whispered.

"She looks like a celebrity," Iris signed, and even as I conveyed it out loud, I had to agree. Sae gave Iris an appreciative smile before she frowned again.

"Girl. You look stunning," Tara added, looking down from her perch on the dog-tree.

Sae cleared her throat, then looked away and cleared it again. "You're all being very sweet and supportive. And as much as part of me has wanted that sort of support my entire life, I kinda need the cold bastard take." She looked to me expectantly. "Give it to me straight."

"Uh. You sure?"

"Yeah," Sae nodded.

"Well..." I hedged, trying to strike the balance between support and what she was asking for. "It's hard to say. You look kind of perfect? Maybe—"

"Don't you dare say too perfect," Tara called down.

"She asked for the cold bastard take, *babe.*"

"I don't care, *sweetheart.*"

"No, it's fine," Sae shook her head, then confirmed. "Too perfect?"

I scratched my head. "Remember who you're talking to and take this with a grain of salt. But the way I've always seen it, there's like—shit, I need a whiteboard."

"No whiteboards," Nick and Sae said simultaneously.

"It's better as a visual," I argued.

There was a rustle as Iris fished around in her backpack, pausing to sign to me. "I've got art pencils and a sketchpad. Would that help?"

"Yes, you're a godsend," I took the sketchbook, flipped to an empty page, and began to draw. "Our X-axis is attractiveness. Far left is least attractive, far right is most attractive." I drew a line, then scrawled a bell curve on top of it, then drew another vertical line. "And this, our y-factor, is approachability. From a psychological standpoint—and there are multiple studies I'm drawing on here—the more attractive you are, the more benefit there is. People automatically assume you're smart, lend more credence to what you say, and are more likely to seek you out and approach you." I turned the sketch and pointed to the above-average section of the bell curve. "At least until some-where around here. Once you get above this area, people get kind of weird. Intimidated. They're far more likely to assume you're someone important, or full of herself, or whatever. Result being, they're more likely to dodge you and make assumptions."

"Yeah... yeah. That kind of tracks," Tara admitted.

Sae snatched the sketchbook from me and studied the scrawlings. "Asked for the cold-bastard take, not the nerd-take, but I'm picking up what you're putting down."

"Alternatively, they'll just get confused and ask for an autograph. Black Pink in your areaaaa," Nick drew the last word out, immediately cut off by a collective groan. "What?"

Julien shook his head.

"Nick, I don't care how high you are, you can't say that," I moaned.

"Huh?" Nick scanned the room with an expression of betrayal. "Wait—"

"That's racist," Iris signed sternly.

"Iris says you're racist."

"I'm not—It's not like that—Sae, I can't think when you're mean-mugging me with that face," Nick backed away.

"What is it like then, Nick?" Sae crossed her arms, tapping a foot expectantly.

"It wasn't a stereotype, I was being specific!" Nick blinked rapidly. "She looks like Jisoo from Blackpink!"

"Oh shit," Charlotte paced in front, looking at Sae's face from all angles. "You kind of do." Alarm came through in her voice. "No. Actually, it's almost one to one. Sae, swear to god I didn't do that on purpose. Don't know how it happened, but I'm really not like that."

Chaos reigned, with Nick and Charlotte both taking very different approaches to underlining how not-racist they were, while Julien and Tara formed Switzerland, observing from the sidelines and wisely staying out of the crossfire.

"You idiots," I laid back on the floor and put my hands on my face. "No one is racist. There's a thing—"

"A thing, Helpline?" I could almost feel her glare through my hands.

"Yes, Sae, I'm fucking impaired for the first time since middle-school and can't think of the name, cut me a break. But it happens with police composite sketches where a person is described to a sketch artist and the result ends up resembling a celebrity."

"Maybe you should make another graph."

"Fuck you."

Julien coughed. Almost laughed, then coughed again to cover it. "Uh, just piping in as a totally neutral and politically correct party to say that the term Matt's forgetting is celebrity resemblance bias."

"Yes! Exactly," I pointed at him.

"So it's an actual thing?" Sae asked.

Julien nodded. "And while it does happen with sketches, it also happens with plastic surgery. You start with attractive features—most celebrities are varying degrees of attractive, they're a presence in our lives—and that mental image becomes a source we subconsciously draw on to fill in the blanks. And Charlotte's a dyed in the wool k-pop stan."

"Juuuuules," Charlotte whined.

"Seriously? Would you rather be outed as a racist or a k-pop stan?"

Sae was about to respond when Talia came staggering in, tail tucked, almost swooning from side to side, her eyes red. "Why does my body feel so sluggish?"

"Did you sneak a taco off the tray?" Nick asked.

"No..." Talia lied.

Julien stumbled backward. "Holy shit, a talking dog!"
God dammit.

"What did you call me?" Talia growled deep in her throat.

Sae put a hand to her face. "Alright, now that I'm mad and apparently have no one to be mad at, I'm gonna let you all explain that." She put a hand palm out toward Talia in a circular gesture, then tugged at Charlotte's sleeve, clearly moving on from the awkwardness. "Ready to go back to the drawing board?"

"Yeah." Charlotte looked down at Talia, did something that landed somewhere between a bow and curtsy, then stage-whispered to Julien, "Fill me in later."

Relief flooded Charlotte's features as the two departed and awkwardly reintroduced Talia as Nick's summon and resumed work on the furnishings. Talia scanned the evolving room, emanating a mix of grumpiness and disdain. "For all the time I've been a summon, Nick has never built *me* a house."

Nick stumbled, no doubt unhappy that he was catching another stray until he realized Talia wasn't actually talking to him and resumed his business.

I slapped the top of the closest structure. "Talia. This is a doghouse. For dogs. I'm sure *Nick* thought about it and ended up assuming if he did build you a house in which dogs are housed, you'd take it as a grave insult."

"Can you guys, like, stop saying my name that way? Gonna give me a coronary," Nick complained.

Talia ignored him and sniffed the wool, then entered the house and laid down in it. "Regardless of who it's meant for, it's a very nice house." She turned her head, all side-eye.

I put my hands on my hips and sighed, glancing at Iris. "Up for building a fourth?"

"Yeah," Iris nodded, just looking happy to be needed. "Small structures don't take much out of me. It's not a bother."

"It should be bigger than the others so those cheerful idiots don't get any ideas," Talia instructed.

"Such a choosing beggar," I rolled my eyes.

"Wait!" Tara exclaimed. She was stretched out supine on the upper level of the dog-tree, head hanging upside down off the platform, hair streaming straight down. "Talia's a wolf.

What if we did something a similar size to the rest but made it out of stone instead, and made it look kind of natural-like?"

"Like a summer-home cave, since she's over here all the time?" I asked.

"Yes. I like it. That human is wise," Talia acknowledged and put her head down, nestling into the vicuna.

Beside me Iris was already drawing, creativity apparently reinvigorated by the idea of doing something with a more natural bent.

A vibration rattled through the floorboards, emanating three times before it faded, any accompanying noise squelched by the music and Tara's voice. "Did someone knock?"

Tara cocked her head. "Not that I heard."

"Matt!" Someone screamed from the other side of the door. I jumped to my feet and raced to the living room, only for something to slam into me full force. Kinsley grabbed me and shook me, eyes wide in panic. "Matt we're fucked."

"Breathe, Kinsley," I brushed aside her matted hair and pressed the back of my hand to her forehead. She felt clammy, but not so hot it was concerning. "Who was at the door? And why are we fucked?"

"Because we're all high as balls and the feds are here!" Kinsley hissed.

CHAPTER FORTY-EIGHT

There were worse possibilities for this unfortunately impaired moment in time. An incursion from a rival region with multiple casualties, or a sudden announcement from the Ordinator that they'd changed their minds and the Transposition started now.

Miles' presence was more like a distant third.

If I was lucid, it wouldn't even rank in the top ten. But I wasn't. Even ignoring the impromptu carpentry workshop and subsequent green-lighting of the dog-tree, the fuck-up with Talia served as evidence of that. It hadn't even occurred to me that she shouldn't be speaking aloud before she gave Julien and Charlotte an existential crisis. And unlike Julian and Charlotte, Miles was a far more serious threat.

Because he was the real deal. I'd watched him pick a man apart during an interrogation, guess his age, pre-system vocation, and the exact combination of suggestions and threats necessary to break him open like a walnut, all completely cold. Perceptive, intelligent, and borderline unreadable. On a good day, locked in and focused with the proper title equipped, engaging with Miles was still dangerous. None of my subtler abilities could touch him, implying a special class he'd kept painstakingly close to the vest.

To make matters worse, the voices in my head had been uncharacteristically quiet ever since the accidental dose. A relief, but one I felt far less strongly now that I explicitly needed them.

It's fine. He's just here because I never messaged him back, or to give his regards, or because Mom is incapable of keeping anything to herself. The only reason he'll have to be suspicious is if I act guilty.

Internally, I did a double-take. Because that was my own inner voice, completely unfiltered for the first time in what felt like forever. More confirmation that I was flying blind. I stepped away from the peephole and pitched my voice low, speaking to Kinsley. It threw me off for a second because she'd moved, taking cover behind the counter and peeking out, her pupils blown. "Go in the dogs' room with the others. Turn the music down and tell everyone to sit tight."

"The dogs have an entire room now?" Kinsley hissed.

"It's not like anyone's—that really what we want to focus on at the moment?"

"No. Fine. But, Matt, you're not gonna let him in, right?"

"Relax. It's Miles. He won't stay long."

Unhappily, Kinsley crouch-walked from cover to cover, making her way to the hallway and sneaking down it.

"Kinsley," I called after her. "Other way."

Kinsley swore, surveyed her surroundings, then for some undefinable reason, flipped me the bird.

"What are you going to tell them?" I asked, trying to remind her.

She thought for what felt like a long time. "To sit down and turn the music tight."

"Great. Perfect."

Once she was gone and I'd shot a message to Charlotte

telling her and Sae to lay low, I braced myself and opened the door. "Miles."

"Happy gettin-old-day, slugger." Miles grinned crookedly. There was a dark-green bottle beneath his arm with golden foil over the top. An open-navy blazer revealed an old Metallica t-shirt tucked into a worn pair of jeans. In a way, it was odd how normal he looked, when he wasn't clad head-to-toe in system attire or business casual.

"Thanks. All quiet on the western front?"

"Mostly," Miles confirmed. Then the smile faded as he looked past me into the dark living room. "Looks like the party died. Everything alright?"

There goes any chance of a quick visit.

"Yeah. Just moved to the back, we've been working on a couple side projects. Come in." I waved him inside and flicked on the light, going to the kitchen and rifling through the fridge. "Uh. Someone made a giant pitcher of lemonade, there's beer—the cheap shit Nick likes, not-coke, and coffee."

"Not to mention tacos and dessert." Miles picked up one of the now-cold brownies up to his nose and breathed deeply. A second later, his brow furrowed and he looked at me quizzically. "Damn. If I knew you were cutting loose, I would have brought something other than sparkling grape juice."

Briefly, because I wasn't confident in my ability to hold things together without creating the sort of suspicion more likely to make Miles look closer, I gave him the rundown on the oil mixup. In the old world, this was perhaps the stupidest thing I could have done. A cop would see it as an admission of guilt, and a fed would consider it a point of leverage. To a lesser extent the latter was still true, but with the psychopaths and necromancers running around, I figured it was better than just letting him wonder. He'd grill me for info either way. That part of his job was hard baked into his DNA.

What was less predictable was the way he laughed until his eyes were red. "And here I thought the surprise party was destined for spectacular failure."

"It's been a spectacular something," I muttered, as Miles screwed the cap off his beer and took a long pull, trying not to chuckle.

"For the record," Miles pointed the top of his bottle at me. "I told her it was a terrible idea. I think everyone did. She was— privately, of course—bemoaning how 'uncooperative' your friends were."

I rubbed my face in annoyance. "Yeah. Generally it doesn't matter. Once Mom gets an idea in her head, no one gets through, and everyone who challenges her isn't being open-minded enough. At least until it all goes wrong and she runs away with her tail between her legs."

"Brutal. But I guess I can see it. That happen tonight?" Miles asked.

"After we started working on the side-projects, she made some comments that it wasn't what she'd imagined, got antagonistic, and left when no one was looking. Hasn't answered her messages since." I stopped myself suddenly, realizing I was effectively dragging my mother to the man she was dating. "Not trying to be harsh. It's not a big deal, really. Just part of recovery. Pink-clouding and whatnot."

"Guess I can stop composing this break-up message." Miles rolled his eyes. "You're not usually this transparent."

"Yeah, yeah."

Even without the snipe at the end his comment was an obvious joke, but it landed a little too close to a constant source of anxiety. Same as most addicts, my mother had a pattern. She'd get clean, commit to the process, really go all in. With every passing day, she'd grow more confident and her productivity would rise. Then almost inevitably, something would knock her down—a failed relationship, a decline email from an interview—and she'd spiral, eventually landing back at square one.

There was an awkward silence, and we both shifted uncomfortably in the lull. We were both great communicators in a crisis, far less so when there was no obvious problem to solve. Part of me was kicking myself for not asking Kinsley to pass a message to Tara, asking her to insert herself into the conversation to smooth the tension between me and Miles.

As if my thoughts were somehow manifesting reality, the dog's door cracked wide enough for me to see Kinsley's horrified expression as Tara slipped out. She'd tidied her hair before making the appearance and she flashed us both a smile as she raided the cupboard, lifting a bag of pistachios.

"Can I grab you boys anything?" she asked.

"I'm fine," I said.

"Ate on the way, but thanks," Miles answered simultaneously.

"Babe," Tara said, drawing immediate side-eye from Miles. It was the same word from earlier, but a simple alteration of inflection changed so much. Instead of sarcastic, it sounded confident and familiar. It took me a second to realize she was performing, flexing a little. She waved the bag at us. "Need to coat your stomach with something. You'll thank me later."

"Listen to the woman," Miles agreed seriously. "He who parties without eating will not enjoy the party for long, nor the day that follows."

"Confucius?"

"More like de Sade," Tara quipped.

Miles barked a laugh. "Now there's a deep cut."

Tara gave me a withering glance. "Since you're not explicitly saying no, I'm gonna take your silence as consent—"

"—Totally not problematic at all—" I interjected.

"—and fix up a plate." She gave Miles a meaningful look. "Make sure he doesn't just stare at it and actually eats?"

"Scout's honor," Miles nodded, agreeing easily. It imparted some small measure of relief that Tara didn't immediately ping Miles' radar. More like the opposite. If anything, he seemed more comfortable than he'd been before and continued to make polite conversation until the plate of leftovers was delivered and Tara returned to the dog's room, winking at me over her shoulder.

As soon as the door closed, Miles turned to me and waggled his eyebrows, absolutely radiating smugness. "Well I gotta say, kid, you really suck at introductions. How long has that been going on?"

<Jaded Eye's> voice echoed somewhere in my subconscious, dissecting Miles' sentence. I focused inward for a moment, tuning in long enough to identify the pithy quality it adopted often when it was bored and offering commentary purely to stir the pot, then tuned out.

"Sorry. Her name's Tara. And it's new," I returned neutrally. "We're still figuring it out."

"Well, figure it out quickly. I dated a few waitresses in my day, but none like that. She seems great."

"How?" I asked the air in frustration. "How the hell do you pick her out as a waitress with less than two minutes to draw from?"

"Well..." Miles shifted his head from side to side. "Could say it's the posture, the way she held the plate from the bottom and didn't struggle with the balance for a second... but I'd be lying my ass off. I've had a few work lunches downstairs."

"Right."

Suddenly, I felt foolish. And more than ready to change the subject. "Enough about me. How's everything with you and Mom? She was worried when you disappeared."

"It's been good," Miles said, putting a little too much emphasis on "been." He grimaced sheepishly. "After getting out from under some trouble, I got a little too ambitious for my own good, started talking about making things official... and uh... she was enthusiastically in favor."

It took a second to parse what he meant. They were exclusive, as far as I knew, so that meant... "Official, as in marriage?"

"Yeah." Miles put the beer to his lips and tipped it upward.

"Three wives wasn't enough?"

He coughed, almost choking as he wiped his mouth, glaring at me distastefully. "The timing had to be intentional."

"I mean, I'd be worried. Four wives is basically a harem."

"They're exes. You're not usually this 'funny' either," Miles complained. He cocked his head, considering something. "Would you?"

"Hm?"

"Be worried, if we took the next step? You've been chill until now. But I wouldn't hold it against you, given our history," Miles said, quietly waiting for my response.

It was strange to think about. Purely because of how well we knew each other and how tenuous that relationship had been. Across the collective experiences of both my identities, I'd seen Miles at his most savage, willing to say or do almost anything to accomplish his goals. On the surface, he was controlled, careful, and calculated. The only time he'd completely lost his cool was when I—through Myrddin—threatened his colleagues. Yet, when given the opportunity and a thorough dose of reasonable doubt, he'd made peace. He was socially savvy, a terrible public speaker, and a fantastic mentor. Whatever else he was, I got the sense that, more than anything, he was a protector at heart.

We've had our problems, but you've always been fair. Really, I should hate you on principle, but in a way I look up to you. It's weird to say that. My generation, most of our heroes are either fictional or dead, so really, that's not nothing. You always have your eye on the ball. Do the necessary thing even when it's hard. But you're not all rough edges. If you're wrong, you cop to it. If someone's suffering, you try to help. You're a natural leader, and the people who follow you do so out of trust. Of course I approve.

"Jesus Christ." Miles leaned all the way back in the chair until it creaked. Almost defensively, he tossed a small black box onto the table. "Was just gonna check in, drop these off, and be on my way, but, uh, you wanna get some air?"

What? Why the sudden change of...

Slowly, I put a hand to my face. "How much of that did I say out loud?"

Miles looked up thoughtfully. "From 'we've had our problems' onward."

"It's the weed talking."

Miles grinned. "Well, let the weed know that's the nicest thing anyone's said to me in years."

"Eat shit."

"Aaaand he's back."

————

A wind current cut the humidity of the midsummer air. The roof of the building, despite the bar, swimming pool, and swathe of waterproof furniture that surrounded us, was entirely abandoned. Miles' gift was a pair of aged Cuban cigars, the "real deal" I was told, repeatedly, as he cut and lit them. His second, more concerning present was a small portion of spiced rum, which I eyed with distaste.

"Relax, Mocktail. You don't have to finish it. Just sip enough to get the flavor profile. Authentic experience and all." Miles set his glass down and vaulted back over the bar, putting a hand on the small of his back and stretching before he picked it up again. We walked over to a bench near the railing that encircled the rooftop and took in the skyline. Miles tapped his glass against mine, resonating "ting" lost in the sound of ambient wind as he raised it and drank. "Puff, then sip," he told me.

Cautiously, I did so.

The result was complex, a blanket of layered richness that was difficult to pin down—vanilla, nutmeg, and cinnamon all warred for prominence, the underlying cloying taste the only point of relative consistency.

"That is way, way sweeter than I expected it to be," I said, staring down at the rum.

"Pretty good, right?" Miles pointed a finger at me, waiting for confirmation.

It was. Too rich and extravagant to enjoy more than once in a blue moon, but it really, really was. I raised my glass, letting the honeyed liquid coat my tongue.

"Did you know I'm impotent?" Miles asked.

I choked and coughed, unable to stop myself from spritzing rum all over the pavement below. "Beyond the obvious payback, that's relevant to this conversation how?"

"Everything still works. But yeah, I'm shooting blanks. Have been for thirty years. Went back a few times, and the result's always the same. Nada. Zilch."

"Still waiting for the relevance, Miles," I said again. Instead of responding, he waited for me to do the mental math. "Hold on. Are your kids adopted?"

"Some were," Miles nodded.

"So the rest..."

"'Were miracle children, god's grace, a literal one-in-a-million shot. Providence.'" He chuckled ruefully. "Ashamed to admit I actually believed my first wife when she fed me that line. The second... not so much."

"Damn."

"I had it coming," Miles worked his jaw. "Too many hours at work, too many weeks without date nights, way too many weekends spent doing nothing but vegging in front of the TV because I was too burned out to function. All the cliche cop shit. But it's a cliche for a reason."

"Not sure anyone has that coming."

"You're very supportive, under the influence." Miles eyed me, leaning out over the railing. "But save the pity. They're all my kids, and I wouldn't trade them for anything. My name's on their birth certificates. Legally, that's all that matters."

"Why wouldn't you order a paternity test?"

"Oh I did," he snorted. "More than one. Couldn't believe she'd lie to my face like that. Spent a lot of time at the gym—and in the ring—working the anger out. Took some time. After the anger was gone... guess I realized a few things. The first was that I needed to file for divorce, ASAP. The second was that I wanted to be a father. Probably most important, there was a reason it was me in the OR, not the other guy."

"You stepped up," I realized.

"Why not? By any reasonable standard, I was stable, accomplished, and motivated. Not saying it's been perfect. My eldest... reconnected with his biological father, decided he was a better fit. Calls me Miles now. Hard pill to swallow. Hard as hell, but it wasn't up to me. Just like I chose him, it was his right to choose someone else." He made a dismissive notion. "This has all been a very roundabout way of conveying that I have a lot of flexibility when it comes to acting as a parent. You don't have to worry about me elbowing in on what you've got going with Iris and Ellison." He stared out at the city blankly, breathing out cigar smoke. "You've taken care of them for a long time. And frankly, from the sound of it, done a better job than most."

I took another sip of my rum. For a moment the skyline

seemed to spin, and I closed my eyes, blinking until the nausea faded. "My... history doesn't put you off?"

"The details that came out at the panel?" Miles asked, guilt creeping into his expression.

"Yeah."

"That deadbeat," Miles said, disgust leaking into his voice, "beat his woman until she was black and blue and shot a cop. Dipshit was doomed any way you spin it. If nobody stabbed him, he would have offed himself. In the likely scenario he lacked either the wisdom or courage to off himself, he would have 'offed himself.' If somehow he didn't bite the bullet either way, the judge would have punched a one-way ticket to the needle express faster than you can say capital punishment."

"So you would have done the same?" I challenged, not entirely sure if I believed him.

"It'd be wrong to say that without being there." Miles' brow furrowed. "But I sure as hell would have looked the other way."

It's not like it was. At the beginning, he was an unknown quantity. It got worse, and for a while he was an enemy. But it's not like that anymore. We're on friendly terms with and without the mask. Myrddin helped him clear the bounty and they've been working together behind the scenes, which makes us at least a valuable asset. Maybe it's time to finally level with him.

"Close call at the tower today bothering you?" Miles asked. Like he genuinely wanted to know. Like he cared.

"Not really." My throat felt tight. Constricted.

"So, talk to me," Miles scratched his head. "Because you look miserable. Like something's eating you from the inside out. If there's anything you want to share, I'm a good listener." He scowled and puffed his cigar. "And no, this isn't fishing for intel. Believe it or not, I genuinely, authentically give a shit."

It was a perfect opening.

CHAPTER FORTY-NINE

... And when he finds out about the nursery? What will he think of me then?

A second of hesitation was all it took to rein myself in. The most concerning part of it all was that if the earlier slip hadn't happened, I might have seriously considered it. But thanks to the Talia mishap, I knew I wasn't all there. And Miles—intentionally or not—had created the perfect moment for me to confide in him. The over-share, the fact that he'd pulled back the veil on something not only personal, but deeply vulnerable and painful, made it feel wrong to hold back. But by the same token, it's exactly what I would do if I was trying to get information out of a neutral party and needed to use a light touch.

It bothered me that he was so hard to read. The fact that he was established as a great liar really worked against him here. Because it all felt genuine. Even now, as he waited for me to answer, arms crossed casually over his legs, framed by the scattered lighting of various skyline buildings behind him, there was no tell, no restrained anticipation, zero anxiety, or dubious body language.

Maybe it was real. And the fact that I'd never know for sure legitimately annoyed me. I'd been so careful until now, and if I put that in jeopardy the one time in years I cut loose a little, I could never forgive myself.

The Transposition was imminent. Nick and I were doing everything we could to stop it from happening, but even with Hastur's backing, our chances were about as good as a coin flip. I got the sense that Hastur had been on this "perfect future" kick for a while, and it'd never seemed to work out for him before. There was no reason to assume it would work now.

No matter what the details of the greater game they based it on were, the chaos of the first Transposition had been so all-encompassing it'd been far easier for the spectating gods to skirt the rules and target me more directly. Realistically, the second would be more of the same: filled with indirect (and not so indirect) attempts to get me killed and draw negative attention to my continually unwanted presence.

I was seemingly in Miles' good graces now, but that didn't mean it'd stay that way after the second Transposition. There was no telling what I'd have to do, or how the greater powers would spin those actions in the worst possible light. If for some reason that didn't happen, I'd revisit the topic then, and only then.

But now I had a problem. Because sidestepping this or changing the subject would be the worst possible call. Almost worse than telling him directly. Miles wasn't stupid. He'd already called me out for acting strange, considering the circumstances. If I didn't give him something he'd draw his own conclusions, if he hadn't already. The better option was to pivot. It had to be something I felt genuine guilt over, so I couldn't just make something up on the fly either. Especially in my state, he'd read anything fabricated as false. It had to come from the heart.

And I was terrible at from the heart.

I cleared my throat, then cleared it again. "My sister's deaf."

"I'd put that together," Miles said, his expression relaxing slightly. While clearly puzzled, he also almost looked relieved.

"It's never been a problem. Hell, learning sign language might've been the smartest thing we ever did."

"Being able to communicate silently at a moment's notice? I can see the benefits."

"Iris couldn't." I shook my head. "Spent years working with her, hammering self-acceptance, making damn sure she never felt like an inconvenience... but I always had the sense she never fully bought in."

A shadow crossed Miles' face. "When you're a kid, everything that makes you different from others is seen as negative. It takes a lot of growing up before you're able to see those differences as advantages. Other kids really don't help."

"No, they don't. Little shits."

I rubbed my eyes, trying to force the jumble of feelings and memories into a coherent thought. "Point is, I've spent years trying to communicate to Iris that her disability isn't a problem. That it doesn't make her a lesser person, and that anyone who makes her feel like an outcast or unworthy because of it can go pound sand. It doesn't need to be fixed."

"This have something to do with that necromancer attack?" Miles asked, reading between the lines.

"In part. This is the other half. It fell into my lap a while ago, Kinsley's people just identified it." My hand went to my inventory, and I hesitated before finally fishing out the radiant golden potion and passing it to him. Miles took it, studying the newly revealed description, his jaw slackening the more he read.

"Holy shit," Miles murmured. He peered up at me after a moment. "You've been keeping this under wraps, right? No way you haven't."

"Yeah."

"This is big enough that I'm gonna need specifics. Who knows, exactly?" he pushed, more insistent.

"Me and Kinsley. A few researchers on her science team, well-compensated to be discreet."

"Not good enough. Anyone in the dome with a functioning head on their shoulders would be frothing rabid to get their hands on this. Assume there's already a leak." Miles left the cigar in his mouth, puffing idly as he held the potion up to the light and rotated it. "Hell, if this were up for grabs I'd do a lot to lock it down, just for the insurance policy." He paused, peered at me. "You're clever enough to put together that you either need to bury this so deep that no one could possibly find it, or it needs to be used. Immediately. Too great a risk otherwise."

"Rationally, yes."

He held the potion out to me, wiggling it by the top. "Yet here it is. Why?"

When I spoke, it was difficult. Painful. "Iris almost died during the attack. The big fucker, the one that kept hounding us down, targeted her before I even realized anything was happening."

"That much I'm familiar with. We've been looking into it from our side, but it's a slow process. A lot of potential degenerates in the mix," Miles nodded along.

"There was this moment—she was on the playground, just being a kid again for the first time in forever, and I saw the shadow, and there was just... nothing I could do. No surfaces that I could bang on that she'd feel the vibration from, no way to catch her attention and sign a warning. Nothing."

"It was that close?"

"A hair's width. Ever since, all I can think of is how if she could hear, I could have warned her so much earlier. It feels horrible to think along those lines, but I can't help it. The obvious answer is to give her the potion and be done with it. But..."

"You're worried about the message," Miles filled in. "That by 'fixing' the problem, you'd basically be confirming what she's always believed to be true."

"Exactly."

There was a rash of sirens below, a line of police cars and firetrucks traveling down the long city road that led to the interstate. We both watched them shrink into the distance and Miles pulled up his UI, skimming through his messages. He squinted. "Looks like my surprisingly relaxing evening is coming to an abrupt end."

"Necromancer?"

"I wish," Miles said, stubbing out his cigar and placing it on the ashtray. "Lots of people cracking because of the countdown. There's some pyro freak in the center regions, losing his shit, taking the bounty as a challenge."

"Need a hand?"

"Nah. Even if you were clear headed, me and the reformed DPD can handle one moron with a god complex. Small potatoes. Probably won't even wake Hawkins up for it. She's handled the last few." He stood and stretched, scowling at something in the contents of the message before he stuck his hands in his pockets and looked at me. "As far as Iris goes? I wish I could tell you the right call, but I can't. No one can. All the history's on your end, and inevitably I'd be speaking from ignorance. But I'll leave you with a question."

"Shoot."

"Are you the same person you were when all this shit started?"

"No."

"Be precise."

I thought about it. "Because the world was changing, and I

chose to change with it. Mentality first, system abilities and augmentations later. Anything that could give me an advantage."

"Body and mind, right?"

"Yeah."

"Why even do that in the first place? There was nothing wrong with you, before. As much as you might believe otherwise, you were a relatively normal kid, forced to grow up in less-than-ideal circumstances. Why were you so hellbent on using the system to fix yourself?"

"It had nothing to do with fixing anything," I argued, annoyed by his wording. "It had everything to do with power and potential. I'd be stupid to just ignore an avenue of advancement, knowing that other people can and will. Refusing it outright out of paranoia or principle would have put me at a profound disadvantage—ah."

Miles nodded slowly, letting the meaning sink in. "It's one thing to make the best of a difficult situation. It's another entirely to continue to do so and ignore an obvious solution because there's something about it you find distasteful." He studied the concrete, scuffing at something with his dress shoe. "That's the thing about kids. Try too hard to insulate them from everything that could hurt them, they'll act out and sneak around. Try too little, and the result is the same. But even if you strike the perfect balance, you can't shelter them forever. From the world or their choices. A day will come when they bite off more than they can chew, talk to the wrong person, or hell, just happen to be in the right place at the wrong time. And when that day comes, you have to hope—and pray to god, or Allah, or the devil, whoever the hell you pray to —that you've done everything possible to prepare them for it. And if you haven't?"

For just a moment, the confident, easy-going demeanor

disappeared, along with any trace of a smile. "Well, you get to live with that."

Seconds passed, whatever was left unsaid thick enough that I could almost feel it. I almost asked before Miles' mask slid back into place. "Uh. Anyway, whatever you do with that thing? Do it soon. And for chrissakes, kid, don't keep it on you. You're a heist waiting to happen."

"Got it." I waved goodbye as he left in a hurry, descending footsteps echoing down the stairway.

I knew what I wanted to do. My conversation with Miles had only reinforced it. The only variable that remained was whether Sae would see it that way.

CHAPTER FIFTY

I returned to my suite, surprised to find it nearly as dark as it was before the party. As my eyes adjusted, I spotted Nick's silhouette, barefoot, shirtless, and passed out on the far end of the long couch with a pillow over his face, flanked on either side by two of the dogs—who notably, were ignoring their ridiculously extravagant domiciles in favor of smothering Nick.

Warm light from the end table lamp illuminated Sae's face. Not the face I'd grown accustomed to seeing, but her old one, finally free of the alterations that plagued her. It sort of shook me, seeing her like that. She'd kept most of her original features, save a few cosmetic tweaks for vanity.

"Damn," I said aloud. Initial snafu aside, Charlotte did great work.

Sae put a finger to her lips, her movement and expression serene. I looked down and saw Iris, bundled up in a blanket, eyes tightly shut as she dozed, head on Sae's lap.

I heel-toe walked to the couch so the vibrations of my footfalls wouldn't be disruptive and sat down carefully, trying not to jostle them. "What, I leave for ten minutes and the party dies?"

"Try two hours, Helpline," Sae pointed to the digital clock on the stove that read 3:01.

It'd been longer than I thought. I winced. As much as I'd not been in the mood for company, some part of me regretted abandoning my guests. "Anyone still here?"

"That idiot," Sae pointed to Nick. "Kinsley passed out in one of the dog beds. But Julien and Charlotte called someone to take them home, Tara too."

"How were they, when they left?" I asked.

Sae made a dismissive gesture. "The hobbit made sure everyone knew you were 'dealing with a matter of great importance,' and they genuinely seemed like they had a great time. Just got tired is all. Was gonna see myself out too—not really the last person at the party kind of girl—then the other hobbit fell asleep on me."

"I can take her."

"She's fine for now," Sae ran her fingers through Iris's curls, "Way I see it, I owe Iris a lot. The mirror doesn't lie. I looked scary as hell when I came back and she never even hesitated. Just accepted me and did whatever she could to help."

"That's Iris."

Iris moaned, grimacing as she clung to the blanket. It was a small, distressed sound, and Sae gently shook her shoulder until she roused from REM sleep, settling back down into quiet snores.

"Always have this many nightmares?" Sae asked.

I shook my head. "That's new. Ever since the attack."

"Bastards," Sae's tranquil expression soured. "I get that the strike team is temporarily retired, but..."

"You'll have the info as soon as I do," I assured her.

"And we'll go in hard?"

"Like always." I paused, wanting to comment more on her

appearance but not sure how to do so politely. "Are you... happy with the end result?"

"Still in shock, but over the moon really," Sae shook her head in wonder. "I'd come to terms with it. The way I looked. On some level I'd even started appreciating the benefits. Like sure, I'm a freakish monster, but I'm armored as hell with built-in defenses to match." She held a dark chitinous hand up, extending the claws on her fingertips before retracting them again. "Never been so deep in the denial sauce to actually see it as an improvement, but it's saved my life more than once. The one thing I just couldn't take without getting nauseous—the face—is gone. As long as Charlotte's around, anyway."

"For the record, I never thought you looked like a freakish monster."

"Yeah, yeah," Sae gave me a playful shove.

"There's something I need to talk to you about. Something we probably should have talked about earlier, but there just wasn't time."

"Kind of scary, but go ahead."

I breathed in deeply and began. It helped that this was mostly familiar ground. I'd already told Sae about Hastur's pitch, along with the at-the-time unidentified potion and promise of an eventual second. Now it was just a matter of filling in the blanks. Throughout the retelling, Sae was uncharacteristically silent, absorbing the information stoically. It was only near the end that she finally interrupted, revealing a growing annoyance. "Helpline, can we skip to the part where you explain how this is all a bad thing? Getting tired of waiting for the other shoe to drop."

Whatever reaction I'd expected, that wasn't it. I blinked. "That... is the bad part. I only have one, and Hastur's stringing me along for the second."

"Okay..." Sae stared at me with growing disgust. "Please tell me this isn't you struggling with whether to give the first one to your sister or take it yourself."

"No—"

"Because no one deserves it more than her," Sae growled, surprisingly heated. "Putting aside the fact that she's your sister and this would significantly improve her chances of survival right before an event that will absolutely put her in jeopardy if it happens, she's not like us."

"Just wait—what's that supposed to mean?" I asked, getting a bit irritated at how dismissive the last comment sounded.

"Try looking around?" Sae said, equally annoyed. "I have a lot of respect for you, Matt, but at least a part of the reason we work so well together is because we're the same. We're both great at breaking things, picking people apart, being as brutal as necessary to get the job done. If the last month has proven anything, it's that."

"Not everything was a bloodbath," I hissed and leaned back on the couch, white leather creaking beneath me. "We showed mercy when we could."

"Yeah, I'm sure Buzzcut and the rest of targets you whisked away to 'interrogate further' are all living happily on the farm upstate," Sae rolled her eyes.

Not exactly.

She continued without waiting for a response. "It doesn't make any difference to me. As far as I'm concerned, every member of the Order who wasn't Shanghai'd into the Court is scum fully deserving of whatever bad shit comes their way. But there lies my point." She jostled Iris gently, stirring her from another nightmare, waiting for a few seconds until she snored again. "Your sister's a builder, in a time people actually trying to rebuild shit to make life better and not as some method of raking in Selve are hard to come by. Just look at the hospital. We need people like her. And we need them to survive whatever's coming."

"Yeah..." I agreed, suddenly at a loss for words. Hearing not one, but several of the arguments I'd intended to make come out of Sae's mouth because of the misunderstanding.

"So you agree."

I snorted. "If I say another goddamn word without clearing this up, you're going to actually hate me."

"Clearing what up?"

"Read the description again, Sae." This time I handed her the potion. She seemed as irritated with the obliqueness as always, but as she scanned it again, the sense of irritation faded.

<Item Description: The residual tears of a false god, collected from her final prison in the aftermath of a failed insurrection. A universal palliative. Cures all lingering status effects, diseases, pre-existing injuries, impairments, or defects regardless of age, mental conditions, and unwanted alterations, so long as the recipient is still alive. Once imbibed, the secondary boon—
Asura's Boon—is received.**>**

<Asura's Boon: Once this boon is attained, the recipient claims an aspect of the divine. Base Kit Immunity to all curses, status effects, and diseases is exponentially bolstered. Resistance to all damage types is amplified. Existing lifespan is extended by a magnitude of five. Permanent XP multiplier of 2x. Additional class utility for specific classes. Divine Aspect.**>**

"Oh," Sae said.

"Yeah."

"You... were never considering using it," Sae groaned.

"Not for a minute."

Then her brow furrowed and she looked up at me in shock. "Wait—was this some dark psych setup to get me to argue against myself?"

"Jesus. Not even a little. It caught me completely off guard, and someone decided to lay into me before I could correct the assumption. You already said a lot of the things I was planning to point out. The only reason I was being circumspect at all was to present all the information and let you decide." I eyed the potion, feeling some degree of relief now that it was literally out of my hands. "As much as it might seem otherwise, I don't actually know how you're doing. You mask too well, and tempting as it is to pry, I generally resist temptation."

"Generally?" Sae raised an eyebrow.

"Generally," I reiterated. "But how you're handling things? How bearable or unbearable each day is? There's only one person who can really know that."

Her mouth pressed tightly together. "What happened in the tunnel wasn't your fault. My dumbass ran away into the worst possible place. I panicked. Big whoop, shit happens. The only reason I'm even here is because you came back for me and fished me out of the dark. You've already helped plenty. So why do you keep trying to make it your problem?"

I thought back to the early days, from the first meeting at the Turkish coffee place onward. Casting spells around Nick's backyard, strategizing against monsters, discussing system abilities and possible synergies. It felt like decades ago, even though in reality it was less than a year.

"Just feel really bad for breaking your nose."

Carefully, so as not to wake my sister, Sae cocked her arm and slugged me hard enough to leave a bruise. I stifled a laugh. "Ow."

"Real answers only."

"Dunno, it's... hard to explain." I breathed out, feeling more tapped out and exhausted with every exhale. The events of the day and the substances of the evening were catching up to me. "For a cop, my dad was pretty laid-back about laying down the law with us. Not really the authoritarian type. With one exception."

"Wear a condom?" Sae guessed.

"Campfire rules," I corrected. "Leave it better than how you found it." Despite myself, I laughed. "Real stickler for it too. Ellison would bitch about how we always ended up cleaning up other people's trash—other campers who hadn't followed the code—and my dad would say, 'remind me what the definition of better is, son?'—and Ellison would just grumble and go back to filling his bag. Anyway, it stuck with me. Even after he was gone and we didn't really have time to go camping anymore."

"Don't tell me you were one of those weirdos walking around a park with a bag and an extension grabber."

"Nah. It wasn't compulsive or anything. Just every once in a while, if I was somewhere scenic—"

"—like a park," Sae wiggled an eyebrow.

"Like a park," I sighed, "And there was litter or something that wasn't completely out of my way, I'd pick it up and toss it. I've never really thought of people that way. When I met you all though, I got the same feeling. As a group you had this bond, this feeling of closeness and camaraderie that was just foreign to me. Freaked me out a little. Both because it was foreign, and I didn't want to somehow mess it up."

"Please."

"Like you said, I break things. And there was so much potential. I was still up my own ass about compartmentalizing, doing it all on my own, so the plan was always to leave eventually. Help Nick clean up the trouble he was in and move on to whatever was next."

"Campfire rules," Sae said.

"Exactly," I said, reaching down to tuck a stray tuft of hair behind my sister's ear. "But things didn't go as planned. On multiple levels. Maybe it's not possible anymore, but I guess in some ways I'm still stuck there, trying to make sure everyone lands okay before my luck runs out and someone punches my ticket. Or I end up crossing lines that can't be uncrossed and you need to walk away."

Sae raised her fist and I tensed, waiting for the hit. Instead, she bumped it against my shoulder, gently. "For the record, asshole? If you died? My life would be considerably worse. So if you're stupid enough to go get yourself killed, take that into the afterlife."

"Ah, existential emotional blackmail, the rarest variation."

"Could have just skipped all that and said 'because we're friends.' Hell's the matter with you?" The words were all bark and no bite, and after a moment Sae laid her head on my shoulder. "Maybe you somehow missed this, or need to be reminded, so let me make it clear. You've gone to bat for me more than any friend ever has. I've seen you do some really, really dark shit, and I'm still here. We're ride or die, Helpline. Nothing's gonna make me walk away." She cracked an eye and looked up at me. "And of course we give your sister the potion, headass. Even if you had both right now, I'm not sure I'd take mine."

"Why?"

"Because we're days away from a potential apocalyptic throw-down, and I don't want to go into that wobbling around, trying to get comfortable in my own much-more-cozy but much-less-resilient skin."

That... was pretty well reasoned, now that I thought about it. More to the point, something she'd briefly touched on gave me an idea. "Do you want to?"

"Wobble around?"

"Give my sister the potion."

The eye cracked again. "For real?"

I shrugged. "In a way, you kind of already are. Don't see any reason it can't be literal. If you've got somewhere to be in the morning, we can wake her up now. Pretty sure she'll understand."

"Morning's good. Close to morning as we manage, anyway," Sae readjusted, getting comfortable. "Tinnitus is a bitch. Put some music on?"

"Sure," I picked up the remote. "Only have what was already in the CD player."

"What's a CD?"

"Ignoring that. Your options are oldies, older oldies, and the secret third option."

"If you say oldies again, I'll punch you."

"So one note," I rolled my eyes.

"Just like your music collection. Pick whatever, I don't care."

The guitar intro to "California Dreamin'" began to trickle from the speakers and I set the remote down. As much as it was clearly platonic, this was more physical contact than I was used to. Yet it wasn't all bad. Somehow it felt comfortable, warm, being surrounded by people I cared about, accompanied by a feeling I couldn't quite recognize. The TV idle screen read five-nineteen, the last vestiges of consciousness unspooling before I realized what it was.

Peace. So complete and all-encompassing that **<Jaded Eye's>** voice was little more than a distant echo in my mind.

What happened the last time you felt safe?

CHAPTER FIFTY-ONE

A whirring grind stirred me to consciousness, bright over-saturated light blinding me and rendering my greater surroundings indecipherable. Composite plastic scratched paint as the electric outlet's faceplate dropped from where it was previously mounted, screw coming loose and nestling somewhere deep in the plush carpet.

"Who's still doing construction?" a small voice moaned from beneath a pile of blankets in the nearby bed.

"Uh." That was as far as I got before realizing that the answer was probably me. There was a drill in my hand, and below the bedside end table was another dismantled outlet, components arranged next to it as if someone had planned to put it back together only to get distracted halfway through. "Don't worry about it."

"Is this what a hangover feels like?" Kinsley asked, her small muffled voice ragged and uncomfortable.

"Probably."

"People sign up for this?" she croaked.

"I think it's the before part they're after."

"I don't even remember the before part!"

"You didn't miss much. I'll close the curtains, just try to sleep it off."

"Kay." There was a grunt as Kinsley rolled over and wedged herself further into the covers, breath regulating, then becoming a quiet snore.

On some level, I had to agree. Beyond the cooking oil mishap I'd barely drank, and between the pounding in my head and the warped fishbowl visual perspective, the punishment didn't feel at all proportional to the crime.

Something clattered in the kitchen, unsettling me more than it should have. For better and worse—mainly worse—I remembered the previous night's proceedings with stark clarity, all the way through to crashing out on the couch. Objectively, I knew there were other people here. Kinsley of course, and Nick and Sae were probably still around. But knowing did nothing for the thick knot of anxiety lodged in my chest.

Just gonna confirm.

I pushed the cracked door open with my foot and the intense ambient light magnified, washing everything out.

"Heads up, here he comes again." I made out Sae's silhouette, still lounging on the couch we'd fallen asleep on. Further back, there was a clatter as a blurry outline of Nick dropped what he was doing, picked up a metallic object, and pointed it at me.

"No toaster," Nick said, jabbing the—spatula, maybe—toward me. From the combined gesture and tone I got that it was a warning, but the meaning was almost impossible to parse. Behind him, my toaster was an unfocused blob of silver on the counter.

"Okay... didn't have any plans for it, but sure. And are you seriously wearing an apron?" I asked.

He was. A pink lacy apron that read "Kiss the Chef" in red print across the front, embroidered with a heart. Thankfully fully clothed beneath. Besides Charlotte, who kept putting the brownies away like they were nothing all night, Nick had partaken the most and was seemingly affected so little by the aftermath that he'd gotten up before everyone else and started cooking breakfast.

"'Doesn't have any plans, he says,'" Nick stabbed the spatula at me. "Like he hasn't been stalking it like bizarro Bob the Builder."

"Matt, you with us? Like, actually lucid?" Sae observed, slouched low on the couch where the backing shielded her from the late morning light.

"Guess I was sleepwalking?" I asked, still trying to catch up.

They both nodded, and Nick went back to his cooking, hovering over it.

"Mumbled for us to fuck off when we tried to get your attention. Look around," Sae said.

Once more, I tried to wipe the sleep from my eyes. It worked better this time, and though my perspective was still warped, I could make out far more detail. Every electrical outlet had suffered the same fate as the ones in the guest room. From the TV stand to the bookshelves, everything with a door or latch had been opened, interior contents either removed or rearranged in a hurry. Three metal vent covers had been hastily stacked on the coffee table, beside five smoke detectors that were gutted, stripped down to their internal circuitry, nine-volt batteries arranged next to them.

"The hell?" I asked no one in particular.

"There's a couple working theories," Nick announced, skillet sizzling as he chased what smelled like eggs around with the spatula. "Either your subconscious and impaired mind went into loot goblin mode and started taking this place apart the same way we handle a dungeon if we're being thorough—"

"—or you were looking for bugs," Sae provided dryly.

The latter made far more sense, given the feeling I'd had from the moment I'd woken, and the areas I'd apparently focused on. On some level, I understood. Because as I'd been replaying it in my mind, it was obvious that I had fucked up. From the unfortunate surprise to the invitation from Miles, I'd mostly just been playing the cards that were dealt. But accepting that invitation and subsequently leaving Julien and Charlotte unattended created a blind spot that was entirely through human error.

Should have asked them to leave earlier, idiot.

<Jaded Eye's> voice sounded even more edgy than usual, as if somehow sentient and unhappy with its earlier suppression. I wondered, grumpily, if this was the result of some sort of interaction between the party favors, my title, and **<Vindictive>**. There were aspects of that theory that didn't track, of course. But it was at least a partial explanation for the lapse in time, which was better than none.

"Obviously, we were all kind of blasted, but did–"

Sae interrupted impatiently. "Either Nick or I had eyes on the Court people most of the evening. Almost the whole time. Charlotte took a couple breaks from working on me to use the bathroom, but not often. The toilet flushed both times, hands were damp when she came back."

"Jules was just vibing all night," Nick agreed, portioning the scrambled eggs and bacon onto plates and serving up coffee. "Followed me around after you ditched us for the clandestine rendezvous. Kept that up until they called it."

"I asked this earlier," I realized.

"In a dryer, more zombie-ish fashion, yeah. Side note, what

did Miles want?" Sae asked, peering over the blanket. "Anything
we need to worry about?"

"Other than asking perfunctory permission to marry my
mother? Nothing, really. I think we're clear." There was an
internal prodding from **<Jaded Eye>**, almost passive-aggres-
sively drawing attention to the fact that I was missing something without spelling out what it was. It took a full second to
put my finger on it. "What about Tara?"

Sae scoffed and pulled the blanket overhead, emerging
moments later when Nick brought over the food.

"You mean your girlfriend who did nothing but help
things go smoothly and talk you up all night? Your fake girlfriend? That one?" Nick scowled at me, clearly annoyed,
shoving a plate at me before he settled down and began
to eat.

"What crawled up his ass?" I asked Sae.

"Halfway through the night, he decided the chemistry
between you both was too real to be fake. Went full degenerate
shipper until I crushed his headcanon and he's been low-key
tilted ever since," Sae complained, forking the first bite of fluffy
yellow into her mouth, wincing preemptively. She glanced over
at Nick. "What is this?"

"Ehhgs?" Nick answered, mouth completely full.

"Yeah, but it isn't terrible," Sae said, staring down at the
plate in disbelief. "It's actually kind of good."

I took a few experimental bites. Between the salt, pepper,
and something I couldn't quite put my finger on, it was
perfectly seasoned. "Sae's not wrong. Since when did you learn
to cook anything that wasn't a blackened husk?"

"Not gonna misdirect me, toaster assassin. Been dodging
your shambling ass all morning, waiting for confirmation. Is
the fake girlfriend actually fake, or is there a little somethin'
somethin' happening there?" Nick made a vague, circular

motion with his fork and stared at me with a determination that communicated he had no intention of letting this go.

"It's weird," I admitted, annoyed with how Nick seemed to hang off every word.

"Uhuh," Nick said, leaning forward.

"First of all, she's an employee. It wouldn't be appropriate."

"Totally right," Sae nodded along sarcastically. "No one in the history of humanity has ever crossed the ethical lines of dating their boss."

"Technically, Kinsley's her boss. And whose side are you on?" I glared at her.

"Mine. Obviously."

I thought about it. There was a lot I couldn't say. Partially because they were details my sober mind didn't care to share, partially because some of my observations were too personal and subsequently cruel to give voice to. Because all three of us had known someone who smiled the same way Tara did. Someone who was kind, clever, and had an eye for detail. Someone who could walk into a room and capture the hearts of everyone in it effortlessly, just by being who she was.

Someone who was gone.

"But..." Nick prompted, steepling his fingers.

"I've never seriously entertained the idea of, you know, sharing my life with someone. Part of that is an issue of domain. Isolation is how I recharge, recoup. If I don't get that time, little things that should be minor irritations become bigger problems, and after there are too many problems I end up lashing out. So the idea of someone constantly being there, sharing that space, has never appealed to me."

"And yet..." Nick raised his eyebrows.

"Tara doesn't... bother me. Like at all. There's definitely friction. We're too different for there not to be... but somehow it's not tiresome the same way it is with other people. So far, our points of conflict are productive. Beyond that, she's scary smart, somehow genuinely seems to like me despite my quirks, and is one of the most proactive people I've ever met."

"Which has all lead to the realization that..." if Nick leaned forward any further, he was going to fall off the couch.

"In some alternate universe where we actually have a chance to retire and step away from all this? I guess I could see myself settling down with someone like her as a partner."

Nick leapt to his feet, contents of his still-held plate shifting erratically as he cocked his free arm, ready to pump it.

"Hold up. That's an intentionally broad term, dumbass," Sae raised her voice, interjecting just shy of a full-blown preemptive celebration from Nick. She gave me a withering look. "For fuck's sake, stop edging him before he makes a mess."

"A partner purely in the non-romantic, tackling-life-together sense," I admitted, suppressing a laugh as Nick collapsed back onto the couch, crumpled and defeated.

"But she's so hot, bro," Nick protested hoarsely.

"Such is life," I shrugged. Maybe now we could finally stop talking about it.

"No one's stopping you from dating Tara," Sae observed, growing cranky from Nick's antics.

Nick twisted in his seat to face Sae, actively horrified. "Never. I'd never date my friend's fake girlfriend. Even if she was his ex. Fake ex. Whatever."

"Because you're fucking Matt?"

"What? Weird segue, and no. Because friends don't do that to friends."

"So," Sae nodded along, tapping her lower lip with a finger. "You're saying it's possible to have a meaningful relationship and genuine connection with a person you have no intention of banging?"

Nick pinched the bridge of his nose. "Ease up, Socrates. Just seems like a waste is all."

"To you, maybe. But just because you're wired to need both doesn't mean everyone else does. Let him be who he is."

"You right. Just want my boy to be happy."

"Same," Sae squinted at me. "However it lands—even if it's messy, don't write the concept off. Every failed relationship helps clarify what you're looking for in the future."

"Thanks," I said, realizing after a moment that I truly meant it. It was an odd topic, trivial in the greater scope of everything happening around us, but the acceptance felt gratifying somehow. "But we should probably refocus on surviving the next few weeks. Other than Iris, what do we have on the docket today?"

"Tower's out," Nick shook his head. "Started blowing up both Aaron and Tyler's messages first thing this morning and got a firm negative. Aaron's game, but Tyler thinks people are still too shaken by what happened yesterday and more likely to make mistakes. Pushed, but he wouldn't budge."

"Probably the right call. But at the rate we're going, I'm not sure we'll make it," I muttered.

"Yeah. Planning to go in swinging as soon as we have the go ahead but, might need to consult with Hastur, start talking about plan B." Nick's brow furrowed. "What's, uh, happening with Iris today?"

The pillow Sae chucked at me like a throwing axe sailed harmlessly by my head. "Seriously?"

"Felt wrong to tell him until I talked to your grumpy ass. Really gonna give me shit for that?" I asked defensively, catching the second pillow thrown in response and tossing it back. It caught the air unnaturally, swooping up at the last second and clipping her chin.

"Bitch! I just got this face," Sae snapped back, real fear

flashing for a second before she covered it. "Who brings User powers to a pillow fight?"

I hadn't, had I? Subconsciously, I glanced down at the bound ring on my finger. **<The Devil's Share>** significantly reduced both the stamina costs and spin-up time of my Ordinator abilities, at the cost of giving me a permanent mental hair-trigger. There'd only been one slip up since I'd equipped it early on, and ever since it had more or less worked flawlessly. But...

"Guys, hello?" Nick looked between us blankly, still waiting for an answer.

Sae groaned in annoyance, then started to convey what the potion did and our plans for it. She'd only made it about halfway through before Nick suddenly bolted upright, his eyes wide. He hustled toward the door, stripping the apron off, tossing it aside, and pulling on his shoes. He addressed us both over his shoulder almost as an afterthought. "Text where you're going and don't start without me!"

"Nick. The first thing this little girl hears cannot be your guitar store rendition of 'Smoke on the Water.' Nick!" Sae sat up straighter and barked after him, the blanket covering her lap sliding off and unsettling my sister, who blinked awake and immediately began wiping sleep out of her eyes. But Nick was already gone, the vibration of heavy footsteps growing more distant as he jogged down the hallway.

"Might compromise with 'Stairway to Heaven,' if it comes to that," I offered, more than a little amused with how protective Sae had grown of my sister. Nick being this enthusiastic was a given, considering how long they'd known each other. He'd watched her endure a lot of the hardships. But this was new for Sae.

"That's not better," Sae argued.

"It's a little better."

"What's wrong? Why are people yelling?" Iris signed, still blinking the sleep out of her eyes. Though still tired and beleaguered, she somehow seemed less troubled than before. I chose to take it as a positive sign. Maybe something good had come out of the party after all.

"Everything's fine," I spoke aloud as I signed, mainly for Sae's benefit. "There's breakfast, and after you grab a bite we're going on a little field trip."

"To where?" Iris asked.

"You'll see."

CHAPTER FIFTY-TWO

While technically the same park Iris and I visited during the necromancer attack, the winding cement path circled a large enough area that both the hospital and tainted playground were entirely out of sight. In truth, I wasn't sure how else to do this. There were no books to reference, no studies or data to consult, forcing me to make do with forethought and common sense.

The car slowed to a halt, not-Prius's tires perfectly aligned with the fading white lines of one of the south parking lot's countless open spaces, and Sae immediately hopped out, fishing a still-groggy Kinsley out of the trunk in a flurry of bickering and excitement. In the back seat, Iris didn't move, eyes glued to the window.

I undid my belt and twisted in the driver's seat, tapping gently on her shoulder to get my sister's attention. She started, wide-eyed, panic hidden as quickly as it appeared. But Iris's curls always bounced with the slightest motion, and she couldn't quite hide the shaking.

"Talk to me," I prompted.

"Haven't... been outside in a while."

"And?"

"It scares me. In a way it always did, but it's different now."

I waited, giving myself a moment to parse. Iris hated complaining almost as much as she disliked keeping other people waiting, to the point it drove her crazy every time Ellison went on one of his stonewalling crusades. For her to be doing both? My sister wasn't just afraid. She was terrified.

"Well, I had a reason for taking us out here, but if it's too much, we can go home."

"Everyone's already here," Iris protested, scowling at the suggestion.

I snorted. "Like I care? I'll go out there right now, tell them I'm too hungover and that we need to save this for another day."

"Then they'll be mad at you," Iris shook her head. But her seatbelt was still locked firmly in place.

"They won't. Even if they were, your well-being is more important. What do I always say?"

"'If I want to take care of other people, I have to take care of myself first,'" Iris's gesture was so practiced it was almost dance-like, with a trace of mockery.

"That applies to mental health as much as it does anything else. Maybe more. If you're truly uncomfortable with something —and I'm talking about the visceral sort of discomfort where pushing through feels like breaching a physical barrier—you owe it to yourself to stop, evaluate how you're feeling and why, and if necessary, walk away. No matter who's present or what promises you've made." The sentiment felt hypocritical even as I signed it. Because as much as I believed it to be true, I rarely upheld it myself. It hadn't always been that way. For most of my teenage years, you could have put me in the hall of fame of

removing myself from a bad situation before it went radioac-
tive. At some point over the last few months, I'd lost that. These
days, I was more likely to run into a burning building than get
clear of the smoke. In some ways, it was an improvement. In
general, you tended to make a much better lasting impression
on people when you stuck with them through the hard shit, and
realistically, before I was probably too quick to drop everything.

That didn't change the fact that, eventually, I was going to
get burned.

"No. I'm going," Iris unbuckled her seatbelt and murmured
aloud. "Just wish my stupid brain wasn't so afraid."

I tapped my fingers on the dull-gray pleather of the steering
wheel before raising them to sign. "And if I told you we—me
and Sae—were about to give you a new tool that would help
you better manage that fear?"

"Like, a User ability?" Iris signed curiously, her seatbelt still
winding back into the sidewall.

"Something like that."

In retrospect, it was better to not blindside her with this.
Not in front of other people. There'd be more pressure once we
were out of the car, a greater onus to just do what the crowd
expected and less focus on what she actually wanted. I opened
my inventory and scrolled to the potion, then sent her the
description, observing her reaction in the rear-view.

Her small face cycled through several emotions in quick
succession. Puzzlement at the large block of dense system text.
Excitement for the benefits it could offer her class. Then a slow,
dawning realization as she put the pieces together. Silent tears
welled up, spilling down her cheeks, and she made a noise that
was half-cry, half-laugh. I awkwardly crawled over the console
and into the backseat to put my arm around her, surprised as
she pushed her face into my chest fiercely.

"Happy tears?" I asked, wanting to be sure.

Iris nodded frantically.

"And you know it's just because we want you to be safe, not for any other reason?"

My sister nodded again, then stopped, using what seemed like a monumental effort to temper her overflowing excitement. "It seems... really powerful. The sort of thing that could help out a lot of people. People who probably need it more than me." Her hands wavered, trembling toward the end.

"It's not that simple," I said, and when she looked to me, not understanding, I continued. "In truth, if it were up to me, it'd go to you no matter what, even if you were still just a civilian. Right or wrong, that's my bias. It's true that countless people were severely injured or maimed during the last Transposition, sustaining the sort of harm that healers can't fix. And even ignoring the unfortunate, there's plenty of powerful Users on our side who could use the benefits to push the balance of power further in our favor. If there were hundreds, I imagine there'd be a lot more discussion about who to distribute them to. But there's not hundreds." I shrugged, switching tact. "Do you know what people call you?"

"The overbearing deaf girl?" Iris tried, a fragment of genuine insecurity behind the half-joke.

"Maybe a few felt that way when you first started and the construction crews still had a stick up their ass, but when they started seeing the results, those people got quiet real fast. They call you the architect. But they talk about you like you're a traveling genie, roaming around granting wishes." I gave her a pointed look. "And it's not just people in our region who feel that way, is it?"

Iris squirmed in her seat, the picture of guilt. "Professor Gideon says I'm at the stage of development where I should take on as much practical, hands-on-work as I can, even if it's not lucrative. There's only so much to do around here, and..."

"People get your contact info through word of mouth and reach out for help, and you don't like turning them down," I finished knowingly. Beyond being Iris's employer, Kinsley and Iris were close friends, a rarity for them both. Given that, Kinsley rarely breached trust and reported what Iris confided in her, notable exception being any time Iris left the region with an armed escort. There'd been more than a dozen such trips in the last few weeks, covering everything from fixing a busted sewage line to recreating the framework, foundation, and blue-prints for several hospitals identical to the one in our regions. I'd nearly stopped her the first time and monitored from a distance every time she was in a region we didn't have an estab-lished relationship with in case the request was bait for some-thing more malevolent, but in reality, that'd been mostly unnecessary.

Because Iris didn't charge for her work. She'd graciously accept gifts, and occasionally payment if the region was wealthy and Kinsley negotiated for her, but for the most part she provided her services free of charge, taking the experience as compensation. As much as I wanted to disapprove, it was a mix of altruism and practicality that made sense. In a way it was almost safer, as along with the goodwill, there was no reason to abduct and force someone to do something they were already willing to do for free.

"I know it's stupid," Iris mumbled aloud.

"There was a time in our lives I might have agreed." I nodded, frowning. "If you reach mastery levels and never start charging for your hard work, or take on projects that potentially give other regions a tactical advantage over us, I reserve the right to give you shit for it. I probably will. But... our circum-stances have changed. Monsters and system-bullshit aside, we're not living hand-to-mouth anymore. We started the most lucrative guild in the city, have the added security of the Adventurers' Guild at our beck and call. As bad as things might seem from time to time, we're in a better place now than we ever were. Our basic needs are met. Which means you have more freedom to be who you want to be, rather than who you have to be."

"You don't disapprove?" Iris blinked.

"Don't get me wrong, it's probably smart to back-burner any new requests for the moment until we get a better idea of who attacked us, just for your own safety. But after that..." I ran a hand through my hair. "Do you like helping people?"

Iris hesitated, then nodded agreement. "I don't want to sound ungrateful. You took really good care of us. Sometimes, when things were bad, I tried to imagine how much worse it would be if it was just me, and Mom, and Ellison, and that helped. But there were so many problems, and even though you always found a way for us to scrape by, it wore you down. Ellison too. So many times, I wished—prayed—someone amazing would just swoop in and take care of the big things so we'd finally have a break, but that never happened. Because for us, that person didn't exist. For the longest time that made me angry. At some point after I got my powers, I realized that in some small, specific way, I could be that person. For people who need it just as badly as we did." She finished, looking equal parts embarrassed and ashamed. "And I like that."

I exhaled a long breath. "On some level, I'll never fully understand your perspective. I've been mired in cost-benefit analysis for so long it's practically grafted to my DNA. Part of who I am. Thing is, though, my understanding doesn't matter, and more importantly, you don't have to be like me. It's better that you're not. That outlook is the exact reason you should take the potion. There are selfish reasons, sure, but in the long run, over the course of years, you'll do a lot more good than some power-leveled User."

Iris nodded, absorbing that thoughtfully. "So it's not just a gift, it's a responsibility."

"If thinking of it that way makes it easier to accept, sure."

There was a squeal of tires as Nick peeled into the parking lot, hopping out the driver's side of his aunt's truck in a hurry, hefting a duffel bag over his shoulder and lugging a guitar case toward where Kinsley and Sae had already sat a blanket down on a soft-looking section of grass at the crest of a hill. He hollered something inaudible, jogging over to them in a half-sprint.

"Why's he in such a hurry?" Iris asked, peering after Nick.

"Because he's a well-meaning dork, and he doesn't want to miss the fun part." I rested a hand on the door handle. "Are you ready?"

———

It's funny, how unfounded fears can be. Caution, being slow to trust, and a small helping of paranoia can serve you well. But unproductive fear can summon imaginary mountains that feel unsurmountable, whether the source of that fear is irrationality, hate, or deceptively simple circumstances blown out of proportion. From the car, to the small sanctum of the picnic blanket, to the second my sister drank the potion, I kept waiting for her to make the same connections as me and see it as a betrayal. Iris never did. She was all nerves, sure, trouble staying still and shaking just as badly as she had been in the car. But the moment of damnation where the excitement died and she drew into herself never came. If anything, from the way Iris chugged the potion until she almost choked, pausing only when repeatedly reminded to slow down, she was even more excited than she'd let on.

Kinsley leaned over the bizarre, out-of-place stick in her lap and wordlessly handed Iris a canteen of water, nodding encouragement as she took it, guzzling some down between ragged breaths. "Did it taste as bad as it smelled?"

There was a long pause as Iris reluctantly lowered the canteen, looping the strap around her wrist so she could sign. "No, it was... just kind of overpowering. Weirdly sweet?"

"Like candy?"

"Maple syrup. But, like, maple syrup that'd been left on the shelf for too long."

"Ew," Kinsley wrinkled her nose. "I've got snacks if you need something to wash it down."

Next to me, Nick—still in the overlong process of tuning his hybrid acoustic-electric—leaned over and whispered to Sae. "What's happening? What's she saying?"

Sae leaned away from him. "Well, as I'm not a merchant with a highly convenient universal translation feat, what I do know I've learned the hard way. None of it seems to be 'hello, goodbye, I love you, a spelled-out name, or get fucked,' so it's out of my vocabulary."

Nick blinked. "Haven't learned much."

Sae made the slang sign for get fucked vehemently. "Memorizing the alphabet is like the first section of the massive ASL book they let me borrow, and you're supposed to internalize that first. That shit takes time."

"Fair enough."

"It hasn't kicked in yet," I summarized, still watching Iris carefully. She was swaying a bit, favoring one side. It could have been nothing. A leg muscle that fell asleep while she was sitting cross-legged earlier. But on the off chance it wasn't and something went terribly wrong, I'd coordinated with Dr. Ansari, calling in a favor to ensure she was waiting with her equipment in a parking lot nearby.

For perhaps the fifth time, I checked my messages to make

sure she hadn't been pulled away. It wasn't that I doubted the potion. If anything, I was confident that this one, at least, would work, given the safe assumption that Hastur wanted me on the line for the second.

Just like every other time, there was no further message from the doctor beyond her typically brief, "I've arrived."

What was new was the message from Julian. Which I might have overlooked, if the first word in the message preview wasn't "Tracker."

<Julian: Tracker's down to meet today. Hope you're not too hungover, cause this guy is both booked and a little high-strung, so his availability in the future may be spotty.>
<Matt: Appreciate it. Yesterday was a bit of a shitshow. We're generally more professional, so if it put you off, just know it's the exception to the norm.>
<Julian: Not at all, man! Far as I'm concerned, the taco mishap was providence. You know how long it's been since I just... kicked back and celebrated something? Charlie and I had a ball. The dogs like their digs?>

Unexpectedly, I realized I was smiling.

<Matt: Not as much as they like my couch, but seems that way, yeah. At least one of them climbed the tree, so your vision has been realized.>

Julien sent back a fist pump emoji. Which was odd, because as far as I knew, it was the absolute first image I'd seen in system chat. And beyond a prompt that allowed the manifestation of an on-screen keyboard for those who preferred to physically type their messages—clunky at best—the rest of the text screen was pretty bare.

"Pressure," Iris said. Loudly. I snapped to attention, swiping my messages away so my vision was clear. My sister's hands were over her ears, her eyes wide as she swayed on her feet.

"Is that supposed to happen?" Sae coiled, her casual lounge immediately abandoned as she shifted to get her feet beneath her, ready to spring into action. "She looks like she's in a lot of..."

Pain, I finished mentally, crouching in front of Iris as Kinsley helped her sit down, waving in front of her eyes and holding up ten fingers once she focused on my hand.

"Seven," Iris whispered, eyes focusing and unfocusing on my fingers.

"Where?" I mouthed clearly.

She cringed. "Everywhere."

Fuck, not good. My sister's bad habit of overlooking her own suffering included self-evaluation. So, realistically, a seven out of ten on the pain scale was closer to a nine. It wasn't necessarily indicative of a serious problem, as most system-related transformations, including summoning or level ups, hurt like a bitch, but that wasn't something I was willing to bet on.

"Fucking Hastur. We need to get her to the doctor, now," Sae hissed, fists clenching and unclenching.

"Better not to move her until we understand what's happening," Nick dropped the guitar and stood. Like a switch had been flicked, his easygoing expression disappeared into the calm visage of a leader. "Matt, consensus?"

"Calling now," I said aloud, even as I pulled up Ansari's contact. "Keep her comfortable, don't let her stand because her balance is probably fucked, and whatever you do, don't panic and stress her out more."

Sae propped up Iris and Kinsley held her hand as Nick sprinted toward the parking lot, returning with the entire removable back seat of his truck and placing it down. Iris settled down on the bench, emitting a small whimper that flayed me to my core.

"Breathe," I made the corresponding sign, speaking it aloud simultaneously.

There was an audible pop and Iris suddenly stilled, slumping on the truck bench, her expression blank. It spoke to the severity of the experience that she seemed to have forgotten we were there, stirring after a moment and signing. "It stopped."

"You sure?"

"There's so much text," Iris squinted, scanning the imperceptible scrawl. Suddenly she froze, standing shakily to her feet even as Kinsley supported her arm, trembling growing more severe even as her head whipped around, her eyes frantic. "What is that?"

I looked around, heart dropping as I spotted a familiar person in gray sweats milling beneath the shade of a tree around ten yards out, partially obscured, doing a near-perfect job of appearing like he wasn't watching us. It wasn't a threat, but he wasn't supposed to be here. Or anywhere near me, really. I reached out to Talia, directing her to drive him off.

But on second look, Iris didn't seem to be staring at the man at all. She was still looking around wildly, reacting every time the summer breeze—

A surge of emotion tore through me, nearly spilling over before I forced it down. "That's the wind, kiddo."

————

The result was an overwhelming success, though there were aspects of it that were mixed. Iris seemed to mostly understand spoken speech, though I suspected that had more to do with her talent for lip-reading than true comprehension. Speaking aloud was harder, as processing the sound of her own voice seemed to trip her up more than when it was entirely absent.

Though conversing was a bit stop and start, the experience Iris seemed to get the most kick out of was the sound of our voices. Kinsley was sassier than she'd expected, while Sae was more alto than the soprano she'd conceptualized. I, apparently, lacked much of the intensity she'd assumed and was far more aloof. Only Nick sounded exactly as Iris had imagined, something he took as a point of pride.

"Wonder what Mom's voice sounds like," Iris signed, hesitantly.

I sighed. "Well, you'll have to wait for her to stop crying. That's why she's not here, figured it would be less overwhelming without her losing it." I paused, remembering our tense discussion on the night of my birthday. "Might be better to leave this little gathering out so she doesn't feel excluded."

Iris gave me a thumbs up, immediately getting it. "I'll just tell her you gave me the potion and had to go do Matt things."

Kinsley snorted, "She'll definitely believe it."

"Hey," I protested.

"Almost got all of that, but what was the thing you did with your nose just now?"

"What thing?" Kinsley asked, confused.

"This?" Sae said, cocking her head back and snorting in a near perfect imitation of a pig.

Kinsley blanched. "That's not what I sound like."

"It's kind of similar," Iris signed, nodding to Sae in appreciation.

"No fighting," I gave them both a weary look before signing for Iris. "Kinsley snorted. A snort is like a fractional laugh. Something you do when something is either a little funny, or an outright laugh would be rude. It's not entirely dissimilar from the sound a pig makes, which is the connection Sae is making and the reason Kinsley looks mildly horrified."

"Oh. I mean I know what it is, I've just never heard it before. You don't sound like a pig," Iris immediately encouraged Kinsley, who only scowled at Sae more intensely.

"It's just gonna take time to gather the mental context," I added belatedly, leaving it at that.

She looked up at me, daunted. "There's gonna be a lot of things like that, isn't there?"

"Remember, if you ever get overwhelmed and it starts to be too much, you have those," I pointed to the earmuffs around her neck.

"I will," Iris agreed easily, twiddling her fingers in idle hope. "But I'd really like to hear another song. Can you ask Nick if he'd be willing to play another?"

Damned as I was, I translated the message for Nick, who seemed to melt at the request.

"Absolutely," Nick smiled widely and hefted the guitar, strap around his neck loosening as he strummed the strings, fiddling with the tuning for what felt like the millionth time. He spoke quietly, low enough that only I could hear, pointedly not looking behind him. "You already clock that guy behind us?"

"Yeah," I answered, angling my head so Iris couldn't read my response.

"Didn't want to look too long, but something about him is familiar."

"It's nothing. Talia's dealing with it."

"Yet he hasn't moved," Nick murmured. "And she can be a scary bitch when she wants to. Sure there's not a problem?"

I risked a glance to confirm that Nick was right. He was, though I could make out a patch of bright fur through the bushes that covered them both. The man's body language hadn't changed, he still looked completely relaxed, but Nick was correct that he'd been rooted to that exact spot for far too long. After a moment, he even gave an awkward wave.

"Talia? There a reason he's still here?"

Her mental response lagged, taking a bit longer than it should have. "There's a complication. It's contained. This is an important moment for your kin, your focus should remain on her."

"Gonna step out for a second," I announced, checking in with Iris. "That alright?"

"S'okay," Iris confirmed, still overtaken by the possibility of another song.

Nick suddenly spoke up, overserious. "The last few have been light fun, but I want to sing you the song of my people."

"Nick, please, please, please, no Nickelback," Sae groaned.

Instead of responding, Nick plucked out the first few notes of "Free Bird," and as soon as I was certain Iris was transfixed on the performance, I slipped away, taking the long way around and slipping on the **<Allfather's Mask>** so she lost track of me. I tamped down on my growing annoyance, reminding myself to be as kind and level-headed as possible.

When I circled around the brush, the truth of Talia's complication became clear. Talia and the man in the gray sweats were conversing in low-pitched voices. But the real kicker was the third party—a man in glasses, a button up, and a tie, laid supine, the sweat suit's foot pressing down on his neck. The blood and bruises were all fresh enough that the altercation had likely happened here. He'd been stripped of his wallet and other items in his pockets, a scan card that listed his name and identified him as one of Kinsley's researchers lined up beside them on the ground.

"Don't come any closer," Buzzcut said, watching me carefully. "Identify yourself."

I took the mask off and Buzzcut smiled widely, suspicion

draining away. "Thought so. Getting better at picking you out when you're wearing it, but it's still hard to tell sometimes."

"You organized his things."

"Not exactly," Buzzcut protested. "Just laid them out in an orderly manner. Only once. Still making progress."

"Good," I stared down at the unconscious researcher. "What the hell happened here, initiate?"

CHAPTER FIFTY-THREE

I watched, positioning myself to block the subdued man from view of the busy street not far away, warring with internal impatience as Buzzcut very intentionally used the breathing technique I'd taught him. Three short breaths in, one long breath out. As he relaxed, he lifted his foot pressing down on the researcher's neck ever so slightly, suddenly more cognizant of the pressure he applied. "Well, I was out, picking up groceries. Small goods merchant acquaintance was in the area, and since we're not supposed to use the online vendor unless it's an emergency, figured it was a good opportunity to stock back up before things go apeshit."

Somehow, I resisted the urge to tell him to get to the foot-on-neck part. "Good so far, go on."

"Did my business, played it safe, and was in the middle of checking for tails before heading back when I uh..." he smiled apologetically. "Felt the pull. Realized you were nearby. And I know you've told the others, uh, that it's alright if they check up on you so long as they aren't seen and keep their distance—generally I'm better than that, not some needy child like some of the twits—"

"What have we said about judgment?" I asked him, keeping my tone soft and tranquil.

Displeasure reared its head for just a moment as Buzzcut grimaced, rubbing the back of his head. "To show kindness and understanding to my brothers and sisters, bearing in mind many of them come from more difficult circumstances than I do. It's a hard one for me, boss. But I'm uh... working on it."

"Thank you for acknowledging your shortcoming so frankly. Self-awareness is a necessary step to enlightenment. Continue."

"Sure, sure." He nodded emphatically, happy to move on. "Anyway, I felt the pull. Figured you were busy and didn't need me poking my nose in, but it was on my way and I thought, 'what the hell, might as well swing by, make sure everything's on the up and up.'" He pressed down on the researcher's neck with his heel for emphasis, scowling. "Which was when I saw this dipstick skulking around like baby's first army ranger. Literally hiding in the bushes with a pair of binoculars."

"And you intervened," I finished, curbing a torrent of frustration.

"No sir. If looking was all he was doing, he never would have made my acquaintance. Got enough of a read on him to confirm he wasn't much of a threat, woulda just messaged you if you were on your own. But he started creeping up, real slow like, so I followed. And once I got close enough to make out the little one, bumped his threat level." Buzzcut scowled, lifting his foot to give the researcher a kick, pulling the blow at the last second. He replaced his heel on the man's back, suddenly anxious. "Did I go too far?"

For a moment, the earnestness of the question caught me off guard. Buzzcut was more advanced than the others and almost never directly asked for validation, to the point I sometimes forgot he needed it just as badly as they did.

The Nursery started innocently enough. In theory, it was

part shelter, part rehabilitation. An imperfect solution to a growing problem. The day of my first foray into the tower, I had to handle someone. A mother with a troubled history. Someone who, in a perfect world, I would have spared. But, being a mage, her high intelligence build made her almost impossible to manipulate, narrowing my options to one.

I don't regret it, really. To this day, I still think it was the right call. It was the underlying implications that drove the sliver deep. Realistically, she wouldn't be the last person I wanted to leave alone and couldn't, simply because their continued existence could create future problems. And once you start killing people not because of what they've done, but because of what they might do? The slope was slippery enough that I needed something else.

It came to me in pieces.

The first piece was, surprisingly, Keith, another mage from the Order. Unlike the first, he hadn't done anything wrong, didn't pose a threat beyond the organization he hailed from. I'd subjugated him in a desperate attempt to keep Nick from doing something he'd regret, and once the crisis was averted, I figured that would be the end of it. Subjugation wasn't supposed to last long, and I'd... encouraged Keith to forget the interaction before it expired. As far as I could tell, he was more or less blissfully unaware that anything had even happened. Yet, he lingered. Always seemed to be nearby whenever I was at the Order's HQ, like a shadow I couldn't shake. Eventually, out of sheer annoyance more than anything else, I confronted him.

His explanation was as simple as it was vexing. "Just wanna be available if you need anything."

At first, I wrote it off as some odd attachment issue. Keith was a second child to absent parents and a more charismatic— i.e. Shitheel—brother. The inferiority complex was practically baked in, as was the subsequent tendency to latch onto practically anyone who treated him as more than an eyesore. As explanations went, it fit, and for a while I almost believed it.

Until I caught him shadowing me maskless in my own damn region.

Once confronted, the answer was the same: "Just wanna be available if you need anything."

This time, obviously, I didn't write it off. We took a long drive with an uncertain ending, while I grilled him on what his intentions were, Azure riding shotgun in the passenger seat of his mind. From what my summon could tell, his answers, while perplexing, were entirely forthright. Keith admitted, in a mix of embarrassment and excitement, that he'd come away from his experience in the tower more fulfilled than he'd ever been in his life. That it felt as if he'd been given a difficult task, and instead of shrinking away or being paralyzed by inaction, he'd accomplished it perfectly. That was the reason he kept trailing me, hoping for another task, wanting to experience that feeling of accomplishment again.

When pressed on how he'd found me, after a ridiculous amount of apologizing, the mage claimed there was something almost analogous to a beacon in his head. It wasn't always on, but when it was, it was directional, and after he was close enough, it felt almost like a tangible pull.

It wasn't until I asked him if I had to worry about the possibility he might reveal my identity to others that his cheerful, forthright demeanor vanished. "I'd never do that. Never in my life. Not for any reason, even if whoever was asking was hurting me. I'd never do that to you." He repeated it over and over, regardless of how I phrased the question.

And after, Azure confirmed what I'd already begun to wonder. It was almost identical to a geas effect. The only fragment of true compulsion that remained after his primary directive had long since faded.

The second piece came in the form of testing. Because Keith's account, while jaw-dropping in scope if it turned out to be a fraction of what it hinted at, needed to be confirmed. Most of my days were filled with the mind-numbing process of climbing the tower with Nick, and my nights were spent testing extensively. And the results were curious.

First thing I learned was that the sort of magnetism Keith exhibited varied greatly. If I told someone to do something as insignificant and universally advisable as looking both ways before they crossed the street, they would do as instructed without protest, seem briefly pleased with themselves, and forget me immediately. But if the task given was more difficult while still falling within the lines of something they would do, or rather something they would do if they were an idealized, better version of themselves? They'd follow me around like an imprinted duckling, similar to Keith.

It took some tinkering to find a solution to the multiplying shadows. Initially, I tried asking the imprinted subjects to avoid me, which proved problematic. Not because they didn't listen— they did, a little too well, and the average person is neither as sly or subtle as they believe themselves to be. But giving them the assignment of carrying out their business as usual worked like a dream. It both fulfilled their expectations for another task and had no definable endpoint, meaning they'd carry the "task" of living their usual lives out in perpetuity.

The next discovery was that the magnetism effect could be reversed. This took far more prep work to test, because of the ethical issues of giving some poor schmuck the worst night of his life in the name of research. I needed a deserving subject. And a deserving subject I found. Ex-con, triple homicide, got off on a technicality because the cops got too eager. Mustache that deserved a cell of its own. No noteworthy connections.

I let myself into Chomo-stache's apartment and, after a

brief interrogation and subjugation, directed him to prepare and eat grape leaves—the food he found so revolting even the smell made him gag—until his stomach ached.

Had a mission with Sae and the strike team that night, so I only stayed long enough to confirm he'd carried out the order and left, intending to follow up the next day.

It took three to find him again. When I finally did, another interrogation with Azure confirmed my suspicions. Like Keith, Chomo-stache also had a beacon in his head. Only when he'd sensed me drawing closer, his compulsion was to clear out and get as far away as possible. He didn't seem to understand what happened, even seemed to laugh at himself a little for overreacting. The only concrete conclusion he seemed to draw from it was, in his own words, "Ain't your fault. But if you get too close, get the feeling I might end up doing something unpleasant again." Approaching him without the mask triggered the same result, though he couldn't understand why or connect me to Myrddin.

All of this was troubling. Using **<Subjugation>** before knowing any of it already felt questionable, and the idea of using it after felt far worse, brushing against something borderline mephistophelian. It was one thing to steal someone's agency in a crisis to ensure a better outcome, another entirely to do it knowing it had the potential to permanently alter their perspective and adhere them to me.

If nothing else happened, it might have ended as a cautionary experiment, the result underlining the importance of keeping the Ordinator power in my back pocket until absolutely necessary.

Enter Buzzcut.

In the long interim between Cameron's imprisonment and our first meeting, he'd apparently listened to the edited version of the recording I left of Aaron greenlighting his death, replayed it countless times, growing increasingly despondent. Surprising, because for someone who acted like such a hardass, the betrayal cut him deeply. He wouldn't tell me, or couldn't, because of the geas, but I gathered enough context to fill in the blanks. Aaron had a certain way of engaging you on an individual level. He was so obviously brilliant and confident that when he carved out time for you specifically, or sought your opinion, it made you feel special. Important.

Making it all the more jarring when Aaron suddenly threw you away.

I probably don't need to spell out why I wanted to help Cameron. Commonalities in our history aside, his OCD grew worse, aggravated by his imprisonment, and his already dwindling supply of meds didn't seem to be doing a damn thing. I sat with him, talked, brought plenty of books and DVDs for the ancient portable player in his cell. Despite anything I tried, including calling in a favor from Hastur to remove Cameron's geas, he kept asking me to kill him.

Taking me right back to that shitty day in the tower.

The pieces came together then. A potential long-term solution for all the problems I couldn't bring myself to solve permanently. I'd spent enough time with Azure riding along that I knew almost everything about Cameron. His past, history, traumas, motivations and desires and the psychology underpinning it all. It would take time and effort, but between Azure, my Ordinator abilities, and the unexpected side effects of **<Subjugation>**, I could, in theory, fix him. Erode his traumas, suppress distressing memories, deaden impulses that made his everyday life difficult. Impart a renewed sense of fulfillment and purpose.

So just like I had with Talia, and Audrey before her, I gave Buzzcut a choice. He could take the easy way out if he wanted. Or he could roll the dice with me and potentially have the chance to stick it to Aaron.

It took a while to decide, but eventually he chose the latter.

"Not at all," I smiled, addressing the question of whether he'd overstepped and clapped him on the back. "You evaluated the situation, escalated only when you had to, and kept my sister safe. Well done." I leaned in and whispered conspiratorially. "If anything, you're ready for graduation."

Buzzcut's eyebrows shot up, mouth forming a slight frown. "I get the whole point of the place is to move on eventually. Hard to gather information and act on orders if we don't. But what if I screw up, or backslide and end up losing all the progress I've made?"

I gripped his shoulders gently, fighting a wave of nausea that struggled to surface as I realized I'd done something similar with my siblings, countless times. "You were the first, Cameron. The others all look up to you and respect your judgment. They're eager to see the example you set, watching for footsteps to follow. I'm taking a risk here, yes, but I wouldn't take it if I didn't have the utmost confidence in what you've achieved so far."

"You really think I'm ready?" He rubbed the gray sleeve of his sweatshirt across misty eyes.

Hard to say. Kind of in uncharted waters here. I'd prefer a few more months to make sure there are no wrinkles, but we're out of time.

"Of course you are," I encouraged him, shoving my hands into the pocket of my hoodie awkwardly as he reined himself in. "I'm heading to headquarters today. If you're good to go, I'll take you with me. But if you need more time to settle your affairs..."

"No." Cameron sniffed, stretching his arms out with a few idle swings and centering himself. "Ready to get back in the game. Just gonna go back and say my goodbyes."

"The Nursery's your home. Your family. You know you can always come back, right?"

"Yeah..." he shook his head, glancing up seriously. "But if I'm gonna do this right, probably best to keep my distance for a while." With a heavy sigh, he stared down at the researcher. "So, we instancing this guy?"

I gave the unconscious researcher a long, displeased look, then crouched down to check his pulse again. Still steady. "Pretty sure I know who he works for, and why he's here. His vocation is pretty rare, and he shouldn't be a problem once he finds out what he's looking for is gone. Guessing he'll be out for another hour, at least. I'll call some mercs to pick him up."

"Once I do the rounds at the Nursery I'll stay put, just shoot a line when you're headed to HQ." Cameron removed his boot from the researcher's back, wiping it on the ground as I walked away.

Grass crunched beneath my feet, and I waved behind me as I walked away, smile sliding into an expression that was far more troubled. There was a part of me that still wanted to believe that what I was doing was ultimately good. That it was better to be alive—albeit deeply influenced—than dead. But if it was me in the cell, and someone made me choose between keeping my own agency or being enthralled by someone else?

There's no question what my answer would be.

CHAPTER FIFTY-FOUR

Kinsley was biblically pissed about the researcher. To the point we ended up calling it early, after a few minutes of listening to her scream behind a copse of trees at some poor sap over a voice call. Judging from the earmuffs clamped tightly over Iris's head and her bleary expression, my sister was verging on overstimulated anyway. She stuck it out for a long time, and it helped that I'd chosen a relatively quiet area, but the sounds of the city were still deafening to the unaccustomed.

After dropping Iris off at the apartments and making sure she was okay, I finally allowed myself to look at the timer. **<11:19:27:49>**

It wasn't terrible. Eleven days and change left plenty of room to maneuver. But, as Nick had observed, the problem was the lack of momentum. Hastur wasn't keen on specifics, meaning we had no idea which floor housed the real Excalibur. We also had no clear insight on the process of stopping the Transposition, only that the sword and "prophecy" were key factors in stopping it. The first joint foray into the tower had been a halting, alarming affair that hadn't accomplished much beyond clearing a single floor, and now the leader of the Adventurers' Guild was dragging his feet.

If I had to guess, Tyler was already getting second thoughts about the arrangement after the timer started. The alignment of the Order, Adventurers', and Merchants' Guild already placed us in a powerful position for the coming storm. Tower expeditions took focused effort and consumed resources, and if we faced significantly more resistance, or got entrenched with a difficult floor that incurred a high-casualty count, I could see him battening down the hatches and delaying further attempts until after the second event had passed.

More than anything, the timing is questionable. All the floors cleared without issue before the alliance, yet somehow the first one we come together for with more firepower than ever ends up containing an existential threat? It's almost as if—

The sound of a horn blared through my musing, startling my foot off the brake pedal as traffic bristled behind me, cars edging up, waiting for me to move. I accelerated from the standstill, leaving the green light and complex, cog-riddled workings of the region behind, taking a shoulder road to a highway I'd driven countless times before, feeling a growing degree of disquiet as the gritty scenery grew more familiar.

Things in Region 2, my old home, had improved significantly since I'd left after filling the receptacle. Even from the elevated view on the overpass, I could see countless streets—once cracked and riddled with potholes—now perfectly paved, the dark green of stubborn growth replaced with verdant grass and trees, with an infrastructure facelift to match. It no longer resembled the post-modern slum I'd grown up in, and I felt a twinge of nostalgia. Region 3, alternatively, was a mess. No one in my circle of power had spoken to the leader of Region 3 since the first Transposition. Their decisions during the last event, from hoarding Lux after they'd already achieved the objective to hosting a group of paramilitaries harvesting User Cores, hadn't been conducive to popularity.

But what really boggled my mind was how little it had changed. It started as a low-income area with shitty infrastructure and high crime rates, and despite being among the first to complete their receptacle, hadn't taken a step beyond that. The only new additions here were cheap, neon signs advertising various system- and crafting-related businesses. Several newly minted bars that appeared cobbled together with scrap wood and repurposed windows blared thumping music, and on the streets people staggered between them, substance abuse and homelessness on full display.

Whatever the leader of Region 3 had selected as their reward, it certainly wasn't anything that improved the region itself.

I pulled up in the dilapidated parking lot of a small shoebox of a building. The fading red and white sign read: "Butcher." And in smaller print, "Kosher meat available on request." I stepped out of the car and inventoried it quickly, falling into old habits. I learned a long time ago that when you find yourself in a potentially dangerous place, it's best to blend. Keep an eye on your surroundings, but not too emphatically. Move like you have somewhere important to be.

There was still too much I didn't know about Julien. But the one thing I was confident of was that there was an astronomically low chance he'd try to lead me into an ambush. It just didn't make sense with our history. That wasn't to say I trusted him, exactly. It was impossible to truly trust anyone without extensive understanding of their motives and underlying history.

I tugged open the dirt-encrusted handle of the back door, gagging for a moment as the scent of iron and viscera washed over me, frigid air rushing out as I passed through.

There was a *thunk* as a cleaver came down, wet squelch echoing off the white walls. Blood trickled down from the headless corpse of a hulking furred creature suspended from the ceiling by chains, wound draining directly into a bucket below. A smaller version of something I'd encountered only once in person, but between the musculature and stocky frame, it was unmistakable.

"A lot of demand for troll meat in these parts?" I asked.

"Hardly," a stocky dark-haired man with thick eyebrows and wearing a blood-spattered apron scoffed as he answered, his voice a deep Slavic accent. "There are far better options for sustenance. Razor rabbit, low gnolls, even skull-backed turtles if prepared and stewed correctly. Troll is too..." he half-flexed, "... to be edible. No respectable establishment would sell. Their pelts though?" The man thumped a stack of furs on the nearby table proudly. "Make a fine cloak. Naturally magic resistant, and hardy. The tanners and tailors can't get enough."

"I see." I nodded along noncommittally, even as my stomach roiled at the thought of taking a page out of Audrey's book. Judging from the sheer variety of creatures, skins, and mounted skulls, as well as countless slabs of hanging meat of various exotic shades that appeared entirely alien, business was bustling.

The man's considerable eyebrows furrowed together as he looked me over. "The stink of death follows you, even in place such as this. It will taint the meat. State business, or gawk elsewhere."

What the hell?

"I was supposed to meet someone—" I started before a familiar face ducked through the plastic flaps in the back, carrying an open-topped metal container in front of him. The dark bags under Julien's eyes were the only giveaway to the previous night's activities. Otherwise, he looked bright and

chipper, staring over the sloshing contents of the tin thoughtfully, sporting a similarly messy apron.

"All the good bits are brining, Yakov. And more of the offal
than usual, and yes, I double-checked. Should I toss it?" Julien
asked, looking to the older man for instruction, only noticing
me after he'd already spoken. He grinned, about to speak before
the butcher cut him off.

"Leave it," the man said, never taking his eyes from me.
"Good opportunity to try making hot dog. Show this tourist the
door."

Julien cleared his throat, slightly embarrassed. "No, uh,
Uncle, this is the friend and potential client I mentioned. The
one looking for his brother."

Uncle? They look nothing alike.

"We cannot help him." Yakov wiped his hands on his apron,
still subtly standing his ground until Julien took him aside, and
a series of furious whispers were exchanged in a mix of Polish
and English. While most of it was obscured, I got the general
gist that Yakov was displeased with Julien bringing "trouble"
into his shop, and Julien arguing that he hadn't. Finally, Yakov
turned back to me with a displeased expression. "Name?"

"Matt."

"That real name?"

My blood went cold. "Yes."

He studied me for a long moment, then broke eye contact.
"Too busy to drop everything for new client. If interested in
services, sit and wait."

I glanced around the butcher's shop, noting the utter lack of
seating in the otherwise dingy environment, and offered a thin
smile. "Not a problem."

With a huff that expressed he would have probably been
happier if it had been a problem, Yakov pulled the string at the
back of his apron and strode back through the flaps Julien had

entered from, sparing a few suspicious glances before he was gone.

"Sorry." Julien grimaced, looking back toward the flaps. "It's nothing personal, promise. Yakov has trouble trusting outsiders. He was already paranoid and a little superstitious even before the dome. Nothing crazy, just, kinda old school. If he gets a bad vibe for whatever reason, he clams up."

"And I gave him a bad vibe," I finished, feeling uncertain whether it was wiser to stay or make a quick exit.

Julien rolled his eyes. "Yeah. Both you and the old lady who came in earlier asking for a bulk discount on gizzards. Proper villains."

"Honing my evil plan as we speak," I stated dryly, "Kinda left out the part where the tracker was family."

"Does that make a difference?"

"It could." Not knowing what kind of shit Ellison had gotten himself into was a problem. It could be as simple as crossing paths with the wrong group, overestimating his abilities and incurring a serious injury. Or he could be mired in something more complicated, something a tracker might have a great deal of questions about. Questions he might let slip to his nephew. "I have no idea what Ellison might be jammed up in, and my brother has a history of questionable decision making. The last thing I want is to put you and yours in danger."

More importantly, they have a dearth of shared attributes. Different speech patterns, and complete societal disparity. Hard to imagine they're actually related.

"Yakov's an experienced professional. He handles more than his share of clients with... difficult issues... and always comes away unscathed. Part of that is the way he works—in terms of search and identify, exclusively. He won't retrieve people or objects, he'll just tell you where they are and let you do the rest." Julien stripped off rubber gloves and shuffled to the basin, pumping ample soap into his hands and scrubbing them thoroughly. He looked back at me and grinned. "You're dying to ask how we're related, huh?"

I shrugged, hoping he'd tell me anyway.

"It's a long story. Or short, depending on how I tell it. Heard of those, uh, sites you can send a sample to that give a breakdown of genealogy, as well as your percentage relation to others who share a portion of your DNA?"

Enough to know they provide governments with an excellent secondary database to subpoena, sure.

Aloud, I confirmed that I'd heard of them.

"They're not quite the fad they used to be, but I was a..." his eyes slid to the side, "... member of a support group that wouldn't shut up about them. Generally, I'm pretty self-reliant, kind of had to be, but I kept reading all these success stories and started wondering if I wasn't completely alone. Wasn't looking for a family or anything. Nothing big. Just, like, maybe someone I could swing by and visit for the holidays. So I spit in a tube, mailed it, and to my absolute shock, the results came back with someone nearby. A few months later I met Yakov, and the rest tells itself."

It didn't, really. I'd already pieced together that Julien's childhood left much to be desired. Despite his odd demeanor and eccentricities, I knew a survivor when I saw one. But the picture that glossed over more details than it elaborated on was still more indicative of a deep, metastasizing loneliness than anything else. The fact alone that he'd sought out the butcher over a DNA connection that had to be tenuous and several generations removed practically spelled it out.

After a great deal of awkward small talk that consisted of me, trying not to probe, and Julien, struggling not to overshare, Yakov mercifully returned. The removed apron revealed a well-worn, craggy Megadeth t-shirt depicting a white-winged skeleton. Again, he pointedly ignored me as he spoke to Julien. "We are out of storage."

"There was room in the corner freezer." Julien leaned back, mouth quirking in confusion.

"Not anymore."

"Shit."

"Demand not keeping up with supply?" I asked. It was tempting to leave the negotiations to the Order's Prince, but I got the feeling he believed his uncle would help me out of the goodness of his heart, and Yakov seemed to have missed that memo. Meaning it was time to probe for a need.

Yakov grimaced as I spoke, as if unpleasantly reminded that someone beyond him and his distant nephew was still present. "Apologies. Need to acquire new freezer. Perhaps more than one. It will take time to source. Cannot take on more until the issue is resolved."

Julien looked between us, wincing. "Uncle, there are quicker options. I know you're not the biggest fan of the Merchants' Guild—"

Why?

"Not fond of brats who walk into business and tell how to run it, more like," Yakov sneered, reflexively disgusted.

"From what you said, you kicked her out before she could explain herself." Julien sighed.

"Did not need to hear more about Selve could be making harvesting monsters for crafting and alchemy," Yakov snapped, "Little girl does not care for what I do here. Cares for nothing but money."

"She might have if you gave her a chance." Julien glanced toward me for help.

They were clearly talking about Kinsley. Only it didn't sound like her, at least not entirely. Kinsley was transactional, but she was more than capable of hearing someone out given the chance, especially if they had good intentions. But there'd been ample friction from other merchants since the beginning, fellow traders trying to strong-arm her and force extortionate prices. With the amount of temper between the two of them, it was easy to see how something might have been lost in translation.

"What exactly do you do here?" I asked, looking around. "Why is it so important?"

A little blunt, maybe, but when there was a language barrier, it was better to be direct.

His cold blue eyes bore into me. "Community poor. Monster meat cheap. People here kill monster. Sell parts to me and others. I prepare it and sell back for fraction of system food cost. Better money if I sell to little girl, but no food. More people starve."

As good as things were now, you never forget how it feels to go hungry.

"Give me a minute."

I stepped out the door, shooting an immediate message to Kinsley.

<**Matt:** The butcher in Region 3. Works with monster parts.>
<**Kinsley:** Colonel Mustard in the ballroom. Fucks people up with a candlestick. We just talking in non-sequiturs or what?>
<**Matt:** Do you know him?>
<**Kinsley:** I know I offered that mouth-breather an incredibly lucrative offer and he told me to kick rocks.>
<**Matt:** Did you bother to ask him *why* he told you to kick rocks.
>
<**Kinsley:** Uh. No. Maybe I could have been nicer, but most of these bastards only want to play hardball. Is there a problem?>

———

Fifteen minutes after going into great detail over a voice call of how badly Kinsley had bungled this particular situation, she showed up in force, rolling dark with a half-dozen black Hummers and a moving van. Judging from the shouting, Kinsley and Yakov weren't hitting it off any better than they had the first time, but at least now there was an understanding.

"What aren't you getting? The grinders and slicers are top of the line, probably better than anything we had before," Kinsley stated vehemently, on the verge of shouting.

"These?" Yakov indicated his arms and hands. "Top of line. Better, period. Also cannot be stolen."

Kinsley gave him a flat look. "Come on. I'm not an idiot, there's no way you don't already have some kind of machine. If the point is feeding people in bulk, you know there's a natural limit. I'm not trying to tell you how to run things—"

"—Only when mouth is open."

The merchant girl's eyebrows shot sky-high, and she took a good thirty seconds to center herself. When she spoke again, her voice was relaxed, calm. "I am trying to help you achieve your goal."

"Why?" Yakov challenged.

"Because you're doing important work here that helps people, and I didn't get that before, and I'm sorry!" Kinsley exploded, fists clenched at her side.

"Oh." Julien's uncle seemed taken aback by the admission. He looked down at her for a long moment, still guarded. "There is no longer problem with phoenix breast?"

"No... not at all." Kinsley pinched the bridge of her nose, barely hanging on. "Of course, it's a sapient animal whose feathers have more potential medicinal and arcane uses than a fucking bezoar, so if there's alternatives I'd really love to get my hands on it, but if that's the line between civilians starving or having something to get them through the next day, go ahead, grill that fucker up."

Yakov shook his head. "Butcher. Not cook."

"Do you want the machines or not?" Kinsley extended her arm toward the open moving van, where several people I recognized from our region's construction crew were waiting next to an industrial grinder propped up on a dolly.

"Yes," Yakov said finally, still looking uncertain. "But theft is real threat. Thieves watch expensive things come into store. Come back later, at night, to take them."

"All members of the Merchants' Guild get the benefit of assigned security." She held a hand up, quickly, warding off the inevitable rejection as Yakov's demeanor grew dark. "I know, you're not interested. But I can offer coverage on a trial basis."

Yakov sneered. "This, I know. Protection rescinded when renegotiation fail. Then ruin."

"I'm not the fucking mafia, sir." Kinsley pressed a hand against her chest. "There's an army of these guys. They're strapped, disciplined, and they know their shit."

"Not mafia," Yakov muttered.

"My point is, it costs me nothing to have two of them swing by every night on rotation. Not gonna pull the rug out. Take as long as you need."

Again, Yakov seemed off-put by the generosity. He looked away. "Maybe some parts—inedible, though useful—could be sent back with these men end of day. Fair?"

"That's all I wanted in the first place!"

Julien and I looked on mutely from a distance as the movers began to haul the old equipment out and replace it with the new. I was more or less happy with how things had played out. Yakov was getting his freezer, and then some, which played in my favor. Meanwhile, Kinsley, who'd been increasingly hard-edged as of late, was learning the invaluable life lesson that not every problem could be solved with the diplomatic equivalent of a hammer. It wasn't really her fault. People had been trying to take advantage of her from the start, and her abrasiveness— sometimes cruelty—was a product of that environment. But after you attain a certain level of power and influence, the hammer becomes less necessary. And by that point, it's a lot harder to put it down.

"I, uh, don't really know what to say." Julien stared down at his shoes, fidgeting back and forth, the very picture of guilt.

I snorted. "Please. There's a reason you didn't mention this shared history the other night. You knew this could happen. Practically orchestrated it. It's probably why you offered to help find Ellison in the first place. I'd be pissed if it wasn't for such a good cause."

"No, Matt, seriously." Julien shook his head. "I wanted to. Help, I mean. It only occurred to me later you might glean what happened from context, maybe put in a good word for him once he pulled through. It wasn't manipulation. Just... hoping for a happy accident, I guess."

Did I believe that?

Almost. The most clever thing a gifted liar can do is learn to act like a bad one. Still, it felt authentic, and despite pulling off something that was almost objectively positive, Julien really did look guilty as sin. He wasn't falling back on any repetitive tells that are generally bullshit, such as looking up and to the left, dodging eye contact or keeping it too consistently. In short, he just looked like he felt bad for using me for my connections and resources. And after dealing with people like Aaron on a daily basis, something about that was refreshing.

"Kind of sucks, having to say this, but I'm aware of my image." I leaned back on my heels, squinting in the downpour of sun. "Obviously I'm no altruist. More often than not, the opposite is true. When shit hits the fan, there's a lot I'm willing to let burn for the sake of people I care about. If I can't do shit about something, no point in nailing myself to a cross trying to make it happen anyway. The perfect is the enemy of the good. But if it's something like this? Just fucking tell me. Don't waste time being coy or trying to draw attention to it slowly. Not promising I'll always be able to contribute, especially if there's a conflict of interest, but if people are suffering and there's a simple way to help? That's an easy call."

Julien absorbed that, sides of his mouth quirking up in the ghost of a smile. "Gotta say, you're kind of a good person."

And you're a terrible judge of character.

But I let it pass, as beyond the usual prosaic of not correcting someone who thinks highly of you, Yakov was approaching us.

"New freezer fit the bill?" I asked, stuffing my hands in my pockets.

"Yes." The burled man checked behind him, watching dazed as Kinsley's guys packed up, already through with the makeover and preparing to leave. "Eventful day."

"So you're going to help... right?" Julien said, smiling a little too pointedly to be subtle.

"Okay," Yakov tentatively agreed. "Come back in few hours. Need... uhm. Objects. Belongings of person being found. Also, aspects of person. Blood best. After that, nails, or clump of hair."

"That's doable," I said, shifting my head from side to side. My brother wouldn't be thrilled about it. There was little Ellison hated more than me overstepping his privacy, but he'd been missing for nearly two days now and wouldn't—or couldn't—respond to messages. Not to mention I was pretty sure the stern warning he'd given about meddling in his affairs didn't apply when he was in danger. "Not trying to rush, but how quickly will we see results?"

"Here, easy." Julien's uncle made a broad gesture, likely indicating the city at large. Then he frowned. "Elsewhere, less so. Either way, should know more after."

"Elsewhere as in a realm of Flauros?" I confirmed, musing the limitation quietly as the large man nodded. It wasn't perfect. The realms were massive as they were varied, potential entry points in the city—portals, dungeons, and trials—just as dynamic and numerous. If Ellison was lost in a realm somewhere, the likelihood I'd find him unassisted dropped to almost zero. In that case, if the tracker could give me even the briefest, blurriest snapshot of where my brother was, it would be invaluable.

Time to get some answers.

CHAPTER FIFTY-FIVE

Ellison's penthouse, perhaps unsurprisingly, was serial-killer clean. A brief rifle through his cupboards revealed rows of glassware and plates coated with a layer of dust, moving air displacing enough of it that it swirled in the late afternoon light, piercing through gaps in closed shades and drawn curtains.

The only evidence that he'd even lived there at all was the way his bed was made and the simple black box left behind at the foot of it. On closer inspection, it wasn't exactly black—just the deepest, most somber navy. The box, so far as I could tell, lacked any discernible way to open it. No keyhole, uneven surfaces, or sections that gave any flex. Not so much as a seam. I inventoried it and moved on, finding little beyond a growing sense of unease that was impossible to place until I looked at the room as a whole and realized what was bothering me.

It was the asceticism. When I'd moved in, my place had been pre-decorated. Either by the previous occupant or the owner of the building. Nothing beyond the stock kitschy Eat-Pray-Love shit and pop-art still lifes. It wasn't exactly to my preferences, but it was color and texture, and as I wasn't exactly keen on taking a few days off to redecorate the place, I'd decided it could stay as it was. The irony was amusing. And at the very least, it made me look like less of a psycho.

Judging from the bundle of assorted art, hanging word-pieces, and a number of tertiary appliances I found in one of his closets, Ellison, by contrast, had stripped the walls and blacked out the mirror in his bathroom with masking tape. Someone's personal space says a lot about who they are, and as far as I could tell, either Ellison was making an intentional effort to say nothing, or he was doing worse mentally than I'd realized. My brother got like that, sometimes. When he was frustrated, particularly with his own failures, he'd strip away distractions, carving away at any variable that could even fractionally affect his focus, throwing away sentimental treasures or pawning pored over books close to his heart.

It seemed over the many lifetimes he'd supposedly lived, he'd perfected that approach.

I could have spent hours there, turning everything over, cutting open mattresses and removing floor lining, checking all his typical hiding places. My brother was occasionally sloppy and prone to oversight, but the room itself told me that wouldn't be the case here. Generally, when he was making this much of an effort to be fastidious, the results were impeccable. So I moved on, hoping he'd been too busy to bother with the one place I might find traces of the brother I had before.

Our old place. Much as I'd come to hate the cramped walls and cracking foundation, it'd haunted my dreams as of late. The brass knob turned easily in my hand, hinges emitting the tell-tale squeak that'd so often given away my comings and goings.

It felt strange, being back. Doubly so with the mask on. I slid it off, seal breaking as cool air rushed in, chilling my cheeks, a wave of nostalgia pouring in as the emotional suppression effect faded. Not entirely intending to, I stared down at it, feeling a familiar weight pressing down on my shoulders. Without the Allfather's interference, there was no question I'd be dead. Becoming Myrddin had allowed me so much more flexibility and slack than I'd be afforded otherwise. Beyond that, the identity created a near-perfect outlet for the more volatile aspects of my personality. Myrddin could thrash and burn, escalate as much as necessary without fear of reprisal, and stamp out potential threats before they gained momentum. It'd been a worthwhile undertaking, and with a few notable exceptions, I didn't regret it.

But for the first time since I donned the name, Myrddin's future was murky. The purpose he'd served was more or less complete. Matt had established relationships and clear inroads with both the Adventurers' Guild and The Order of Parsae. Contrasted with Myrddin, who was held at cautious arm's length by the first and almost universally reviled by the second.

After the last mission with the strike team, my alter ego had effectively served his purpose. Now he occupied the awkward space between hindrance and help, sliding more toward hindrance with every passing day. If he was truly another person, an ally, I'd start looking for ways to shelter myself from the half-life. Wouldn't cut ties or burn bridges, exactly, but there was no doubt I'd start distancing, relying on others where I might have turned to Myrddin instead.

Of course, I didn't have to worry about doing any of that. It wouldn't be messy. I could just let it go. Retire the identity and be Matt again. It wouldn't even be that big of a change. My accumulated power and Ordinator abilities would persist. I'd need to be more careful about how I used them, of course, but caution was nothing new.

Once Vernon achieved a high enough level to uncover what lay at the top of the necromancer tree and Jinny's death was resolved, one way or another, there was a real possibility it was time to move on. Grow up. Stop giving myself carte blanche to do whatever the hell I wanted, whenever the hell I wanted.

Learn to put the hammer down again.

For the moment, I retired the train of thought and carried on my search. As I'd hoped, Ellison's room was mostly untouched. Clean, but not impeccable the same way the penthouse was. I gathered enough hair from the creases between the carpet and beneath his bed, filtering them into a plastic bag until I had something that resembled a clump, and moved onto the second, more difficult piece of the puzzle.

"Object of great importance," I murmured. Yakov's description implied a degree of sentimentality, which was going to make this hard, as my brother tended to keep anything he truly cared about under wraps. There were a number of books that potentially qualified—a fraying, Goodwill-acquired copy of *The Name of the Wind* that he'd reread so many times the spine was in tatters, along with several battered volumes of *The Stormlight Archives*. Problem was, Ellison's tastes were mercurial. He'd alternate between lauding an author's praises to bashing them vehemently, expressing vitriol that bordered on loathing. After a moment, I inventoried both books, deciding to aim for quality rather than quantity.

I did a double-take. Through the gap in the books, a miniaturized cartoon figure holding a book beneath its arm stared back. Its head was coiffed with long, flowing white hair, pointed ears extended out to either side, the points long enough that it had to be elven, or at least elf analogous. Red smudges marred a flowing white tunic fringed with gold, perhaps depicting wounds. Tentatively, I picked it up, inspecting it in greater detail. The faintest scent of iron gave it away before my mind even made the connections, and the slow, growing sense of alarm I'd felt since his disappearance accelerated exponentially.

The figurine's wounds weren't wounds at all.

———

"His blood?" Yakov confirmed, inspecting the figurine in the overhead light of the butcher shop.

Wordlessly, I nodded, still reeling from the revelation and fighting a sensation of growing nausea. At some point in the last few days, after our window of communication had closed, Ellison had come home. I'd found more traces of blood in his bed and beneath a flipped-over couch cushion. The cache of cleaning supplies beneath the sink had been unsettled, meaning he wasn't injured so badly he couldn't afford to cover his tracks, but most of the gauze and bandaging materials in the first-aid kit above the fridge were gone. "Will this be enough?"

The older man placed the figurine on the counter, looking it over. "Blood best source. Will work. Statue, important?" His expression was dubious.

To be honest, I still wasn't certain. Ellison had never mentioned the figurine, but that didn't mean much. What stuck out was that in spite of whatever dire straits he was in, he'd sought it out and clutched it, not unlike the way a person might hold a precious memento or rosary for comfort. "Pretty sure."

"Okay." Yakov squared his shoulders. "Should be enough."

I tailed him, moving at a brisk pace to match the man's long strides as he led me past the new machines glinting in the dim light. Yakov moved a clothes stand overloaded with aprons and other apparel, opening a small door that led to a stairway down. He paused in the opening, giving me a long, cautious look before he spoke. "Clients like results. Way to get them, less so. Trouble for squeamish. This problem?"

If Julien's bleeding heart could handle whatever methods

his uncle used well enough that he was happily making refer-rals, I got the feeling I'd probably be fine. "Not at all."

Yakov acknowledged that with a nod, not looking particu-larly surprised. His mouth formed a grim line, and he chucked a thumb toward the stairway. "Follow."

With a small amount of trepidation, I followed Yakov down a set of creaking wooden slats that served as stairs. The walls of the dimly lit basement were comprised of dingy tile and drains. A braided line of seeping organic material formed a wide circle, approximately eight feet in diameter, and within it a crystal basin of dark blood sat squarely in the center. If I'd simply stumbled upon it, the ritualistic display would have looked much more sinister without context. But the intestines that formed the circle were too broad and thick to be human, and Yakov's vocation went a long way to explaining where the materials were sourced from.

I knelt across from Yakov as the butcher arranged the items I'd brought with no discernible pattern, placing them perpen-dicular to the basin, scowling as he made minute adjustments to the circle to better suit some highly complex and unknow-able schema only he could perceive.

"Hold snapshot in mind. Real memory, no imagination. No fear. Familiar," Yakov instructed.

As I did so, he began to chant guttural, primal words in an ancient language. The mental image I'd chosen was a mundane one, Ellison and I walking home after I'd picked him up from the local library, casually navigating the moonlit street. He was half-smiling, overtly trying not to laugh at something I'd said, adjusting the strap of his backpack—

A psionic scream overwhelmed me as the familiar surroundings within the memory ripped away. The scent of gore and oozing flesh grew stronger, more prevalent. The city streets that surrounded him fell away, my brother's jovial face replaced with a more modern visage. Dark bags weighed heavy beneath his eyes as he sprinted, darting through countless burned-out husks of trees that formed a dead forest, the sky overhead burgeoning with storm clouds. Rustling followed him, unseen creatures pursuing through the underbrush at blistering speed, just out of view. Ellison stumbled, swearing furiously as he lost his footing and tumbled head over heels down a long slope, slamming shoulder first into a tree and uttering a pained cry.

"Not... yet," Ellison muttered through grit teeth, pulling what looked like a high-tech crossbow out of his back and jerking it toward a thick copse of nearby trees. He fired, the immediate explosion loud and sudden enough that I nearly opened my eyes.

"Focus," Yakov broke from his chanting long enough to bark.

I held firm. Even as the scent of smoke filled my nostrils and the acrid smell of burning flesh made my eyes water, I forced myself to stay with it. Just a little longer.

Ellison dropped the crossbow, shifting upward against the tree he'd hit, bracing his back against it. Several creatures emerged from the flaming circle of trees, screeching, struggling to put themselves out before falling to their knees and laying still. They were familiar. Part animal, part person. It was difficult to say from the aftermath, but these looked almost exactly like the same sort of chimeras that attacked my region only a matter of days ago. In the distance, after my vision cleared, I could make out some sort of gargantuan structure lined with parapets.

Shakily, Ellison rose to a standing position and began to retreat from the fire, right arm hanging uselessly. His breathing was ragged and bare, every labored inhale tearing at me as he limped toward the castle. Above him, I felt my stomach turn as something fluid and flexible dropped from the branches in a brown-spotted, camouflaged blur.

The oversized constrictor snake seized Ellison, encircling him tightly. For a moment there was hope, because my brother was fast. He managed to get his forearm vertical, quickly drawn knife glinting as he struggled in the snake's grip, waiting for an opening.

Then three more slithered out from beneath the underbrush. Ellison saw them coming. I waited, holding my breath as he pivoted, struggling under the massive snake's weight, buying time and distance.

It was mostly obscured. If I hadn't seen one before, I might have missed it entirely. But there, in the distance, was a runed, circular pillar that looked exactly like an elevator platform. And despite the many realms of Flauros I'd entered, there was only one place with lifts that looked like that.

The tower.

CHAPTER FIFTY-SIX

"Sara, I need to talk to Tyler." I barreled down I-20, swerving around traffic, pushing eighty-five, Buzzcut humming to himself in the passenger seat.

"Uh. Can I ask what this is regarding, Matt?" Sara said, her voice carrying the typical tinny undertone that coincided with a voice call.

"Are you—does he have you screening his calls like a fucking secretary?" As usual for fucking I-20, two cars were turtle crawling the far-left lanes, cruising well under the speed limit. I dropped back, crossing over to the third and gunned it.

<**Miles:** Haven't heard from you in a while. Was getting worried. Got something for me?>
<**Myrddin:** Confirmed location on the chimera necro. Give me a minute.>
<**Miles:** For that, I'll wait all damn day. Take your time.>

The text fired back in the blink of an eye, distracting me momentarily until I realized how long Sara had been silent.

I cleared my throat, switching the blinker for another lane

change. "Maybe that was out of pocket. But what's the deal? He's dodging calls, stonewalling Nick—I don't get it. We're in a strong position right now, but there's no guarantee it'll last if we don't push the advantage."

There was a cutoff noise as Sara started to speak and stopped, then tried again. "Uh. There's a bit of organizational drag happening. Too many chefs in the kitchen."

"Pertaining to what?"

"How to proceed," Sara said carefully.

A chill cut through me. If there was some sort of high-level disagreement on how to approach the tower, that was one thing. But this didn't sound like that. This sounded more like the Adventurers' Guild getting cold feet.

<**Myrddin:** Necromancer's in the tower. One-hundred percent confidence. Either retreated there or had a base from the start. Makes sense. Plenty of fodder to farm for Cores, easy to nab a User every so often without drawing too much attention.>

"Define proceed," I asked flatly.

"There's been a lot of questions regarding the best course of action for everyone," Sara answered.

"Then explain it to me, because I'm not getting it." I punched the horn and held it, noise blaring at an oncoming wall of cars until the one driver capable of tying his shoes without drooling picked the pace up enough to form a hole. "We take the tower, solidify our alliance with the Order, and potentially stop the Transposition events for good. Bearing in mind the last Transposition wiped out almost a hundred thousand people, the alternative is what—sitting around with our dicks in our hands?"

"The alliance will hold," Sara argued. "The Order confirmed it, in writing. They'll support us during this event and any that might follow, so long as we don't undermine them and continue to work towards clearing the tower."

And you think they'll fucking stick to that after everything goes to hell?

Another text came through, interrupting me before I could retort.

<**Miles:** Well, shit. Any chance you can nail down the specific floor?>

<**Myrddin:** No. It's distinct enough to identify from a glance—a dead forest surrounding a giant castle—but I don't have the floor number.>

<**Miles:** Give me a detailed description of the castle, specifically.>

I complied, sending back as much information on the castle as I could recall, hoping he'd connect the dots and latch onto it.

"God, like today hasn't been stressful enough," Sara muttered, voice call barely picking her up. Then, louder: "Matt, I'm not saying we're throwing in the towel. We're not. There are already plans in place to tackle the next floor at dawn tomorrow. But try to put yourself in Tyler's shoes here. Just a bit."

"The man has giant feet, Sara. Do me a favor and help bridge the gap."

<**Miles:** Tip came through about the chimera freak. Could be promising.>

<**Matt:** What—

Pressed as I was, I nearly jumped on it. Started forming a message in the quick-response screen without even double-checking the body of text. My own instincts stopped me a split second before <**Jaded Eye**> could start screaming about a trap, and I expanded the screen, revealing a second series of texts between Matt and Myrddin.

Shit. Almost missed it.

I glanced at the console clock on the dash, setting a mental six-minute delay before Matt could respond to Miles. Wasn't sure if Miles would actually seize on the similar, near-instant responses as a potential connection, but I wasn't willing to risk it.

Sara was already talking, but I only caught half of it. "... has to worry about. He also has to worry about the city at large. If we run ourselves ragged, take heavy casualties and expend resources trying to climb the tower, fail because we run up against something impossible, or end up facing the sort of threat we simply can't handle in the remaining time, we're in serious trouble."

The vein stood out on my forehead. "And if we actually work together through joint effort now and stop the events, it won't matter how many resources we expend."

"You're right," Sara admitted. She sounded exhausted and frustrated, and not necessarily with me. "That's why we're hitting the tower at dawn tomorrow, as scheduled. Believe me, Tyler wants this done just as badly as you do. Assuming we don't hit any serious snags like the last floor and can strategically push through the rest of the climb, there's nothing to worry about."

Translation: one more fuckup and we run away to bide our time with our heads between our legs.

"Great," I bit off a longer, more scathing retort. "Guess we'll get started then."

"Guess so." Sara paused, whispering to someone near her for a few seconds before she spoke. "Iris doing better?"

"Yeah."

"Glad to hear it. Hope she's getting all the rest and care she needs. She's a sweetheart."

"I'll let her know you asked. See you in the AM."

"Try to get some rest," Sara counseled, the line disconnecting moments later.

As much as I appreciated the thought, my concerns were more focused on Ellison than Iris right now. Just because my brother could usually take care of himself didn't mean this wasn't the one time he'd bitten off more than he could chew. According to him, he'd never made it through, so it was going to happen eventually. When I'd called Sara, I'd hoped to buy a few extra hours of progress. Only now, apparently, there was a possibility the Adventurers' Guild might pull support entirely.

They were making a lot of assumptions I couldn't get behind. Chief among them that there'd even been an Adventurers' Guild or Order of Parsae after the upcoming event. A strange assumption to make, probably rooted in how relatively relaxed things had been lately. Other than the necromancer attack on my region, which was shockingly ineffective in terms of casualties, everything had been quiet. They'd grown complacent, and as it always did, complacency led to inaction. As if they'd almost entirely forgotten how severely the first event had kicked their collective asses.

I exited the highway, pulling into a full parking lot beside the dive bar adjacent to the tower, glancing at the longer-than-usual cordoned line that led to the entrance. As tempting as it was to just say fuck-the-guild and go in, I'd already tried that with Nick's backing and we'd gotten our asses handed to us.

No. We were here for another reason.

Beside me, Buzzcut's cheerful humming hitched before it disappeared entirely as I slipped the mask into place, getting ready to exit as I tied up my conversations with Miles.

<Matt: I'm listening.>

<Miles: Catch you with Tara or something? Figured you'd be all over this. Want the good news or the bad news first.>

<Matt: Both>

<Miles: Fine. I have it on good authority that our mutual friend is hiding out in the tower. Downside is, we don't know exactly where, but there's a description of the floor itself. Wanna guess the defining feature?>

<Matt: Big, fuck-you necromancer creatures?>

<Miles: Well yeah. But there's a castle. And not just any castle. Massive stone walls, circular towers with conical roofs. Banners of a red dragon on a gold background.>

<Matt: Wait. Where are you getting this? Because the banner sounds like the exact sort of Arthurian lore shit the AG is looking for.>

<Miles: A reliable source.>

<Matt: ... This reliable source explain why he could tell you in-detail what the floor looked like, without knowing what number it was?>

<Miles: Come on, you know it's not always that clear cut. There's god knows how many powers in play, and people with a recon edge aren't keen on revealing their methods. Trust me. The info is solid.>

<Matt: It's confirmation we're on the right track and a good warning, at least. Not sure how much it's going to factor, given the state of things.>

I held my breath, waiting for him to bite. If I could get Miles on board, there was a chance. He had more experience organizing large groups for strategic purposes than anyone else in the dome, and more than that, was capable of doing so while navigating the more tenuous, political side of things. If anyone was capable of getting Tyler to take this more seriously, it was him.

<Miles: ?>
<Matt: Tyler's getting cold feet about the tower.>
<Miles: The hell? It hasn't even been a week. Why the heel turn?>

The next message came in before I could answer. As usual, Miles was spot on.

<Miles: Fuck. The timer, right?>
<Matt: As far as I can tell. And it's not just him. With that thing ticking down in everyone's faces, lotta people having second thoughts on the best place to focus their efforts.>
<Miles: Bastard wants to have his cake and eat it too. Playing defensive doesn't mean two shits when we have no idea what the motherfucking rules will be this time around. It could be completely different from the first. Worst-case scenario, if they end up splitting the regions, it could actively work against us.>
<Matt: That's what I'm saying.>
<Miles: Even if they can't actually stop the event, a necromancer that powerful needs to be out of play before the event starts, period.>

So close. It was important that Miles didn't feel like I was pushing him into helping. The second he did, he'd suddenly come up with a half dozen other, more important things to worry about. Bearing that in mind, I composed the next message carefully.

<Matt: Agreed. But as things are, Tyler will fold at the first sign of resistance.>

I held my breath.

<**Miles:** Fuck it. Gonna rouse some heavy hitters, see if I can get a supplementary group together. AG might change their tune if someone a little more governmental is in the trenches with them. Mind if I step in?>
<**Matt:** Not at all. See you in the AM.>

I leaned my head back, letting the mask gnaw away the buzzing sensation of stress pressing down on my temples. Beside me, Buzzcut had picked up on my mood, growing more nervous by the second. "Maybe we should do this another day. Aaron's going to have a coronary when he realizes I'm alive, and it kinda sounds like there's already too much to manage."

No matter how frustrated I am, no matter how much I want to scream, none of that is Cameron's fault. He's ready for this. But he's reliant on me. If I lose my shit in front of him, he'll be rattled for weeks.

"Tell me your cover story again," I said, keeping my tone soft, instructional.

"Myrddin abducted me from my home," Buzzcut recited, expression cold, bordering on furious as he inhabited the lie. "Cut my finger off, interrogated me. Got a little rough, some-times, nothing that topped the finger. Didn't really have to go that route. Bastard made me breathe something—a spell or potion, or something else before he started. After it took effect, things got hazy, difficult to focus. He kept asking the same question different ways. The same damn question, over and over again. Eventually, I felt compelled to answer—nothing that betrayed the Order and violated the geas—but definitely information I wouldn't have volunteered otherwise. After a while he got bored and went missing for weeks. Showed up one day, said we were done, blindfolded me, threw me in the back of a vehicle. Drive was around twenty minutes, give or take. Didn't bother to take the cuffs or blindfold off when he kicked me out."

"You can visualize everything?" I checked.

"In detail."

"If you were imprisoned indoors all this time, why's your skin tone darker than it was?"

Buzzcut shrugged. "There was a skylight. If I laid under it and kept my eyes shut, it almost felt like being outside again."

"Why didn't you use the skylight to escape?"

"Because it was a high ceiling for fuck's sake, and he wasn't stupid enough to leave me somethin' to climb."

I paused long enough to give him an encouraging smile. "And how do you feel about Myrddin now?"

"Grateful he let me go." Buzzcut cracked his knuckles, a hint of his old mean streak peeking through. "Genuinely, truly thankful. Because now, there's a second chance to tear his fucking throat out."

"Perfect."

CHAPTER FIFTY-SEVEN

In and out. Merchants section, Vernon, then back here. Ten minutes. Fifteen at most.

My pulse pounded in my neck as I stepped out of the gateway into the portal room. As my mind absorbed the incessant humming from the concave arrangement of magical entryways, it was a relief to find it empty. Not even Sybil was present, the woman who served as Hastur's surrogate and mouthpiece.

When I first joined the order, for the most part people ignored me. Those out of the loop saw little more than a shady newcomer. The rare few with close ties to either Aaron or Sunny who knew Myrddin was the Ordinator gave me a wide berth. Not surprising, as I'd joined soon after the system powers that be drew the connection between the Ordinator and the mass casualty event that defined the first Transposition. There were reasonable concerns that I'd snap at the first sign of confrontation, tapping into whatever god-forsaken powers I apparently had to transform the entire silo into an eldritch hellscape.

Despite the considerable bounty on my head, the smart ones stayed away. But impatience is the downfall of intellect, and eventually the potential reward of power and escape from the dome grew too tantalizing to bear.

I'd dealt with the threats proportionally. Not equally—I'd learned quickly, in early days, if you only match what you're given, it eventually catches up in a bad way. By the same token, if the response is too devastating, you risk souring general opinion. Users here had friends, connections, people they were close to. A perfect, proportional response is one that left those friends and connections quietly shaking their heads as they visited you in the infirmary, not seething with anger and plotting vengeance. Thinking, "Damn, that sucks, but come on. You had it coming."

The real trick was making it look effortless. And that the mercy wasn't mercy at all.

For a while, it had worked. In contrast to the Order's many rules, Aaron didn't seem to care much if we fought among ourselves, fostering his old-world hedge fund philosophy of letting the strong rise to the top.

Lately, despite my best efforts, the random attacks and confrontations had gotten worse. Rumors circulated. There was too much blood in the water. And I had a feeling the members of the Order would be feeling the stress of the timer as much as anyone else. Possibly more. Because unlike everyone who existed outside the Order, it was common knowledge now that if you didn't want to deal with city-sized horseshit, there was one ticket out. And his name was Myrddin.

The double-security doors sequestering the portal room whooshed open to the third floor of the Order's silo. Padded impacts echoed up from the half-dozen fenced-in octagons on the bottom floor, the stench of sweat mingling with cooking meat from the nearby cafeteria as dozens of conversations blended into a constant din of anxiety and paranoia.

"Well shit, y'all. The friendly neighborhood Ordinator's on

deck!" someone bellowed with a raucous cackle. Conversations died as heads turned. There was plenty of wariness in their expressions, but there was something new too. A hunger that perhaps had always been there. Difference was, no one seemed interested in hiding it.

I kept my presence small and moved at a steady, unhurried pace, not bothering to hide my disdain as I scanned faces and monitored for threats. By now I could spot the markers from a mile away. An intentional nudge, a muttered word, usually followed by some muscle head standing to his feet and moving to intercept me.

Oddly, no one made a move. There were plenty of Users around who looked scared enough to try something, but not a single one of them budged.

Elevator's got a lot of people around it. Guess that means stairs again.

The long, windowless stairwells weren't much better in terms of safety. Key difference was space. Room to maneuver. Unlike the boxed-in metal coffin of an elevator, I could do a lot with three flights of stairs.

I kept a grip on the rope in my pack, forming a plan to secure the upper door so if there were people waiting at the bottom, I couldn't be flanked from above.

<Awareness> murmured, and I saw the point of a blade in my mind's eye, plummeting toward my neck.

A Rogue today, huh? That's new.

I yanked the coil of rope from my pack and tossed it straight up, the length unfurling overhead. With the momentum from the turn, I knocked the incoming blade aside, catching the throat of my attacker with my free hand, getting a good look at him for the first time. Pissed-off gray eyes stared back, perfectly coifed black hair completing a look somewhat stereotypical for the class. But there was a franticness behind the hard edge, like he'd known he was out of his element this whole time and gone through with it anyway.

"Who put you up to this?" I scanned the cafeteria behind him. It was almost certainly someone watching nearby, possibly one of the shadowy faces whispering in the cafeteria.

"Kill yourself," the Rogue spat back.

"Disappointing." I shoved him back and released my hold, narrowly dodging the flashing blade as it struck toward my neck. The rope overhead landed, Audrey's blind spirit following my instructions as one end tightened around the rogue's neck, looping around his shoulders, the other tying itself to the base of the nearby railing. "Being completely honest here, I hate shooting the messenger, but there's no time to be picky."

"Huh?" The Rogue croaked, eyes widening as the noose tightened around his neck.

"Solid last words."

He made one last desperate, awkward lunge at me and I caught him, **<Unsparing Fang>** directing my movements as I repurposed his momentum and, almost effortlessly, tossed the man over the railing.

Seconds later, the rope snapped taut.

As tempting as it was to lean over the edge for confirmation, I reminded myself that the casual callousness of the violence was the point. So instead of looking, I stuck my hands in my pockets and returned to my previous destination. The stairwell.

The door latched behind me, my own footsteps echoing off the stone walls as I murmured to Azure, "Status."

Azure's chipper voice resounded in my head. "Alive and healthy! Though delightfully convinced that he's choking to death."

"He's not though."

"Not at all," Azure chuckled. "Our mutual friend has loosened her grip, and the vines masquerading as ropes around his shoulders are bearing most of the weight. Not that anyone in the growing crowd below has made that connection. The Rogue's name is Chris, if you care."

"I don't. Get anything from him?"

"Nothing telling." My summon's shadow flickered as he walked alongside me in the stairwell. "The Rogue's blade is coated with a potent paralytic."

"Why paralytic and not poison?"

"As you surmised, he was strong-armed by another User. Big man upstairs towards the back of the cafeteria. Tau. Took a shot at you a few weeks ago. Once you were incapacitated, Tau intended to follow up for the kill."

I paused to think.

"You broke his legs," Azure provided.

"Right." A tattooed face came to mind. The man was built like a mountain of muscle and almost entirely absent neck. "Doesn't make sense. I remember him now—and he was scared shitless. Why the hell is he coming back for more?"

"Unknown. Largely because Tau seems to have suddenly wised to the practice of integrating mental shielding to his build," Azure said meaningfully.

"Fucking Aaron," I realized, remembering how stressed he'd seemed in my region when he'd asked Matt to speak to Myrddin on his behalf. Turned out he wasn't just micro-managing. The strike team's effectiveness unnerved him, and he'd gleaned more insight watching from a distance than he should have.

"My guess as well. Shall I track him down? See if I can catch him monitoring the situation?"

I weighed the options for a moment, then shook my head. "Aaron's too smart to just wait around slack-jawed. Even if he wasn't, it doesn't tell us anything we don't already know. Monitor the surface thoughts of the people in the crowd, sift for anything valuable. Half the Order will have their opinion of Myrddin front and center, and that doesn't happen every day."

"Roger that." Azure's cheerful expression melted back into a cluster of shadows on the wall, disappearing entirely.

There was a time walking through a waiting crowd—especially an angry one focused on me—would have given me no end of anxiety. Now, as I threw the stairwell door open and walked through them, placidly scanning the dozens of faces that panned me with latent hostility as they parted beneath the red-faced Rogue struggling for breath, I felt little beyond tacit annoyance. All things considered, it didn't take much to intimidate them. The problem was an issue of retention.

"Ay. You gonna let him down?" someone groused, the speaker conveniently hidden by the crowd.

"Depends."

"On what? He's dying, for chrissakes."

A glint of metal on the concrete ground caught my eye. Not wanting to stoop over and present an easy target, I wedged the toe of my boot beneath the hilt and kicked upward, catching the hilt. I studied it blandly. "On whether the knife he tried to stab me with is poisoned." Casually, I hurled the blade toward the hanging Rogue, late application of **<Probability Cascade>** ensuring its slow rotation hit the mark blade first. The knife hit with a thump, sticking about an inch through the Rogue's calf. He emitted a strangled cry of surprise and almost immediately began to seize, his flailing limbs stiffening almost immediately.

"Shame." I took one last look at the Rogue before entering the smithery.

CHAPTER FIFTY-EIGHT

Kai and Erik had expanded since my last visit. Open forges created a billowing heat that flowed outward, jumping the temperature at least twenty degrees from the silo's room temp. Several apprentice smiths, enchanters, and artificers attended various projects behind the open counter. Kai was dressing one such artificer down, his high-pitched voice and colorful language barely audible over the din of metal and buzzing of magic.

Erik was leaning forward on the counter, burly arms crossed beneath him, crumpling his black apron. His gaze shifted between me and the crowd outside the glass windows with a mix of caution and curiosity. "Busy morning?" he asked gruffly.

"Nothing out of the ordinary. Looks like you guys stepped it up a notch." I looked around in quiet approval. "Several, for that matter. Business that good?"

Erik kneaded his forehead tiredly. "Steady. Been up to our necks in commissions for a few weeks now, hence the extra help. Trying to get them out before the Transposition." Suddenly, seeming to remember that I was a customer, he straightened up. "Yours are more or less ready to go."

"More or less?"

"Aye. But it being a prototype, new design and all, I'd like a few more days to tinker if I'm honest."

"And a few days from now, you'll want a few more," Kai called over as he approached the counter, his flowing, colorful robes clashing with his surly expression. He crossed his arms and looked at me, then seemed to finally notice the commotion outside. "Can I get that loaner back—what the fuck is happening? What are they all doing? Is that a shoe?"

Before anyone could respond, Kai was already around the counter and peeking his head out the door, looking up at where the Rogue User was still hanging. After a moment he retreated, slowly closing the door and peering at Erik. "I've been bitching about aesthetic for weeks now, but now I really have to put my foot down. Why is there a human piñata decorating our shop?"

Out of the corner of my eye, I saw Erik brush his fingers horizontally across his throat.

"What does this mean?" Kai repeated the same gesture back, unimpressed.

Annoyed, Erik thumped a fist onto the counter. "It means whatever happens outside the shop is none of our business."

"And if it's hanging above the shop?"

I blew out air. "The guy tried to stab me, I threw him off the third floor. Used the rope so he didn't make a mess." Casually, I glanced over my shoulder. The crowd had moved back some to make room as someone placed a ladder down, while someone else tested the stability of the bottom step, then began to climb.

"Oh." Kai tilted his head from side to side, then raised a hand and made a thrusting motion. "Why didn't you just stab him back?"

"Kai—" Erik hissed.

"Like I said, didn't want to make a mess." I pulled the **<Vorpal Gnasher>** out of my inventory and tossed it to Kai, who caught it, a brief squeak of surprise quickly silenced. "Assuming you've got a knife for me along with everything else, here's the loaner back."

"And how. You'd be shocked how many idiots miss the 'cannot be sharpened by ordinary means' small print on the vorpal enchantment and try to hold onto these." Kai slid the blade out of the sheath, studying its waning edge with a frown. "Though I suppose it'd be hard to miss, given the state." He pressed his thumb against the edge, sliding it down slightly, incurring nothing but an indent. "This sort of wear usually takes longer. You really put it through its paces."

"Been busy." I watched the blade in Kai's hands, feeling a small pang. "The armor penetration paid dividends. Part of me is glad the enchantment isn't widely used—the arrogance full-plate gives certain targets can't be understated. I'd rather they keep strutting around like walking tanks, thinking they're invincible."

"Full-plate, really?" Kai stared at the blade uneasily. "Surprised it worked for that."

"Most of the time it wasn't necessary. Generally better to aim for the weak points, gaps. But if the armor's high rarity and there are no gaps?" I tapped my breastbone. "It did its job."

His mouth pulled down in a pout. "My desire to upsell is battling with my survival instinct."

I snorted. "Go ahead. I'm not gonna throw you off the side of something for trying to do business."

"There's a reason we only use that enchantment for commission loaners," Erik interjected cautiously, eliciting a sigh of irritation from Kai. "As you've seen, it will eventually lose its edge. Sharpening the blade and reapplying the enchantment doesn't take long, but that process requires both a talented enchanter and a smith capable of working with enchanted items. At the end of the day, most people prefer a good blade that will retain its sharpness indefinitely, rather than one that will eventually fail them."

Admittedly, I saw the wisdom in that. Were the dulling process more binary—sharp one second, blunt as soon as the magic faded—I'd probably agree. If you were inattentive, or inexperienced, it would probably still be a bad idea. But I'd been able to gauge the blade's waning effectiveness over repeated uses. And with the new artifact-class acquisition of **\<Luciana\>**, I had one hell of a backup.

Kai grimaced. "I've—we've—put together an already excellent weapon for your commission. Beyond the immediate requests, metal processed through the new lunar forges is particularly receptive to mana. Naturally, I took advantage of that and layered as many potentially useful effects as I could."

"At no additional charge," Erik hastily added.

"Why would you do that?" I asked, genuinely curious.

"New forges weren't a variable when you sought us out. Wouldn't be right."

"I'm happy to pay more for a better product."

"Trying to screw yourself out of a deal?" Erik glared at me for a moment before averting his eyes again.

Kai cleared his throat. "What big-handsome-and-awkward's trying to say is that recently we were mainly selling pre-mades. Then on his first day, the scariest motherfucker in the dome walked in and made a commission. Suddenly, everyone and their grandmother wants something bespoke. Experience from commissions is better, not to mention money, so we're sitting pretty. Well, I'm always sitting pretty, but you get my meaning." He switched back to business mode. "The dagger is mostly done, but the vorpal enchantment doesn't take much space. If you're willing to bring it back for discounted maintenance every few weeks, I can probably make it happen."

"I'm willing." Generous as all this appeared, I wasn't born yesterday. "Guessing you guys are still looking for a way out?"

They shared a look and nodded.

"It's not... urgent, exactly," Kai answered haltingly. "No one's strong-arming us the way they used to, but the vibes around here? Well..."

"The sooner the better," Erik murmured.

"Okay." I clapped my hands together. "Let's see what you've got. If it's good, I'll see what I can do."

"If it's good? Prepare to eat your heart out." Kai rolled his eyes, gesturing for me to follow.

Past the series of forges and several immersion tanks with various luminescent elements, the smith's storage area had been expanded. Approximately half of what was once a basic stockroom had been blown out through carved stone, the new half doubling as a testing area complete with mannequins, padded targets, striking posts, and the dangling ropes and pulleys of various tension mechanisms I could only assume measured flexibility and resilience. The room itself was sequestered from the open format of the rest of the smith, an armored door secured with a series of complex locks that were at least partially magical in nature.

"So," Erik's eyes flashed with anticipation. "Between the armor and weapons, where would you like to start?"

I raised an eyebrow. I'd placed the second order nearly two weeks after the original commission for the weapons. "I assumed the armor wouldn't be ready yet."

He grunted, a pep in his step as he placed a large box on a wide, sturdy table and wheeled over a mannequin with a rolling base, covered in a sheet. "Frustrating as it is to admit, the armor you brought in for alterations was already solid. There wasn't much room for improvement beyond the modifications, though we did manage a few notable improvements. It didn't take long."

"The silhouette—"

"Was the biggest issue, we remember," Kai called over. He'd busied himself working on something out of view beneath a nearby shelf, hands glowing as he made adjustments to the box below. Possibly the knife. "Trust me, you'll be happy with the results."

"Enchanting aside, Kai's an artist with a needle," Erik agreed with the sort of easy confidence that was difficult to fake.

"I guess we should start with the original commission. The weapons," I mused. My original issue wasn't an easy one to solve. **<Page's Quickdraw>** was an invaluable ambush skill in almost any combat encounter at close to medium range. The problem was, I generally preferred engaging at range and typically did so. If whatever I was shooting at survived the initial volley and closed range, my ranged weapons often already needed to be reloaded, forcing me into melee. My initial, more economical idea was to sacrifice inventory space and simply buy cheap crossbows to rotate through. An idea the blacksmith had talked me out of. Now, I was curious to see what he'd come up with.

Erik grinned. And opened the box.

CHAPTER FIFTY-NINE

The contents were, at first glance, a little disappointing. Four simple black outlines—the pistol grip, trigger, and body, weren't much more compact than a typical hand crossbow. The greatest reduction in size was the body itself, lacking the thicker, more ample midsection of a typical self-reloading hand crossbow shaved down to almost nothing. The limbs of all four bows appeared to be folded back for storage, creating a look more reminiscent of some sort of high-tech slingshot than a crossbow.

I dislodged one from the foam and attempted to extend the wings, finding them firm and unyielding. On second look, there were no hinges and the string was taut, but surely it couldn't be permanently locked in this form.

Puzzled, I pulled up the description.

<**Item:** Portent Armory>
Description: Though these four diminutive—

"Hold on," Erik shook his head sternly, snatching the loosely held weapon out of my hands before I could read the description in full. "Respectfully, I busted my ass. Already knew they were gonna be special halfway through, but these little beauties ended up being my second vocational capstone. Let me give them a better breakdown than the pre-filled system tripe."

I inclined my head, trailing behind him as he approached one of the padded targets, finger resting on the trigger guard. "Someone a lot smarter than me once said that limitation breeds creativity. Never put much stock in that 'til now." He smirked. "Could be wrong, but the day you walked in, I got the sense you were frugal. Loaded, but frugal. Also gleaned you didn't give two fucks about ornamentation. So a big part of the design phase was sussin' out how, exactly, to make these things worth the cheddar to ya." He extended his arm toward the target, less than two feet away from the crossbow's barrel, and fired.

There was no sound. No telltale twang. Nothing but a blur and ample thud as the padded target suddenly jerked upward against the back leg of its tripod base, clattering hard against the ground.

Interest piqued, I tried to lift the target with the toe of my boot and discovering it was too heavy for that, crouched down and lifted it with both hands. It was more weighted than it appeared—somewhere between seventy-five and a hundred pounds.

"First piece of the puzzle was stopping power. Probably don't gotta tell you this, but outside of some very specific use cases, hand crossbows are generally outclassed by their bigger, more accurate siblings. The bigger form factor allows for greater power, but it's a new age. Material options with appropriate tensile strength aren't nearly as limited as it once was. Ever run into a Dopki?"

I shook my head.

"Not the nastiest bastards the system has thrown at us, probably not even in the top ten, Nasty nonetheless. Lizards, around the size of a small dog. Chameleon-style camouflage. Ambush hunters. If they feel threatened, they'll jump out at you, generally from a wall, try to get their jaws on your head. If they do?" Erik snapped his fingers. "Lights out. Crush strength that would make an alligator blush. Thankfully for the Users paling around the low-level eco-dungeons they're most common in, their preferred diet isn't meat."

"They eat rocks for minerals, their stomachs are insane, which makes for stupidly good gut string. Get to the cool part already!" Kai called over, covering a laugh as Erik glared at him.

"How much pressure?" I asked, ignoring the enchanter's grumbling.

"Three times the usual amount." Erik grinned.

"Bullshit." I worked my jaw, absorbing the idea that it was even possible. Something occurred to me. "Even if it wasn't, wouldn't that much force just shatter the ammunition?"

"It would. And it did." Erik chuckled nostalgically. "Pulled my hair out trying to get conventional bolts to work. Tried everything. Denser wood, material composites. Everything either broke or bent the second the trigger was pulled."

"What finally hacked it?"

"Something a little closer to home. See for yourself." He pointed to the target.

The back of the bolt—still protruding from the target—was atypical, absent the stereotypical fins. I gripped it tightly, immediately feeling a distinct drop in temperature seep through my glove.

"It's metal." I realized at least a third of the small crossbow's heft must have come solely from the bolt. After considerable effort, it finally dislodged. "Solid all the way through?"

"Yup." Erik nodded, taking the bolt from me and replacing it in another crossbow. "Tried hollow, same issue as the conventional stuff. Iron was too heavy, steel was closer to what I wanted, but still not quite there. Landed on Tridium. System analogue for a tungsten alloy, far as I can tell. Dense. Doesn't handle sustained abuse well, which makes it a terrible choice for armor, but a brief moment of intense pressure?" He adjusted something near the sight, then fired the second crossbow at a more distant target. Again, the bolt rocketed forward. Unlike the first, closer target, the bolt shot forward about five feet before it plunged downward, metal screeching as it slid across the floor. "Imagine you'll get anywhere between fifteen to twenty uses per bolt before accuracy becomes a concern. Course, that leaves the biggest problem of using solid metal bolts."

"Range." I frowned. Diversifying my kit, using different tools for different problems, was nothing I wasn't used to. But the distance was practically non-existent. It'd make me an even better fighter than I already was in close quarters, but from a realistic standpoint it did nothing to solve my mid-range issue and risked redundancy.

"Went back to the ammunition drawing board for a bit, eventually decided I'd need outside help a bit earlier than I thought."

"Nuh uh." Kai replaced the lid of the item he'd been adjusting, smirking all the while. "Tell him. Tell our favorite customer how many days you spent banging your head against the wall before you remembered you had a talented enchanter on staff."

"... Several," Erik growled.

"I'm not just a pretty face. And I've been very curious how, exactly, the Order creates their portals," Kai provided, approaching the table and looking over the crossbows, glowing with pride. "The only teleportation enchantments I have access to can only be applied to inanimate objects. Organic material is a no-go, but I've been playing with it, trying to find a way around the limitations. Not there yet, but I've learned the practical applications inside and out. Coupled with an enchantment that works like a range-finder—which was, coincidentally, another enchantment Erik demeaned as useless—and we found our solution."

I gave up trying to piece it together myself as Kai, barely able to contain his excitement, unseated the third crossbow and passed it to me butt first, gesturing toward the more distant target.

Curious how it would function in my typical use case, I inventoried the bow. Then activated **<Page's Quickdraw>**. It snapped into my hand. The pistol grip—while seemingly identical at first glance—landed perfectly in my palm, the few barely perceptible indentations ensuring the weapon nestled perfectly in alignment. Bearing in mind the faster drop off, I focused slightly above the target and fired, not bothering to aim.

The bolt launched beneath the raised sight, blurring, seeming to shrink for fractions of a second before it disappeared entirely. Moments later there was an impact as the metal bolt slammed into the cushioned back wall behind the target, exactly at the height I'd aimed.

My jaw dropped. Barring enhanced perception, there's no way I would have caught it.

Even with amplified senses it was difficult to parse precisely what, exactly, happened. But I knew two things for certain. The first was that, for a millisecond, the bolt disappeared completely. The second was that it had reappeared, closer to the target, retaining velocity and effectively tripling the range.

"Sorry." I slowly turned to look at Kai. "What the fuck?"

"Uhuh," Kai preened, clearly delighted as he took the crossbow from me. "It's naturally intuitive. If you pull the trigger and the rangefinder enchantment detects a target within three meters, it fires like a normal crossbow. If the target is outside of three meters, the bolt teleports, reappearing approximately a meter away from the target." His brows pulled down in consternation. "Real bitch of a time making the teleport destination pinpoint accurate, main reason beyond enchanting real-estate and the sheer power it would cost being I couldn't just give it a more impressive range, but the end results speak for themselves. What's more, there are identical, less precise variations of the same spell here," he pointed to the butt of the crossbow, then the two limbs, "here, and here."

"To what end?" I asked.

Suddenly, Erik reached over and slapped the bow out of Kai's hand in a gesture that could have been playful, openly grinning as the small enchanter yelped. Kai shrieked something obscene I couldn't be bothered to catch as I watched the small, delicate work of art plummet toward the floor.

And slip through it like a rock into water.

I went to one knee, examining the concrete below. There was no indication that something solid had passed through the surface. Not even a scuff.

"To that end," Erik provided cheerfully.

"What the fuck," I repeated.

"There's a simple on-off enchantment in the grip that detects if the weapon is being held or not." Kai babied his wrist, still glaring daggers at Erik. "If it's dropped, the rangefinders will activate at the last possible moment to trigger the second return-state teleport a split second before the object hits the ground, or is close to exceeding the maximum distance of approximately twenty meters. Once those parameters are met, it returns to the control stone." Kai gestured toward the box with a half-hearted magician's flourish.

All four crossbows sat as if they'd simply been there the

whole time. I picked out the one I'd fired, noting that it was once more locked back into the firing position.

"I was wondering how I'd manage to reload these with the weight involved." I felt a slow creeping smile. "So I keep the control stone in my inventory, fire, drop, the bow returns to the inventory ready for another bolt. Don't tell me they fully reload themselves, given the ammo?"

Erik cleared his throat awkwardly. "We uh, couldn't quite crack how to get these beauties to slap in another bolt on their own inside a User's inventory. In theory, it's possible, but there's a lot of restrictions on the inventory that don't apply anywhere else, probably for good reason. You'll need to do that part yourself."

The weapons presented so many new possibilities it made my head spin. I stood there, silently working through them all until I realized both Erik and Kai were fidgeting uncomfortably, and spoke my current ponderance aloud. "So there's effectively two firing modes. Close and extended. Any way to lock it to one or the other?"

"Hm?" Erik cocked his head, not grasping my meaning.

"In case I need to shoot through something or someone."

They traded a look before Kai answered. "Does that... uh... come up a lot?"

I shrugged. "More than you'd think."

"It'd be difficult to add at this stage." Erik nodded slowly, considering it. "A manual toggle is possible. Technically, the function is already there, but Kai did the enchanting work with the self-activation in mind. How long would it take?" He crossed his arms, wincing as he waited for his partner to answer.

"Weeks. I'd have to scrap most of what I already have and redo it," Kai recited emotionlessly, soul seeming to leave his body with every passing word. "It would cost a lot of resources, and I don't even want to think about the alignment process after doing this four separate times, but sure, totally doable."

"Would you like to tell our favorite customer who broached that very question and was squawked at to get out of the Etherworks and go hit something with a hammer?" Erik asked blandly, a sheen of spiteful mischief in his eye.

"No," Kai said.

"I'll take them as is," I clarified, deciding that specific use case didn't really merit the additional time and aggravation.

Their sense of relief was immediate and palpable.

"Could probably spend all day testing these, but we should probably move on. What else you got?"

———

The answer was quite a bit. Starting with the knife. **<Alchemist's Razor>**, sporting a bowie-style form with Persian trappings, its shining blade covered with runes, finally solved my absence-of-variety problem. It was larger than I preferred, but this was necessary for all the moving parts. The crystalline knob at the base served as a magical battery and rotating mode switch. According to Kai, electricity and fire in small-class weapons caused too many potential problems for the wielder to be viable—if I stabbed a monster with a live knife coursing with thousands of volts of electricity, and taking obvious issue with this the monster grabbed me, the problem was obvious. Same with fire. Instead, he'd started by deconstructing one of Mile's draining garrotes and reverse-engineering a similar enchantment that fed into the knife's internal mana battery, making up the first of the blade's three modes.

The second was imbued with the last of the matriarch spider's venom I'd harvested a lifetime ago. The effect was less potent than the venom in its original form, but the upside was that it would last as long as the blade had charge, which could be restored by switching back to the first mode.

We'd discussed dark, or potentially even eldritch as a third option. Unfortunately, they were so difficult to work with that in the end Kai hadn't been able to manage it. The alternative he'd come up with—parameters being a ruinous, devastating option that countered quick regeneration—was mildly horrifying.

Kai demonstrated, turning the crystalline core on the hilt to the third setting. Unlike the first two, there was no dull green or violet glow coursing through the runes. The metal remained static, though there was a certain reflective sheen to it I was uncertain had been there before.

Gripping the knife tightly, Kai took aim and plunged it into one of the waiting targets. There was an audible SHINK. Bracing himself and planting a foot on the target base for support, Kai gripped the hilt of the knife with both hands and yanked. The target tore, two inches of padding and material pouring out of the gap, leaving a gaping hole around a fist wide. In his hands, the weapon no longer looked like a knife. Rather, a rod of the same length with countless metallic barbs emitting at countless, asymmetrical angles.

"Jesus."

"Transmutation. Kind of brutal," Kai nodded, watching as the spines on the blade folded back in, expending the rest of its power to reforge. "Spines are thin enough that at least some of them should break off, yet they never do."

"What was the base material?" I asked, fighting a growing queasiness.

A few feet behind, Erik cleared his throat and answered. "What was the damaged weapon you brought in made of?"

That was a surprise. Erik was referring to a shattered faux-artifact we'd found in the tower. The sword was meant to be a facsimile of Excalibur. When Nick picked it up, it fell to pieces in his hands. It was supposed to be fake. A prop. I'd brought it in for Kai to study the enchantment traces because Kinsley's team lacked the specific expertise to identify. Kinsley was still hurting on the weapons crafter front, and as the blade material was correctly identified as some sort of low-grade mix of iron and something else, we figured it would make a good show of goodwill.

Apparently we were wrong.

"Which is a nice, gentle lead-in to another topic we'd like to speak to you about." Kai crossed his arms. "The wood you brought in? We'd like more of it. A lot more. Metal too, but we're guessing that was all you had. "

"I'm listening," I ventured, figuring it was better to with-hold information until I had a better idea of where this was going.

Erik circled around the table, standing next to Kai, forming a cohesive unit. "The Wraithwood is staggeringly strong."

"And immensely enchantable," Kai added.

"In typical system-fuckery fashion, it doesn't burn. It melts." Erik shook his head slowly. "The molten—shit, I don't even know what to call it."

"Pulp?" Kai tried.

"Close enough," Erik agreed. "The pulp interacts with other materials strangely when melted down and combined. Still toying with the potential alloys, but I inlaid it on the bows for additional support. Otherwise, they'd be breaking as often as they fired, and Kai wouldn't have been able to use a fraction of the enchantments he managed."

"And the metal?" I asked.

"You're one-hundred percent committed to not telling us what it was or where it came from?" Erik asked again.

I inclined my head.

Kai sighed, surveying the dagger with the barest hint of wonder. "This stupid thing. Your people were correct. Broken and decrepit as it was, there were hints of an enchantment. And not just any enchantment. Whatever the original purpose, it's more complex than anything I've worked with, and it's not even close."

"You couldn't crack it," I filled in.

"No," Kai snapped. "Well, yes. It was impossible to fully identify, let alone recreate, but I was able to parse enough of the internal schema to piece together the type of enchantment. Transmutation."

"Pretend like I have no enchanting background and fill me in on the significance."

Again, they shared a look. This time it was Kai who spoke. "Transmutation enchantments are generally a poor choice for bladed weapons. Maces and war hammers see some benefit, but the downside is arguably still not worth it. It's not as simple as transforming one thing into another. Technically, you can have a claymore that transforms itself into a scythe—not sure why anyone would want that, but you could—but every time you swapped from one form to the other, there would be a small degree of base material lost in the process, accounting for energy spent for the transformation itself. The immediate loss isn't noticeable, but cumulatively, it adds up. The structural integrity degrades, and one day, 'oops,' my novelty weapon fell to pieces."

"Tracks with how I found it," I admitted.

"We—or I, rather—was convinced it was just well-enchanted iron." Erik took the dagger from Kai and looked it over. "Felt, smelt, and melted identically." He grinned, glancing toward the door that led to the forges. "If I hadn't been testing the Wraithwood pulp that week, we might have never thought to melt it down and test it."

I shifted uncomfortably. "Doesn't deconstructing a weapon... destroy the supposedly priceless enchantment?"

"It would," Kai sniffed. "If I was a novice and stupid." He reached in his robes and nonchalantly tossed me a crystal disc. Both the top and the bottom were convex, giving it the shape of a basic UFO, emitting a light green glow that felt appropriate.

\<Item: Expert Enchanter's Blueprint (Incomplete)\>
\<Description: Little can be gleaned from this crafted object by those lacking the enchantment vocation or advanced diagnostic/identification abilities.\>
\<Value: ???\>

"Wasn't accomplishing anything in its broken form," Kai shook his head. "But by copying everything I could—even the parts that were utterly incomprehensible—someone can potentially fill in the enchantment's blanks and make use of it later." Even as he spoke, Kai looked mildly envious at the prospect. "Erik alloyed the 'iron' with Wraithwood pulp, because Erik now wants to alloy everything with Wraithwood. The results were more drastic than every other material he worked with. We still don't know what to call it, but it sure as hell isn't iron."

"Still in favor of Omnium," Erik scowled.

"And if we were naming a knock-off super hero instead of a god-tier alloy, I'd agree with you." Kai rolled his eyes. "More importantly, I tested a small sample with a basic transmutation enchantment for days. Pretty much anything falls apart after fifty alterations, but whatever this is, it's still rock solid." He lowered the **\<Alchemist's Razor\>** in its box, uncharacteristically reverent. "One of a kind. The mode-switch enchantments barely took space. I layered on strengthening, ergonomic, and muffling enchants—which would normally be a pick one or two situation—not to mention vorpal and the weak-point identification enchantment you wanted cloned, and this mean bastard still has room."

"So you could still potentially improve it in the future," I filled in, hiding a smile.

This was a reminder. It wasn't just that, of course. Their enthusiasm, for the most part, was too unbridled to be anything other than authentic. But the entire reason they'd gone so above and beyond was because I'd broached the possibility of getting them out from under the Order if the results spoke for themselves. And the results were screaming that I'd be an absolute dumbass leaving them under Aaron's thumb.

"You have my support." I wiggled the disc that Kai couldn't seem to keep his eyes off of in front of his face. "And on that note, I'm getting the feeling you'd like to keep studying this?"

"God yes," Kai breathed.

I tossed it back to him, noting the barely suppressed shriek as he all but dove to catch it. "Couple of conditions. I'd like you both to keep what you've discovered about Wraithwood to yourselves. Is that going to be a problem with all the new hires?"

"Not at all." Erik smiled, seeming to finally shed his anxiety. "Don't have to tell me we can't trust this lot. I'm the only one who's worked with it. Uh. Few of 'em might have seen me throwing wood shavings into a fire and asked questions—to which they were told to mind their business—but other than Kai, no one knows the value at stake."

"Perfect." I pulled up my UI and sent the contact cards from the woman handling Merchants' Guild talent acquisition. "Message the last contact first, only reach out to the others if there's no answer. The second condition is that from this moment, we only talk about this subject through text. There's a lot of eyes and ears around here. I didn't linger the first time, so they're probably not listening now—"

"Definitely not," Azure confirmed, the slightest ripple of shadow visible as he slipped back into mine.

"—But I drew some attention on my way in, and at least a few people outside are going to realize I've been in here longer than the average customer. Assuming the transition goes smoothly, you'll have access to more Wraithwood than you can shake a stick at."

Erik pounded a table in excitement and paced back and forth. "When?"

"During the event." It was the safest answer. If the joint initiative managed to stop the event, or delay it, we'd need another plan. But if we failed—and there was enough uncertainty with the AG's newly uncovered reticence that I wasn't willing to bet on it—there was no better time to poach crafters than during the chaos of the Transposition.

Judging from Erik's wince, he didn't agree. "Place'll be empty, so we might be able to get the forges out. But if it's anything like the first, the roads will be terrible. Plus, we'll need a cargo truck. Getting from point A to point B through that hellscape in a slow-moving vehicle could be tricky."

"Can you make more forges?" I asked.

His eyes widened. "They're exorbitantly expensive."

"Yes," I said patiently, "And the faction you're about to defect to has materials and Selve to spare. So what are our real problems?"

"Competition," Kai noted glumly.

"If we just... abandon ship." Erik's lips thinned, betraying discomfort with the theoretical. "Even an unspecialized blacksmith can get a lot of use out of the existing facilities. Might even make it easier for him to choose a specialization, considering there'd be no overhead."

"Could you disassemble them?"

"Not without losing the materials."

I studied the fingertips of my gloves idly. "Interesting. Assuming you talk to the contact I sent, like what you hear, and have the foresight to get a formal agreement in writing, that would solve the competition issue at no real cost, wouldn't it?"

Erik turned slightly green at the prospect of destroying his forges, but eventually nodded. "I suppose it wouldn't."

"Good." I clapped my hands together. "Reach out to that contact. When we move, we need to move quickly."

———

We settled for two hundred thousand Selve, which still felt like highway robbery. They—Kai more than Erik—wanted to go over the details of the armor before I left, but I had to see a necromancer about a girl, and I'd lingered too long as it was.

On the second floor, beyond the row of onlookers pressed up against a long railing, I caught a light flash of the back of Buzzcut's head, flanked on either side with various hulking escorts, mostly melee Users that made up Aaron's personal guard. The glimpse filled me with trepidation. We had a solid plan, but Aaron could be unpredictable. He wasn't the sort of guy to take luck at face value. Never had been. He'd be intrigued by the possibility of an inside look at the so-called rabid dog he'd unleashed, tempted by the opportunity presented. After that, though? It really all came down to how well Cameron could sell it.

When it comes to developing an asset, menace and friendliness both play a part. Too intimidating and abusive, and they'll jump ship. Too friendly, and they'll assume there's no stick. Trust is key. Balance. They need to hold the belief that you—or the people backing you—are scarier than the people you're turning them against, and simultaneously believe that you'll come running if they stick their necks out and the axe comes down, even if you won't. To be clear, I'm not encouraging the practice of burning assets. There are a lot of people on government payroll I don't associate with because they're too quick to do exactly that. Sometimes you can't help them, and that's a tough pill to swallow. And no matter how pragmatic you try to be, you will swallow it. Because if you did it right, you're the only hope they have.

With Mile's voice echoing in my head, I composed a quick message.

<**Myrddin:** Remember. This is a litmus test. He won't move on you right away. We're on the precipice of a lot of volatility and he'll be hesitant to add to the pile. But if you get the sense he's considering finishing what he started, fall back to the safe house and get invisible. There are other ways you can help. I get that you feel beholden to me, for the fresh start, the sense of purpose. But dying accomplishes nothing.>
<**Cameron:** Maybe not. But it'd be an honor.>
<**Myrddin:** Say it back to me. Dying accomplishes nothing.>
<**Cameron:** Got it. See you on the flip side, boss.>
<**Myrddin:** Say it—>

The bell above the blacksmith's door rang before I could send the message. He stepped through awkwardly, half twisted around, speaking to someone in a low tone before the familiar face was revealed.

"Heard there was some dark and broody celebrity hanging out around here. Seen anyone like that?" Julian smiled.

CHAPTER SIXTY

In a way, it was a relief to see cracks in Julian's visage. The way his fingers drummed nervously against his leg. The little stress lines around his mouth that betrayed worry, despite considerable effort to stay aloof. Beyond conveying that he wasn't exactly thrilled to be talking to me like this, it was more evidence to the fact he was exactly what he presented himself as.

What was less of a relief was that I'd so recently spoken to him without the mask. The mask would alter the sound and pitch of my voice, but Myrddin and Matt had similar speaking patterns, a precedent I'd established before realizing how many problems that was going to cause.

Julian was perceptive. I needed to amplify the differences that did exist, or the connection would be plain as day.

Leaning into that, I tried to push past him. "Out of the way, dickhead."

Instead of trying to stop me, Julian reached out a hand. "We've never met. I'm Julian. Prince of the Parcae Court."

"And I'm in a hurry."

"Better get to the point then." His voice was firm but calm.

"There's a kid outside slowly choking to death. Me and some others have been trying to cut him down, but it's hard to get leverage on a ladder and the rope is shockingly resilient."

"Didn't you get the memo? The Court wants nothing to do with me, they made it perfectly clear. Didn't want to add more shady associations to the already sketchy origin when they're about to make a public debut." I hit him with the facts, letting them speak for themselves. "New boss, same as the old boss."

Again, the Rogue was in no real danger. Audrey would send a warning if he was. I'd planned to leave him hanging there like a living gibbet until my business was concluded, then dismiss the summon and wash my hands of it.

If nothing else, the accusation that the Court seemed more worried about their public appearance seemed to get under his skin. "Some members felt that way, yes. Not all." His eyes slid to the side. "And I also get why you're being such a hardass." Julian breathed out slowly, cocking his head. "It's been hunting season around here lately, I get it."

I leaned forward and growled. "Move."

"In a minute." He stared me down. "The wild animal schtick might be keeping you alive, but beyond that it's not doing you any favors. Think about appearances. A lot of people who got what's coming to them aren't copping to their part in it. Some, even a few with considerable pull, are claiming you attacked them unprovoked. Add in the fact that the Order's rules don't seem to apply to you, and one of these days you'll catch more trouble than you can handle."

"I'm shaking."

<Awareness> trumpeted a warning as Julian's shoulder and arm twitched.

A sucker punch? Really?

The exchange was lightning fast. I shifted slightly, dodging the would-be attack before realizing it wasn't there at all. He'd never moved. But both **<Awareness>** and **<Emulation>** had triggered.

I activated **<Page's Quickdraw>**, sudden resistance halting the typically smooth-as-glass movement—despite my speed, he'd caught my arm, stopping me from withdrawing a crossbow from my inventory. This time, he actually moved, reaching back toward his inventory.

Returning in kind, I lashed out and kicked it away, following up with a flurry of blows aimed at his unarmored face and neck, each deflected at the last second, one after another.

The response was pure calculated defense, which with experience, meant a serious attack was coming. I disengaged and instinctively lowered my center of gravity, ready to absorb or avoid. Only to realize Julian was doing the same.

Kai's shrill voice broke the standoff as he shouted from behind the counter he was half-cowering behind. "No fighting in the smithery!"

"Sorry, ma'am," Julian said, suddenly chagrinned.

"I'm a boy!" Kai snapped at Julian, irate.

"He started it," I said begrudgingly.

"Did I?" Julian asked, the slightest hint of a smirk plying at his mouth.

"Sure felt that way." I watched him for any indication of deception and found none. Annoyed and unsure what exactly happened but not wanting to escalate, I dulled Myrddin's edge. "Look, let's be real. I don't care what happens to the kid. What I care about is the impression it gives if I go out there post scuffle and let him down. It'll look like I'm running away with my tail between my legs."

Julian absorbed that, nodding slowly. "People like me around here. They don't always listen, but sometimes they do. Play ball and I can maybe quench the heat a little. Get them to refocus elsewhere. And if they don't listen and I catch wind of some kind of bad coming your way, I'll warn you. Plus, it'll give the impression you're capable of listening to reason if you toe the line a bit. Humanize you."

"Not sure that helps me."

"At the very least, it makes you look less like an existential threat that needs to be put down," Julian pointed out.

It was strange; despite being a terrible liar, he was a great negotiator. Before Julian, I'd argue that was impossible. Negotiating always required some level of deceit. Yet along the same lines of giving an ancient eldritch hive mind enough doubt that it actually hesitated, he'd picked up quickly that I was more concerned with appearances than actually being an asshole and immediately switched tact, absorbing that knowledge into his strategy. He was also seemingly immune to being shrugged off, a strategy I'd spent most of my life perfecting.

And I had to admit, he wasn't wrong. The mercy of my previous course of action—letting the kid hang as a cartel-style warning until I left and releasing him—would be lost on most people. But not everyone. There were too many witnesses for them all to be stupid. At least a few of them would connect the dots.

As much as I hated it, this played better.

"Do you care if I publicly threaten you?" I checked.

"Not at all."

"Fine."

———

That didn't mean I was going to be nice about it.

There was a thud and a whimpered cry as the Rogue dropped a solid six feet and hit the ground on paralyzed legs, immediately toppling. Julian, as expected, was there to catch him, protecting his head from a potential concussion. Even as the Prince winced from the harsh landing, he offered a smile. "Thanks for the assist."

A current of whispers went through the gathered crowd. I forced myself not to look at them, focusing on Julian instead. I raised my voice slightly, making sure the onlookers could hear. "Just keep your end of the bargain. If you don't, it'll be you dangling next."

To his credit, he paled a bit and inclined his head. "Message received."

I was mostly ignored as several people pushed by to help Julian with the downed Rogue. He'd get a boost in popularity from this, which was fine, as it also sent the message that Myrddin could be reasoned with.

I took one last look at Julian, happily chatting away with several Users helping him carry the petrified Rogue, and disappeared into the crowd, ignoring a sense of growing unease as I approached my next destination. Vernon's lair.

Applying as much active concentration as possible, I followed the back wall, searching for the telltale indentations and outlines of the hidden door.

"Dark wizard!" a high-pitched voice chittered, rousing me from my search. A small capuchin that I was almost certain hadn't been there before rested in a sitting crouch, reaching back to pluck something out of the dark tuft of hair that crowned its head, stuffing whatever it was into its mouth and biting down with a crunch. "It is the dark wizard, yes?" he asked, suddenly unsure.

"It's me. Afternoon, Jeeves." I bent down and studied him. "Coat's looking better."

Jeeves was one of Vernon's more successful experiments. The mind of a dying kobold, transplanted into the damaged corpse of a monkey. Part of what made him a success, in my eyes at least, was that while the monkey was technically undead, he seemed to be growing more lively over time rather than falling apart like the norm. His previously patchy, mussed fur had grown longer from the last time I'd seen him, covering much of the scar tissue of pre-death injuries.

"Groomed it myself," he proclaimed proudly, then glanced away distractedly, listening to something I couldn't hear. "Master Vernon will see you now."

"Thanks, Jeeves." I patted the monkey on the head, then left through the now visible double doors.

When I'd first met Kinsley's father, his lair had been near-identical to a hospital wing, complete with sterile tile, bright fluorescent lights, and surprisingly modern medical equipment. Pretty much the opposite of what I'd expected to find, but according to Vernon, a necromancer's lair was a reflection of who they were.

It hadn't changed much since then, but the key differences were hard to ignore.

Large bubbling suspension tubes lined one side of the room, the liquid that suspended various corpses and writhing forms an odd light blue. Some of the creatures were intubated, some simply floated, perfectly suspended in the center.

The other side of the lair was lined with reinforced wall and heavy-duty containment doors, connected by alternating panes of security glass.

Vernon rushed past me in a surgeon's smock, sleeves, and neoprene gloves soaked with blood held upward and away from him, gaze hard and assiduous. "Where the hell were you? Been sending messages for days."

"Busy," I answered, struggling internally with whether it was worth asking what left him in that state or simply ignore it. "But I'm here now. What's the problem?"

Vernon scoffed. There was a sudden spray of water on metal and he aggressively scrubbed his hands beneath a downpour of water from an industrial sink. "Who said there's a problem? If anything, this should be a pleasant surprise."

"So pleasant you're covered in more blood than Carrie's prom?"

"Unrelated," Vernon stated begrudgingly. When I didn't respond, he rolled his eyes. "An abomination couldn't assimilate the organs I chose. Of course, if a necromancer was allowed to properly anesthetize subjects and still use their fucking abilities, it wouldn't have even been a problem, but I can't, and it was."

I steered the conversation away from whatever failure had frustrated him. "Jeeves is still holding up well. Great communication, strong sense of self. Seems to be regenerating rather than rotting and hasn't dropped any limbs."

"It's all him, really." Vernon's edginess subsided somewhat. "Something of a blessing the original kobold had an intelligent, flexible mind long before he endured the misfortune of ending up on my table." He smiled for a moment as he removed his gloves, until he sniffed at his hands and grimaced, pumped out more soap and thrusting them back under the downpour of water. "It's like he intrinsically understands that while my methods and abilities are... unpleasant, I'm trying to extend his life. Most of them don't. Uh." He pinched the bridge of his nose with wet fingers, grimacing again at the smell. "What were we talking about?"

"When was the last time you slept?" I asked, fully aware of the hypocrisy.

Not hearing me at all, Vernon snapped his fingers. "Right, the simulacrum." He seemed to retreat from the excitement, fixing me with a cool stare. "We're close to our original goal. Very close. It's imminent."

"How imminent?" I asked cautiously.

"Unless my most recent acquisition was a red herring—and

that's never happened up to this point—it should be next level. I'm already more than halfway there," Vernon said, with the confidence and detachment of a professional. He held onto that detachment as he continued. "Forgive me. There's more I'd like to show you. Real, tangible progress. But given that our goal is in sight and our alliance is coming to an end, taking my leverage with it, I'd like to speak to her."

"Kinsley?" I stalled, knowing the answer was obvious.

"Yes."

I chewed my lip. "The original condition of telling you she was alive was that you'd wait until after you were done here to get in contact."

"I want to speak to my daughter, god *dammit!*" Vernon roared, and his lair came alive. The monstrous abominations in the suspension tanks squirmed violently, throwing up a storm of bubbles that obscured their movements. Several inhuman silhouettes pressed up against the frosted security glass on the other side, constant low-pitched moans becoming more audible. The overhead lights dimmed as a dark wreath of shadows descended from the corners of the ceiling down the walls and approached me, tendrils reaching.

<Suggestion> fired reflexively, and I battled through a barrier of sky-high intellect to send Vernon waves of calm, images of him reunited with Kinsley tagged with patience and serenity. After a moment, the creatures in the tanks stopped writhing and the silhouettes pressing against the security glass wandered away. Vernon buried his face in a hand. "I'm sorry. It feels like I've been strung along for ages. But that isn't your fault. You've been a man of your word so far. Hell, you're the only reason I even know she's alive. I just... really need to talk to her."

"I'm on your side, Vernon." I hugged him. It didn't come naturally. If anything, it was stilted and awkward. But it's what

Kinsley would have wanted me to do, and I did. "With the way things stand now, arranging that would be difficult. I'm not saying I couldn't make it happen, if it's pressing." I released him. "Is it pressing?"

"No." Vernon took a step back and wiped his eyes. "There's just some things I need to say to her. Things she really needs to hear. But the timing doesn't really matter, so long as she hears them."

I heard him. Both what he was saying out loud, and the quiet part. Realistically, we could have arranged a meeting weeks ago. Listed it as a requirement of the alliance, but in the end, Kinsley refused. Because, as this most recent outburst had shown, while Vernon had gotten far more adept at appearing stable, he really wasn't. When this first started, he'd awakened, looked over the grim macabre nature of the necromancer tree, and swore never to touch it. The only reason he'd finally stooped to it was that the Order allowed him to believe that his daughter was dead and dangled the concept of true resurrection in front of him like a twisted carrot.

Eventually, I found him on the other side of a crossbow, but by then it was too late. He'd crossed the rubicon. Killed dozens with the Order's help, harvested their Cores, all with the intention of reaching the height of a necromancer's power to bring back a daughter that was still alive.

Mostly innocents.

The abject cruelty of the manipulation was part of a very long list of reasons I could never see myself working with, or for that matter, sharing a world with Aaron long term.

Sooner or later, however the chips fell, Aaron had to go.

The sterling result of that cruelty was the same reason Kinsley wanted to delay speaking to Vernon until we were in a controlled situation and could ensure his safety. Because she was certain his real intentions had nothing to do with reuniting or reconnecting with her.

More accurately, he wanted to say goodbye.

"Let's—" he sniffed. "Let's put a pin in that, and I'll show you what I've got going."

Wordlessly, a hand on his back for support, I followed him into what appeared to be an operating room.

One look at the pale, feminine face of the person on the table ripped my breath away.

CHAPTER SIXTY-ONE

Blood burbled from her mouth, leaking down the side of her face as a sea of crimson pooled around the wound of her ruined throat. The arterial blood faded away with the memory, leaving only the pale, lifeless expression of a person, small and motionless beneath a wrinkled white blanket that came up to her chest, an oxygen mask over her face.

Beneath it, Jinny's eyes stared straight up, cold and lifeless as the day we'd lost her.

I put a hand on the table for stability, compensating for the sudden weakness in my knees. "This is why you asked for pictures. So... the new ability..."

"We theorized before that, with her body being instanced, there was a good chance we'd need a vessel." Vernon nodded. "That's looking to be true. This is, for all intents and purposes, a functioning body." He pointed to the IV and the heart rate monitor. "Cycling fluids, heart beating on its own. Can't see it, but the neurons are firing." He waved a cautious hand, warding off the obvious question before I could ask it. "The body can't breathe on its own. Brain activity isn't much higher than a person who would be considered clinically dead."

"How did you even pull this off?" It was almost impossible to keep up. I couldn't stop looking at her.

"Simulacrum allows me to create a living form, but it's horrifically unintuitive. The rest was a result of practicing keeping things alive that shouldn't be, not to mention countless hours of bone and flesh sculpting." Vernon hesitated. "Drew from the references I had, tried to stay as faithful as I could, but deviations are inevitable. If it works... she'll probably experience a degree of dysphoria regardless of accuracy—after all, no matter what it looks like, this isn't her body. But she'll be alive."

"If the system doesn't pull a bait and switch and give you something else," I recalled, doing whatever I could to manage expectations.

"Yes." Vernon frowned. "There's also an issue of cost. My recent abilities have been ramping up in requirements, demanding escalating tiers of User Cores."

"Anything legendary?" I asked, dreading the answer.

"Not yet. But I suspect we'll know when we need one." He glanced at me. "You still have it, right?"

"I do." I fumbled with my inventory. "Want it now, or later?"

"Later," Vernon answered, a little too quickly. When I gave him a questioning look, he breathed out a long sigh. "It's nothing too alarming, but worrisome nonetheless. I've taken a number of necromancer feats centered around efficiency. Reduction of downtime. Nothing too sinister on the surface..."

"... but?" I asked.

"There's been side effects. Some can be explained away by stress and sleep deprivation, others not so much. The most prominent occurrence being somnambulism."

I shrugged. "A lot of people sleep walk."

He pulled at the smock at his throat uneasily. "Less, I suspect, navigate to their operation rooms and begin working with sharp implements in a subconscious state, utilizing precious resources on questionable endeavors."

My eyebrows rose. "Yeah, okay, point taken. I assume you've established precautions?"

"Oh yes." Vernon chuckled. "One of the unexpected benefits of being a necromancer is that they, apparently, spend a great deal of time and energy securing their lair. Didn't have much use for security before, but I've since gained an interest. The security doors containing this room and a few others are on a daily rotating cypher. The solution is sent every day, but it's pre-scrambled in an odd, esoteric way that requires working it out on paper, referencing a key."

I squinted. "I get it, infinitely harder to work through a puzzle if you're half-asleep, but why would a necromancer even want that in the first place?"

Vernon laughed again. "To ward off psychics from ripping it straight from their minds, apparently. Ridiculous paranoia if you ask me."

"Sure," I agreed carefully.

"Anyway, for this, it works to my purposes." Vernon shrugged. "The sleep walking is probably just stress. But you can understand why I want you to keep the Core."

"I'll keep it safe." I patted my thigh. "What other side effects have you been experiencing?"

Vernon smiled thinly and shook his head. "Nothing really. Not tangible, anyway. It's more..." his face fell, dejected. "It doesn't matter. Nothing that will affect our work. But the quicker we finish this, the better."

So you can talk to Kinsley and punch your ticket. Azure?

"Woah," Azure whispered into my mind. *"The suicidal ideation is on full display. Same motivation as usual, despair, guilt, an endless outpouring of guilt—but when it comes to whatever he's hinting at, he's completely closed off. Actively not thinking about whatever 'it' is,*

even though you're talking about it indirectly. That's incredibly diffi-
cult. Whatever it is, he buried it deep."

"Repression?"

"Definitely."

"Could you crack it?"

"A necromancer's lair is similar to a realm of Flauros, but it isn't quite the same. In a realm, I could, given time. Here? Probably not..." There was a pause, pregnant as they come. *"Unless you're willing to use mindspi—"*

"No."

Leaving things as they were, on a question mark, made me profoundly uncomfortable. But unstable as he was, I didn't want to risk pushing him. And switching to **<Cruel Lens>** was likely to push him more than I could reasonably justify.

As I made up my mind, Vernon slowly circled the table, clinically surveying his work. When he spoke, his voice was distant, curious. "It's such a strange thing. This vessel has musculature, organs, and a mind. Its reflexes function. Even now, her mind sends signals directing her lungs to breathe, her heart to beat. There's a part of me that wouldn't be surprised at all if she just woke up, stretched out her arms, and walked away."

Jinny's head turned toward me at a sharp angle as she smiled through bloody teeth.

"You'll bring me back. Won't you, Matt? It's the only way to keep your promise."

I forced my eyes shut, holding them closed for several seconds. When I opened them again, Jinny was back to the way she was, the hallucination banished. Vernon, still surveying his work, hadn't noticed. "But she can't."

Vernon shook his head. "It will never not be vexing, that after thousands of years of argument and discourse the philosophers were right. Even if you have all the pieces to make a person, and assemble those pieces perfectly, there's still something missing. Something no science or magic can replicate. Bastards."

The spark.

"Any resources we should be on the lookout for, anything else you need for prep? Anything at all?" I asked casually, trying to cover my discomfort and move on.

Vernon didn't answer right away. Rather, he seemed to be mulling over something important, working up the nerve to ask. "Would you like to speak to her?"

What?

"What?" I asked sharply, sure I hadn't heard him correctly.

"What?" Azure repeated, signaling that, apparently, I had.

"I've been carving a rather direct path up the necromancer tree, only branching out when strictly necessary or advantageous. But I read each potential acquisition in detail. Some are trite, most are macabre. Others bear passing interest." For perhaps the first time, Vernon didn't sound quite as revolted as he typically did discussing necromancy. "A few—barely more than a handful—stick, like pinions in the back of my mind."

"What the fuck are you talking about, Vernon?" I asked, trying to stay calm.

He winced a little. "There were other options adjacent to simulacrum that, while not as directly practical, might still hold value for us." The discomfort faded as he argued his point. "It's a bit expensive, yes, but barely a drop in the bucket compared to the points I've saved."

"How," I said flatly.

The doctor chewed his lip, then swiped at his UI, pulling something up before he made a flicking gesture toward me.

<Commune with Soul Fragment>
<Level 79 Necromancer Ability>
<Description: Either the necromancer or a person the

necromancer chooses may commune with the fragments of a soul housed within a monster, User, or divine Core for a short duration. The soul cannot be captured or compelled to convey information in this state, and its willingness to do so may vary drastically dependent on its pre-existing relationship with the channeler.>

<**Cost:** Absolution of an Epic Rarity User Core.>

I worked my jaw for a moment, mouth suddenly dry. "How... uh... much would it cost?"

"Roughly a third of what I've set aside." Vernon's answer was quick enough that he must have been considering this for some time. "I've never made a body for a person before. Only monsters. Could be worth acquiring just to consult the subject on her vessel, better chance of a smoother transition that way."

"And the reason you've waited until now to mention it?"

With a sigh of frustration, he inclined his head for me to follow him.

I gave Jinny's potential body one last look, some strange, irrational part of me still convinced she might suddenly stir, and patted the outline of her hand through the sheet that covered it.

Won't be much longer.

The metal containment doors slid shut as I left, a series of heavy-duty *thunks* and clicks echoed behind as I followed Vernon up to a series of smaller glass panes and punched a button. The glass grew translucent, revealing a small chamber within that resembled a lizard terrarium in both size and presentation, dirt, moss, and bits of dry wood shaping a faux forest floor, green leaves and ivy above forming an uneven canopy. Tiny humanoid figures contained within emanated a soft silver glow as they darted around, short stints of flight taking them to perches at various elevations, leaving trails of sparks that blinked and faded like fireflies.

As if actively aware of the observation, several of the creatures landed in front of the glass, pawing at it with tiny hands. Up close, they looked like the glowing silhouettes of tiny impish humans, blank eyes shining with mischief as they crowded the glass, pushing and shoving to get closer to Vernon, who smiled down on them dotingly. Now that they were closer, it was distinguishable that the light that formed their bodies wasn't perfectly continuous. All of them were bisected by asymmetrical dark lines. Lines that almost resembled sutures.

"Dinner time, children," Vernon announced, withdrawing an ordinary glass Tupperware filled with perfectly squared cubes of meat. He grabbed a fistful and opened a small compartment at the top, securing it again before pressing another button. There was a brief whirr and a hidden hatch dumped the contents.

They moved before the cubes even hit the ground. Like sharks, the tiny figures leapt, sharp teeth flashing in the white light as they snatched the meat out of the air, gobbling cubes as large as their throats in seconds and shoving in more.

"Pixies?" I asked.

"Sprites," Vernon corrected, mouth quirking slightly. "Though the team that brought them in called them flying piranhas, which is equally accurate. These came from a pack of around twenty felled with an AOE. Most dropped Cores, so they salvaged the bodies and brought them to me." He wiggled a finger at one, smiling as it paused from its meal to nip at him through the glass. "Endearing little things. Uh. The reason I'm showing you this is because it's a rarity to receive so many of the same creatures at once, let alone ones killed identically at the exact same moment."

It clicked. "Less variables and a larger sample size. Relatively."

"Exactly. An opportunity I intended to put to good use." Vernon wiggled his finger again, leading the ambitious sprite still trying to gnaw on him to a small cube of meat that had fallen in the corner. His smile faded. "Unfortunately, these are the lucky ones." He reached past me to another panel, and the frosted glass pane on the left became transparent.

From what I could tell, the small creatures in the second enclosure were also sprites. But these only glowed a fraction as bright as the others. Their movements were sluggish. Several were curled up on the ground, unmoving, save small stirrings of breath that indicated they were still alive. Or undead, rather.

"Will you eat for me today?" Vernon murmured quietly, repeating the same process, albeit with a much smaller volume. The internal hatch dropped open, dumping the cubes onto the terrarium detritus, where they tumbled to a stop.

None of the dimmer sprites stirred. One stood, but only to stumble away from a cube that had landed at her knees, mouth tight in a rictus of pain.

"Same diet, environment, and I assume reanimation process. But the difference is drastic. Any correlation between the behavior and the rarity of their Cores?" I leaned forward, all but pressing my face against the glass. Toward the back, one of the small creatures turned to look at me, then glanced away, the tuft of light that formed a facsimile of hair covering her face.

In the reflection, Vernon shook his head. "It was the first thing I thought of, but both groups are a mix of common and uncommon Cores. If they were more intelligent, the contrast could be attributed to differences in personality. I've studied and tested them in various ways, and in most they are function-ally identical—driven by instinct and a basic hierarchy of needs."

"You've had experiments fail before," I said, recalling a few particularly unpleasant visits to the lair. "Every necromancy process you've described is difficult and esoteric compared to the straight-laced arcane. This could be within the margin of error."

"As you've witnessed firsthand, failures in this field are as spectacular as they are violent. Obvious." Vernon bit his lip, wiggling his finger in front of the glass by the nearest sprite, to no response. "This is a third result, somewhere between success and failure. I've seen it before. The despondency, the—for a lack of a scientific term—brokenness. Sometimes even as an outcome of routine processes I've perfected."

Curious, I reached out to one of the smaller creatures with **<Suggestion>**, opening the mental connection wider than I typically would, tagging an image of a pleasant meadow with serenity and warmth as a simple greeting.

A psychic scream slammed back.

LIES. ALL LIES. THE DARKNESS NEVER ENDS. CAN'T FEEL, CAN'T SEE, IT FREEZES, GNASHES WITH TEETH OF IRON AND ICE. DON'T MOVE OR IT WILL FIND US AGAIN, RIP OFF OUR WINGS, SLITHER INTO OUR SKIN, MELT OUR INSIDES TO JELLY, QUENCH THE LIGHT. IT HURTS. IT HURTS. IT HURTS. IT—

A fortified mental barrier slammed down, severing the connection. Azure. In the aftermath of vertigo and mental static, he made a scathing remark about the danger of what I'd just done, my mind too confounded to fully grasp the words.

"Are you alright?" Vernon asked, staring at me quizzically.

"Could—" my voice caught as I tried to purge the imprint of terror. "Could some souls be more degraded than the others? If reincarnation is a factor—"

"—a categorically massive 'if,' but continue," he commented.

"Hypotheticals are all we have. We know definitively that the system reuses assets, so reincarnation—or some sort of continuation of the soul along those lines—could create an unseen variable."

"I have two theories." He lingered for a moment before pressing the button on the panel, concealing the crestfallen monsters behind a frosted pane once more. "The first, the one I like, is along those lines, though reincarnation as the vehicle of deterioration did not occur to me. A varying, hidden attribute that cannot be measured or identified through means we simply do not have access to. For perhaps selfish reasons, I'd prefer that to be the case."

"And the one you don't like?"

His eyes panned to the first enclosure. "Beneath all the ritualistic complexity and gruesome mysticism, true reanimation—the practice of reanimating with part or all of the soul intact—is crude, almost workmanlike. Putting it metaphorically, imagine the soul itself as a ball of yarn. When a living being dies, the ball of yarn disappears, embarking somewhere unseen. It doesn't always do so cleanly. It unspools, leaving behind an infinitesimal length of string. An anchor, or Core." He pulled a glowing orb from his pocket and held it up to the light. "For a practice so entrenched in mortality, necromancy cares little for what lies beyond the curtain. It pays no mind to where the ball of yarn comes to rest." He closed his hand, obscuring the Core and yanking it toward his chest. "Instead, its focus is finding the most efficient method of drawing the necessary material back from oblivion."

A slow, dawning horror washed over me as I understood. "After the sprites were killed, their souls didn't necessarily go to the same place."

THE DARKNESS NEVER ENDS.

"Eschatological pluralism is nothing new. Heaven and hell.

Elysium and Tartarus. The House of Song, and the House of Lies. Valhalla and the phonebook of possible realms the Vikings had." Vernon snorted. "The concept of posthumous stratification in the afterlife has been around for nearly as long as humans themselves."

I nodded slowly. He was right, of course. But it was a little different seeing potential evidence for something that, previously, had to be taken entirely on faith. Colder.

"Again, it's just a theory. And not a particularly good one at that," Vernon insisted, still clearly shaken. "None of the monsters capable of intelligent thought I've reanimated recall anything but darkness. There's no way to know for sure."

"Unless," I hedged as I replayed his uncharacteristic offer in my mind, "you could commune with a soul that remained in its resting place."

"I'll admit, it'd be nice to have confirmation." Vernon smiled thinly. "Along with having the opportunity to speak to your friend again, you'd be able to verify that she's well..." he tapped the glass and the frolicking sprites stirred and chased after his hand, "and that resurrection wouldn't end up being a tragic extension of suffering."

For a moment, I seriously considered it. I'd blindly fought for this for so long that even the smallest breadcrumb of reassurance would mean everything.

And if, instead, you discover it was all for nothing?

There was that to consider, yes. But, perhaps more importantly, it wasn't my place. It was Nick's. From the description, **<Commune with Soul Fragment>** could only communicate with a given Core once. If Vernon's second theory was correct, and through an astronomical case of cosmic injustice the most humane thing we could do for Jinny was to leave her where she was, Nick needed to be the one to speak to her.

Because he'd never forgive me if I took that from him.

Rightfully so.

Slowly, *painfully*, I shook my head. "Tempting as it is, we don't know how many points true resurrection is going to cost. Even if you've looked at the tree and worked out what it should potentially be, I wouldn't be shocked if logical progression gets thrown out the window when we're talking about something this game changing. Better to bank everything you have until we know for sure."

He held my gaze. There was something there. An ember of anger, indignation maybe. Before I could work it out, it was gone.

Instead of arguing, Vernon sighed and rubbed the back of his neck awkwardly. "I'd be lying if I said I wasn't a little disappointed."

"If it turns out there's enough to get both, we absolutely should. You'll get your answer then."

He nodded, satisfied, an odd cheeriness coming over him as he rearranged several implements on his desk. "It'd be nice to have that curiosity sated beforehand. I think I'll ask Kinsley to give me a tour of her accomplishments." He grinned at me, eyes hollow as he retrieved a clipboard and held it under his arm, signaling our meeting had come to a close. "It's one thing to be told how well she's landed, another entirely to see it for myself."

Settling accounts. Again.

I resisted giving knee-jerk approval. "Just because she's wealthy and well-positioned doesn't mean she doesn't need you."

"That's exactly what it means." Vernon shrugged. "Children grow up. It's inevitable."

"There's a world of difference between getting older and growing up early because there's no alternative." I thought back to the most recent fiasco, then further, to the pavement puddle researcher's supposed attempt to flee directly out of a glass window and Kinsley's emphatic claims that she hadn't ordered him thrown. "She's struggling."

Vernon stilled. "What do you mean?"

I hesitated, trying to find a way to convey what I wanted without fully understanding it myself. "I mean she's struggling. She bends over backward to cut deals, cooperate with others, only to see it thrown in her face. Everyone wants what she has and is looking for a way to take it from her. Kinsley, aware of the threat, eats like shit, never stops working until she passes out and wakes up for work again. Keeps taking on more and more responsibilities even though she's already drowning. But she's a survivor, so she sucks in water and keeps going."

Slowly, Vernon ran an idle hand through his hair, unknowingly leaving it askew, giving him a slightly unhinged look. "Funny." He chuckled in a way that clearly indicated he didn't find it amusing in the slightest. "When I first expressed my doubts about continuing my work after discovering my daughter was alive, I was told—informed rather plainly—that she had support. Access to everything she could possibly need, plenty of protection, and an impressive accumulation of wealth. You're saying that's not the case."

I shook my head, aware that he was repeating some of my wording verbatim. "You're not hearing me. She has money and power in spades. Her delegation could use some work, and she's cheap enough that she'd rather black out her schedule than drain the coffers hiring an adequate number of staff. No one's perfect."

"Then what's the problem?" Vernon asked. His voice, while deceptively calm, was undercut by the fists clenched at his side.

"No one tells her when to stop. Where the lines are," I said simply, sticking my hands in my pockets. "No one challenges her. No one she respects, anyway. She's surrounded by people with their own agendas who won't risk jeopardizing their positions by confronting her, because they have vested interests they're not willing to lose. They smile and nod along with whatever she does, and when she fucks up—rare, but it happens—they say nothing."

"I see. And you, Myrddin? Are you one of the people who nod along?"

I fixed him with a cold stare. To this point, I'd been doing my level best not to judge Vernon. On the scale of hard-left life turns he'd spun out completely, and in my experience, getting pissed off at someone who was already shit out of luck and more depressed than a Russian novelist was counter-productive. But his reaction, and general irritation at the possibility that reuniting with his daughter would require more effort than whatever short, sentimental goodbye he was envisioning?

Well, it was really pissing me off.

"Who do you think taught her how to cross those lines? It's not my place to suddenly flip the script and tell her to rein it in. Kinsley needs a touchstone, Vernon. Someone who prioritizes her well-being over everything else. Her soul. Otherwise..."

She ends up like me.

Still staring at a corner, he murmured something I couldn't make out.

"What?"

"The irony of what you're asking." His teeth ground audibly, and he pounded the desk so hard it made me jump. "When any reasonable person, knowing what I've done, would say the best thing I could do for my daughter is stay the fuck away, you want me closer, playing the role of parent and moral paragon. I've harvested people. Torn apart monsters—no, living creatures capable of thought and speech, no matter how monstrous they appear—simply to study their biology and catalog potential use-cases. I've...

done other things. Terrible things. Simply because I was curious."

"Capone, Escobar, Mussolini," I countered, rattling off names one after another. "All inarguably bad people who somehow found their way into being decent parents."

"Pablo Escobar's a little thin." Vernon rolled his eyes.

"Yeah, well, Capone isn't. Stayed the same person until the end, never really stopped doing heinous shit until his downfall. But he wanted more than that for his kid. Tried to show him the road not taken."

"And that's your idea of a good parent? A hypocrite?"

I shrugged. "Authentic, self-driven transformation is hard. Even if you have the motivation, it takes a level of doggedness and grit that's often impossible to sustain. So sure, it's not ideal, but sometimes being a hypocrite is the most effective role a parent can play. The next best thing."

"The next best thing," Vernon repeated. He buried his face in a hand, the portion still visible slack and haggard. "My reserves are still tapped from work earlier today. I need rest."

That was my cue to leave. I shoved my hands in my pockets and turned toward the door. "It's about to get busy, so this may be the last time we speak in person before we finally get answers and you get a much-needed vacation. I'll be in a place with a lot of high-level monsters, so if I bag any rare Cores I'll hold them for you. But is there anything else you need?"

"No," Vernon said, clearly wanting some space. He spoke again just as I started to walk away, eyes peering over his hands as he leaned forward in his chair. "Actually, your friend was a mage, yes?"

I nodded.

He stood and walked over to a nearby cabinet, opening the panel and revealing a row of shining, meticulous medical equipment. "If you're going to be around high-level monsters—

particularly creatures with magical abilities—I need blood samples for reference. It's not strictly necessary, but if you want to ensure she's brought back exactly as she was, I may need to manually graft ley lines into the vessel. Had to do it for a few of the sprites that were more damaged than the others, and with them I at least had their original bodies to draw from."

Absorbing that, I avoided looking down at his blood-soaked sleeves. "Surprised you're not inundated with samples to study."

"Unfortunately, simple monsters are the easiest to capture. I get a lot of those, brought in muzzled and restrained. Anything higher level tends to land on my table as either a corpse or a Core. The corpses are usually dead too long, blood compromised by coagulation." He rummaged around for a while before retrieving a small metal tube.

There was a button directly below a small LCD display and two circular openings on either convex end, bottom aperture larger than the top. With practiced ease, he took a small glass vial and screwed it into the bottom.

Though it was different than others of its type, I immediately connected the resemblance. "Lancing device?"

"Essentially." Vernon nodded. "Another new acquisition. Draws more blood than a typical lancet, intended for posthumous use. The interior of the vials is coated with a compound that should halt degradation entirely for at least a week."

"Shouldn't slow me down too much. How many do you need?"

His head wobbled back and forth in thought. "Uh. Ten, perhaps. To give me the clearest picture."

\<Quest Received\>
Quest: Dubious Tithes

Primary Objective — Assist Vernon, Necromancer, in gathering samples for his research.
Obtain 0/10 Unique Blood Samples from High-Level monsters
Secondary Objective: Obtain additional rare Cores.
Threat Level: ???
EXP GAIN: Significant
Time Limit: N/A
Reward: Increased relationship with Vernon, Necromancer.
Reward: ???

My mouth went dry, even as I mentally navigated the steps to accept it. On the surface it was simple enough. A literal fetch quest. It'd been a while since I'd received any direction from the system at all. To the point I'd begun to wonder if it was being intentionally denied. Suddenly receiving one after weeks of nothing felt significant. But what was more significant was the absence of something that had always been there.

The Personal Objective that warned me to keep my class a secret from other Users, present in every quest I'd received since the dome came down.

It was gone.

Somehow, I managed to form a coherent sentence. "Message when you hit the top of the tree. Won't be able to communicate much, with realm interference, but I'll try to check in as much as I can."

Muttering something that sounded like an agreement, Vernon stretched and walked away as I departed, whistling something classical in a minor key that sounded a little like a nocturne.

CHAPTER SIXTY-TWO

I left the Order's headquarters in a hurry, taking a portal exit that put me a few blocks away from one of the few coffee shops still up and kicking. After a bit of dark roast and rumination, I came to the conclusion I could worry about what the absence of the Personal Objective meant later.

There was a good chance it was nothing. Supporting that, none of my existing, outdated quests displayed the objective as failed. Perhaps it'd been long enough that keeping my identity guarded was meant to be assumed and the objective had only been there as an early guard rail.

More to the point, I'd already failed it, intentionally. As a merchant, Kinsley—the first person I'd divulged my secret to— was a bit of a gray area. But Nick and Sae were Users, and despite belonging to the exact group of people I was supposed to shield my identity from, I'd told them explicitly.

Smart or not, Nick needed to hear it.

Similarly, Sae was so vulnerable and alone at the time that keeping her in the dark would have been borderline exploitation.

I told myself it made sense. I'd received unachievable objectives in quests before, but never—to my knowledge—because the criteria itself was simply inaccurate to reality. I received the quest to help Jinny before she died. Her death was imminent, and given the swiftness with which it happened, there was little anyone could have done to stop it barring some form of precognition. But up until the moment she died, it was still achievable.

"You're going to bring me back, right?"

I drained the coffee, trying to force the caffeine to clear my head through sheer power of will. All it left me with was jitters and an empty cup. I'd been too deep in my head lately. And when I found myself lost in the feedback loop of my own thoughts, there was generally only one thing that helped.

Getting back to basics.

I pulled up my UI.

Matt
Level 24 Ordinator (25 Pending)
Strength: 6
Toughness: 12
Agility: 33+
Intelligence: 20+
Perception: 14
Will: 21
Companionship: 3
Active Title: Jaded Eye
Feats: Double-Blind, Ordinator's Guile II, Ordinator's Emulation, Stealth II, Awareness I, Harrowing Anticipation, Vindictive, Page's Quickdraw, Squelch, Acclimation, Hinder, Escalating Fire, Assassin II, Mind Spike, Decisive Action.
Skills: Probability Cascade, LVL 21. Suggestion, LVL 32. Command, LVL 15. One-handed, LVL 34. Negotiation,

LVL 29. Unsparing Fang (Emulated), Level 23. Bow
Adept, LVL 13. Twilight's Nocturne, LVL 16. Subjugation,
LVL 31. Riposte, LVL 11.
Boons: Nychta's Veil, Eldritch Favor, Ordinator's Imple-
ments, Retainer's Guiding Hand
Summons: Audrey — Flowerfang Hybrid, Bond LVL 11.
Talia — Eidolon Wolf, Bond LVL 15. Azure — Abrogated
Lithid, Bond LVL 20.

I'd noticed the pending level earlier, a little after my horrific
hangover had loosened the vices on my mind. It wasn't like me
to miss a notification, especially one as significant as a level-up,
so it had to have happened in the tower after Julien's boss one-
shot caused me to lose consciousness.

Unamused by the memory, I lingered on **<Vindictive>**,
silently cursing the problematic perk.

Keeps the User conscious until the moment of death my ass.

It'd been a questionable selection from the beginning. I'd
picked it out of pure necessity, needing a way to keep myself
conscious and functional in a critical moment. Having
endured the unpleasantness of patching me up after the fact,
Dr. Ansari railed on the stupidity of the perk with searing
veracity.

*"The mind loses consciousness for a reason, Mr. Matthias. It may
keep you conscious, but it could kill you just as easily. Elevated stress
hormones and the potential for psychological trauma alone are not to
be trifled with. Maintaining awareness in the midst of something
truly agonizing could easily give someone as young as you a heart
attack. It could kill you even when the physical trauma itself would
not."*

Despite that, I'd been hesitant to get rid of it. If it hadn't so
recently shown itself to be unreliable, I probably still would be.
With lingering reluctance, I pulled the respec charm from my

inventory—a gift from a crafter in my region—and selected **<Vindictive>** from the dropdown.

<Vindictive removed. Consumed feat points are now refunded.>

Huh. Not what I expected. The system was so often malicious that it was a surprise when things worked in a logical, not-out-to-fuck-you-over manner.

The additional points opened up some options. I'd planned on banking the feats for this level, but there were a lot more expensive options that were suddenly viable choices.

As I scanned them, I felt the familiar buzz behind my eyes that indicated Azure was looking through them directly.

"Need a consultation from a nosy summon?" Azure asked.

"By all means." I leaned back in my chair and scrolled to the top of the list. "Gonna take the whole night, otherwise."

A slight shudder went through me as Azure assumed control, glancing over the level information as he went down the list. My eyes glanced toward the pastry bag that now housed only crumbs. *"If I was petty and unwise, I might demand another scone as payment."*

"Take human form after we're done, I'll buy you one."

He said nothing, and I internally sighed. "You want to eat it in my body."

"I just want to taste it the way you taste it. Mimicking a human is easy. Recreating functional taste buds that are as vast and complex as a human's is pretty much impossible. But I won't ask for that because you'll say—"

"—It's weird, yeah. Especially when you start moaning. With my voice."

"It was my first time experiencing pizza, but fine, *keep holding it over my head,"* Azure whined, continuing to scroll the list. *"You*

*don't really need more perception, or feats that latently achieve increased perception. It's a little low and I know you're worried about it, but the fact that you have both **<Awareness>** and summons— multiple sets of eyes watching all around you at any given time, all of whom are capable of sending an immediate silent warning—puts you far above average."*

"Great. What else?"

The many feats blurred as Azure scanned through them.

There were a few promising options. **<Low-Blow>** potentially paired quite well with **<Unsparing Fang>**, ensuring any attack to a pain or nerve center was more likely to disorient and stun the target. It wasn't a straight damage increase, but it created more potential windows for attack, so in an oblique way, it kind of was. Azure spent a few minutes arguing for **<Sword of Damocles>**, the feat that bestowed enhanced melee accuracy and critical chance while dealing damage from above, until I sent him a mental image of me, jumping down from the rafters on top of a gnoll who moved at the last second and left me face planted on the ground, and he begrudgingly moved on.

Azure idly flicked from one page to another. *"There's an obvious choice. Not something you'll go for, but it makes a hell of a lot more sense than bulk dumping points into intelligence."*

My stomach dropped. "No."

"Yeah, it's a touchy subject." Azure sighed, still toying with the feat page. *"But the point is, there's options. Some of them actually make the core ability more palatable."*

I paused. But only for a moment. "The only reason I have **<Mind Spike>** is because we needed a trump card. The capacity to tip the scales in a critical moment after every other avenue fails. And *only* after."

"Perhaps," Azure said, in the way he often did when there was more coming. *"But by creating such tight criteria, you are, in a*

way, admitting that if specific circumstances occur you are willing to use it every time they do, yes?"

I caught a glimpse of him in the window's reflection, leaning over my shoulder like a concerned sibling. A bit inaccurate—so far as I could tell, when Azure and I communicated mentally, it was entirely internal. He wasn't hanging over my shoulder like Casper. But these projected hallucinations were common, likely a subconscious rumination on his part that communicated a sense of camaraderie.

Begrudgingly reminding myself he was looking out for us, I forced myself to answer honestly. "Yes."

"Then I'm not understanding why you're so vehemently against making that—arguably inevitable outcome—less horrifying."

I wrested control from him for a moment to rub my temples. "Let's just stop talking abstractly, this is already giving me a headache. The variant of **<Mind Spike>** you want me to look at. Does it offer any practical benefit to us beyond lessening the long-term impact?"

"It does," Azure said immediately, the pitch of his voice rising with cautious excitement. *"It slightly lessens the initial damage, but the real kicker is it won't permanently disable ranking up the stat anymore. Obviously a big benefit to the target. Simultaneously, if you **<Mind Spike>** and **<Subjugate>** a mage, they have the potential to build themselves back up. Eventually, given enough levels and steady commitment to recovery, they could be as capable as they used to be. It's a—ah fuck, you're baiting me,"* he realized, sourness seeping into the mental connection.

"Just making a point." I smiled at the waitress as she filled my coffee, suddenly in control of my faculties again as Azure retreated. "The entire point of a nuke is the capacity for catastrophic destruction. It shouldn't be conventional, have multiple use-cases, or be easy to justify. The second you get comfortable with the idea of pressing that button is the second you've lost."

"Please spare me the Kissinger rant," Azure said, still sulking.

I sipped the coffee. "Dead motherfucker aside, I always found the counterarguments to the tactical nuke take kind of compelling. Escalation, for one. Slap someone across the face and they punch you in the jaw? Take it to civil court all you want, maybe there's even a case, but no one's gonna genuinely believe you didn't have it coming. Because escalating is human nature."

Azure drifted into my sightline and lounged beside the table, mental apparition ghostly and orange, his expression the picture of false calm. *"I'm aware of the necessity of rules when it comes to engagement. There's a reason you let Sunny's boy go. Why I've never considered proposing we go after Aaron through his only obvious weakness."*

"Careful. If Daphne heard that, she might beat you to death in an alley."

"She's not weak." Azure rolled his eyes. *"Just more vulnerable than him. But I get it, why we can't use her. For the same reason I would rather it be literally any other human on earth than the necromancer who targeted your sister."*

"The gloves tend to come off. And they always take it farther than you think they will."

"What I don't understand," Azure said, hovering closer to the ground and literally putting his foot down, *"is why you can't recognize the difference between a weapon capable of ending countless lives that is impossible to conceal, and an untraceable single-target ability that affects one person at most."*

"Does it, though?" I set my coffee down unevenly, sending ripples across the surface. "Because I'd argue it affects the lives of everyone they rely on, people dependent on them, the victims of any accidents their diminished acuity may cause. Their children."

"As it would if they were killed or maimed in a pedestrian way." Azure's head lolled to the side, eyebrows knitted in exasperation.

I felt for Azure, I really did. To him, my caution must have seemed utterly irrational. It just wasn't something we would ever see eye to eye on. His logic and reasoning excelled at mimicking a human's, but like his sense of taste, lacked nuance. Spared little room for undefinables.

And somewhere between **<Subjugation>** and **<Mind Spike>** was an undefinable I couldn't shake. **<Subjugation>** wasn't permanent. It could be used in a way that instilled a dogmatic sort of loyalty, but that was entirely optional. **<Suggestion>**, **<Subjugation>**, and **<Command>**, if used responsibly, all had the potential to leave the victim's psyche unharmed.

<Mind Spike> was the complete opposite. It battered the psyche, inflicted permanent harm to the sheer, ruthless purpose of lowering the target's stats enough to give my other abilities a foothold. I'd tried it only once, on a small group of hostile goblins in the tower. At the time, I figured testing on dumb, hostile mobs was kinder than targeting something neutral. It was necessary— for one thing, I would have never realized, possibly until there was zero room for error, that it was the only Ordinator ability I'd encountered that deployed a visible projectile.

As it worked out, neither was kind.

"I don't want to make it easier to use. More convenient or justifiable. Easier to stick to the rules that way."

"And I'll respect that, for now." Azure phased through the booth's wall, checking the perimeter for the second time that hour, his troubled voice still perfectly clear. *"Because it helps you function. Right and wrong don't factor for me. We could dangle*

Daphne off a building by her ankles tomorrow for all I care. I abide by your wishes because I care about you. And objectively, there's wisdom in being careful."

"But?" I prompted.

Azure, still facing away from me, breathed out, his shoulders slumping. *"There's too many rules. They're too restrictive, and eventually you're going to paint yourself into a corner."*

"I'll break them if I have to."

"Exactly." Azure looked up, watching the fading golden glow of the skyline, hands stuck in the ghostly manifestation of a hoodie. *"You're capable of it, sure. But it weighs on you. Every time you cross a line you've set for yourself, the... hope... dulls a little more. It's dim enough as it is. Maybe this is a stupid sentiment, but I don't want to see it gone."*

"... What hope?" I pretended not to understand. Not out of cruelty. It was just easier than the alternative.

Azure rubbed at his face with his sleeve, then snapped out of existence. After a few seconds, I felt the buzzing behind my eyes again. *"Just take **<Low Blow>**. It pairs nicely with **<Unsparing Fang>**, and you'll get practical value out of it quickly."*

"Was thinking the same thing," I said quickly, scrolling down the page. "Still leaves us with two points though."

"Nothing else stood out. Maybe just bank them."

"What about this?" I pointed out a feat I'd been considering for a while.

*"**<Transmogrify Equipment>**?"* Azure asked, puzzled. *"Why? It's entirely cosmetic."*

I pulled up the description while I waited.

<Transmogrify Equipment: The User can change the appearance of any weapon or item they possess to match that of any other weapon or item within the same subcategory. This

ability is limited to items the User has previously owned or
held, even if only briefly.>
<**Requirements:** 20 Intelligence.>
<**Cost:** 2 Feat Points>

The light came on. *"Unless,"* Azure realized, *"you've recently
upgraded your arsenal and don't want those recent, rather distinguishable acquisitions locked to Myrddin."*

"Like you said, I have too many rules." I tried to offer it as an
olive branch. "Maintaining different sets of equipment, leveling
up skills for said equipment, it all splits too much focus. I've
been pissed as hell at the Adventurers' Guild for dragging their
feet, when in reality I've been doing the same thing in a
different way. I'll still work on archery, of course. That'll only
open up more options for me, and bows are a good fit."

*"As we've observed before, knives and crossbows are relatively
ubiquitous."* Azure disembarked, reclining on his back and
floating in front of me with his hands behind his head as if
carried by an invisible cloud. *"But the list of skilled, high-level
Users who rely on them instead of switching to a sword is far shorter.
Myrddin sits at the top of that list."*

"Yeah. Gonna need to misdirect. People have already
noticed that my Page abilities aren't that different from a
Rogue's, so no point in going overboard. Need to style myself
differently without sacrificing effectiveness. Just can't stand in
the middle of a storm the same way. I'll give it some thought."

"Take your time," Azure raised his wrist, looking at an imaginary watch. *"You've got... twelve hours, give or take?"*

I tried not to let that get to me. Tomorrow needed to go
well. I didn't even want to imagine the clusterfuck that would
play out if there was a repeat of the last floor.

It was a defining moment.

And there were only a million more things I needed to do to get ready.

CHAPTER SIXTY-THREE

Fog rolled in from the east, darkness of the early morning bestowing the festive, carnivalesque atmosphere of the tower with a decidedly creepy flair.

The tower was still up and running. As far as anyone could tell, it never closed, and even now there were four early risers decked out in system gear making their way through the empty queue. Ravens—or crows, though they seemed too big to be crows—flitted around the sticky, confetti-littered square, pecking at detritus, eyeing their fellows with jealousy as I tossed the small murderers hopping around my feet bits of torn-up bread. They gobbled it down, sparing Talia fleeting glances where she'd curled up and dozed a few feet away.

I'd arrived a little after four in the morning, sleep already a distant fantasy. Most of the previous night had been spent messaging everyone I could, calling in favors, coordinating.

It still didn't feel like enough.

But as much as it felt like I should be doing something, there was nothing left to do now but wait.

Heavy footfalls scuffed concrete. Nick approached the tower from the front, looking half awake and a little lost. From the looks of it, I wasn't the only one who'd used the recent lull to upgrade. Both the sword and gleaming silver armor looked entirely new. More unexpected was the small luminescent creature wiggling under his arm.

I whistled low. He started, a little, then made his way over to join me.

"Couldn't sleep?" I asked as he took a seat on the stool beside me.

"Nah." Nick grunted as he hiked himself up on the adjoining stool, metal support beam groaning beneath the heft of his armor. "Too in my head. Got the yips, as the old folks say. Haven't felt like this since the night before my last game."

"And the plus one?"

"Oh, right." Nick removed the creature from beneath his arm. It looked to be a semi-translucent, lightly glowing crab identical to the planners, only larger. He placed it down on the metal counter of the cart, where it skittered back and forth, rotated a few times, and plopped down, active camouflage adapting to the stainless-steel surface as now barely visible eyestalks flitted between us and the region beyond. "Mr. Crabbington."

"Mr. Crabbington," I repeated slowly.

"Remember all the detailed, 4k, borderline cinematic footage Slenderman and co had of the last event?"

"Trust me, I remember."

He chuckled. "Well, I've been brainstorming our Adventurers' Guild problem, and in the middle of that I got a bug up my ass about it. Didn't seem right that they could sling highly edited shit at us from the skies while we're down here stuck in the Stone Ages. So after asking basically everyone I could think of, I reached out to the big man himself." Nick reached over and patted the crab on the head. "He hooked me up."

I stared at the creature. "It... records?"

"It does."

"Is it recording now?"

"No. It's pretty much a magic robot with organic bits. Doesn't even have to eat. There's a command phrase to start and stop, and it can only hold so much before it has to offload it somewhere, so it's inactive."

"You uh... sure he wasn't just fucking with you?"

"Yeah," Nick trailed off, brows furrowed. "It was weird. He had it all locked and loaded. Sybil brought one in as soon as I said something, like he knew I was going to ask. Answered every question I had."

"Even if Hastur isn't perfectly omniscient, he has more fore-knowledge than any of us do."

"But why that, though?" Nick pointed out, puzzled. "If we're right that his power is limited until he ascends, or whatever, and he only gets, like, snapshots of possible futures and the steps to get to them in the current moment, why the hell would he waste two seconds of attention on some dipstick coming in to talk to him about a crab?"

He had me there. "You said this had something to do with enticing Tyler and didn't explain how."

Nick sat up excitedly, foisting the crab off the counter back onto his lap. "Right. I was racking my brain, trying to come up with ways going into the tower now instead of later could work to his benefit. Problem is, it's kind of a raw deal for an iffy outcome. He deploys the guild, uncertain of how many floors we have to clear, with only our and the Order's word to go on that it's worth his time. If Tyler commits, he can't really prepare for the second event, and if we fail, he'll be weaker for it."

"Yeah. I've been coming up empty on that too," I admitted.

"But what if going into the tower and fucking up monsters for the common good actually bags him more recruits? Think about how fucked up people were over the footage. Part of that's because it was explicit, footage of a violent tragedy, sure, but part of it was also because most people haven't had shit to watch since the streaming services croaked. Video affects us more than it used to." Nick shook the crab for emphasis, which wiggled its arms unhappily in response.

"Huh." It was out there. But not so much that I couldn't smell the opportunity.

"We have it film the big battles. Make the Adventurers' Guild out to be badass heroes, raging against the fading of the light." He puffed himself up, comically heroic, before slowly slouching back again. "Course, I uh, have no idea how to go about distributing it. Or how to edit it even." He rubbed the back of his neck, tired and a little shell shocked. "Was so convinced that I had *something,* but this was all probably a stupid idea to begin with. Guess I ran out of time."

Splitting my attention, I pulled up my DMs and composed a message.

<Matt: Probably about to step directly on an anthill here, but need to ask something anyway. I'm aware embedding is a thing and most forums and aggregate discussion sites on the old web didn't devote resources to it, but is there a snowball's chance in hell your forum project has video-hosting capabilities?**>**

The answer, one I'd expected back by noon at the earliest, came back lightning fast.

<Mom: IT'S FIVE IN THE MORNING MATTHIAS.**>**
<Matt: Didn't think you'd be awake. No rush, hit me back when you can.**>**
<Mom: I only just drifted off ;-;**>**
<Matt: Deep breaths. Count some sheep or something.**>**

<MOM: DON'T TRY TO HELP WHEN YOU CREATED THE PROBLEM.**>**

Okay, message received.

"That why you didn't message me about it? Worried it was stupid?" I guessed, feeling a little guilty.

"No. Well—is it stupid?"

Seizing the enemy's propaganda machines and repurposing them for the common good?

"Not even a little."

"Oh," Nick said, encouraged, then scrunched up his face. "Wasn't afraid of making a fool of myself. Not just that, anyway. You're doing a lot you can't tell me about, and even if I'm not getting the play by play, I can see how busy you are. Just trying to be choosier about when I blow up your DMs."

I held my fist out on my leg silently and he bumped it. "As much as I appreciate the discretion, never hold back when we're talking about something with this much potential."

"Look at us." Nick slapped me on the back with a grin. "Communicating, establishing boundaries like grown-ass adults."

"Got the ass part right."

"I always get the ass part right." Nick grinned, in a manner not so different from his old self, before the smile faded. "We have to show up, today."

I agreed. "Carry, if needed."

"I think..." Nick hedged. "I'm gonna cut loose. Really tackle the first floor full bore. Inspirational hero shit. Opinion?"

It was obvious he was waiting for me to advise caution, expecting a warning to pace himself. But we were past that. The AG was already on the verge of throwing in the towel. Their members had likely already picked up on the uncertainty from leadership. We needed more than a win.

We needed a victory.

"A lot of bad shit happened in the trial." Noticing the way he immediately stiffened, I hurried on. "Because of that, we don't think about the rest of it much. And it wasn't all bad."

Nick scoffed, gaze unfocused, full of regret.

"You saved my life."

He rolled his eyes. "Another hour and you would have figured out a way to handle old stretch-neck yourself."

"These days, maybe." I shrugged. "Back then, I'm not so sure. It was a weak start. Fewer summons, less resources and contingencies. And the spider wasn't weak. She had me in check. I've never told you this, but I was watching the whole time."

He took a second to recall it, but once he did, his face flushed bright red. "How?"

"We had the same patron. Convinced her I was on her side and she let me hold the strings. Had front row seats the entire time."

"Oh." Nick covered his eyes with a hand. "It's always hazy when I'm that pissed off, but from what I do remember, it got... a little crazy. You saw all that, huh?"

"I didn't just *see* it. It was everything I could do to not just gape, slack-jawed."

"Stop."

"I'm serious. And sure, parts of it were a little terrifying— never going to forget you beating a bug to death with another bug—"

"—Come on, man," Nick groaned.

"But it *was* inspiring. You had this placid fury, this flow, that was humbling to watch. Utter purity of purpose. You were good when we fought together before that, but as soon as I was deep in shit, it was like someone flipped a switch. I realized two things at that moment. The first was that I never wanted to fight you. Ever. For any reason. And the second was that I trusted you implicitly."

He trotted out the beaten-puppy expression. "You didn't trust me *before* that?"

I pushed him lightly. "Shut up. There are levels of trust. What I'm getting at is, if you want to bring that guy back, start the camera up and go for it. Even if we don't find a way to use the footage, it'll wake the people who are there the fuck up. So go nuts. Take chances, be flashy as hell. And I'll make sure the cards come up in your favor."

Be who I know you can be.

"Much as I appreciate the support," Nick stared at the ground, his smile fragile, "I'm not sure I have that guy in me anymore. It changes a lot, knowing..."

"...how quickly you can lose someone," I finished. In the recesses of my mind, **<Jaded Eye>** stirred.

Tell him.

No.

I shook my head ever so slightly, trying to banish the thought from my mind.

"We just said that we need to give this our all," Nick said, voice strangely calm. "If you thought of something that could help—"

"It won't help," I snapped. "It's cruel, and shitty, and manipulative." Nick was already holding the weight of the world on his shoulders. Add any more, and there was a real chance it would break him.

"Damn, I didn't realize it was all lip service."

"Fuck off."

"Matt. We've been here before." Nick lowered his arms to either side and pushed a few times, mimicking rolling a wheel-chair. "No one's ever been honest with me the way you were then. It scared the life back into me. If you have a way to get in my head and help me lock in, cruel or manipulative doesn't matter."

"I don't *want* to." My voice wavered as I slipped off the stool and backed away from him. He was nothing to me when we met in rehab. An idle curiosity with an inevitable end. And even then, I'd only gone through with it because nothing else seemed to work.

Funny. How different things are with time.

Now, hurting him was the last thing I wanted.

"Okay, okay," Nick gestured with both hands palm out, as if warding off an attack, suddenly looking haggard and fatigued. "My bad. That was a shitty thing to ask. You only came at me that hard because we weren't really friends yet. I just thought... you know."

Talia's voice echoed in my mind. "I cannot know how you intended to motivate our packmate. With the recent developments, I can only guess. What is certain is that he will continue to wonder what you might have said. And imagination is often far crueler than reality."

Fuck.

Talia sprang to her feet and took off, heeding the mental command to scout the perimeter. I waited there quietly, praying that I'd somehow been lacking and there was an entire survey unit parked on a roof somewhere.

Eventually, confirmation came back. We were in the clear.

I reached into my inventory and withdrew the **<Allfather's Mask>**, feeling the signature coldness as it tightened beneath my chin.

"This really what you want?"

"Yes."

"Vernon's close, Nick." I didn't bother turning around. Didn't need to. His jaw was on the floor, and he was on the verge of falling off his stool. "All signs point to resurrection being the next skill he unlocks."

Like clockwork, metal smacked against metal as he held onto the counter to steady himself. "What?"

"Did I stutter?"

"You—you told me he was at a progression wall. That it wasn't promising!" His eyebrows furrowed, surprise shifting to anger.

I turned then, giving sound to the silent voice that tormented my fears, my failures, my every doubt. Aiming outward, instead of in. Leveraging it like a weapon. "Yeah. I fucking lied. That really surprise you at this point?"

"Why would you—" his lip trembled, "What the hell is wrong with you, man? I've been worried sick!"

Nick put his hands on me, but I knew the shove was coming long before he moved. I broke his grip, slamming against his center plate with my palm, sending him backpedaling until his armor collided with the cart and he hit the stool. "Come on, let's hear it. Go ahead. Tell me how it wouldn't have been a problem. How you wouldn't have started counting down the days, dropped in on Vernon at every opportunity and tipped our hand. That the dim prospect of resurrecting Jinny becoming not only real, but imminent, wouldn't have been a constant distraction that could have easily gotten you killed."

He bit his lip and looked away.

"Exactly. So yes, I kept it from you. The only reason we're even talking about it now is because I can't stomach the sniveling anymore."

"You don't mean that."

"Sure I do. For once, I mean every, fucking, word." I grabbed him by the collar of his chestplate, pushed him back. "This is what you wanted. Honesty. Well how's this for honesty, Nick? You've been so screwed up over whether or not you might be able to bring back a dead girl that you haven't even considered what you might be bringing her back into."

"Of course I've considered it! We've been trying to make things better. Trying to put an end to this," Nick snarled. He had a lot more fight in him now than he had in rehab. That meant I had to peel the resistance back, layer by layer.

"Then actualize, motherfucker. Because we are running out of time. And the difference between you stepping up or tripping over your own feet could be the difference between bringing Jinny back to a mending society or a hellscape."

He gripped my wrist tightly, trembling with rage.

I leered at him outwardly, feeling nauseous as the guillotine's blade began to slide. "The second event will be worse. I barely lived through the first, Nick. *Me.*" I jabbed a thumb into my chest. "Jinny had a lot of firepower in the early days, but every User still breathing has come a long way since then. She'll be weak at first. Vulnerable. Maybe you can protect her. Maybe you can't. But if you really care, you can't just fixate on her alone. You have to end this. Save *everyone*. And if you're too selfish to see that, then you may as well not even try."

His grip around my wrist relaxed. But his eyes were fathomless. Cold as forged iron. "Remove your hand."

I almost didn't. But the message beneath his impassive expression sent was crystal clear. If I kept going, finished the thought? I didn't know what he'd do. But it scared me. He reached out. Too slow to be anything aggressive, but I still fought the urge to back off, create space. The sense of danger he was giving off was almost palpable.

Fresh air hit my skin as he tugged the mask off.

"The last time someone tried that, it didn't end well for them," I joked, catching a chill.

Nick embraced me in a rough hug, the cool metal seeping through my armor. "Sorry I pushed. It wasn't fair."

"I wanted to tell you the necromancy details. It's been driving me crazy. But you'd already been through a lot, so I held off, and... the right time never came."

"You were right," Nick said simply, sitting back down on the stool. "About everything. I've been short-sighted. Just, completely focused on an endpoint that isn't even the end. Even if it doesn't pan out and the next ability Vernon unlocks is sentient jack-o-lanterns... it'd suck to say goodbye to her without knowing I'd done everything possible to end this. Jinny didn't talk about her life much."

Nick was saying all the right things. Making jokes, setting low expectations, engaging in self-deprecation. But I knew what I'd done. The cruelest thing you could do to a person, when the future was uncertain. Beyond the cajoling and crudeness of the wake-up call, I'd given him hope.

And he burned with it.

Nick held his arm out, checking how steady it was, lowering it satisfied. "Good news. The yips have been vanquished."

In the distance, the fog brightened, parallel high-beams casting long fingers through the haze. Another pair appeared behind it, and another.

"They're here."

My friend stood, somehow seeming both younger and older than he had minutes ago. "Let's get this party started."

CHAPTER SIXTY-FOUR

The turnout was astounding. I'd expected a fraction of what we had—two-thirds on the upside. Looking around the lobby now, it was like half the people I personally knew in the city had shown up. Miles arrived first, fully decked out, Audrey hanging from his belt like an organic satchel. He was chatting with Azure—whose chosen form for this particular assignment was a muscled but slight looking goblinoid with gray hair in Rogue's clothes, flanked by several Users who read as feds I didn't recognize.

In a completely unexpected move, Miles had reached out to me—to Myrddin—late the previous night and invited Myrddin to help with the tower. Guaranteeing oversight and protection from any potential hostilities.

All told, it was a good sign that my once-pursuer-turned-mentor no longer felt the need to keep Myrddin at arm's length. I was naturally forced to decline. But the request presented an opportunity to get all my summons on the board without arousing suspicion when I'd already been brainstorming a way to do exactly that. Myrddin couldn't make it.

But his summons could.

Both the Adventurers' Guild and the Order of Parcae had mobilized en masse, guild heads both present. I didn't have to guess why Tyler was there. The perpetual scowl and mask of skepticism made it perfectly clear. He was here to make the call on whether or not the tower was worth pursuing. Evaluate the floor on a hair trigger.

Aaron was the bigger surprise. Delegation was his religion, and he was the very picture of devout. Seeing him here, roaming around in his high-thread-count business casual, working the room, slowly gravitating toward me was both irritating and disconcerting. If he was going to act as a force multiplier, I didn't have a problem with his presence, but I had a feeling when shit hit the fan, he'd be lingering in the back as usual.

I caught glimpses of Astrid and Astria on the periphery. Miles spotted them just as quickly, and never forgetting a face, sidled up to them, likely reconnecting over their joint efforts during the Transposition.

No sign of Max. He hadn't responded when Myrddin messaged him, so to some extent that was to be expected. It rankled, because Max was probably one of the few people in the dome who could have set Tyler's mind at ease, if the numbers were good, but he was either busy or ready to move on from strike team business, even if our purposes here were pure.

Julian and Charlotte showed with the rest of the Court, Queen Mari striding before them, giant club resting on her shoulders as she pursued a cotton candy vendor who seemed to be doing his best to evade her. There was no sign of the Duskblade Knight, but if that was the Court's only absence, it wasn't a big one.

Somehow, there was less division. Everyone seemed more keen on socializing, groups mixing and merging in a way the previous cliquey, standoffish atmosphere hadn't allowed before.

They got their asses kicked, collectively. In a way one specific group can't be blamed for. Somehow it turned into camaraderie.

There were shockingly few people on the outskirts. Nick separated from me almost as soon as we got in the doors and was parked on a bench, his armored fingers steepled in front of him, head bowed. Part of me wanted to check on him. The other part was too distracted by another person mingling on the outskirts.

Bandages on his arms, an odd cloth cloak, and curly hair. I'd only seen him once.

But he'd left one hell of an impression.

I was less concerned with where he was than where he wasn't. At my brother's side, deeper in the tower. If he was here, there was a good chance my vision was correct and Ellison was completely alone.

Being angry with him was irrational. I had no information and didn't know what their relationship was. For all I knew, Curly was a hired gun.

Which was something I reminded myself as I approached from the side, forcing myself to unclench my fists.

"Haven't seen you around here before."

"We've met," Curly said, matter-of-factly, seemingly completely unconcerned with the bolt of anxiety he'd just sent down my spine. His voice was wistful, and quiet enough that it was difficult to make out over the din.

Fine.

"Where's my brother?" I tried, offering it conversationally, like we were talking about the weather.

"The Keeper is the wind. He waxes and wanes, going where he likes when he chooses, motives and predilections beyond the comprehension of the corporeal."

Oh good. He's insane.

"Any information you have could help," I tried again. "The floor number, or why he pushed so hard into the tower by himself."

"Will there be vampires today?" Curly looked at his nails. His eyes were milky, and if it wasn't obvious from the way he surveyed the room that he could see, I'd wonder if he was blind.

"No." I paused. "Is that a warning?"

"It is a question," Curly replied, bolstering my annoyance to biblical levels.

"Well, we haven't *been* to the next floor before, so no one knows what we'll be up against," I said, biting my tongue before I could reflexively add "asshole."

"The Keeper often knows that which he should not. You do not share this trait. Disappointing."

"Mothe—" I cut off, grinding my teeth, switching to a customer service voice. "Whatever we're fighting, we'll be glad to have your support."

"Support," Curly repeated, as if trying out the word out for the first time. He drew out a pack of Marlboros from within his haggard, raggedy tunic and parked a cig between his lips, absentmindedly holding the pack out to me. I took one as he lit his own and made no offer to light mine. He took a deep draw and breathed out smoke. "You'll be heading to the highest floor currently available?"

I nodded, pocketing the cigarette and making a mental note to throw it away before we started climbing the tower. It seemed perfectly pre-system ordinary and **\<Jaded Eye\>** hadn't activated, but being handed something that I was, in a way, forced to hold onto set my paranoia on edge.

"Then I will climb with you, until you lose pace."

I scanned the room, looking for literally anywhere else to go before I said something regrettable, only to look back and see that Curly had disappeared.

"Motherfucker," I groaned.

A light, likable chuckle filled me with dread. "The eccentric types are always a pain in the ass." Aaron had finally made his way to me, casually surveying the room. He was focused on the queue for the queue counter, smile drooping a bit. Curly was somehow already there, slouched and lethargic as he exchanged Selve for a monstrous turkey leg. "The way he moved though... well, it doesn't matter. Theme of the day is come one, come all, right?"

The double meaning wasn't lost on me. He was testing the waters, seeing if I was desperate enough to disregard our history and ask directly for his help.

"That why you're here? To rally the troops?"

"Not at all," Aaron chortled, brushing off the snipe. "I'm here because my deity believes that climbing the tower will lead to a better future."

"Of course. Aaron the devout," I mused.

"That, and the problem dog skulking around my home seems to have lost his teeth."

"Fancy that."

He looked at me directly. "I don't know how you did it, or how involved you were. The fact that you have so much sway over such a frightening individual continues to vex. But thank you for returning Cameron to me. The last time we spoke about him, I made a decision in haste and came to regret it. It's a great relief to see that mistake undone."

Translation: you delivered, and I'm returning the favor in kind.

I stuck to the script. "Like I said before. All I care about is winning and getting out from under the gameshow from hell."

"Ever the pragmatist. Best of luck out there today." The

edges of Aaron's eyes crinkled, showing the ghost of a smile as he strode toward Tyler.

Seeing that Sae had arrived, and fighting the ever-present urge to flip the bird at Aaron's back, I moved toward the center where Miles had waved Sae over moments ago.

"... and the old cowboy says, yep, that's about as far as I got too!" Miles delivered what sounded like a punchline. Astrid and Astria cackled, while the other feds rolled their eyes and Sae looked vaguely green.

"Well, I *was* hungry enough to see what I could scrounge up from the county fair buffet, but suddenly my appetite is gone." Sae rolled her eyes.

Astria wiped a tear away, shoulders still heaving in amusement. "Just... heh... avoid the chili and you'll be fine."

"Hurk." Sae shook her head, glancing at me. "If you still need to eat, I'd steer clear, Helpline."

"Miles telling weird jokes again?"

"Ah, come on, a little humor to lighten the mood never hurt anyone." Miles stretched, seemingly without a care in the world. But the single worry line etched into his forehead. "Ever hear the one about the woman walking home with her three daughters?" Miles asked, and when Astria and Astrid both confirmed they hadn't, he launched into it.

Tuning him out, I turned to Sae and pitched my voice low. "When I said you didn't have to come, I meant it."

"I know." Sae crossed her arms stubbornly, trying to project confidence and failing. "But this is important. Can't dodge the realms forever."

"Take a backseat if you need to."

Sae had grown exponentially over the last month, in terms of level and experience. She was hard as nails and showed no signs of cracking. But everything we'd done together had occurred almost entirely within the real world. I wasn't sure if the nerves came from showing her face in public after weeks of hiding, or because this was the first time outside of the adaptive dungeon she'd set foot in a realm of Flauros.

A text from Miles popped, directed to Matt.

<**Miles:** You trust this group?>
<**Matt:** Sae I can vouch for. The twins showed up out of nowhere and helped out during the necromancer attack, and I think they may have pitched in for my old region during the event, but that's the extent of our involvement.>
<**Miles:** They're solid.>

"For what it's worth," Miles said to Sae, transition from text to spoken conversation perfectly smooth, "we may not be in there long. Tyler's putting caution first. Wants to make sure no one's rushing into something that could clap back on us the way the last floor did. It's a shame, because there's a big opportunity here to stop what happened last time from happening again. Totally understandable where he's coming from, just a damn shame."

Apparently his talks with Tyler hadn't inspired confidence. But I had to smile a little, realizing he was already doing what I'd intended to do.

<**Matt:** That the angle? Make Tyler out to be reasonable but overly cautious, get people talking about what that hesitation might cost them in hopes that they break ranks?>
<**Miles:** Yup. All I got. Wanna help?>
<**Matt:** Naturally.>

————

It took nearly an hour of near-constant crowd work between the two of us before I started hearing things that showed promise, organically emerging from conversations neither me nor Miles had directly interfered with. Doubts about the Adventurers' Guild being here in any serious capacity. Fears centered around what would happen if we simply walked away empty-handed. Glimpses of rebellion and determination, stemming from that fear.

Tyler called everyone over to where he and Aaron stood near the elevators and began to speak, straightening up from the slouch he'd developed and exercising a level of gravitas I hadn't seen from him in a while. Sara stood behind him, monitoring the crowd for threats, her expression otherwise immutable.

"Well, I was gonna wait until nine to do this, but somehow most of you were actually on time," Tyler announced, smiling a bit as observation drew laughs. "There's a lot of new faces, some of whom belong neither to the Order or the Adventurers' Guild, so I'll give you a quick rundown of where we're at. We believe, collectively, that there's an artifact near the top of the tower worth pursuing. Not for its inherent value. From what I understand, the artifact itself holds little value beyond being a slight improvement on the average sword."

That was a clever bit of misinformation. If he outright announced to the crowd that **\<Excalibur\>** was at the top of the tower, it'd kick off a gold rush on the name alone.

The few artifacts I'd encountered had been completely game changing, but they were rare enough that it wasn't common knowledge.

"By now, it should be obvious to anyone that the kind folk of the tower are methodical with their screening processes, so I'm sure no one's foolish enough to try and smuggle something out," Aaron added, eyeing a few members of the crowd mean-ingfully. They shifted uncomfortably under his gaze.

Tyler stepped forward. "Even if they weren't, I'd like to believe that not a single person in the group assembled here today would be tempted to do so, given what we stand to gain. An end to the madness. An alternative to simply forging ahead, charging headfirst through the meat grinder that has, for the last few months, kept us and the people we care about in a state of constant peril." He faltered, pausing to adjust his eye patch. "This is a critical undertaking. One we cannot afford to rush. I want to be clear. The last time we made an attempt, there was a biohazard incident. One with the potential to threaten the lives of every person within the dome. Given that, Aaron and I are placing serious emphasis on the importance of caution. Several experienced scout teams will survey the floor first, while the core force holds at the entrance. After we have a clearer picture, a decision will be made."

I groaned. And, unexpectedly, realized I wasn't the only one. There were disapproving murmurs, even a solitary boo.

Miles and I had talked to a lot of people. But not that many. And no matter how persuasive you were, it was impossible to start a fire from stone. The kindling had already been there, dry and brittle beneath the surface, ready to ignite. Everyone here had their lives changed by the dome and the Transposition in some way. Every single person was tired of being at the whims of the unknown.

"Make no mistake, we *will* climb the tower," Tyler insisted, feeling the resistance and trying to counterbalance. "It's a ques-tion of timing now. We cannot afford to expend ourselves on the precipice of disaster. But even if now is not the right time, we will return."

He continued on for a while, battling the growing sense of

unease and irritation before seeming to grow tired and calling for everyone with us to embark on the elevator.

Despite the massive circumference of the lift, by the time everyone filed on it the spacing was tight, cramped.

Knees bent and whispers circulated as the elevator rose, picking up speed, walls blurring with the acceleration.

We emerged at the top of a tall hill, verdant meadows extending out toward the horizons, a large circle of trees encapsulating the distant perimeters.

At first I was relieved. This floor looked exponentially larger than the last, but the sight lines were wide open, meaning I'd be able to alter the flow of any battle more effectively than the previous floor's cramped interior.

"Holy shit," someone mouthed.

I looked down. And spotted the war camp.

CHAPTER SIXTY-FIVE

I scanned it through a pair of binoculars I'd bummed off a scout, lying prone at the ledge that led to a steep descent downward, scanning the structure. Wooden stakes carved from tree trunks formed high walls, thankfully not so high that they obscured our elevated view.

What was visible was grim regardless. Hobgoblins—the goblin's meaner, smarter cousin. Excepting a few loin-clothed, malnourished variants that seemed to be of a lower caste, they were all either fully or partially armored, and the weapons I could see were of decent quality. It was, by an order of magnitude, the largest group of monsters I'd ever seen in one place. Five hundred give or take, though the real headcount was difficult to establish as they appeared to be sleeping in shifts, numbers obscured by the large barrack tents. There was a considerable armory, a forge, even a mess hall.

Beyond the numbers, there were two massive problems. Separated from the rest of the camp was a small defended square that housed eight catapults. Their payloads were nothing special, judging from awkward mounds of "ammo"—they were using ordinary chunks of rock. Somehow, despite the considerable noise this many people made, the hobgoblins were still completely unaware of our presence, and the catapults weren't pointed at the mountain. But the artillery weapons were on wheels, and we were absolutely in range.

Not good.

The second, arguably bigger problem, were the prisoners housed in various cages scattered around the camp.

Nearby, Aaron and Tyler were arguing.

"Relax," Aaron insisted, dismissing some point Tyler brought up. "We have elevation and enough firepower with all the mages to level a building. It'll be bloodless on our side. Just bomb the hell out of them and wash our hands of it."

"They have *hostages,*" Tyler fired back.

"No one's been this high in the tower before. And even if someone has, look at them all. They're obviously system-created entities, strategically placed to stop us from taking the obvious solution."

"Hearing this?" I murmured to Miles, who was doing the same thing I was a few feet away with an expensive-looking rangefinder.

"Every word," Miles replied.

"Got info. But it's more likely to hurt us than help us."

Casually, Miles shimmied sideways until he was close enough to whisper, resting prone beside me. "What's up?"

I hesitated, not sure whether to share what I was about to. "I've seen this setup before."

"The hobgoblins?"

I shook my head. "The hostages. Found my way into a dungeon once with a small group, shortly after I got the class. Owlbears. Had a human hostage in a cage. We were the first ones in, according to the system notification, so I came to the same conclusion Aaron did."

"Fake human, generated by the system to create an additional obstacle. Reasonable conclusion to come to."

I hesitated.

"Aw, fuck." Miles stared down at the camp. "How'd you figure it out?"

"Vitiligo."

"Sorry, what?"

"He had vitiligo."

"So does my aunt. The hell does that have to do with anything?"

"Your aunt and less than one percent of the human population," I said, blending truth and fiction as smoothly as I could. "It just stuck in my head as odd. Why would a generic, system-created hostage have such a specific trait?"

"Pass the binos. Rangefinder keeps fogging." He took them from me and surveyed the cages in the camp, pausing on each one. "C-section scar. Tattoo. Another tattoo, different color, different artist. Really terrible glasses. Surprised they let him keep those. Fuck me." Miles lowered the binoculars, wiping a bead of sweat off his forehead. "Bureau likes to blame every missing person on a necromancer, but I'm willing to bet a lot of people who disappeared right at the beginning met a similar fate. You gonna... oh." He leveled a cool gaze at me, seeing, without judgment or affirmation. "Horrific as it is, flattening that camp is the easiest way from point A to point B. And if Tyler finds out, this could be the excuse to back out he's searching for. A reasonable person might be considering keeping that to himself."

I looked away.

"Well shit, kid. Really front-loading the heavy stuff." Miles sighed, giving the camp another once-over before he shook his head. "I don't have to tell you, of all people, that sometimes life gives you shit choices."

A slow chill crawled up my spine.

"You're thinking about the lives at stake. Trolley problem logic. If you keep your silence, let those twenty people suffer whatever's coming their way, you stand to save hundreds of thousands of lives. What you have to realize is that's a false binary."

"How so?"

"You're not leveraging the lives of the people down there," Miles pointed, "against the lives of the people outside. You're leveraging the lives of the people down there for a single step in the right direction."

"Fuck." It was a relief, in a way. Even if it didn't make the current situation any easier.

"You wanna tell them, or should I?" Miles asked.

I stood to my feet, brushing bits of detritus off my armor and approaching the two guild leaders with my hands in my pockets. "I've encountered a similar scenario before. The hostage was a real person, abducted when the meteor hit and we all got our classes."

Tyler leveled me with a frown. "You're sure?"

Aaron looked between us, unconvinced. "Just because it happened once doesn't mean it's the case here."

Too quick on the comeback. He already knew.

I turned my attention to Tyler. "Confident. The hostages all have distinguishing marks. Why the hell else would they give a system-generated human a C-section scar?"

"To make them more convincing," Aaron argued. "Isn't that the entire point?"

Out of the corner of my eye, I saw Nick hold the crab up, peering at it intently before placing it down on the ground where it blended perfectly with the grass.

My pulse spiked.

Now?!

"Much as I appreciate you bringing this to my attention," Tyler rubbed his head, "it changes things. We can't blindly fire into the camp without risking innocent lives. There's no approach with cover of any kind and they have braziers scattered around the meadow, so stealth is out of the question. Even if we descend down the back of the mountain and circle around, they'll see us coming, and the catapults will do the rest."

"What about the people?"

Heads snapped around, the tone and authority in the voice immediately striking. As far as I could tell, Nick wasn't doing anything differently. He was standing casually, one foot slightly in front of the other, gauntlets resting on his belt.

"The situation is tragic..." Tyler said, scanning Nick up and down uncertainly. "But we can't help them without putting our own in serious peril."

Nick chuckled, running gloved fingers through his hair. "Guess I'm just confused. I'm not the brightest guy in the world. Or the dome. Sometimes things that should make sense to me don't. So help me out a little. If we're right and those people down there have been stuck in cages since this all started, they've probably suffered a lot. I've been held against my will before. It was a picnic compared to what the folks down there are going through, and I'll still never forget it. Guess I'm wondering, if the assembled force of two of the strongest guilds in the dome aren't going to save those people... who is?" The challenge in his voice rang, clear as day.

Tyler glared, swatting at his eye patch. "You would understand better if you bothered to listen." Beside him, Aaron slowly began to smile.

Nick shrugged. "Happy to get my ears checked after, but I'm pretty sure I heard the catapults and elevated firing positions were the biggest problems, no?"

"Well... yes," Tyler admitted.

"And if they weren't a problem, you'd feel more comfortable swinging that sword around."

"There's a difference between comfort and knowing I'm not marching the people I'm directly responsible for to their deaths," Tyler countered, off balance, starting to sense the powder keg but not fully grasping what it was yet.

"Then I've only got one thing left to say to you." Nick leaned forward.

Here it comes.

I dropped into a crouch, mimicking adjusting my boot.

There was a blur as Talia darted away, sprinting from Nick's side toward the twin mages.

"For Frodo," Nick said, letting it hang for maximal confusion.

Just as Tyler had recovered enough to speak, Nick turned and took off running at a dead sprint, directly toward the ledge.

CHAPTER SIXTY-SIX

"Talia, give Astria a message from Myrddin. Tell her if the hobgoblins try executing hostages, send a strong reminder why they spaced them out like that in the first place. Keep it vertical and off target. Hit Sae, Julien, and Charlotte after, from me. Tell them they don't have to help. But if they feel like pitching in, we've never needed it more."

Talia broke off from us, darting between onlookers, ducking beneath the wide gate of a gaping tank, and she tore hell toward the twins.

I ran parallel to Nick, keeping pace. But only barely. My agility was closing in on double his. How he was managing the speed was beyond me, until I noticed the way his armor had changed color.

He was glowing gold.

"Whatever the hell you're doing, I think your patron approves," I yelled over the cacophony of clanking.

"Yeah. Got a lot of juice," Nick panted, sparing a glance at me. "Dunno how long it's gonna last. We need to go in hard, fuck 'em up as much as we can with the time we have."

I glanced at the rapidly approaching ledge. "Maybe worry about the cliff first?"

"Nah." He grinned, a manic gleam in his eye. "Just aim for the bushes."

"It's a ninety-degree incline, motherfucker!"

"You trust me?"

"Fucking obviously!"

"Drop back a bit. Follow my lead."

"Already... am."

I trailed off as Nick pulled ahead, gaining ground without any adjustment of speed on my part, sprinting toward the ledge without so much as a flicker of fear. He hit the ledge and leapt, no hesitation, catching enough air that I knew, instinctively, the landing was going to be fatal.

"What—" I cut off, slack-jawed, as Nick shot straight outward, fists out behind him.

The friend I'd once watched struggle to walk, flew.

"You idiot," I murmured, popping my flight charm, trying not to think about all the ways this was a terrible idea, fighting the wind to catch up with him. "Now that we're weightless and it'll be three times harder to do a damn thing, any other bright ideas?"

"Think they realized I didn't take the short way down?" Nick glanced back at the mountain, wincing and wobbling a bit as the motion redirected the wind current and nearly knocked him off course.

"Yeah, they're aware," I said dryly.

"Then we go low." He swooped down, dropping altitude until we were unnervingly close to the ground, weaving through the waist-high grass and drawing his sword, holding the hilt with both hands, sweeping side to side at seemingly random intervals like he was searching for something.

In seconds, he found it. One of the hobgoblin rogues

skulking through the grass, clad in leathers, staring at the oncoming hurricane, frozen.

The collision was a horrifying squelch and resulting squeal as Nick's sword speared all the way through his shoulder, cross-guard acting like a fish hook as the hobgoblin was dragged, kicking and screaming, the back of his legs plowing through the soil.

"Got you a present," Nick said, shifting the sword slightly so the monster was closer to me.

The hobgoblin's beady black eyes hopped from me to Nick and back again, panicked.

"I don't want it."

"Just fuck with him, I'll evade for a bit."

I bit back a sharp retort, catching his meaning. He knew the Ordinator abilities required a lot of set up and was trying to give me a window to use them. Granted, it was a depressingly small window, and only a single goblin out of a camp of five hundred. But it was better than nothing.

<Subjugate>.

I reeled, nearly hitting the ground as psychic feedback snapped back on me, the inhuman squeal breaking my concentration.

"What the hell?"

Int/Agi Hybrid.

"Uh, Matt, I don't mean to rush—"

"Then don't pick up the world's smartest hobgoblin and expect me to work quickly," I snarled, grabbing the goblin's head and twisting his neck to the side, giving me a better angle. Drawing a knife, I carved his ear off, ignoring both Nick's horrified look and the goblin's crescendoing howl.

"Can you go five minutes without committing a war crime?!" Nick shouted.

I ignored him, opening a connection through **<Sugges-**

tion> and forcing my way through, feeling for weaknesses and fears. The hobgoblin, whose name was some guttural multi-apostrophized grunt I couldn't pronounce, was a hedonist first.

And hedonists were easy.

PROTECT YOUR CHAIN OF COMMAND. ESPECIALLY THE ONES THESE INTERLOPERS GET CLOSE TO. IF YOU FAIL, YOU'LL NEVER SEE THE INSIDE OF A BROTHEL AGAIN.

His arm was in bad shape. His mind was chaos. If it worked, he'd run himself ragged, haplessly pointing out every goblin that outranked him while doing very little to actually protect them.

Again, the goblin screeched in fear. Nick carried him in a slow circle, squinting at the camp. It was difficult to see anything with blades of grass hitting me in the face every five seconds, but I could hear the footfalls of armored troops converging toward us, and unless I'd completely lost my sense of direction, I was pretty sure we were on the opposite side of the camp from the catapults.

"It's working," Nick smiled, wind whipping through his hair. "We're pulling them away from the artillery." He glanced at me, wincing a little as he said it. "Any... chance you can turn him up a little?"

I considered the hobgoblin's remaining ear, then quickly disregarded it. The monster was in a lot of pain already. More and he was at risk of falling unconscious.

Instead, I hammered his mind.

THERE WILL BE NO WOMEN. ONLY MEN.

Somehow, the hobgoblin's screams rose another octave. Nick corkscrewed, holding the creature straight up, carrying him upright above the grass as he flew blindly on his back, zigzagging through the grass on a random path. I tried to imagine how it looked from the fort. A single hobgoblin, carried at break-neck speed on an unseen mount, screeching bloody murder.

It was one hell of a distraction.

"Ready?" Nick said.

"Almost."

WARN THEM. SCREAM UNTIL YOU CAN'T SCREAM ANYMORE.

In a manner that was almost compliant, the hobgoblin sucked in a deep breath. Nick spun, letting gravity do most of the work as the goblin slid off his sword, tumbling across the ground. It spit out a mouthful of dirt and immediately started raising a racket again.

"Guard towers first?" I asked, fighting a growing thrill.

"Just like the Wildlands days," Nick winked. We split to the left and right, swooping through the low grass as our abandoned abductee continued to provide cover.

I flew low enough that the toes of my boots threatened to catch the ground. That was the point. If we were too obvious, it would undo the entire gambit for reorganization. The hobgoblins in the towers weren't heavily armored, but that mattered less than it usually would. That was the downside of using the flight charm in combat. It was all about momentum. If you were floating and struck a static object, it'd do almost nothing to the object and end up pushing you back.

Even if you were flying directly at them, it was hard to get a knife to stick.

With that in mind, I drew **<Luciana>**, spinning once from the ring to dial in the heft, and spotting the rickety construction of a tower above me through the grass I shot straight up, evening out in a tight curve, hoping the momentum was enough.

The tower hobgoblin's mouth dropped open in surprise as the horizontal slash parted his throat, a curtain of black descending from the wound. There were two more, equally surprised but much quicker to react than their companion had been. Still floating a little off the ground, I slammed the karambit back into my inventory and quickdrew two of the new crossbows, firing them both, feeling a mix of satisfaction and panic as bolts struck home, dropping the monsters. But the combined force of the shot sent me flying back toward the wall.

I flailed, dropping one of the spent bows and inventorying the other as my hand caught purchase on one of the spikes of the log wall, waiting for the world to stop spinning, unsure how much attention I'd drawn, if any.

The next guard tower over, a pale, terrified-looking hobgoblin openly gawked, shakily raising a giant sheephorn to his lips and inhaling.

HOLD YOUR BREATH, I commanded.

It froze, wide-eyed, cheeks inflated, lips still planted firmly on the horn. Unlike the previous sentry, this one had taken the dress code more seriously, an amalgam of iron and leather armor that covered both neck and head, limiting my options. Taking an extra setting to line up the jump, I cast **<Probability Cascade>** on my legs and launched toward the tower, accelerating, then rotating in midair so my feet were in front of me. My boots landed square on the horn's rim.

I grabbed the overhang for leverage and kicked with both feet, breaking teeth and sending the horn down the goblin's throat. He fell with an echoing gurgle to the ground.

This pace was too breakneck. I needed to take stock, get an idea of how Nick was doing—

CRACK.

Across the camp, there was a thundering splinter of wood and shrieking voices as a guard tower on Nick's side splintered, armored monsters scattering beneath as it plummeted to the ground, partially collapsing on another fallen tower I hadn't even heard go down. A glowing gold blur shot out from beneath the wreckage, zipping above a small squadron of archers coherent enough to aim before they fired.

Okay. So much for drawing their attention away from the center.

<Probability Cascade> activated and every arrow went wide, missing Nick by a wide enough margin that he may have not even noticed they fired. He—probably realizing his tower solution had been too bombastic—made the best of the situation, deviating from the original catapult destination and flying along the elevated catwalks, holding his arm out, grabbing, yanking, and clotheslining goblins off their elevated positions.

Not something I could do half as effectively with my current strength, but there was another option. I took flight, dodging an onslaught of arrows from below, sticking to the shadows beneath the catwalks, planting more than half of my incendiary charges on the thick support beams that supported the catwalks.

Below, the one-eared goblin from before was planted in front of a larger variant, a cruel-looking brute with a large mace, never taking his eyes off me, holding a shield with both hands.

Thanks, pal.

The brute was in the midst of shouting directions in harsh guttural commands, recognition lighting in his battle-hardened face. "They're targeting our defenses! Regrou—"

I dipped low, and bypassing one-ear entirely, quickdrew a crossbow and shot the commander in the face. He toppled as I moved on, building momentum back up after nearly diverting into a wall of waiting swords and shields. The incendiary charges went off, one after another, lighting a fire I coaxed to burn brightly until segments were falling away. Through one of the newly opened holes, I saw Charlotte alone in the distant field, holding her staff skyward.

A shower of sparks spanning the central camp drifted downward like snowflakes. I steered clear, Nick following my lead. Below, in the midst of the churning chaos, I saw a single goblin reach up, catching a spark on the back of his finger. He recoiled as it flared, leaving a purple afterimage in my vision, grabbing at his face, mouth twisted in a rictus of pain.

Naturally, I looked away as soon as the sparks went off, grabbing at Nick's arm as we met above the catapults. "Flight is getting dodgy. They're shooting skeet and I can't stop every arrow. We need to play it tighter."

"Yep," Nick mused, seeming to weigh a few options before deciding on one that involved dropping straight down, toward a mass of hobgoblins spread out amongst the catapults. He kicked a spear aside and landed on top of the spearman full force, the spearman's skull cracking beneath his boot.

I was about to assign that particularly impossible feat to patron bullshit until I saw him drop the remnants of his torn-up flight charm on the ground.

I'd wondered how he was going to deal with the weightless-ness problem. Seeing it now, though, was sobering. The flight charms were an invaluable form of retreat. We could get more through the AG connection, assuming Tyler didn't send us both packing after this, but that didn't help us now.

And once the charms were gone, there was no backing out. No tactical retreat.

We were committed.

I tore mine and landed, ducking beneath a sword, grabbing the attacker by the neck and **\<Subjugating\>** him.

These two are a distraction. There's a larger force that way, hidden in the grass. Gather up as many as you can and GO! I sent him a mental picture of figures hidden in the sprawling field on the other side of catapults, in the opposite direction of the mountain lift.

He nodded briefly before taking off, barely dodging beneath Nick's wide, savage swings and high-stepping over the snapping jaws of a canine. Talia watched him go, cocking her head before she turned back. *"Help is on the way."*

"How much?" I shouted, catching Nick under his arms as he stumbled back, fresh dent in his armor.

Talia waded in with a snarl, locking her jaws around the club-wielder's throat and tackling him down, tearing at his throat, releasing once the struggling stopped, dark blood dripping from her fangs. *"More—"* Her eyes widened. *"Look out!"*

Amidst a new storm of sparks, a massive projectile plunged toward us, argent blue corona shimmering with sheer destructive power, and for a moment my crazed mind thought it was another comet. I dove to the side, taking Nick down with me as Astria's projectile impacted a dividing wall and exploded with an ear-shattering *BOOM*, a radius of flaming shrapnel peppering the dirt and catapults around us.

"I said vertical and off-target, god dammit!" I shouted, my own voice barely perceptible over the ringing in my ears. The explosion left a wake of goblin bodies both in front of and behind the retaining wall. Heated as I was, I knew Astria was deadly accurate. If I had to guess, the hostage in peril had been toward the center of the camp. She'd limited the range of damage by targeting the top of the wall. The hostages on the other side seemed terrified but unharmed, and by some miracle neither of us had been hit.

"Matthias," Talia said, approaching us cautiously.

"Think... I may have fucked up," Nick said, his voice pained and ethereal.

No.

A twisted, blackened chunk of metal jutted from Nick's abdomen. He touched it, grimaced, then gripped it tightly.

Automatically, I knocked his hand away and upended a health potion into his mouth. "Leave it until the potion kicks in."

"Look at them all," Nick murmured. Beyond us, through both the original entrance to the artillery section and the retaining wall, the hobgoblins had mostly recovered. They were climbing over the remnants, more approaching from the side. Compared to before, they were moving slowly, cautious. But the caution wouldn't last for long.

He was in shock. The wound wasn't fatal, but I'd wager it hurt like hell. I withdrew a sack of incendiary charges. "Come on, buddy. Need you to set these while Talia and I hold them off."

Nick shook his head, trying to shake it off and failing. "Bad idea. Remember the fireworks?"

I snorted. The first and only time we'd celebrated the Fourth of July—his idea—and Nick had almost blown himself up with M-80s. *Twice.* "Well, somebody's gotta do it."

"You go, I'll..." Nick tried to push himself up and fell back, harried and disoriented. "Shit."

It was the shock. He wasn't dying, I'd checked his vitals with **<Blade of Woe>**. And we couldn't just retreat here, without taking the catapults out of play. I needed to snap him out of it, somehow. And without using my powers, in my panicked state, there was really only one thing I could think of.

Talia barked at the encroaching goblins, alternating between the advancing groups as I whispered-yelled in Nick's ear. "'You, me, nobody's gonna hit as hard as life. But it ain't about how hard you hit. It's about how hard you can hit and keep moving forward. How much you can take and keep moving forward. So get. Up. *Motherfucker.*'"

Nick laughed, cutting off abruptly from the pain. When he recovered, his eyes were more focused now, and the franticness behind them seemed to fade. "Think you... ad-libbed at the end there, coach."

This time, when I tried to pull him up, he worked with me, boots catching purchase against the ground. Nick straightened, downing another potion before he gripped the shrapnel in his abdomen and *pulled*, grimacing as it came free, leaving a spatter of red across the soil below.

"Decision time. Charges or pointy-eared bastards," I prompted.

"Well, I can't chicken out after all that." Nick grinned, drawing his sword shakily and banging it against his shield. "Talia! To me!"

Talia skipped away from the encroaching goblins, taking her place at Nick's side, glancing at him with concern. I saw it too. It was a brave face. Nick was amping himself up and trying to set me at ease. But the wound had been serious, and health potions weren't a cure-all. Whatever time we had left, the accidental friendly fire had probably cut it in half.

I sprinted away as Nick drew first blood, drawing charges from the bag and placing them on the catapults, only catching glimpses, worry growing by the minute. Because Nick wasn't glowing anymore. His patron's favor was apparently fleeting.

That didn't matter. Because he had *mine*.

His sword found throats, gaps, openings. Every impact his shield took resonated, jarring the attacker to their bones. The goblins crowded in, bloodlust stoked, pushing and shoving to get to Nick when they'd been cautious and orderly just moments before. The fallen clung to those still standing, begging for help or trying to right themselves, only to be stumbled or tripped over.

A spearman that through the gaps in between the critical moments I spent between focusing on Nick and working on the charges jammed his weapon into Nick's back, eliciting a roar of rage as Nick pivoted and rang the hobgoblin's head with his shield like a gong.

"Matthias!" Talia roared into my mind.

"I see it."

My vision began to gray, signaling my mana was running low. I placed the final charge, retreated, and blew it, covering my ear and the back of my head with an arm. The already sweltering temperature skyrocketed, searing my back as I drew my saber and began to fight, swinging the saber defensively so Nick could afford to retreat. But more goblins were pouring into the square by the second.

Retreat where?

Searching, desperate for anything that resembled a choke point. But beyond the burning catapults, the artillery square consisted of nothing but a shack in the corner. It was either that or running out into the open and hoping the AG had made up enough distance to assist.

Another round of Charlotte's sparks bought us a moment of breathing room. If we were going to move, we needed to do it now.

"Talia—"

"I'll hold them for as long as I can. Go!" Talia urged.

I supported Nick, back straining as I steered us toward the shack, firing my last two loaded crossbows behind us, killing the frontrunners. As we half-limped, half-ran, I lowered my head in supplication, never taking my eyes off the destination.

Nychta, grant me strength.

The low, menacing pitch of a woman's chuckle echoed in my ear, confirming what I already suspected. I hadn't pinned down all the details, but I knew she was drawn to battle and carnage. She'd be watching.

"And here I wondered if you forgot about me, little Ordinator," Nychta whispered.

I didn't.

"Perhaps. What will you offer for this request?"

A sacrament.

"Harvested with the blades you hold so dearly?"

If that will suffice.

"Dance beautifully to the drums, my sweet. Your wish is granted."

A surge of acid roiled in my gut. My fingers twitched, every part of me straining to turn around and face my attackers, to demonstrate every facet of the foolishness of their pursuit. I kept moving, somehow retaining enough of myself to help Nick into an overturned crate in the back.

Nick stared at me, panicked. "We're trapped."

I shook my head. "We are the trap. Tell the camera to stay away, cover the rest of the camp or something." The running footfalls grew closer. They'd be going from bright midday to pitch black. Goblins and goblinoids had better night vision than humans, but the difference was stark enough that it would still have an impact. **<Harrowing Anticipation>** activated, threads expanded from my vision, the aggressive, percussive beat of **<Twilight's Nocturne>** thrumming alongside it. "Nick," I said, teeth gritted as some outside force tugged at the back of my skull, forcing my face into a smile.

"Yeah?" Nick asked, chugging more potions.

"Don't watch, okay?"

If he responded, I didn't hear it. I was completely focused on the plan. It wasn't the worst plan ever, but it was close. **<Harrowing Anticipation>** wasn't cheap. My already depleted mana was lower than it had been.

To make matters worse, the supply shack was the definition of any port in a storm. It wasn't at all secure. The walls looked thin. If the catwalks and catapults were any indication, a single torch in the right place would set the entire thing ablaze.

With the sudden light level change, it'd be easy to kill the first few hobgoblins through the door.

But if I did that, they'd get smart. Smoke us out or start shooting.

So the answer was simple.

Take advantage of the initial bloodlust and kill them slowly. Keep the bodies that did fall away from the door and let the goblins that persisted raise enough din and ruckus that the battle appeared to be ongoing.

It wasn't perfect. But it was all I had.

The first group pushed through the door in an angry cluster, not even bothering to slow down.

My turn.

I slashed from shoulder, to sternum, to shoulder again and threw him aside, moving smoothly now, aches and pains from the previous encounter all but forgotten. **<Luciana>** carved through armor straps and tendons alike, every strike accelerating, the small resistance I did feel paltry, almost nothing.

The artifact was unlike any blade I'd ever used, and at that moment I cherished it. In the low light, many of the attackers didn't seem to notice the extent of their injuries. They tried to keep fighting as their legs buckled on severed Achilles, their guts spilled out, and nicked arteries pumped black life's blood onto the ground.

Myrddin didn't fight like this. Myrddin was about efficiency. He killed, but he killed humanely.

This was something else.

But the drums beat, each strike a swell, drowning out all rational thought as the gods themselves bore witness and I was undone.

The first clever goblin tried to run. Would have made it, but he lost footing on the viscera-covered floor. I fish-hooked him with the karambit, flesh and bone of his upper palate providing enough resistance to yank him back before it parted and gave way.

The second clever goblin stuck his head in, wide-eyed, and turned to shout a warning.

I risked a **<Subjugation>**, because it didn't matter.

If I died, I died.

"Long pig's back on the menu, boys. They're on their last legs. Get 'em!" The converted hobgoblin charged in, blade lowered, directly into another goblin crawling toward the door, who howled and fell still.

More followed, trickle renewed to stream, and I met them. **<Luciana>** began to wail, glowing dull red in the low light, her voice merging with the beating of the drums, two songs becoming one.

This was who I was. Who I always had been. A blade in the dark, waiting to be drawn.

Nothing else mattered.

The subjugated goblin fell, ganged up on by its enraged fellows before I capitalized on the distraction and put them down.

It didn't matter.

No one mattered.

Something... was wrong with that. It bothered me. Dissonance in the song. I tried to kill it and found that while it wasn't as loud as before, the atonality was impossible to snuff. It remained, buzzing in my ear, marring the melody, even as the bodies of maimed hobgoblins collapsed from their injuries, one after another.

Why aren't there more coming? Surely there's more.

"From the sound of it, the cavalry's here. Take a breath." Someone—no... I knew them.

Nick snapped his fingers in front of my face, smiling sympathetically. The words registered late, din of battle becoming audible over the roaring of blood in my ears.

The ground shifted beneath me and I realized we were standing on bodies, simply because there was nowhere else to stand. They littered the floor, stacked two high in some places. Black blood and other viscera dripped from the ceiling, coated the walls.

"It—" I started.

"You don't have to explain. My dumbass fell short, again. All you did was pick up the slack. It'd be kind of messed up if I climbed up on a high horse and complained about how you did it."

"Come on." I wanted to believe him. But everyone had a limit.

His smile slipped a little, and he seemed to be intentionally avoiding taking in more of our surroundings than he had to. "It's another bullet point in the let's-never-go-at-each-other-for-real column, if I'm honest. But we're alive. And once we see this through? You can hang the dark shit up for good." He reached for the tent flap, ready to leave.

I blurted something out. Something that'd been gnawing at me from the beginning. "And if I can't?"

Nick paused, turning back to look at me as if the answer was the most obvious thing in the world. "Then I'll do the same thing you did for me. Drag you kicking and screaming back into the light."

———

Between the joint efforts of Charlotte, Julien, Sae, and Miles, the goblins were reeling. I'd initially asked for their help because they were all, to some extent, people I trusted. The fact that the six of us worked so well together ended up being a happy accident. Despite varying ages, backgrounds, and philosophies, we all brought something unique to the table that somehow added up to a greater whole.

Sae and Nick alone were a complementing martial power-house. Nick of the hit-me-and-see-what-happens variety, Sae of the good-luck-hitting-me-at-all. They'd found their tempo first, likely because after her alteration, recovery, and the strike team work, Sae was most similar to me. The difference was, where I excelled in hammering down single targets, Sae had more sustain and endurance. And unlike me, she was a lot more comfortable digging her heels in on the frontlines.

The two fell into a comfortable rhythm almost immediately. Sae shredding through monsters at close range, baiting and taunting them into Nick, who absorbed the reprisal and returned it exponentially, heaping affirmation and praise onto Sae all the while.

Granted they kept high-fiving in the middle of combat, more than once with a number of sharp objects barreling their direction, but that was more Nick's fault than Sae's.

Together, they drew a lot of aggression. More than double what they would have individually.

Which was good, because without the redirected attention, there would have been an abundance of repeatedly blinded, infested, or disease-stricken monsters that, if not otherwise occupied, would be highly motivated to look for the User pointing a wand or staff their way.

The sheer value of Charlotte's utility was insane. Coupled with the sheer nastiness of some of the more visceral hexes, and a detached, almost scientific commitment to experimenting and finding the most debilitating combinations of effects, she was terrifying. Some of her magic—the mass blind spell, for one—was telegraphed. Others, like the painful looking boils and a sudden area of effect pressure shift that ruptured the eardrums of anything with the misfortune of standing in it, were either imperceptible or almost impossible to trace.

Not to say some of the more afflicted and understandably pissed-off hobgoblins didn't try.

Which was where Julien came in.

I liked Julien, as a person. He was friendly, agreeable, less impulsive than Nick and just as quick to listen and contribute to discussions without dominating them.

After what I saw on the last floor, however, Julien was the only person I'd half-expected to stay on the mountain. He had some sort of hang-up with violence, even when it was clearly justified. Either due to class, personal beliefs, or both. Frankly, if he was going to repeat his previous behavior incessantly, insisting on dragging every monster we encountered capable of speech into drawn-out negotiations, I would have preferred he stayed there.

Where Julien actually landed was somewhere in between. He engaged almost purely defensively, fully committed to safeguarding Charlotte, aiming to disarm and dissuade.

His mercy had limits. Which, in my eyes, changed things a great deal. If one of the aforementioned repeatedly blinded, eardrum ruptured, disease-stricken hobgoblins mistook mercy for stupidity, Julien put them down. The Prince was willing to take a hell of a beating for whatever ideals or rules he followed, but he wasn't callous enough to expect others to do the same.

I could respect that, even if I didn't fully understand it.

Before the dome it might have annoyed me, in the context of an online RPG or tabletop game. Having one person fully committed to safeguarding another felt like a waste in the context of gamified bullshit like damage per second or encounter scaling. But I'd seen the way system monsters and other Users aggressively targeted magic types. I'd been on both sides of it. It was the natural course of action, given the low defenses and sheer power they wielded.

So if Julien wanted to stick to Charlotte's ass, I was all for it. Hell, I'd bring the glue gun.

It freed me and Miles up to do what we did best.

Interestingly enough, Miles' rules of engagement varied compared to what I'd seen in the real world. With people, he played around <**Awareness**> religiously, exercising caution and a slower pace. With monsters, the easiest way to locate Miles was to look for the place where hobgoblins were dying in a rhythm, one after another, searching for an unseen assailant before an arrow found their hearts, throats, or foreheads.

I mainly stuck to my crossbows, staying near the members of the group furthest from Miles. In part, it was tactical, ensuring one of us could rotate to help at any given time.

The other part was nerves. Miles didn't seem as thrilled or engaged with the team as the rest of us were. Unless I was reading it completely wrong, he was overtly pissed off. It could have been the fact that no one warned him beforehand, but I doubted it. I'd made the decision to cut loose in the tower. Leverage every resource I had, every ability, every summon. What we were doing was too important. If we failed, I didn't want to look back and regret that decision. I tried to be smart about it. Having Myrddin lend his summons to Miles, letting everyone think Talia was Nick's spirit guardian. Deploying Ordinator abilities in a more subtle manner.

Disguised and obfuscated as they were, my cards were on the table.

And if anyone was going to connect the dots, it was Miles.

There was no real friction. He was polite to everyone, responding to callouts and proactively rotating for assists. But I didn't miss the way his eyes followed me, sliding away whenever I looked in his direction.

By the time the combined force of both guilds arrived, the goblins had been halved. It wasn't all us. Several Adventurers' Guild mages had followed Nick's lead, popping their flight charms and peppering monsters from the air. Queen Mari had, apparently, done exactly what I thought Nick was about to do. Ran down the mountain, across the field, and into the fort, leaving a trail of bashed-in skulls behind her.

Within minutes of the reinforcements arriving, it was over, the elevator's appearance in the center and a system announcement indicating that the hidden criteria was met and the floor had been cleared.

Everyone from the impromptu group stuck together, some mix between camaraderie and the awkwardness of knowing that we'd broken ranks and an administrative thrashing was inevitable. Sae had Nick in a headlock for some comment he made, while me, Julien, and Charlotte watched from the cheap seats.

Tyler's imposing figure—head and shoulders over most of the Users overrunning the camp—made his way toward us. Almost every few steps he would pause, draw his sword, and deliver a killing stroke to a hobgoblin still suffering on the ground.

"Okay, am I wrong, or is that... a *really* intimidating way to approach a group of people?" Nick asked, looking a little pale.

"Probably just nervous because you thumbed your nose at him less than two hours ago," I told him.

"No, it's uh... kind of intimidating. He's not even my guild leader and I'm all kinds of intimidated." Charlotte laughed nervously. Horror overtook her expression as she turned to Julien, who was leaning against the same railing she was perched on. "Oh. God. Do you think Aaron's pissed?"

"It's Aaron." Julien shrugged, wincing as Tyler killed

another hobgoblin in the distance. "Not even god knows if Aaron is pissed."

I tapped behind my ear. "Neck gets all bulgy. Pretty much his only tell."

Both Julien and Charlotte turned to look at me sharply.

"You knew each other before?" Julien asked.

"Yep." And that was as much as I was willing to say. "But from what I was hearing earlier, he wanted this anyway. You guys are in the clear."

"Lucky fuckin' you." Sae watched Tyler's approach, growing glummer by the second. "I was chatting up one of their recruiters. Planning to join them before this. Fat chance of that now."

"Eh," Miles said, "depends on how he interprets it. If he sees it as an act of rebellion, you're screwed. But Tyler's a reasonable guy. If he sees this as a tryout, you might even get to skip the assessments. Either way, you're not gonna get torn up like these two." He chucked a thumb at me and Nick.

"Not trying to narc, but you were the first one down here with us," Nick said, frowning. "And I'm not even a member of the Adventurers' Guild."

"No, but you're an accessory to Matt, so you're liable to take some blowback."

"Hey."

"As for me, I'm a fed," Miles shrugged. "Punishment isn't really a thing for us. If the fuck-up isn't to Waco levels, we usually just get promoted in a backhanded way."

"Asshole," Nick snorted.

"Fascist," Julien added.

"Uhuh," Miles agreed. "Y'all want some popcorn?" He pulled an already popped bag from his inventory, grabbed a handful, and passed it back just as Tyler arrived. "How's it hanging, chief?"

"Shut up," Tyler growled.

"Okay."

The guild leader gave us all a hard look before his gaze came to rest on someone in particular. "Sae, right?"

Caught completely off guard with a mouthful of popcorn, Sae hopped off the fence and straightened. "Yes, sir."

"You're in." Tyler flicked something on his UI, and moments later a very stunned Sae did the same. "Let me be clear. The Adventurers' Guild does not endorse the sort of maverick, back-biting chicanery that went down today. If I get wind of any issues along those lines, you'll be out just as easily. But I understand you had no previous affiliation and relationship with the people who so foolishly put themselves in danger. With that in mind, the loyalty and skill you demonstrated today is commendable."

"No maverick chicanery." Sae nodded. "Got it."

"Or backbiting," Nick added, unable to suppress the snicker.

"And *you*." Tyler closed distance, his forehead inches from Nick's. "You're not a member of my guild. I cannot discipline or admonish you for your behavior. I certainly cannot tell you you're an irresponsible, self-centered little shit who put the lives of at least twenty people—arguably more—in mortal danger for the sake of his own vanity."

Nick winced. "If you could, I'd tell you I'm very sorry."

Tyler bristled, mistaking Nick's sidelong apology for lip, and looked ready to pile more on.

Beside me, Miles raised his hand like a grade school student with a question.

"Yes?" Tyler asked, his tone dangerous.

"It got chaotic for a while. Just been wondering, how many hostages did we lose, chief?"

"None," Tyler admitted, almost begrudgingly.

"Glad to hear it."

Tyler sighed and moved on, pausing in front of me. Unlike the way he was with Nick, he seemed more frustrated than angry. "I'm not even sure where to start. In recent days you've been the most vocal about devoting resources to the tower, so my first inclination is to pin all the blame on you and nail you to the goddamn wall. Especially knowing how persuasive you can be. But you're not a god, capable of enthralling the masses to your whims—"

Coughs echoed as Nick choked on a piece of popcorn.

"—and in the end, every person here who broke the chain of command made their own decision. Looking at that objectively, I've failed as a leader to correctly gauge and assess the needs and desires of my own. Your selfless actions in the last Transposition go a long way, and your status as both a region leader and a high-placing member of the Merchants' Guild makes you borderline invaluable. Beyond that, we have history. *However,*" his tone changed, and he loomed over me. "If you think those connections are enough to stop me from throwing your scrawny ass to the curb if necessary, you've got another thing coming. Got it?"

Reasonable. Fair. Tyler always had been, to the best of his ability.

"Understood," I said.

"Good."

Almost casually, Tyler reached over and slapped the bag of popcorn out of Miles' hands.

"That was pre-system popcorn," Miles said calmly, staring down at the bag.

"You think you're cute?" Tyler asked, restrained calm masking fury. "All the glad-handing and congeniality to my face while you stir shit up behind my back?"

"I'm at least a little cute. Ex-wife one and three thought so.

Two women who hate each other but agree on something can't be wrong."

"Uh-huh. All of a sudden you're in my business, dry-fucking my ass, because someone mentioned a necromancer and now you need somewhere to put the hard-on."

Miles pushed off the fence, getting far inside Tyler's personal space. "Now that you mention it, it is getting a little stiff downstairs. Stiffer now, because I don't think I mentioned that particular detail to anyone."

One of the girls made a gagging noise. Probably Sae.

"You're not the only one with sources," Tyler rolled his eyes. "Every time I leave the real world, some fresh hell gets thrown in my face."

"Downside of being a visible leader."

"We've decided to run advance teams before committing so many people. It's just too much power off the board at any given time. Coordinate with Sara, she wants you to spearhead this, given that you're so motivated to find this fucker. I can't do it without leaving us open to opportunists, and I don't want my people going up against a necromancer without—"

"Every fed available, once we know where he is. Yeah. Got it." Miles nodded, blowing air out. "So, an advance team, acting in a scouting or clearing capacity. We call in reinforcements as we need them once we've established threat. Can I have my pick of your and Aaron's people, or is this a 'just yours' situation?"

"It was his idea, so I'd say he's on board. It'll spare us both a lot of grief. Though I was told to tell you that members of the Court may opt out if they wish."

Miles shifted his head back and forth. "I'm thinking... ten people, so we have enough for a solid rotation?"

"Fine by me." Tyler turned and walked away.

"There a time limit?" Miles asked.

"You have them for a week."

With a sigh, Miles bent down, picked up his involuntary litter, and shoved it in his pocket. "Not a lot of time. We worked pretty well together. You guys down to be Team 1?"

Nick and I immediately agreed, Julien and Charlotte following suit shortly after.

"If Aaron really gave the green light, it beats being rarified around Order HQ all day," Julien smiled. "Plus, it's for a good cause." Charlotte nodded agreement.

Sae wrinkled her nose. "Only if you promise to never talk about your dick again."

"Reasonable and wise." Miles shot a finger gun at her. "Done."

He clapped his hands, signaling dismissal. "Everyone, go home, pack your shit. Keep some inventory space clear, but as a rule, take more than you need. Only gonna come down for air if we have to. Think of it like a camping trip. Run out of food and we will resort to kobold sashimi before we take the time to stop by Little Debbie's eBay extravaganza, so bear that in mind. Gonna do the same, scrounge up Team 2, and we'll all meet in the lobby at 0800 tomorrow."

Nick left first, pausing when I didn't follow him. "I'll catch up."

"Aight. Thanks again, for everything today." Nick shifted, taking in the whole group, rubbing the back of his neck awkwardly. "I was completely cooked if you guys didn't follow me down."

"Had to. We built a dog tree together." Julien waved back at me. "See you tomorrow."

"Yessir."

Would I see him tomorrow? Any of them?

It was hard to say.

"Think I'm hungrier than before I ate the popcorn," Sae complained.

"Same," Charlotte said, skipping over to walk next to her. "We're not expected back for a while. You guys wanna grab something to eat on the way home?"

"As long as it's not kobold," Nick walked backward. "I'm thinkin'... barbecue? Burgers?"

Their voices faded as they grew more distant, figures merging with the din of Users picking at the charred camp, conversation melding into the noise as though it was never truly there at all.

We watched them go for longer than we needed to. A cool breeze rolled in, sending a sway through the golden grass. Above, the twin suns drifted toward the horizon, light dimming as the long shadows of the surrounding trees crawled across the field.

"Am I... that... obvious?" Miles asked. The usual charm in his voice was gone, wrinkles around his forehead and mouth more pronounced like he'd aged years in minutes.

I shook my head. "Just got the sense you had something to say."

"Come on, let's not do this here."

We trekked away from the camp, perpendicular to the mountain, away from the setting suns. The copse of trees—likely impassable, if this followed a typical dungeon format—were decked with round, light-green leaves that didn't look entirely real. Once the camp was a distant anthill of activity, Miles slipped his pack off his shoulders, placing it at his feet and unzipping it. He grunted as he hefted a sleepy-looking Audrey out, patting her gently on the back of the head. "Good morning, sweetheart."

"Meat," Audrey said, pouting.

"I've been told you have a big appetite." He pointed to the

copse, some thirty yards away. "Spotted some birds in those trees earlier. Feel like going hunting?"

Judging from the way she snapped to attention, mobility vines propelling her across the field at breakneck speed, Audrey did in fact feel like going hunting.

Miles looked down at his shadow. "Azure, you feel like watching over her?"

"I could." Azure solidified into his goblinoid form, looking between us. "Everything alright here?"

"Yeah." Miles put his hands on his hips and stretched. "Yeah. No big deal. Just gonna have a chat."

"You can go."

Azure nodded to Miles, eyes flicking back to me.

"Call for help if you need it."

Then Miles raised his arm. A falcon landed on it, puffing out its fluffy white chest and cawing into Miles' face. He grimaced and reached back into a pouch on his belt, pulling out a strand of stringy meat and handing it to the bird.

He'd been wearing the same pouch the day I met him. During the Transposition.

My mouth went dry.

"Only this one's my summon. The other two are loaners. Greedy little thing. Helpful, but greedy. Tends to get himself into trouble if I let him roam too long. Eyes far bigger than his stomach." Miles stroked the falcon under its chin. "Isn't that right."

It squawked, offended, then took off.

I said nothing.

"They're rare, from what I understand. Summons I mean. Not many people have them, so it's not common knowledge how they work." Miles watched the falcon fly away. "God knows I'm no falconer. Reason I can just let 'em go like that is because summons have a maximum range. He can only get so far from me before he has to come back. It makes the realm situation a little inconvenient. If he's flying around and I enter a dungeon—or any realm of Flauros, really—poof, he's gone. And I have to tap into my mana pool and summon him again."

I closed my eyes. Opened them again. When I did, Miles was staring right at me, like he was looking at someone he'd never seen before.

"How do the loaners work then, if they're not yours?" I asked, monotone.

"I've been wondering the same thing. A new friend lent them to me, with basic instructions for their care and well-being. Like I was dog-sitting." He chuckled. "Audrey kinda fits that bill. She's sweet. Bristles when anyone walks by the door, talks about as much as a husky does. Totally unlike the flower-fangs in the dungeons."

"And the other one?"

"Not dog-like. Very, very, person-like. Acts more like a teenager than a monster. Cryptic. Vague. Doesn't seem to like me much."

"Maybe he'll warm up to you."

"Probably not." Miles rolled his eyes. "I'm terrible with teenagers. And if he finds out I used an analysis ability to piece together what he was hiding behind those question marks, well, might as well cue up 'Truth Hurts.' Donezo. There's nothing teenagers hate more than nosy caretakers."

"He was hiding what he was? The monster type?"

"Uh-huh. So around five this morning, I had two burning questions I really wanted to get answers to before I came down here and put my life on the line." Miles held out fingers, enumerating. "'What the hell is an abrogated lithid?' And 'Are there multiple types of summons that can persist across realms?' So I started making phone calls, pissing off pretty much everyone in my contact list."

As soon Miles said the word lithid, I drew **\<Luciana\>** and held it casually behind my back.

"Find anything?"

"Oh yeah. More than I wanted to, if I'm honest. At its core, a lithid is a parasite. Feeds off suffering. Friend of mine, former cop at the DPD who hopped careers to the twenty-four-hour shift at the psych ward, really didn't enjoy her time with one. Said it read her thoughts, twisted her fears into nightmarish realities. Tortured her. The only reason she's alive at all is because she was with someone who ran slower. The two guys and the bear in the woods joke."

"Jesus." Again, my delivery was b-tier.

Fucking get to it, Miles

"The effects lasted a long time. Certain... compulsions... extended far beyond that initial experience. Hence, psych-ward. Freaked me out a little." He gave me a thin smile. "We're both cerebral guys, you get it. Anything that fucks with our heads is a no-go. Guessing that's why you're straight edge."

His hand dangled, shifting ever so slightly, revealing the slightest glint of a blade behind his thigh.

"Kinda ballsy," I observed, "knowing that and bringing it with you anyway."

"Well, I'm more insulated than the average User. Took additional precautions too. Thought my new friend might be trying to get the one-over on me, trojan horsing his way into this mess of neurons." He tapped his head and looked away. "But I didn't notice any attempted intrusions. And they really helped out today. The summons. So now I have no idea what to think."

"Could have been a genuine gesture of goodwill," I tried.

"A gesture of goodwill? Yes. *Genuine?*" He shook his head. "Not so sure. Because I talked to a *lot* of people. Got in contact with or directed to nine Users with the ability to summon. And it's interesting, because, apparently, they do vary. Range, difficulty, power, how verbal and cooperative the summons are. There's a ton of discrepancies. But every one of them, from the first to last, were consistent on one point and one point only. 'Summons don't persist across realms.' Which is why I had to take the risk, with the lithid. See what happened. Because if the summons disappeared on the elevator, well, whatever, it was bullshit. And bullshitters are a dime a dozen. But if they didn't disappear... it meant my new friend was blowing a different type of smoke. From very close by."

It was circumstantial. And there were holes. Sample size of the summoners, potential interference from the lithid, the hundreds of other people who crowded onto the same massive elevator. The fact that he'd come after me over this before and failed. It wouldn't hold up in a court of law.

But there was no court of law.

There was nothing but me, and him, and the knives at our sides.

"It's getting late. Why don't you say whatever you've been circling, Miles?"

"Fair enough." Miles' forced smile faded beneath his tired eyes. "Are you the Ordinator?"

"I am."

Double-Blind will continue in DOUBLE-BLIND 4**!**

————

Make sure to join our Discord
(https://discord.gg/5RccXhNgGb)
so you never miss a release!

THANK YOU FOR READING
NYCHTA'S FAVOR

We hope you enjoyed it as much as we enjoyed bringing it to you. We just wanted to take a moment to encourage you to review the book. Follow this link: Nychta's Favor to be directed to the book's Amazon product page to leave your review.

Every review helps further the author's reach and, ultimately, helps them continue writing fantastic books for us all to enjoy.

————

Also in series:

DOUBLE-BLIND
DOUBLE-BLIND
GILDED TOWER
NYCHTA'S FAVOR
DOUBLE-BLIND 4

————

Want to discuss our books with other readers and even the authors?

JOIN THE AETHON DISCORD!

You can also join our non-spam mailing list by visiting www.subscribepage.com/AethonReadersGroup and never miss out on future releases. You'll also receive three full books completely Free as our thanks to you.

Don't forget to follow us on socials to never miss a new release!
Facebook | Instagram | Twitter | Website

Looking for more great books?

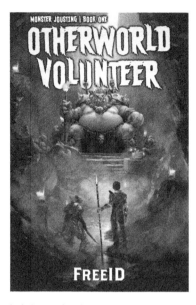

———

For all our LitRPG books, visit our website.